SO NEAR—AND YET SO FAR AWAY

When Sir Jeremy Dole kissed Perdita after they had been solemnly pronounced man and wife, she thought herself the happiest of brides.

Ever since she had first spied Jeremy when she was a chit of a girl, she had adored him from afar. But never in her fondest dreams did she dare hope to share his name and feel his lips on hers.

Then their honeymoon began—and her dream ended. For that kiss before the altar was the last kiss she received. And in the glittering world of sophisticated Paris and then amid the elegance and intrigues of aristocratic London, Perdita learned that she was truly her actor father's daughter as she feigned unquestioning acceptance of her husband's coolness. And no one ever suspected how cleverly she was employing all her wits and wiles as she searched for its reason—and plotted its remedy. . . .

PLAY OF HEARTS

PLAY OF HEARTS

CORINNA CUNLIFFE

A SIGNET BOOK

NEW AMERICAN LIBRARY

SIGNET, SIGNET CLASSIC, MENTOR, PLUME, MERIDIAN AND NAL BOOKS
are published by New American Library,
1633 Broadway, New York, New York 10019

First Printing, February, 1986

1 2 3 4 5 6 7 8 9

PRINTED IN THE UNITED STATES OF AMERICA

For Molly and Rebecca Fox,
great researchers and greater friends,

and for Bambi,
who never gets books dedicated to her

— 1 —

"If love's divinity be such
That I remain outside its holy ring,
Let me not rue it overmuch,
But teach my heart a different song to sing.

"Oh dear, I don't really like that at all, Frolic. 'Holy ring' sounds too much like church bells."

Perdita Chase looked down at the little Italian greyhound as she spoke, and the dog looked back at her expectantly as it heard the sound of its name. He was used to being the first to hear Perdita's poems, and she found in him the perfect audience—one who offers no criticism, but yet seems interested and appreciative.

"I have no doubt that you agree with me," she continued, leaning down to pat the sleek beige coat, "but the trouble is that you have never been very helpful in suggesting other rhymes."

A strand of pale blond hair, which almost matched the dog's coat, fell forward from the hood of the girl's red cloak as she bent down. They were an elegant pair, both lithe and fine boned, and with their pale coloring brightened by startlingly fine eyes. The dog's were a lustrous brown, but the girl's a deep gray, with a fringe of thick black lashes that seemed to make the eyes almost too big for the pale face with its high cheekbones and wide brow.

This brow was now creased with a frown as Perdita tried to find an alternative phrase for "holy ring."

The girl and dog were walking across one of the fields that formed one boundary of the property of Hangarwood House, which for the past thirteen years Perdita had regarded as home.

7

The house lay at the edge of the village of Byfold in Surrey and had originally been a large farmhouse. When Matthew Chase had inherited the property, he had extended the house so that it would be large enough for a gentleman's residence. Even so, it was still modest compared to its counterpart, Shotley Park, which was the seat of the Dole family in the neighboring village of Idingfold.

Though Perdita's mind often dwelt on castles and Gothic mansions, she was perfectly content with the more modest comfort of Hangarwood House provided she could spend a lot of time living in her imagination. It was this imaginary world which occupied her now as she trudged on through the cold outdoors.

It was late afternoon and the evening air was beginning to spread the field in which Perdita walked with a gray glitter, as though someone were scattering millions of sequins across the grass. Here and there vivid green tufts, which had been in the faint sunlight all day, gave emphasis to the monochrome silver of the landscape. Beneath the leafless horse chestnuts the grass was a deep metallic gray. The trees stood like feathers against the sullen yellow-gray of the sky, and at the horizon, earth and sky lost their definition in a swirling white haze of low-lying mist.

It was not a day to draw anyone out of doors, and Perdita had in fact spent most of the day inside, cozily ensconced before the fire in the old schoolroom reading a collection of Lord Byron's works. Although she was a great admirer of the poet, she had been mulling over a long dramatic poem of her own which she thought should involve dungeons, several lonely castles, a lost heir, and perhaps even a ghost. By lunchtime, Lord Byron's efforts seemed less exciting than her own embryonic work. However, the characters proved stubborn in finding their ways through the maze of action and Perdita had abandoned them to their fate and turned her mind to a short love poem. These she had usually found flowed happily from her pen, but this one was giving her some trouble and at half past three she had gone downstairs, taken her old red cloak from the hook in the hall, wrapped it tightly around her, and calling for Frolic had stepped out into the cold air, hoping that it would clear her head and offer fresh inspiration.

It was Perdita's custom in any case to walk in the afternoon

with her step-cousin, Jane de Marney. The relationship of
step-cousin had long ago been transformed into something
closer, both by law and by affection. When Perdita had been
officially adopted by her uncle, Matthew Chase and his wife,
Charlotte, Jane (Charlotte Chase's daughter by her first marriage) and Perdita had effectively become step-sisters, but the
closeness which had quickly developed between the two girls
had soon erased the word 'step' and no two people, linked by
blood, could have found a truer sisterhood.

Both the girls looked forward to their afternoon walks,
where the exercise was often enlivened by Perdita outlining
the plot of her latest epic poem or novel and asking for Jane's
opinion. The two girls were virtually inseparable, spending
all possible waking hours together, but Perdita was surprised
to find that she was not missing Jane as much as she had
thought she would. Jane and her mother had been called away
suddenly to attend the sickbed of one of Jane's aunts in
London. There had been no time to make arrangements for
Perdita to visit friends while her aunt and stepsister were to
be away, and although the house would be empty of all but
the servants (Perdita's uncle, Matthew Chase, had died some
months before and her cousin Robert Chase was away at
Eton), Perdita had seen a certain luxury in being left to her
own devices.

"You can always call upon Lady Dole for company, you
know," Mrs. Chase had said anxiously as she stepped into
the carriage which was to take her to London. "I do not like
the thought of your being alone."

Knowing her aunt to be one who craved constant company
and who could never believe anyone else happy in solitude,
Perdita assured her that she would call upon Lady Dole
during the next few days.

Even so, the last sight Perdita had of her departing family
was that of her aunt's head sticking out of the window of the
carriage and saying, "If we are not back within the se'ennight,
pray ask Lady Dole if you may stay at Shotley."

Perdita had nodded, smiled, and waved, but the thought of
having a few days alone in which to pursue her writing,
uninterrupted by her aunt's imploring her to put down her pen
for a second and join her in a game of piquet or a visit to a
neighbor, was a treat that Perdita meant to enjoy. She also
felt diffident about inviting herself to Shotley. The main

reason for this was the thought that she would be constantly in the presence of Sir Jeremy Dole, Lady Dole's eldest son.

Jeremy had been Perdita's idea of manly perfection since she had first set eyes on him at the age of five.

The bewildered little girl had found nothing but kindness in her uncle's home, and Uncle Matthew and Aunt Charlotte had done all they could to make her feel welcome, but the difference between the formal atmosphere of Hangarwood House and the life of the theater, which was all Perdita had known before, had left her confused and shy. Her uncle's admonition that she should never again refer to her father, and particularly not to the fact that he was connected with the theater, had increased her confusion and driven her into an imaginary world where she felt more secure.

The obvious horror with which her uncle and aunt spoke of the theater and the way they had told her that to mention it would set the whole country talking about her, had made Perdita realize that to have an actor as a father was a very bad thing indeed. She had come to realize that it was almost as bad as if he had been a murderer or a convicted criminal, and she had developed a habit of avoiding all questions about her father, or if pressed, inferring that he had been a soldier who had died in some foreign land.

But in the inner reaches of her heart, her private recollections of her father never changed, and she could still conjure up pictures of a warm-hearted man with a great booming voice and a way of generating excitement all around him. She had delighted in the fantasy of the theater—the costumes, the characters, the lighting, the scenery, and the way fairy tales came to life. When she had come to Hangarwood House the sudden banishment from this fairyland had been too abrupt and she had taken to making up stories to herself into which she could disappear whenever her new life proved too confusing or dull.

There had been nothing malicious in her uncle's instructions to forget her former life, and Perdita had somehow been aware of this. She knew that he sincerely believed that he was doing his best for the his dead sister's only child, and felt that to give Perdita the haven of his home and the upbringing and advantages of a lady was to save the child from a life which could only have brought her unhappiness.

The fact that his sister, Lavinia, had been blissfully happy during her short marriage to Edmund Wycoller had somehow become confused in his mind with the fact of his own unhappiness when she eloped with the actor she had met while staying in Suffolk.

Perdita's uncle's refusal to let her talk about her life with her father was the only shadow in Perdita's otherwise sunny childhood. Her aunt and uncle had treated her exactly the same as the child of their marriage, Robert, and Mrs. Chase's daughter by her first marriage, Jane. The diverse family had been welded together by Mr. Chase's sense of justice and fair play, and Mrs. Chase's easy-going and affectionate heart. At his death eleven months before, Perdita had found that she had grieved over her uncle as much as if he had been her true and only father.

The chief blessing of her adoption, however, had been the relationship which had quickly developed between her and her step-sister, Jane de Marney. Although the latter was two years younger than Perdita, from the moment Perdita had entered the house the two had become inseparable. Jane's high spirits and Perdita's dreamy but imaginative mind were perfect foils for one another. In barely a month after Perdita's arrival it was virtually impossible to find one without the other.

The only other person who had been allowed to enter the inner sanctum of this affection was the younger of the two Dole brothers, Christopher. Christopher was only three years older than Perdita and had been of an age to enjoy the girl's games, to be the perfect leader of many a reprehensible escapade, the imparter of local gossip, an advisor on problems, and a friend with a ready laugh and an easy temper.

But it was his older brother Jeremy, ten years older than herself, who caused Perdita's heart to flutter. The age difference made him seem an adult to Perdita and his good looks, his kind, protective air, made him seem to her to have all the characteristics of a Galahad. This age difference placed a barrier between him and the younger ones, but it in no way lessened the love that Perdita lavished upon him.

There was a sheaf of poems at the back of the drawer in which Perdita kept her handkerchiefs. These, tied neatly with an appropriate blue ribbon, were all dedicated to Jeremy. Even the one on which she was now working was destined for that same package.

Perdita had been six when the seal had been set on her worship of Jeremy. Still shy and unsure of how to behave in the restrained atmosphere of her aunt and uncle's milieu, she had been the obvious butt of the taunts of a particularly obnoxious little boy of ten who had found out that she was adopted and immediately told her that her parents could not have liked her if they had let her go. Perdita had not been able to refute these taunts and her eyes had filled with tears as she stood immobile with misery while the sneering words poured over her. The little boy was taking great delight in having such an easy victim, but his amusement was short-lived, for Jeremy, coming upon the scene and hearing a few words, assessed the situation and acted. The fist planted squarely on the fat boy's jaw had knocked him flat and he had looked up at the tall sixteen-year-old who was saying in a frighteningly calm voice, "Don't ever, ever let me catch you being unkind to Perdita again or I'll make you sorry that you were ever born."

The boy beat a hasty retreat and decided that perhaps he would leave Perdita be in the future. Jeremy put his arm around her without mentioning the incident and she was able to compose herself and rejoin the company without anyone being the wiser about her near total loss of self-control. Jeremy had smiled at her and told her not to worry, that no one would hurt her again and that if they did, she was to tell him at once. From that moment her heart was completely his.

Her adoration had survived Jeremy's absence at Cambridge, and later when he joined the 15th Hussars and she saw him in his dark blue uniform with the silver lacing, he had looked so breathtakingly handsome that he had instantly become the face she saw on all the crusaders, Scottish lairds, wandering minstrels, and knights errant who peopled her novels and poems.

For the next two years he was with Wellington in the Peninsula, and apart from his infrequent letters home, Perdita heard nothing of him. He had been sent home to recover from his wounds after the battle of Vittoria, and much as she yearned to soothe his fevered brow with a cool and silken hand (which she soaked for hours in cucumber water so that it would be white enough when needed), she and Jane were sternly told by Mrs. Chase that they were to leave him in peace.

In her mind, though, the fourteen-year-old Perdita had seen herself nursing him, being the only one from whom he would take the nourishing broth and gruel she would have made for him, saw herself reading inspiring and invigorating books to him, arranging his pillows, and generally being the one who could bring him back to health. She had invented conversations in her mind in which he would, smiling weakly, tell her that it was only the thought of her which had brought him through the nightmare campaign and his illness. However, when she had had the joy of being sent over to Shotley with some peaches from the Hangarwood hothouses, she had been so dumbstruck by the sight of his gaunt face and the suffering in his eyes that she had barely been able to answer his questions in monosyllables.

She did not dare embark on her imaginary conversations with him and it had not seemed suitable to tell him of the new calf born on the farm that day, nor that she was trying to tame a jackdaw she had found fallen from its nest that spring. Most of all, she did not dare ask him to tell her of his experiences for fear of awakening unhappy memories which might jeopardize his recovery, but she longed to be able to take away the strained, haunted look on his face.

He had been gentle with her shyness, trying to draw her out, but her short, self-conscious answers had discouraged him from pressing for information. In a few minutes he had laid his head on his pillows and closed his eyes with exhaustion, and after a lingering look of adoration, Perdita had tiptoed quietly away.

When he was recovered, he had put on his uniform again and ridden off to rejoin Wellington. He had been through the battle of Waterloo and had become an aide to Wellington through the early days of the occupation. Then his father, Sir Percy Dole, had died and Jeremy had left the army to take up his duties as the owner of the large estates.

When Napoleon had been sent to St. Helena and peace had returned, it had not brought with it the ease and prosperity everyone had been waiting for. Instead, the rural areas suffered from deprivations they had never known before and every landowner found the need to tread carefully through the violent changes that were taking place.

Jeremy found his time taken with trying to manage the estates and keep them from suffering too badly from the terrible conditions. His absorption in his duties made him even more remote from the two girls and Christopher. He did not begrudge them their frivolous pleasures, but he was unable to join them. Perdita, however, would have given up every picnic or party had she been asked to share his problems with him, and saw clearly in her mind's eye his look of wonder and admiration as, with a wisdom beyond her years, she solved them for him. She had visions of his suddenly seeing her as a mature woman, and being amazed at the perspicacity of her remarks. Unfortunately, Jeremy never discussed the details of his responsibilities with her and she found herself fated to be an unrecognized sybil.

Jeremy was filling Perdita's thoughts now as she walked along the edge of the field which ran parallel to the lane. She had long since given up hoping for him to see her as a wise child, and now at the age of nineteen, wished only for him to see her as a mature and lovable woman. It was true that when they met at dinner or one of the local assemblies he was unfailingly polite and treated her with charm and consideration, but at the local balls he spent more time introducing her to suitable partners than he did in dancing with her himself. He was kind and protective, but Perdita knew that he saw her only as a child, and she yearned for him to see her as a woman to love, not as a child to protect.

These tender thoughts were soon rudely interrupted by a distinct feeling of cold and damp from the wetness of the ground seeping through the soles of her halfboots. She must go home if she did not want to catch cold and receive a scold from Aunt Charlotte when she returned from London. Perdita called to Frolic and started to turn for home.

Frolic had run ahead down the hedgerow in pursuit of some enticing scent and was now snuffing eagerly, and digging with frantic paws, at a frosted clump of grass. He obviously had no intention of answering Perdita's call, so she started down past the gate to the lane and along the hedgerow to fetch him. Just as she passed the gate she heard it creak and turned to see two men coming through it. She recognized neither of them as belonging to the village. The larger of the two had a face that was as red and massive as a slab of raw beef, though the top half of his face was shaded by a cap pulled well down over his forehead. A stubbly growth of beard covered his square jaw and a scar ran down from beneath his right eye to just above his chin, making a track like a footpath through a hayfield. His mouth was narrow and formed another line at right angles to the scar. He had obviously suffered some injury to one leg and his wide shoulders heaved at every step, as though it were they rather than his legs which propelled him over the ground.

His companion was half his size, wiry where the red-faced man was thick-set, and the smaller man had a sly ratlike face, with two yellow teeth protruding through a mouth set in a perpetual but unfriendly grin. His pointed nose was blue with the cold and a drip glittered on the end of it. He carried a sack and a cudgel.

The sack and cudgel immediately suggested poachers to Perdita, and she was puzzled that they would walk so openly and with such confidence on private land in daylight, but before she could think of a suitable admonition, the beefy man said, "Be you from Hangarwood House, miss?"

Surprised, Perdita answered, "Yes."

"That's she then," the beefy man said, and before Perdita could think what he meant he made a lunge for her, pinning her arms to her side while his companion pulled the sack off his arm and in one practiced sweep pulled it down over her head.

She tried to cry out, but her gasp for breath only filled her lungs with dust and she fell into a fit of coughing. Before she could recover, she felt ropes being tied around her body and then jerked tight so that in seconds she was trussed as tight as a chicken for the spit. She felt an arm like an oak branch go around her and she was dragged through the gate to the lane beyond.

Other hands then picked up her legs and with a heave she was flung in the air. Before she could brace herself for the inevitable fall she landed on a pile of hay and immediately felt more hay being piled on top of her. From far off she could hear Frolic barking and she suddenly thought that he would be sure to die of exposure without her to take him home. She tried to cry out again, but before she could begin there was a sound of a whip cracking and the cart lurched forward down the rutted lane.

The difficulty Perdita had in breathing through the dusty folds of the sack and the hay on top of her, plus the acute discomfort she felt from her tightly tied limbs made it difficult for her to get her mind to work rationally. Her heroines in a similar situation would have been filled with brilliant ideas for escape, and would be even now plotting how to outwit their captors, but every rut the cart hit seemed to bruise Perdita's body and she could not take the time to work on plans while she was futilely trying to brace herself against the incessant jolts of the cart. She bumped about in the hay in an uncomfortable and ridiculous manner as the cart creaked onward through the gray wintery dusk.

There was no sound that she could hear from her captors, and she soon realized that she would have to work out for herself why they had kidnapped her, where they were taking her, and what they planned to do to her. Here again, the young ladies in her books would have had some brilliant thoughts, but Perdita regretfully found that she could not come up with any sensible ideas. She knew that there were many people so desperate with starvation that they would do anything to get a crust of bread, but she had never heard of any young lady, deep in the country, being snatched as she had been. Besides, neither of her captors had been in the least bit interested to find out whether she was wearing any jewelry or carrying any money. The only clue she had was that they had asked whether she was from Hangarwood, and having ascertained that had immediately set upon her.

A small ray of light began to penetrate Perdita's brain. Jane's father had been an extremely rich man, and being his only child, Jane would come into a fortune when she became twenty-one. It was likely that somehow the two men knew about her and had assumed that Perdita was Jane.

Perdita's first inclination was to try to get their attention and tell them of their mistake. Then she realized that they would hardly be likely to apologize profusely, untie the ropes, and speed her on her way. It was more likely that their disappointment would turn them sour and that they would harm her when they found out their mistake. Perdita lay rigid with fear. Her only hope lay in letting them believe they had the right girl and praying that their demand for ransom could somehow be met.

Time ceased to have any reality. The pain in her wrists and ankles and in her knotted-up body was gradually turning to numbness. At one point the cart stopped, but no one came to get her out of the back and after what seemed to be hours the horse was whipped up again and the journey continued.

The numbness turned to a new sort of agony which soon became the only thing in Perdita's mind. If she could survive it she swore she would never again have her heroines so lightly swung across saddle bows or tied up to trees in woods. Time had blurred into a continuation of pain, and in the darkness under the hay, Perdita had no idea whether it was late evening, the middle of the night, or dawn. Suddenly the cart stopped again and she felt it sway as the men got off the front of it.

The hay was scraped off her and she was roughly pulled out of the cart by her feet. The ropes were untied, but her legs were so numb that she nearly fell, and the beefy man grabbed her quickly and pulled her to her feet. He pulled the sack off her head and she gulped in the cold air, revelling in its freshness even though it felt as though someone were filling her lungs with icy needles.

After taking a few deep breaths she dared to try to move her arms and legs. The numbness was leaving them, but being replaced with the agony of pins and needles as the blood returned to her extremities.

"Can ya' walk?" the beefy man growled.

"I think so," Perdita answered, tentatively putting her full weight on one foot and gratefully finding that it supported her.

"Come on then." The big man jerked her arm and pulled her toward a dilapidated shed which stood in a clearing in the wood in which the horse and cart now rested.

The moonlight sifted down between the spikey bare branches of the trees, which looked like hobgoblins, arms outstretched waiting to pounce. There was no landmark by which to identify the place, though Perdita gave a quick glance around the clearing before the beefy man pulled her into the shed.

The interior was damp and musty and even colder than the outdoors. Perdita shivered and the beefy man called over his shoulder, "Get a fire going, 'Enry, we don't want this prime 'un dyin' on us yet."

There was a small fireplace against the back wall of the shed, and a heap of dried leaves in one corner. The beefy man spread the sack which had covered Perdita's face on the leaves and roughly pushed her down on it. "Now you stay there and you'll be all right and tight, but kick up a dust and your chances of a long and 'appy life won't be great.''

Perdita had no intention of kicking up a dust. Her good sense told her that to scream as loudly as she might in this out of the way place would call up nothing but the rage of her captors, so she sank down on the sack and started to chafe her wrists and ankles to try to get the blood flowing more freely and to warm them.

The man called Henry came in a few minutes later, his arms laden with twigs and branches of wood, and he carried an old rusty iron kettle in one hand. Within a few minutes he had laid a good fire and had started it going with the aid of a tinder box and flint. He then set the kettle on an iron hook over the fire and sat down on a small stool to wait for it to boil.

The fire crackled and hissed and the shadows flickered over the dirty walls of the shed, but neither of Perdita's captors spoke. The beefy man leaned against the chimney piece as though, without his role as prop, the whole shed would collapse, and Henry gazed intently at the fire, every now and then poking the logs and sending a shower of sparks racing up the chimney.

After a while the kettle began to rattle and Henry picked it off the hook, wrapping an exceptionally filthy bandanna around the handle. Then, like a conjurer, he produced a small packet and two chipped mugs from the tail pockets of his coat. He divided the contents of the packet between the mugs and then poured the boiling water on them. He then gave the brew a quick stir with a twig he picked up from the floor and walked over to where Perdita half lay, half sat on her pile of leaves.

'' 'Ere, drink this. It'll help to keep the cold out, and we've a good way to go before we gets to our final lodgin'.''

The discomfort of the ropes on her body and been replaced with a marrow-chilling cold, and ignoring the filth of the cup, Perdita drank gratefully. The warm herb tea seemed to bring back some life to her, and she began to feel that it was remotely possible that she would not die of the cold.

Henry held the other mug out to the beefy man. '' 'Ere, you can take your sup first, George, but don't take it all. I don't have more o' that stuff and 'avin' less flesh on me bones I 'ave more need of it. Cripes, with this cold I could do with a tot of blue ruin, or at least a good mulled ale.''

"You'll get that soon enough," George growled. He took a long drink from the mug while Henry watched the liquid go down his throat with the intensity of a dog waiting for tidbits.

"That's enough now. 'And over the mug. Gawd'struth, you're a greedy cove. Never think of the other fella. Take what you want and to 'ell with anyone else."

His voice fell off to a mutter as George, with a scowl, handed over the mug. Henry's weasle face took on a more relaxed expression as he warmed his hands around the mug before drinking off the remainder of the tea.

Perdita would have been glad of another cup, but knew that there was no hope of getting it. She sat trying to control her shivering as the penetrating cold worked its way through her red wool cloak and the dress underneath. The two men said little, staring silently at the burning logs which seemed to do little to ease the overwhelming chill of the room.

The logs had burned down to faintly glowing coals when Henry finally got up. "Well, we'd better be on our way. The 'orse should be rested by now."

George came over to Perdita and pulled her roughly to her feet. "Come on, your ladyship. Time to get back into your carriage."

He picked up the rope that had tied her so uncomfortably before, but before he could put it around her she said, "Oh please, don't tie me again. The rope hurts so much. I promise not to try to escape. You don't have to tie me, or to put that horrible sack over my head." Then with more boldness she added, "Don't think that my mother will pay any ransom for me if I have suffocated, or my arms and legs have frozen off."

George looked at her for a moment and then gave a sneering laugh. "Oh my, I am sorry that your ladyship was inconvenienced in any way. 'Enry, we forgot to bring the silk rope with us. Aren't we the forgetful pair then?"

He started again toward Perdita, but this time Henry intervened. "Don't tie her so tight this time. You bleedin' near crippled 'er the last time. Besides, she's not goin' to broom on us. With both of us watchin' 'er, she wouldn't. She's not so beef-witted. She knows we wouldn't take kindly to her makin' off. As for the sack—oo the 'ell's goin' to 'ear 'er under all that 'ay?"

George shoved Henry roughly out of his path, but Perdita

was grateful for his intervention, for the ropes were tied more loosely and they did not cut into her wrists and ankles, and although George picked up the sack, he did not put it over her head.

"Awl right," he said, "but the first peep from you and the sack goes back on—and tighter than before. Now come on." With that he picked her up as though she had been a feather and slung her over his shoulder.

They went out into the dark clearing once more, where the farm cart, with its defeated looking old horse, stood in the waning moonlight. Perdita was once again unceremoniously flung into the cart and the hay piled over her, then she felt the two men get up onto the front of the cart, heard the whip land on the horse's hide, and the cart lurched forward again.

The herbs in the tea, the long tension of fear, or simply the relative comfort of having her arms and legs more loosely tied somehow produced a lethargy in Perdita so that after a while she slept. She awakened once or twice as the cart hit an abnormally large rut, or when George cracked his whip, but through the journey Perdita floated in and out of sleep so that the whole ugly drama just became like a bad dream. The hay kept her warm and the darkness that engulfed her made her lose all track of time. She did not know whether they had been traveling for an hour or for a day when finally the cart lurched to a stop and her captors got down and pulled the hay off her again and untied her ropes.

There was just the first faint hint of dawn in the sky as she got out of the cart this time, and Perdita saw that they were taking her to another building in a wood. This time, smoke was already coming from the chimney and the sight of it cheered her. The shocks that she had undergone had made reality as insubstantial as a cobweb and she had a vision that she was about to be turned over to someone like Mrs. Parkin, the gamekeeper's wife at Hangarwood. Even as the thought crossed her mind she realized that her mind was playing her false, and as if to underline the deception the door of the cottage opened and a third man came forward.

"You got 'er then," he said with a malicious grin.

"So you can see," George answered crossly, pushing Perdita so roughly that she stumbled and would have fallen across the threshold had not the third man put out his arm to catch her.

He looked down at her face with an expression that did nothing to still the panic in Perdita's heart and said, "A pretty little thing, ain't she. Well, if 'er loving ma don't come up with the ready, I fancy that Peg could make use of 'er in the kip shop. But not before I've 'ad a taste of 'er. Wouldn't mind breakin' in this little filly, I wouldn't.'' His leer became more pronounced and he brought his pock-marked face toward Perdita's.

She drew back from the filthy face and his disgusting breath, and his expression became angry. His fingers closed painfully around her jaw. "Don't fancy me, eh? Well, perhaps I'll teach you a few fings you never knew before." His grimy hand dropped to her shoulder and he pulled the cloak roughly away from her. What he would have done next Perdita shuddered to think, but Henry stepped forward as though to hit the man and stopped him with a growl.

"Leave 'er be, Crib. She may be our ticket to 'eaven on earth, but not if you start playing your stupid games wiv 'er. Don't forget, me and George 'as our rights too. She's not yours, so keep your daddles off 'er.'' As he said this he wrenched Perdita away from the glowering Crib, pulled her into the cottage, and closed the door on the other two men.

"In 'ere," he said, pushing open a sagging door in one corner of the room. Perdita was thrust forward into a tiny room little bigger than a powder closet. In one corner, there was a rough mattress made of sacking stuffed with straw, over which was thrown two extremely dirty blankets. There was a pail beside the bed, but apart from that the cobwebs and filth on the floor formed the only other decorations. Once she was inside Henry slammed the rickety door, and Perdita heard a key turn in the rusty lock. Far from being dismayed at being locked in, she could only hope that Henry would keep the key hidden on his person and that the lecherous Crib would be locked out.

There was no light in the room, but the wall boards had warped, so that here and there the light from the fire in the main room flickered through and saved Perdita's prison from being in total darkness. It was warmer than the other shed in which they had made their brief stay, and Perdita could feel grateful that at least one creature comfort was available to her.

She sat down on the sacking bed and pulled the blankets

around her. She had long since lost her fastidiousness and was only grateful for the warmth that the blankets gave. Besides, she had far more important things to think about than whether or not she was sharing the blankets with other and smaller inhabitants.

The sickening fear which Crib's attack had produced was beginning to quiet and she was able to think back over the snatches of conversation she had heard on the last part of the journey and realize that it was as she had suspected, her kidnappers had mistaken her for Jane. She could only pray that her aunt would be able to comply with the ransom demands, but as the men had thought they had abducted an heiress they might well ask for a sum which it was beyond her aunt's power to pay.

The alternatives were too horrible to contemplate. The man Crib, the reference to Peg's kip shop—Perdita could hardly allow herself to think about those things. Peg's kip shop was only a vague threat to her, as it was only her imagination which told her what sort of place it might be, but Crib was a much more concrete threat, and she had no doubt that if her aunt failed to come up with the ransom, Henry would no longer try to protect her from the lustful advances of the revolting pock-marked man.

She turned over in her mind the possibilities of escape, but she could not see how she could get out of the locked room, let alone the house, without one of the three men seeing and stopping her. Her best hope seemed to be in buying as much time as she could in the hopes that the constables could pick up her trail and release her. Crib had so completely terrified her that she had no wish to make him angry, and by being quiet and compliant she might even hope that he would forget that she was in the tiny room. George seemed less of a threat, vast and oafish but with an oxlike wit. Crib was passionate and loathsome, but did not seem to do much thinking. It was obviously Henry who was the brains that had organized her kidnapping, and who kept the other two under control. If she could keep on the right side of Henry, perhaps she could find the time she needed.

There was a scuffle in the corner of her straw mattress and Perdita turned quickly in the direction of the noise. A large rat sat in the corner staring at her. She stifled a terrified scream and flicked the corner of the blanket in its direction. The rat turned and disappeared down a hole in the corner of the cupboard, and Perdita realized that none of her heroines had ever known the real meaning and extent of fear.

— 2 —

The pair of match-grays wheeled in at the gate of Hangar-wood House as the dark-haired gentleman in the curly-brimmed beaver and the multicaped coat looped the reins deftly. The air was cold and one of the horses, well fed and underexercised, shied at a white painted stone edging the driveway. The thong of the whip caught him swiftly between the collar and the pad and he went forward briskly, matching steps with his partner.

Sir Jeremy Dole had been busy all morning trying to come to a compromise with one of his more cantankerous tenant farmers, but at the back of his mind had been a determination to call upon Perdita Chase later that day. His mother was disinclined to face the cold of the March afternoon, but sent him off with sincere entreaties to Perdita to come to Shotley for a few days.

The new grays, which had been bought at Tattersalls the previous week, were the ostensible excuse for the visit. Jeremy had determined that she would be pleased to have him ask her opinion on them, but his real reason was to allay the anxiety he had felt the moment he knew that she would be left on her own while her aunt and step-sister were in London.

If Jeremy's brother, Christopher, had not been at Cambridge, he would have been the one to make the five mile drive to Hangarwood. Jeremy knew that Perdita would have taken more pleasure in his brother's light-hearted company but hoped that he might make at least a tolerable substitute. Jeremy had often watched the way in which Christopher could bring forth the laughter and chatter from the tall, blonde girl, and he had taken delight in watching her animation as she spoke to his brother, but Jeremy acknowledged that he did not have Christopher's ease of manner and that with him Perdita was more shy and reserved. Nevertheless, he had long ago assigned to himself the role of Perdita's guardian and champion. It had been the sight of her bravely fighting back tears as an obnoxious Tommy St. Dawes had been teasing her about being adopted which had first aroused Jeremy's protectiveness. From that day he had seen Perdita as someone who was his special charge, and although he did not think of this consciously, it was these inner promptings which had caused him to have the grays put to his curricle that afternoon.

He drew the grays to a stop in front of the shallow stone steps at the entrance of Hangarwood House, and almost before the wheels had stopped moving, Clamp had jumped down from the seat behind his master and was holding the grays' bits.

"Keep them walking, Clamp. I won't be long, but I don't want them getting cold. If I am delayed I will send word and you can take them 'round to the stables."

Clamp gave a brief nod and a "yes sir" and waited while his master looped the reins around the whip and got out of the curricle. Clamp's eyes followed the tall figure as Sir Jeremy climbed the steps of the house and rapped on the door. The languid movements of the tall man Clamp knew to be deceptive. If ever there was a bully trap, he thought to himself, his master was one.

Sir Jeremy had developed a fine art with his fists when defending himself from bullies at his prep school, and he had continued to follow the science of boxing throughout his life. The slender frame was covered with hard muscle and Sir Jeremy was regarded as one of the stars of Gentleman Jackson's boxing salon in Bond Street, and one of the most outstanding members of the Pugilistic Club.

If anyone were fool enough to be deceived by Sir Jeremy's lazy manner, Clamp could tell them that they were the ones to be proved buffle-headed clunches should they see fit to try to take advantage of Sir Jeremy.

The groom's face creased into a grin as he remembered his first meeting with Sir Jeremy, when they had both been serving with the 15th Hussars during the Peninsula War. They had been bivouacked outside Badajoz just before Wellington's army had fought the bloody and hard battle to take the town. A captain of the 28th, who had just joined his regiment from England, had been berating one of his men for

not being dressed properly. The lack of uniforms and even
sufficient clothes and blankets had long been a fact of life to
the officers who had served through the earlier months of the
campaign. They all were well aware that it was as much as
the men could do to find enough coverings to keep them from
actually freezing to death. Morale was low enough as it was
without ignorant officers making life more difficult for their
men, and Jeremy had taken the new arrival to one side to
explain the predicament of the men in the ranks. His effort to
intervene had produced a cold, "I'll thank you, sir, to mind
your own business, and I'll mind mine."

Jeremy had shrugged his shoulders and started to turn away
when he saw the officer reprimand the man again and accompany his words with a savage blow with his whip across the
man's face.

The fist that had knocked the young captain back into the
oozing mud had come so fast, so unexpectedly, and with such
force, that the captain could hardly believe that the man
standing over him with a murderous glint in his eye was the
same one who had been coolly offering advice to him but a
moment before.

Clamp, who had been watching the whole proceedings,
had seen and admired. He himself was no stranger to the
lightning use of the fists, having been a notable member of
the fancy before a run of back luck had given him the choice
between the workhouse or the army. There had been many
moments in those months in Spain when he had felt that he
had made the wrong choice, but now the rain, the mud, the
cold and hunger were forgotten as he saw the man he wished
to serve.

The next morning, before the camp was fully awake, he
had presented himself at Major Dole's tent and had asked to
be considered for the job of his batman. Jeremy had looked at
the round deceptively jovial face with its boot-button eyes,
noted the squashed nose and cauliflower ear, and said slowly,
"Clamp—you must be the Clamp who went fifteen rounds
with the Surrey Bantam in 1810."

"Yes sir," Clamp replied, only a slight reddening of his
cheek betraying the pleasure he felt in Major Dole's having
remembered one of his more notable successes.

"That was a good fight, Clamp. It may be some time
before I see another man as good with his left hand. All right,

present yourself to the Regimental Sergeant Major and tell him that I wish you to be assigned to me as my soldier servant, and then come back here and I'll have things for you to do.''

Clamp had saluted smartly and left the tent. But that day was the beginning of a deep friendship and mutual trust. Though neither would have felt it seemly to admit it, each would have laid down his life for the other, and Jeremy knew that his life had indeed been saved by Clamp when he had been wounded during the battle of Vittoria.

Jeremy had been vaguely conscious of the wiry little man's half dragging, half carrying him behind the lines after he had been hit by the musket ball, and his last conscious impression had been of hearing Clamp haranguing the surgeons to attend to his master before anyone else. When Jeremy had at last regained consciousness he had found himself in the unknown luxury of a decent cot, covered with no less than three blankets, and with a miraculous feather pillow beneath his head. He did not dare ask Clamp where he had obtained these rarities, but had accepted them gratefully. Clamp's magic had even extended to producing chicken broth in the midst of an army which had long since subsisted on stringy goat or donkey meat and a few weevily biscuits.

It had been Clamp's untiring nursing which had pulled Jeremy through the fever which had attacked him three days after he had been wounded. The surgeons had shaken their heads and given up all hope of saving his life, but Clamp had set his jaw and dared Death to lay a finger on his master. Through the mists of his fever, Jeremy had been aware of Clamp's cajoling and threatening him, and willing him to live, and he had even then been grateful for Clamp's devoted care.

As Jeremy had regained strength, Clamp's manner had become more astringent, but Jeremy had noted an unaccustomed brightness in the batman's eye when they had said their goodbyes before Jeremy was shipped home to convalesce.

They had been together again as soon as Jeremy had rejoined his regiment. The pair had been at the battle of Waterloo and in the army of occupation then established in France. When finally Jeremy had returned home upon the death of his father to take up his duties as heir to the title and estates, he had bought Clamp out of the army so that he could act as his groom and valet.

While Clamp had been reliving the past, Jeremy had been waiting on the doorstep of the house. As the minutes passed, a frown gathered on his face. He was about to raise the knocker again and was framing a suitably curt remark to make to the butler, Bonder, when the door was opened by that very gentleman who was looking decidedly and unaccustomably ramshackle for the butler of a gentleman's residence.

When Bonder saw that the caller was Sir Jeremy, the worried expression on his face lightened and before the visitor could step through the door he had launched into a wild and disjointed speech.

"Oh, Sir Jeremy—Oh, I am that glad to see you! We are all at sea here, sir . . . the most terrible thing—or at least I fear a terrible thing, sir—I have sent for Mrs. Chase, though I'm not sure what she can do about it—at least I felt it necessary to send for her . . . of course I have had the coachman and the men from the farm set up a search, but there is not a trace—no trace at all, sir. The dog was found this morning about half a mile away, but no trace of her, sir, not a scrap . . ."

"Bonder, have you taken leave of your senses?" Sir Jeremy said coolly, pushing past the distraught butler and firmly closing the front door behind him. "Perhaps you would be good enough to show me into the drawing room—and perhaps I might impose upon you to take my hat and coat."

He turned his back to the butler so that the latter could lift the heavy driving coat from his shoulders, and then he followed the agitated butler into the drawing room.

Jeremy noted with some displeasure that the fire had not been lit in the room and that it was distinctly chilly, and he hoped that Perdita had not suffered from this sort of neglect throughout the entire absence of her aunt. However, he said nothing about the room, but turned to the butler and said, "And now, Bonder, perhaps you would take a deep breath and tell me what it is that has turned you into a complete rattle?"

"It's Miss Chase, Sir Jeremy. She's disappeared."

For a second the calm expression left Jeremy's face and was replaced by one of sharp interest. "Disappeared? Explain—

and be quick and coherent. When did she disappear? Who was the last to see her? Did she leave any note to say where she was going?"

Bonder took a deep breath. "No one actually saw her go out of the house, but her red cloak is missing and the dog, Frolic, was found, as I said, some half mile from the house, down beyond the Ten-Acre meadow, the other side of Matcham's Lane. Betty, the second housemaid, had taken Miss Chase tea at three o'clock. Miss Chase was in the old schoolroom then, writing. She had said nothing about going out, but she and Miss de Marney nearly always walk out in the afternoon. We didn't find any note, but when she didn't appear in her room to dress for dinner at six o'clock, and when Susan, her maid, went to look for her in the schoolroom, the room was in darkness.

"Susan very sensibly sent for me then, sir, as it was quite dark out by that time and Miss Chase should have been back, so I had everyone out looking for her around the grounds. I feared that she might have twisted her ankle or had some accident and been unable to get home, and when we didn't find her in the gardens or the nearby pastures, I sent 'round to the stables and the farm to have every man looking for her. I knew that Miss Chase couldn't have intended to go far, it being so late when she set out and so cold, but the lads searched all evening and well into the night and found no trace of her. We resumed the search at first light and I had all the villagers asked if they had seen anything of her, but no one had seen a thing. One of them found the dog at eight this morning, but there was no sign of Miss Chase, so I sent the coachman up to London to bring back Mrs. Chase. But oh, sir, I am at my wit's end. I can't think what can have happened to Miss Chase."

"You've done very well, Bonder," Jeremy said soothingly, though he looked worried. "You have done everything you could, but I think we must alert the constables. If the dog was found without Miss Chase, I am afraid we must assume . . ." Jeremy's jaw clenched and his frown deepened. He found suddenly that he did not want to put his thought into words. He was silent for a moment and then he said, "Just where was the dog found, and did it appear to have been there all night?"

"I don't know exactly, sir, but I could find out."

"Do that if you please, Bonder. I will wait here—and Bonder, perhaps you would be good enough to send in one of the maids to light the fire?"

"Oh yes, Sir Jeremy. I am sorry, sir, but we have been in such a state . . . I do hope that you will overlook this ommission . . ."

"Quite, quite, but be so good as to tell Clamp that I will be with him directly."

Bonder gave a half bow and nearly ran from the room. A few minutes later a maid came in, gave a bob curtesy to Sir Jeremy, and proceeded to attend to the fire. Sir Jeremy was scarcely aware of her presence. He had walked over to the window and was frowning at the view outside. Only the slight tapping of the toe of one of his immaculate boots gave any sign that he was suffering from acute impatience.

Within five minutes Bonder had returned, though to Jeremy it seemed that the butler had been away for hours.

"Well?" Jeremy said, turning from the window as soon as he heard the door open.

"Fred was the one who found the dog, sir. He says he was cowering in the grass near the gate from the Ten-Acre Meadow into Matcham's Lane. The dog was just wimpering and shivering, but was not running about, sir, and from all appearances it seems to have been there some time."

"Very good. I will return as soon as possible, but I want to go down to Matcham's Lane to see what I can find. If you hear anything further, send one of the boys to fetch me instantly."

With this, Sir Jeremy strode out of the room and, pausing only long enough to pick up his coat and hat, ran down the steps, climbed into the curricle, and, before Clamp was settled in his seat, had whipped up the grays and set them at a gallop down the drive.

"It's Miss Chase, Clamp," he said between clenched teeth. "It seems she went out for a walk yesterday afternoon and has not been seen since. Her dog was found by the gate onto Matcham's Lane. We're going to see if we can find any sign of what happened to her."

Clamp did not reply, but his beady eyes fastened speculatively on his master. There was not much that Clamp did not know about Sir Jeremy, and he was well aware of his master's feelings for Miss Chase. For any other emergency, his master would have been unwilling to spring his cattle, but the new grays had been set at a headlong pace without regard for their vulnerable legs.

It took less than five minutes to reach the gate and Clamp was barely at the horses' heads before Jeremy had swung out of the curricle and was through the gate. Clamp watched over his shoulder as Jeremy bent to examine the ruts and grass around the gate and to look closely at the hedgerow on either side of it. He looked intently for some minutes and then said, "Ah, yes." He picked something off a bramble by the gate and held it out to Clamp. It was a small piece of red cloth, but from the look in Jeremy's eye it might as well have been someone's lifeblood.

"She was wearing a red cloak," he went on, almost to himself, "and see, here are some trampled branches—no footprints, but the ground was too hard for those—and, yes, the grass here has been trodden down hard. There's no doubt she was taken away by force. Not even the slightest chance that she went off with someone she knew. Well, there's nothing more that we can do here, Clamp. We must go back to the house and await developments. If she was abducted it was for a reason, and ten to one that will be for a ransom."

He had swung himself back into the curricle as he spoke, and was turning the grays deftly in the narrow lane when a horse rounded the corner being ridden at a hard gallop. Sir Jeremy drew the grays to a halt as a breathless groom pulled up beside him.

"There's been a message, Sir Jeremy. Bonder says to ask you to please come back at once, sir."

Jeremy gave the boy a curt nod and set the grays once again into a gallop. Clamp clung like a limpet to the arms of his seat and prayed that they would live long enough to help Miss Chase. His prayers, or Sir Jeremy's skill, proved adequate and within minutes they had drawn up once more before the steps of Hangarwood House.

This time there was nothing languid in the way Sir Jeremy went up the steps, and he was in the house almost before Clamp had time to get to the horses' heads. Jeremy entered the hall to find Bonder staring at a small boy who was backed into a corner. There was an uncanny resemblance in the tableau to a large sheepdog holding a lamb in a pen. As Jeremy entered the hall, Bonder turned quickly and said,

"This lad's got a message from the man who took Miss Chase, Sir Jeremy."

Jeremy went over to the boy, who was looking as though he wished himself anywhere but in the hall of Hangarwood House.

"It's all right, my lad. You have nothing to fear from us if you tell us the truth. What's your name?"

"Billy Larkin, sir."

"He's Tom Larkin's son. The ploughman over at Hartdale Farm, Sir Jeremy," Bonder added helpfully.

Jeremy nodded, and then turned his attention to the boy.

"Very well, Billy, give us your message."

There was something in the expression of the tall man which made the boy pull himself up into a reasonable facsimile of standing to attention. He fixed his eyes on the tall man's face, took a deep breath, and launched into his recital.

"This man comes up to me yesterday afternoon and 'e says as 'ow I was to wait until this afternoon to come 'ere, and then I was to speak to someone in the 'ouse and tell them that they 'ad taken the young lady, but she was awl right and would be so long as they got the money for 'er and no funny business. The man said 'ow as to tell you that you was to get two thousand guineas in gold and put it in a bag and take it to . . ." Here Billy screwed up his eyes in an agony of effort to remember the details. ". . . the 'ollow oak which stands by the fork of the road just the other side of Otley Green on the road to Ashford from Maidstone. The money was to be left in the tree before midnight on the twenty-fifth if you ever wanted to see Miss Jane—"

"Jane?" Jeremy said. "Did you say Jane? Are you sure that was the name?"

Billy opened his eyes wide. "Yes, sir, the man said 'Jane.' I know 'e did. I remember 'cause it's the name of me youngest sister."

"Very well, go on."

"That's all 'e said to tell you."

"Where did you see this man?"

"Down the far side of the Longacre. I was doing some stone picking and 'e came up to me in the field and asks me if I knows 'ow to remember things. I told 'im as 'ow I reckoned I remembered as good as anyone, and 'e said 'e'd give me a shillin' if I'd do as 'e said. 'E told me what I just tolds you, sir, and then 'e gave me a shillin'.'' The boy reached a dirty hand into the worn pocket of his breeches and pulled out the shilling as though to verify the whole of his story by this action. '' 'Ere it is, sir, and I did like 'e said, didn't I? 'E said as 'ow I wasn't to tell no one I'd seen 'im until today afternoon, and then I was only to tell someone in this 'ouse. 'E said 'e 'ad spies and 'e'd know if I talked to anyone, even my ma. 'E said—''

"Yes, well you're quite safe now, Billy," Jeremy said, cutting off the spate of words. "Tell me, had you ever seen this man before?''

"No sir, I never seens 'im until 'e came up to me in the field yesterday. 'E didn't say 'is name. Just told me as 'ow I was to tell you—or someone 'ere—what I just tolds you. Then 'e gives me this shillin' and—''

"What did he look like?" Jeremy interrupted.

The boy looked bemused, '' 'E was just a man, sir,'' he said, as though in his eyes God had not only created all men equal, but also indistinguishable.

"Was he tall?"

The boy tilted his head on one side and looked first at Jeremy and then at Bonder. '' 'E wasn't as tall as you is, sir, nor yet as tall as 'im,'' he said, jerking his head toward Bonder, "but 'e was taller than me Dad.''

"Was he fat or thin?"

'' 'E wasn't really fat, but then not thin neither. Least 'e didn't have a belly, but 'e was big like.''

"Good, now did you notice anything else about him? What was he wearing?''

"I don't remember, sir. 'E 'ad on an 'at, and a coat and breeches and leggin's. Sort of ordinary things, sir.''

"And you said he was alone? There was no one else with him or nearby?''

"I didn't see no one, sir."

"There was nothing else you remember at all? Think. It could be worth a guinea to you.''

The last statement made the boy's eyes and mouth open into large O's, then he shut them tightly and an expression closely akin to agony came over his face while he thought. He was silent for a moment, then he opened his eyes again and said slowly, "I can't remember nothin' more sir, 'cept as 'ow 'e 'ad a long scar goin' down 'is face, and 'e walked with a limp. But that's all I can remember.''

"Good boy, Billy," Jeremy said, pulling out a guinea from his pocket and handing it over to the delighted boy. "If your mother asks about this, tell her you came by it honestly, and if she doesn't believe you, tell her to ask Sir Jeremy Dole."

The boy managed a shy tug at his forelock and muttered "sir," and then his eyes flew around the room as though looking for escape before this strange gentleman should change his mind and take his guinea back.

"All right," Jeremy said, "you can go now, but if you think of anything else about the man, or if you remember seeing anything else unusual yesterday afternoon, come back here and ask for Mr. Bonder and tell him. He will give you another shilling if you tell him something that he finds interesting."

As soon as the boy had left the room, Jeremy turned to the butler. "Bonder, when Mrs. Chase gets here, tell her that I have taken the matter in hand. Try not to let her worry unduly. I will do everything possible. I must get up to London tonight so that I can get the money from my bankers in the morning. The message said that the money had to be at Otley Green on the day after tomorrow, so we haven't much time. I will leave word at home where I can be contacted, so send over to Shotley if you hear anything else."

Jeremy was walking toward the front door as he spoke and Clamp, when he saw his master come out of the house, brought the grays up to the steps. Clamp turned an inquiring glance at Sir Jeremy as the latter stepped into the curricle, but he got no answer until they were out of the driveway and heading toward Shotley Park.

"They've taken her, Clamp. At least, only one man has been seen, but I surmise that there must be at least two involved. She was not with the man who delivered the ransom message, so she must have been held by someone else. They think they have Miss Jane, apparently. I can only pray that they don't find out that they have the wrong girl. If they think that they won't get the ransom, God knows what they might do."

Clamp saw the muscles in Sir Jeremy's jaw tighten and the latter was silent for a few minutes, then he continued, "When we get to Shotley, get Hughes to have Fuego saddled for me. I must get to London tonight so that I can arrange to get the money for the ransom early tomorrow. Then I want you to have one of the horses put to the dog cart and take it to The Stag at Maidstone and wait for me there. I will come down with the money as soon as I can. It has to be delivered to the fork in the road at Otley Green by midnight the day after tomorrow.

"Once you get to Maidstone, you might make discreet inquiries as to whether there have been any strangers around. I am particularly interested in a man of medium height and stocky build who has a long scar down one side of his face and a limp. He is the one who delivered the ransom message to Billy Larkin. If we find a man answering that description, we'll know we're on the right track."

"If you'll excuse me, Major, may I make a suggestion?" Clamp asked.

"Certainly."

"Might I suggest that you get one of the grooms to take the dogcart over to The Stag, sir? I fancy I might be able to find out something if I was to come up to London with you. I still have some friends, as you might say, in some of the rookeries. I could spend the night visiting some flashhouses. If you asks me, it sounds like quite a bit of planning went into this kidnapping—not just a fly-by-night job—and since they kidnapped the wrong lady, my guess is that it wasn't local chaps neither. In that case, it's ten to one that someone in The Smoke will know somethin' about it.

"I'll spend the night asking some questions, and if I hears anythin' before nine o'clock tomorrow, I'll come 'round to your 'otel in Bond Street. If I don't hear nothin', I'll head down to Maidstone and meet you at The Stag. I'll be able to ask all the questions I want after I gets there."

"Very good, Clamp. I think that is an excellent plan. I had forgotten that you might still have useful connections in London. I hope that you may turn something up, for once the villains have the money they will have no use for Miss Chase so we will have to act quickly. Our only clue is the description of the man who gave the instructions to Billy Larkin. Even so, the mere fact the man took such little pains to hide his limp and scar makes me think that he was confident that we would never find him. I don't like that—not one bit, Clamp."

Clamp nodded his head. He was not happy about the state of affairs at all. He might have seemed confident when he spoke to his master of rekindling old friendships in The Smoke, but the purlieus of the dark parts of London were intricate and widespread. Were it not for the amazingly efficient word-of-mouth information system that worked in the rookeries and gin shops, he would never even have suggested his plan.

Lady Dole was no more confident than Clamp that Perdita would be found before the deadline of her ransom, but she too understood Jeremy's feelings for the girl and she was not going to add to his troubles by burdening him with her misgivings. When he had told her of his intentions, she put a hand on his sleeve and said, "I am sure that you and Clamp will manage. Why, you have overcome worse difficulties than this in the past."

"There was never anything as serious as this," Jeremy said shortly, and Lady Dole allowed herself a brief smile at the thought that he could dismiss so cavalierly the entire Napoleonic Army, but she was well aware that he was in no mood to see the humor of his remark at the moment, and she kept silent.

"You would help a great deal, Mama, if you would go over to Hangarwood and try to keep Mrs. Chase from getting herself too upset. I should hate to have Perdita find everything at sixes and sevens when I bring her home."

Lady Dole told him that she would set off as soon as he had left so that she might be at Hangarwood when Mrs. Chase arrived, and with that Jeremy left the room. A few minutes later she saw him riding down the driveway on his black Andalusian stallion, closely followed by Clamp on a serviceable cob.

— 3 —

There may have been consternation at Shotley and Hangarwood House, but it was as nothing to that felt by Perdita in the inactivity of her tiny room. She had spent the first part of the night sleeping only fitfully. Every small noise had made her think that the rat had returned, or worse still, that Crib had taken the key from Henry and was going to attack her again. However, these problems, as the night proceeded, began to pale beside the constant attack of the fleas which inhabited the rotting blankets. Here again was a problem which none of Perdita's heroines had ever had to face, and she realized that the distresses of reality were often based on incidents which would seem ludicrous in a romantic novel.

Her bites tormented her, but in the end it was the placid snores of her captors which she found most irritating. Unable to sleep herself, she found their easy slumbers infuriated her more than the kidnapping itself.

The men had done little talking the night before, so she was none the wiser as to why they should have singled Jane out to be the victim of their kidnapping. It was true that Jane's father had been a very wealthy man, but he had lived in Dorset so it was strange that someone who knew of him would have taken the trouble to come up to Surrey to seek Jane out. There were plenty of other rich families in Dorset with daughters to kidnap. It had therefore become clear to Perdita that there must be some specific reason why Jane had been the intended victim.

The mystery had helped her to keep her mind off her present condition and her acute discomfort. It also helped her to stop worrying over how Aunt Charlotte would ever discover her in this remote cottage in heaven knew what area of the country, a thought which produced nothing but deep despair.

The room, which had seemed warm last night in comparison with the icy cold of the outdoor, was now bitter cold and in the first light of morning Perdita could see the frost, which had formed on the top of the blanket where the moisture in her breath had congealed into ice. The room was too small to permit her to move about and warm herself, and the wall that divided it from the larger room, although flimsy enough to let some light through its cracks, effectively prevented the heat from the fire from penetrating the room.

When Henry brought her breakfast, she was ravenous, but the dry piece of black bread and the single cup of water did little to take the edge off her hunger. She had started to ask him what they intended to do with her, but he had looked at her with his little red rat eyes and said shortly, "Don't ask no questions."

Sometime during that day she heard one of the men whistling and then the door being unlatched and the whistling fade as the man went off down the track. A little later she heard Henry say, " 'E never struck me as an 'appy man before."

" 'E's got 'is 'eart's desire now," Crib answered.

"Not yet 'e 'asn't," Henry replied. " 'E 'asn't got the money yet."

"You and me's waitin' for the money, but George 'as got the girl. That's what 'e wants. 'E only wants to see 'er family suffer. I wouldn't like to be in 'er shoes."

Perdita felt her body freeze. The thought of George with his filthy hands and ugly scarred face planning some sort of torture for her made her feel physically sick. She looked around to see if she could find some sort of weapon. She knew that she could not defend herself against the three of them, but she would feel happier if at least she could inflict some injury to even one of them. However, there was nothing that could do the least damage, and even her clothing was without any sort of pin or brooch.

She curled herself against the far wall and tried to stop the shivering which had started when she had heard Crib's words.

There was a long silence, then she heard Crib say, " 'E's been gone a long time. What the 'ell can 'e be doin'? We don't need much stuff. We'll be movin' on by tomorrow night. The less 'e 'angs around the town the better."

" 'E's not been gone that long," Henry answered. "You

know wiv 'is limp 'e doesn't cover the ground like you and me does. It takes 'im a bit of time to get anywhere.''

'' 'E never was a swift one, even before The Nile. When we was servin' together the officers was always after 'im to get movin'. Took 'im three times as long to get up the mast as it did the other coves. Gawd, no wonder 'e caught that shot in 'is leg. 'E couldn't get out of the way of a snail, let alone grapeshot.''

"Was that why de Marney turned 'im off then—because 'e was so slow?" Henry asked.

Perdita pricked up her ears and moved as quietly as she could to the wall that divided the room from her cupboard. She looked through one of the widest chinks in the wall and could see the two men sitting on either side of the fireplace. They looked warm and relaxed and she felt hatred flare up within her at the thought that they should be so comfortable while she was so miserable, but she waited intently to hear the answer to Henry's question.

Crib took a draw at the long clay pipe he had between his teeth and his next words seemed to be formed of a long plume of smoke. "Seems like George 'elped 'imself to a few things. Mostly the oats what was to 'ave gone inside Mr. de Marney's 'orses. George found 'e could make a bit on the side selling them, but the 'ead groom caught 'im at it and Mr. de Marney turned George off without a character. 'E couldn't get a job down in Dorset after that. There was enough honest men with good references looking for jobs. 'E was just the sort the press-gangers was looking for, so 'e joined the Navy you might say.''

"You would 'ave thought 'e would 'ave forgotten about de Marney after the time 'e 'ad in the Navy," Henry mused.

"The Navy make our George forget de Marney—never. It just made 'im 'ate 'im more. Wasn't cut out for the Navy, our George. 'E was seasick whenever we was at sea and when we was at anchor he was in trouble. They say 'e was flogged more often than any other man in the King's Navy, and that scar on 'is face wasn't won in any battle with the Frenchies. 'E got it in a fight with another man over some duty 'e didn't want to do. Always was a lazy so and so, our George. I reckon de Marney wouldn't 'ave kept 'im even if 'e 'adn't been caught stealing. Mind you, de Marney was gener-ous compared to most masters. Most of 'em would have seen

George transported. But George didn't see as 'ow 'e 'ad anything to thank de Marney for. George 'olds a grudge longer than any man I ever knew. That man what gave 'im the scar, 'e went missing nearly a year after they'd 'ad the fight. They said a wave must 'ave took him overboard in the night when we was in the Bay of Biscay, but if you asks me, the name of that wave was George. I never seen George look so 'appy as 'e did the day after that chap was lost.

"Still, I'll say this, if George didn't have such a long memory and wasn't so determined to pay de Marney out, we wouldn't all of us be 'eading for a comfortable old age, so 'is grudge is our gain so to speak."

"Nevertheless," Henry replied, " 'e's got windmills in 'is attic. 'E'd never 'ave been able to arrange the matter 'imself. It's lucky you sent 'im along to me. George couldn't work 'is way through a mutton pie without 'elp. Left to 'isself 'e'd make a mess of anyfing."

There was silence again for some time and then Crib spoke again. "Gammy leg or no gammy leg, 'e's taking 'is own sweet time. What's keepin' 'im?"

Perdita saw Crib rise to his feet and go toward the door. He went out of her line of vision, but she heard Henry say, "Where d'ya think you're going?"

"I'll just go down the track a bit and see if I can see 'im."

"No you won't. It's bad enough that one of us 'as to be seen. Don't you do it. If it does go wrong, this way there'll only be one man that people will 'ave seen and you and me'll be all right and tight."

Perdita heard Crib answer from the door, "Is that why you got 'im to send the message by the boy and get the 'orse and cart? I wondered why 'e 'ad to do everything'."

"It was 'is idea in the first place, wasn't it?" Henry answered.

Crib laughed. "You're a sly cove. What you goin' to do if 'e's picked up? They may 'ave someone waiting to see who comes to collect the money tomorrow night. If they get George, there's no saying but 'e might talk."

"George won't be collecting it," Henry said shortly.

" 'oo will then?" Crib asked.

"I will. They'll 'ave someone staked out to see 'oo collects the blunt. They'll be lookin' for a stocky cove with a limp, not a little one like me, so I'll be able to get closer and see when the coast is clear. George 'asn't got the wits to make sure there's no one around before 'e snatches it. I'll see to the money side of the arrangements. You and George will be on the way to London as soon as I'm sure that the money is in place, then I'll wait until you're well on your way and the coast is clear before I takes it. Then I'll lay low for a couple of days and then come up to The Smoke and meet you at Peg's place."

"What we goin' to The Smoke for? I thought we decided we'd 'ead for Dover and slip over to France."

"We might be noticed in Dover, but we'd never be bothered in the rookeries of London. Besides, we've got to get rid of the girl. You didn't think we was going to take 'er over to France with us, did you? What's the use of that when she could be making us a pretty penny in Peg's kip shop. Besides, she'll be better 'idden there than six feet underground. If she causes trouble, Peg can always teach 'er to swim in the Thames." Henry gave an ugly cackle, and Perdita, in her hiding place, hugged herself to try to stop the tremors running through her body.

Crib's remark last night had been unpleasant enough as an idle threat, but now with Henry's sinister planning behind it, the threat was very real. Perdita was not acquainted with the underworld of London, but even a gently reared girl gets hints of some of the more prevalent criminal activities. She could only guess what Peg's kip shop was, but there was no doubt in her mind that she would do well to avoid all intimate knowledge of it.

Perdita heard no more of the conversation in the next room. She sat huddled on the straw mattress against the far wall unable to control the shaking of her body. She knew that the cold was only partly to blame for the shivers that ran through her. She had never before known real fear. Her life had always been surrounded by loving protection, first by her father and mother, who, for all their vagabond life, had kept their daughter safely protected from the seamier side of the theatrical world. Later, Perdita's life at Hangarwood House had been that of a gentleman's daughter in a small village where everyone was known and could be counted upon as a friend. Until George had stepped up to her in the Ten-Acre Meadow, she had never met anyone who had posed any kind of threat to her. She had certainly put her heroines into many

perilous situations, but she knew now that the reactions she
had described of pounding hearts and stifled screams were not
the genuine reactions of leaden coldness and difficulty in
thinking rationally.

That night she did not sleep at all. Rats rustled in the
corners of the cupboard, the fleas bit with renewed vigor, and
the three men in the next room snored stertorously and inter-
mittently, but it was none of these things that kept Perdita
from sleeping. Every time she closed her eyes she saw the
awful face of Crib coming close to her, saw his gleaming
eyes and mocking leer, and almost felt his hands tearing her
clothes from her body.

Between her bouts of shivering and the waking nightmares
she tried to pray, but the God to whom she had been taught to
direct her prayers seemed remote and irrelevant, known only
in the peace and sanctity of her home or the tranquil old
church in the village. She found that the only vision that gave
her comfort was that of Jeremy standing over the fat little boy
at the party so long ago and saying, "Don't you ever, ever let
me catch you being unkind to Perdita."

The object of her prayers changed and she heard herself
whisper, "Oh please, Jeremy, come and get me."

Meanwhile, Jeremy and Clamp had reached London, but at
the outskirts of the city they had parted, Jeremy to go toward
Westminster and Clamp toward the east and the less salubri-
ous quarter of the city.

Jeremy could do little that night. His bank would be closed
at this hour and there was nothing to be gained by camping
out on its doorstep. The activities which he usually pursued
while in town seemed objectionably frivolous when set beside
Perdita's danger. Neither his club, nor any other surroundings
filled with people, suited his frame of mind and he made his
way to the Stevens Hotel in Bond Street. There he saw to the
stabling of Fuego and then, seeking the solitude of his room,
he ordered a light dinner to be sent up to him. After dinner he
tried to read a book, but he found that his mind would not
concentrate on the pages and instead went around and around
his conversation with Billy Larkin seeking some clue which
might give him a lead as to where Perdita was being hidden.
After a time he realized that there was no grain that he had
not sifted, examined, and found useless, and increasingly the

visions of the sort of men who would be holding Perdita suffused his mind. He had seen enough of unprincipled, conscienseless ruffians in the ranks of the raggle-taggle army which had marched through Portugal and Spain, men who would kill or rape, steal or maim for a moment's amusement, and Jeremy felt physically sick at the thought of Perdita in the hands of men like those. His jaw clenched and his hands formed into fists and he cursed with impotent fury. Never had he know such anguished frustration and he paced the room torn between an insane need to get out and simply *do* something and a more rational hope that Clamp was having better luck in finding some clue to Perdita's whereabouts.

In fact, Clamp was having considerably more luck. Having stabled the cob, he had changed his clothes in the hayloft of the livery stables and had emerged no longer the gentleman's gentleman nor the ex-soldier, but a rough and slightly sinister figure, despite his round face. He was now dressed in ragged trousers, a coat of his master's that had seen many better days, a pair of roughly mended boots half a size too large for him, and a filthy cap. His hands had acquired an amazing amount of grime, which seemed to have been on them for several years. Thus transformed, he made his way toward Whitechapel.

Once there, he threaded his way through the refuse-strewn narrow streets to the Nag's Head, where he proceeded to order himself some of the home-brewed beer which he privately described as "belch." Halfway through his first pint, he fell into conversation with a couple of men who were obviously regular visitors to that public house. A couple of beers later he was certain that no one in the pub had seen a thick-set man with a limp and a scar, and Clamp moved on through the darkness to another hostelry.

It was not until the early hours of the morning and in the fourth place he visited that he got any response to his seemingly idle questions. He had been inquiring of a man with a patch over one eye whether he had seen a man with a limp and a scar. Clamp got a negative response from the one-eyed man, but a man in a dusty blue coat sitting on an adjoining bench leaned over and said, "There was a cove like that in 'ere Monday sennight. 'E was lookin' for 'Enry Wigsworth. 'Enry came in a few minutes later and 'e and the cove with the limp sat over there in that corner for nigh on an hour. Vey didn't seem keen on keeping company with no one else neither. Joe tried to sit down beside them and 'e was shuffled off in an 'urry.''

Clamp turned to the man in the blue coat. "I'd be hobliged if you could tell me where I might find this 'Enry Wigsworth. The cove with the scar said 'e might 'ave a job for me, and to meet 'im in 'ere. But it don't look as though 'e's comin' in tonight, so I'd better go looking for 'im.''

"I couldn't say where 'Enry is. I 'aven't seen 'im for a day or two, but if I was you I'd go ask Peg Diver. She's 'is doxie. She works down The Wattles, just off 'A'penny Street. She's more likely than anyone to know where 'Enry is, and 'e may know where the cove is what you are lookin' for.''

Having taken more explicit directions and having caused some ribald laughter at the inquiry as to whether it would be too late to call on Peg Diver that night, he paid for his information with a round of beer and took himself off toward The Wattles.

As he progressed toward his destination the streets became even more filthy and the grimy houses turned into little more than hovels. The stench of old refuse mingled with the rotting muddy smell of the Thames as he approached the river, and the miasma of odor made even Clamp's strong stomach start to rebel. He had to resort to pinching his flattened nose with his fingers before he eventually reached the place he was looking for.

In the house to which he had been directed there was a candle burning in the dirt-covered window, casting a flickering light into the outside world, and Clamp picked his way around a decomposing dog and rapped at the door.

A voice from within called, "I'll be wiv you in a second, deary. Don't go away.''

Clamp waited by the door. Noises from the adjoining houses and the coming and going of a considerable number of men of all kinds, told him that Peg wasn't the only one engaged in business in The Wattles that night. He did not have to wait long before the door opened and a rough looking man came out and Peg, dressed in a grease-stained wrapper, stood framed in the doorway.

"Come in, me darlin'. Sorry to 'ave kept you waitin', but I've got some luvley girls 'ere.'' She let out à cackle which exhibited several broken and blackened teeth, and entering the house Clamp thought to himself that she would have to have plenty of information to make his visit worthwhile.

Peg was a little dismayed to find that Clamp, having declared that only she would do for him that night, was not interested in her usual wares. But when he flashed a bright new guinea and told her of the reason for his visit—being careful to emphasize that it was the man with the scar and not her Henry with whom he had business—Peg became more forthcoming.

"What's 'e taken then, this scarred cove?" she asked

"I 'ad this locket belonging to me dead mother," Clamp said in a choked voice. "The only thing I 'ad to remind me of the best mother a man ever 'ad, and that thieving cove took it off me as soon as I closed me eyes for a bit of a kip." Clamp's expression of woe was miraculously genuine considering that he didn't even remember his real mother, and the woman that had brought him up had turned him out of the house with a kick and a clout when he was eight.

But Clamp could not have chosen a better story to appeal to Peg. Under her paint and dirt beat a heart that revered motherhood with the passion of one who has spent her life avoiding it. Motherhood to her was white-haired old ladies waiting at cottage doors, and she leaned forward and patted Clamp's hand.

"Dirty beggar," she said. "My 'Enry would never demean 'isself to take somefink of sentimental value like that. 'E'd 'ear from me if 'e did. Awl right, I'll tell you what I know. I saw 'im last Saturday. 'E said 'e 'ad to go down to the country on a job and 'e wouldn't be back for a little while. 'E said someone had put somefink to 'im in the pub which was worf 'is while to pursue, so to speak. I suppose this cove you're looking for turns 'is 'and to a bit of anyfink, cos 'Enry 'inted that we'd be on easy street after 'e'd done this job, so it must 'ave been a big one."

"Do you 'ave any idea whereabouts in the country 'e was planning to go?" Clamp asked.

" 'E didn't say, dear."

"Is there anywhere that 'e might go to? Anywhere that 'e 'as used to 'ole up in before?"

"I don't think so, dear. 'E usually does 'is work 'ere in Albania. The only place 'e's ever talked about in the country is the place 'e was born in. Somewhere near Maidstone, I think it was. A place called Otley Green.''

Clamp's heart missed a beat, but his face remained impassive.

"Do you think 'e would have taken the man with the scar there?'' he asked casually.

"I couldn't say, dear, but I know 'Enry's old mother died a few months back and 'e did say somefink about 'er 'aving a small cottage down there. 'Enry was raised there. 'E's talked about it once or twice. It was outside the village, in a wood. Sounded like a pretty little place to me, but I wouldn't care to live in one of them out-of-the-way places. Too quiet. Y'd need nerves of steel to live in a place like that.''

Clamp spent the next ten minutes trying to hide the fact that he found the cottage in Otley Green the most interesting thing he had heard about in the last twenty-four hours. He tried to curb his impatience to be off and down to Otley Green on the instant, but while Peg was regaling him with tales of her life in London and the hardships of her profession, Clamp's mind was whirring with plans for getting back to the livery stable, getting a message to Sir Jeremy, and getting down to Otley Green as soon as he could. However, he did not want to arouse Peg's suspicions by being too eager to leave and it was a good hour before he left Peg Diver's house.

By the time he walked out of The Wattles, the sky was lightening to the east and a cold wind from the river was chivvying the garbage in the streets. A few mangey looking dogs were competing with flea-ridden cats for the edible pickings left in the gutters. Clamp strode on, stopping only once to kick a cur which was trying to take a moldy crust of bread from a tiny child huddled in a doorway. As he moved westward there was to his gait a confident strut which many a member of the fancy would have found disquieting.

The cold morning air helped to dispel the evil effects of the pints of "belch" he had been forced to consume in his pursuit of news, and by the time he had saddled the cob and made his way to the Stevens Hotel, he was feeling quite himself again.

He had not seen fit to change out of his nighttime clothing, and the doorman at the Stevens Hotel gave him a haughty look and told him to be off. It took some persuading before the doorman would even call out the major domo, but once the latter arrived on the scene, he sent at once for Sir Jeremy, having been given explicit instructions the night before that if a man named Clamp came looking for him, Sir Jeremy was to be told immediately.

Jeremy's almost instantaneous arrival and the look of dismay on the doorman's face did much to restore Clamp's good humor, but he did not have much time to gloat. The alacrity with which Sir Jeremy directed him to proceed to Otley Green gave Clamp little time but to attend to business.

Clamp was to make discreet inquiries in Otley Green and to then return to The Stag in Maidstone, where he was to meet Sir Jeremy as soon as the latter had been able to get to his banker and follow Clamp down to Kent with the ransom money. Sir Jeremy knew full well that the presence of two men in a small village making inquiries would cause a lot of talk, particularly if one of the two was obviously a gentleman. He therefore reluctantly sent Clamp off while he remained behind to deal with the financial transaction.

After Clamp had left, Jeremy's impatience precluded his enjoying the excellent breakfast provided for him at the hotel, and it was only just after nine o'clock when he had Fuego brought to the door and he proceeded quickly to Messrs. Coutts in the Strand. He had to pound on the big doors for a few minutes before he was allowed in, but after that it was only a matter of minutes before he had the money and was once more in the saddle.

Weaving his way among the traffic that was already filling the streets, and ignoring the calls of street sellers and beggars, who were quick to notice an elegant gentleman riding a good horse, he made his way toward the city, crossed London Bridge, and was soon in the squalid surroundings of Southwark. Turning eastward, he skirted the elegant buildings of Greenwich and then as Fuego's trot became a canter, as the more heavily populated parts of town were left behind, he began to see the county of Kent opening out before him.

At Farningham, Jeremy stopped at The Crown and Anchor to allow Fuego a breather and found that Clamp had been there only an hour before. A half-hour's rest gave Fuego new zest for his work and it was as much as Jeremy could do to prevent the stallion from covering the next nine miles at a hard gallop. He made one more short stop at Wrotham Heath and arrived at The Stag in Maidstone shortly before noon.

The groom from Shotley Park was lounging in the stableyard talking to some of the ostlers when Jeremy rode up. He touched his forelock and was able to inform Jeremy that Clamp had arrived about half and hour before, had stabled the tired cob, hired a horse from the inn, and had ridden off.

"He said to tell you, sir, that he was going to get on with inquiries and that he would be back 'ere by two this afternoon."

With that Jeremy had to be satisfied, but he knew Clamp well enough to know that he would cover the ground thoroughly, and he also knew that if Clamp could find out anything, he would. Jeremy then found that he was famished, and having time to kill before Clamp's return, he settled himself in a private parlor in the inn and ordered himself a good luncheon of roast duck and turnips, washed down with the innkeepers best claret.

The journey down from London had helped to remove the lassitude of despair that Jeremy had felt the night before, and though he longed to be out in the countryside seeing if he could find a trace of Perdita, he found the wait less difficult than he had expected. In any case the warmth of the fire after the cold of the journey, and the good claret relaxed him and, propping his feet on the fender before the fire and gazing into the flames, he waited for the return of Clamp.

— 4 —

It was only four miles to Otley Green from The Stag, and Clamp covered the distance on the hired horse in less than half an hour. The village proved to be a small one, barely extending beyond its green. The roofs of the houses were mainly tiled, but here and there one of thatch added its shaggy texture to the skyline. All of them looked neat and well cared for and the Norman church stood steadfast inside its circlet of old gravestones, which, tilted by age, looked like giant's teeth guarding the sanctuary.

The green itself held the usual complement of donkeys and cows grazing on what nourishment they could find in the brown grass, and several geese, like a pile of gray stones, sat on the banks of the icy pond in the middle.

Clamp did not want to make his presence any more noticeable than necessary and was debating whether it would cause less comment to make inquiries about Mrs. Wigsworth's cottage at the vicarage which stood beside the church or to follow the sound of hammer on metal and disturb the blacksmith in the smithy the other side of the church. He had decided upon the latter and was about to turn the horse's head toward the green when a small girl carrying a pail almost as large as she was, came out of a cottage behind him.

The child started toward the village pump which was situated on the edge of the green a short way in front of Clamp, but as she started to pass him, he leaned down from the horse and said, "Would you know where I can find Mrs. Wigsworth's cottage, lass?"

The child stopped in her tracks and looked at him with such wonder that it seemed that the noise of his horse's hooves had not penetrated her mind. She stared at Clamp silently for a moment with big brown eyes which glowed from the pinched little face shadowed by the threadbare shawl pulled over her head. Clamp began to think that the child must be deaf and was about to repeat the question in a louder voice when the child spoke.

"She be dead."

For a heart-stopping moment Clamp thought that she was speaking about Miss Chase, and then with relief realized that she meant Mrs. Wigsworth.

"She went to 'eaven," the child continued. "Me mam told me she'd 'ave a pauper's funeral, but she 'ad a big coffin pulled on a farm cart with a big bunch of flowers on it. Me mam says they didn't know she 'ad any family, but she must 'ave. She says Mrs. Wigsworth might have put away a bit for 'er funeral, but she wouldn't 'a sent 'erself flowers."

Clamp waited impassively for this piece of news to be imparted and then started again. "It must have been a grand funeral, but do you know where 'er cottage is?"

"Yes," the child said with the finality of one who is sure of her knowledge. Her eyes stayed fixed to Clamp's face, but she volunteered no more.

Clamp began to feel that he needed some training in dealing with village children, but he decided to try a more straightforward approach. "Could you direct me to the cottage?" he said curtly.

The firmer tone did wonders. The little girl's eyes opened wider and she said quickly, "You go straight on until you see a fork in the road with a big tree with an 'ole in it. Then you go down that way," she said, waving vaguely to Clamp's right, "then in a little while there's a path into the wood, and you go down that and then you'll see the cottage."

"Is there anyone living there now?" Clamp asked.

"I don't know," the girl replied thoughtfully. "I don't expect so. Mrs. Wigsworth's dead."

Before she could launch again into her description of Mrs. Wigsworth's funeral, Clamp leaned down and pressed a penny into the child's hand. He rode on quickly, leaving her standing in the middle of the village street, pail in hand and staring in wonder at the penny.

The child's directions proved to be accurate enough, and Clamp passed the oak with the hole in it with a feeling of satisfaction. It was yet another sign that the trail he was on was the right one. Less than half a mile on, he found the path which the child had described, but Clamp turned the horse and rode back a few hundred yards before turning the animal into the woods. He rode into the wood for some way and then he tethered the horse to a tree before making his way through the underbrush toward the path.

He reached the path, but did not go on to it, only using it as a guide and following his own line several yards into the woods. Within a few seconds he saw the roof of the house between the trees and could see a thin string of smoke coming up from the chimney. Once again he felt a sense of elation as the threads and snippets of information and evidence started to complete the picture begun in Peg's kip shop. The cottage was most certainly inhabited, but if the word had not reached the child yet, it could not have been in use for more than a couple of days at the outside. Clamp knew that it was impossible to keep hidden in a small village for long, no matter how remote one's hiding place.

He made his way cautiously around to the back of the house, keeping well out of sight of its small windows and moving in a crouch so that the leafless undergrowth would give him as much protection as possible from any eyes which might be looking out of the cottage.

There was a small door at the back, but no windows. A large rain butt stood at the corner by the door to catch the water that dripped from the eaves, and Clamp crossed the few yards of clearing between the house and the woods to press himself against the butt. He could hear movements from inside the house but no voices, and he waited, his ears straining for the least sound, conscious of the dripping of the condensing mist from the trees onto the sodden brown leaves, of a rustle of a mouse or bird moving a twig in search of food. He could feel his heart beating and his nerves seemed to stretch halfway across the world.

He waited for what seemed like an eternity, debating whether he dared move around the house to the windows and peer in, and finally deciding the risk was too great. If Miss Chase was in there. and if he were seen, the kidnappers would be quick to get rid of her one way or another.

The minutes ticked away and Clamp still heard no voices.

He had just decided to make his way back to The Stag to tell
Sir Jeremy that he was almost sure that he had found the
place where Miss Chase was being kept prisoner when the
door at the back of the house was opened suddenly. Clamp
had only time to dodge to the other side of the rain butt,
praying that whoever was coming out was not looking for
water.

As the door opened Clamp heard a voice from inside say,
"Where're you goin' now? You're not goin' back to the
village, are you?"

The man at the door answered with a gruff, "Don't be
such a windpate. I'm just goin' out to do the needful."

Clamp heard a third voice say, "Gettin' nervous, are you,
George?" Then the man who had opened the door appeared
around the rain butt and set off for the woods. As Clamp
watched him go, the final piece of the puzzle fell into place
and the picture was complete. The man heading for the
woods walked with a limp.

Clamp waited only until the man was out of sight and
then he turned back into the woods. Within a few moments
he had collected the horse and was heading at a gallop
for The Stag.

Clamp's face when he walked into the inn parlor twenty
minutes later told Jeremy that Clamp had been successful.
The parlor was deserted except for the two of them, and
within a few minutes Jeremy had heard all that Clamp had
discovered.

"But you saw no sign, nor heard anything of Miss Chase?"

Clamp's elation dimmed for a moment. "No, but they
must 'ave 'er there. If they'd of got rid of 'er, pardon me
saying so, Major, they wouldn't all be 'anging about. They
don't need three of them to pick up the money, so it stands to
reason that they're all there so that someone can guard Miss
Chase. Besides, they'll want to keep 'er until they know the
money 'as been delivered."

"I hope you're right, Clamp. But in any case, you've done
wonders. I couldn't hope that you'd have so much success.
Now we've got to plan how we get her without the kidnappers having a chance of harming her. Can Jim use his fives?"

"I don't think 'e's much good," Clamp said, mulling over
the few times he had seen the young groom having a tussle

with the other lads. "I wouldn't think 'e'd be too much good in a tight spot, but 'e might be better than nothin'."

"Well, he can make a diversion anyway." Jeremy said. "Still, I think that we had better make plans as though we were on our own. Now, draw me a plan of the house from the outside. I need the position of the doors and windows and any cover near the house."

He pushed a pen and paper over to Clamp, who sat down opposite Jeremy and proceeded to make a very rough drawing of what he had seen of the house. Jeremy watched with some amusement the effort Clamp put into the proceedings. The man's tongue was clenched between his lips and his brow was furrowed, making him look like an elderly pugdog. Finally he raised his head and handed the paper back to Jeremy.

"You'll see, Major, there's a door at the front and one at the back. The one at the front has windows on either side, and the clearin' in front is larger than the one at the back, so it's not easy to get up to the front door without bein' seen."

"That's all right," Jeremy said, and then proceeded to outline his plan to Clamp.

Within half an hour Jeremy was driving the dogcart out of the stableyard and had turned toward Otley Green. Clamp and Jim, on the cob and a hired horse, had already set off across country making their way toward the cottage in the woods.

When the two men reached the spot where Clamp had tied his horse before, they dismounted and tethered the horses. As they proceeded on foot, Clamp adjusted the length of rope he had slung around his body, and passed a thick cudgel to Jim. As he did so he said, "Remember, if you see anyone but Sir Jeremy, me, or Miss Chase, 'it them over the 'ead with this. Don't wait to find out if they're your mother's best friend. Just 'it as 'ard as you can. You don't want them coming back for more. But be sure you don't 'it one of us."

The young groom laughed. "I won't do that," he said scornfully.

Clamp gave a snort. "Don't be so sure. I've seen better men than you lose their 'eads in a tight situation. Just remember, if you get it wrong I'll show you 'ow to use a left 'ook, and you'll be at the receiving end."

The smile left the young groom's face and he followed

Clamp silently through the wood. They made their way to the edge of the clearing at the back of the house, but did not attempt to cross it.

There was no sign of activity within or without, but the thin thread of smoke still rose in the damp, cold air. Clamp shivered but it was not from the cold; he had felt this way before he went into the ring with the Surrey Bantam, and he could have described every muscle in his body.

Once again the silence was only broken by the dripping of moisture from the leaves and the activity of an animal in a thicket. A small wind blew a flurry of drops onto the two men, but they remained as still as the tree trunks around them.

Suddenly Clamp raised his head a fraction and looked down past the house to the path to the front door. A second later he could make out the misty shape of Sir Jeremy casually walking up the path as though, for all the world, he was sauntering down St. James's Street. Clamp touched Jim on the shoulder and the two of them eased forward across the clearing at the back of the house. At a signal from Clamp, Jim crouched behind the rain butt and Clamp took up his stance on the other side of the door.

Almost as they got there they heard a rap on the front door and inside the cottage the sound of chairs being pushed back. There was a low murmur of voices and then someone walked toward the front door.

"Now," hissed Clamp, and, taking the latch and putting his shoulder to the door, he flung it open and in one quick movement was in the room almost as soon as the front door had been opened for Jeremy.

Clamp did not wait for instructions but launched himself at the nearest man. He was not playing by any rules, and a fist like a piledriver sank into Crib's soft belly, and another one that the Surrey Bantam would have remembered, caught the man on the point of the chin as he doubled up. There was a noise like air going out of a balloon and Crib lay on the floor staring sightlessly at the ceiling.

Clamp turned around in time to see Jeremy land a blow that Gentleman Jim would have soundly approved of, and the limping man also fell to the floor.

The third man, seeing his two companions felled within

seconds, decided that cowardice was a valuable asset in the circumstances.

"She's in there," he said, pointing toward a cupboard at the far end of the room. "I wouldn't let 'em 'urt 'er. I've seen to it that they treated 'er right."

Jeremy barely looked at him, but it was not an encouraging glance. "Tie them all up, Clamp," he said shortly as he strode over to the cupboard and wrenched the door open.

Perdita was cowering in the corner. The noise of the fight had done nothing to calm her, and even when she had heard Jeremy's voice a second before, she had not had time to assimilate the fact. The long hours of dreaming that Jeremy would come to rescue her had made her think that even this was a dream and she looked up at him framed in the doorway as though he were some ghost.

He reached out his hand to her without a word and she tried to rise to her feet, but her legs seemed to have lost all their strength, and it was not until Jeremy pulled her up into his arms that she could stand. Even then, she was trembling so hard that she would have fallen if he had not held her tightly.

"Did they harm you? Tell me," he said in a voice that sounded almost angry.

"No," she answered, the word coming out in a shaky voice which she hardly recognized as her own. "I'm—I'm just cold and filthy and—and—" She found she could not finish the sentence.

He looked down at her, and his eyes were filled with anxiety, but his voice was firm. "You're safe now. The men have been taken care of. I'm going to take you home. Do you think that you can walk if I help you?"

"I think so," Perdita said, but she found that her legs were not obeying her orders and Jeremy reached down with a swift motion and swung her into his arms. He carried her into the room where Clamp and Jim were trussing up the men like chickens ready for the pot.

"Clamp, you stay with these men," Jeremy ordered, "and Jim you go quickly and fetch the constables from Maidstone. I'll take Miss Chase back to The Stag. Jim, as soon as you've seen the constables, I want you to take my horse and ride as fast as you can for Hangarwood House. Let them know that Miss Chase is safe and that I will be bringing her home as soon as she is fit to travel. She should be fit enough for that in the morning. In any case, if there is any change of plan, say that I will be sending Clamp with a message."

"And I'm to take Fuego, Sir Jeremy?" the boy asked, scarcely able to believe his luck in being allowed to ride Sir Jeremy's charger.

"Yes, but don't lame him," Sir Jeremy answered, and the boy turned quickly and had the door open, afraid that Sir Jeremy might change his mind and spoil his chance to boast that he had ridden Sir Jeremy's charger when he got back to Shotley. He was stopped in his headlong flight by Sir Jeremy's speaking again.

"Steady there. I want you to stop first at The Stag and tell them to prepare a room for Miss Chase. I want a good fire in it and the bed warmed and some hot bricks left in it. Tell them to have some fresh broth made, too. All right, now you can go."

As Jim raced out of the front door, Jeremy nodded at Clamp. "Can you manage these three until the constables get here? I want to get Miss Chase to The Stag as soon as I can."

Clamp nodded and touched his forelock. "I reckon, Major, that it'll take more than these three gull-gropers to see me all abroad," he said.

Jeremy allowed himself a smile at Clamp's assurance, and holding Perdita firmly in his arms, he turned and walked out of the door with her.

Perdita was finding it hard to assimilate all the events of the past few minutes. The two days and nights she had been held by the kidnappers had left her with a feeling that nothing was real anymore, but through the haze of unreality she was sure only of Jeremy's arms around her and his face against her hair. It might be a dream, but it was one that she was in no hurry to wake from and she snuggled her face into his shoulder and relaxed in the strength of his arms.

In dreams, short journies can take a long time, and long ones only seconds; to Perdita's sorrow the journey down the path to the waiting dogcart took only a few seconds as Jeremy's long strides covered the ground. She found all too soon that she had been placed on the seat of the dogcart and that Jeremy had walked around to get in on the other side. However, she was greatly relieved to find that once he had settled himself in the dogcart, he put the reins in his right hand and drew her against him with his left arm.

Almost as soon as they started on the road to Otley Green, Perdita's teeth began to chatter with delayed shock and cold. Jeremy, looking down at the blond head tucked into the crook of his shoulder, drew the horse to a halt.

"I'm a damned fool," he said. "I should have had the forethought to bring some carriage rugs." He slid his arm from around Perdita and started to remove his greatcoat. "Here I'll wrap you up in this. We won't be long. It's just over four miles to Maidstone."

Perdita protested faintly that she would not take his coat, but he overrode her protestations with a smile and said gently, "You need not worry for me. I have survived worse weather in more threadbare clothing than this, and for far longer than it will take us to get to The Stag."

Perdita could not tell him that her fear was mainly that he would now feel it unnecessary to keep his arm around her, but when he drew her back against him again and said, "You'll soon be tucked up in a warm bed with some good hot soup," she found that her protestations faded quickly.

The rest of the journey passed in silence. Perdita concentrated on the fact that she was being held tightly by Jeremy, and blissfully realized that sometimes real life did behave like novels and that heroes really did rescue heroines. With him so close, she could shut her mind off from the horrors of the past few days and concentrate on this wonderful moment. Her shivering lessened and the steady clip-clop of the horse's hooves lulled her into a state near sleep. Jeremy bent his head and gently laid his cheek on the ash-blond head cradled on his shoulder.

By the time they arrived at The Stag the warmth had come back to Perdita's legs and feet and she was able to walk into the inn supported on Jeremy's arm. In a daze she heard him issue commands and saw maids and porters run to carry them out.

Gently, Jeremy helped her up the stairs and into a room which looked out onto a quiet garden at the back of the inn. There was a large feather bed against one wall which looked more inviting than anything Perdita had ever seen. A vigorous fire was burning in the fireplace and a maid was busy filling a hip bath with steaming water. The maid turned and curtsied as Perdita came into the room and Jeremy gently freed himself from Perdita's clinging hand and said, "After you have had your bath you are to get into bed. I have ordered some food to be sent up to you, and I will come back to make sure that you eat it all. But first you must get warm. You will be surprised how much warmth and good food will do for you, and after a good night's sleep you will be feeling much more the thing. I'll leave you now, but I'll be back as soon as they bring your food."

Perdita hated to see Jeremy go, but the hot bath and the ministrations of the maid helped to take the tension out of her body and she felt her muscles begin to relax. When her hair had been washed and dried before the fire and the maid had produced a deliciously clean nightgown, she climbed into the huge bed and snuggled under the thick eiderdown, finding the luxury of hot bricks against which to warm her toes.

As soon as she was settled in bed the maid left, shortly to reappear with a tray laden with food and a steaming mug of mulled wine. Jeremy followed the maid into the room and smiled to see the improvement in Perdita's color. There was a flush of pink in her cheeks and some of the terror had left her eyes, but Jeremy was too old a hand in cases of shock to think that Perdita had put her bad experiences behind her.

"Now," he said, drawing up a chair beside the bed as the maid busied herself tidying up the room, "I am going to see that you eat everything before you. It will do you a power of good to eat. You will see. You have been through a hard battle, but I have seen men who have been through bad times recover amazingly after a hot meal. I remember one chap—in the bad winter before Salamanca . . ." He talked on, watching Perdita eat, and knowing that the sound of his voice was more important than what he said.

Perdita found that her tired brain could not assimilate the stories he was telling her, but the sound of his voice was like a soothing hand stroking her tangled nerves and making them straight again, and like an ointment on her raw senses. She surprised herself by eating all the food on the tray, and sure enough, found that the warmth and a full stomach brought about a relaxation that she had thought she would never attain again.

When at last she had finished the food and the wine, her eyes were beginning to close, and Jeremy gestured to the maid to remove the tray. When she had left the room, he got up quietly and pulled the bedcovers up to Perdita's chin.

"I will leave you now," he said softly. "Sleep well. Tomorrow I will have you safe home with your family. But if you should need anything in the night, I am next door, so just tap on the wall and I will hear you. Now good night."

Perdita's eyelids were closing over her gray eyes. Jeremy turned from the door to see the black lashes finally lower themselves onto her cheeks and he went out of the room and softly closed the door.

Perdita slept and in the deep warmth of the bed she felt herself still held in Jeremy's arms. He was bending down to kiss her and she smiled in her sleep, but then his face became covered in a stubble of filthy beard, she could smell the foul breath and see the malice in the eyes that were coming closer to her face. She tossed in the bed and moaned, but the vision of Crib closed in on her. He had her pinned in his arms, his hands were tearing at her clothes. She couldn't get away and she screamed.

The evil face of Crib began to fade as a voice said, "It's all right. You're safe, my love. It's only a bad dream. Perdita, wake up! It's all right."

Jeremy's voice went on soothing her, though she could not stop shaking. He sat on the bed and took her in his arms and, like a child, she pressed her face into his chest, drawing courage from his warmth and strength. His hands stroked her back and hair and his voice murmured comforting words, and gradually the bedroom in the inn and Jeremy became more real than the nightmare of the dreadful cottage and the evil Crib.

After a while she realized that she was not behaving as one of her heroines would have done, and that Jeremy must think her terribly namby-pamby to be so lacking in spirit.

"I'm sorry," she murmured, pulling away from his arms. "You must think me so terribly stupid. It's just that I dreamed that the man, Crib, was—was—Oh, Jeremy it was so awful . . ." But the recollection brought with it a renewed fear, and she started shaking again. Jeremy pulled her close and rocked her in his arms.

"Hush, my sweeting, hush. Of course, I don't think you are stupid. You have had a horrible experience. No wonder you have nightmares. Everything is all right now." He shifted his position to ease a cramped muscle and Perdita clung to him urgently. "It's all right, sweetheart, I won't go away again. I'll be here to drive away the nightmares. I won't let anything hurt you."

As her shaking lessened and then ceased, he gradually lowered her back onto the bed. Her eyes were beginning to close again, but every now and then they would open and she would draw herself close to him. Finally she slept, but she held his hand tightly. Jeremy eased himself into a reasonably comfortable position beside her and spent the rest of the night watching and dozing.

The morning sun was streaming between the cracks in the curtains when Jeremy awoke. He looked down at Perdita sleeping soundly beside him and gently unloosened her hand. She stirred slightly but did not waken, and Jeremy tip-toed quietly to the door. With his hand on the latch he turned back to look at the figure in the bed, but she did not move and he opened the door and walked out into the hall.

"Why, Sir Jeremy! Sir Jeremy Dole! What a pleasant surprise. I had no idea that you were intending to stay at The Stag. Why, had I known I should have insisted that you share my carriage from Idingfold."

Mrs. Banistre-Brewster was blocking Jeremy's path back to his own room, her face alert with the joy of finding someone to question and hound. She was well known in the villages of Idingfold and Byfold as being the nonpareil among gossips. Jeremy had made a joke of the fact that her information service was infinitely better than that of Wellington's. Of all the people he could have wished not to meet on that particular morning and in that particular place, Mrs. Banistre-Brewster was at the top of the list.

"I had no idea that you were planning a journey from Shotley Park," the lady went on, her hands reaching out to clutch the sleeve of Jeremy's dressing gown in a gesture which had become automatic over years of preventing her victims' attempted escapes. "Had I heard that you were to travel, I should have sent my manservant immediately with an invitation to accompany me." She tugged his sleeve and gave him an arch smile.

"Now, in which direction are you going? I am on my way to Folkestone to stay with my sister for a month. If you are going in the same direction, I would be pleased to take you up in my postchaise. You can send your man on with your conveyance, and we can pass the journey in a nice coze. Now I will not hear of you refusing. I assure you it will not put me out in the least and I am sure that you find the journey passes much more quickly in pleasant company."

Jeremy tried to interrupt, but Mrs. Banistre-Brewster held up her hand. "Oh, of course. How stupid of me. I had forgotten that you would have your own traveling carriage. In that case you may put some of your luggage in my postchaise and I can move into your conveyance. I am quite sure that your carriage will have much better springs than the one I have hired. Now I will go straight downstairs and make the arrangements so you will not be troubled at all."

"I am very sorry, madam, to have to forego the pleasure of your company," Jeremy said urbanely, "but my business is in this town and I must excuse myself as I am late for my appointment at this very moment."

"Ah, Sir Jeremy, I am sure that it is important business to do with your estates. Such a lot to manage, but you know we are all agreed in the neighborhood that you do not leave enough to your man of business. You must not wear yourself out. You must forgive me for saying so, but attention to duty can be taken too far, dear Sir Jeremy. After your gallant service to your country, you owe it to yourself to take time for pleasure. Why only the other day, Mrs. Munster and I were saying that you make a slave of yourself to your duty. Fie, I declare that if everyone had attended so well to their duty during the war, the country would not be in the state it is today. Your duty now is to delight us ladies with your presence. Why it is time you looked for a wife. I know that your charming mother would like nothing so well as to have to relinquish her place as the mistress of Shotley Park to a daughter-in-law.

"Now out upon it! I declare I have raised a blush to those handsome cheeks. I am sure that you already have some delightful young lady in mind! Now I will not rest until you have divulged her name to me."

Jeremy found his irritation hard to keep in check, and the blush that Mrs. Banistre-Brewster had discovered on his face was in reality a flush of anger. However, his one desire was to remove the lady from the door of Perdita's room, which he was all too aware she had seen him leave, in his dressing gown, only moments before.

"You must excuse me, madam," he said in an icy voice which had reduced many a young officer to jelly, "but I have urgent business to attend to and must find my man to shave and dress me."

"Oh, indeed, Sir Jeremy, I will not keep you. I do so understand your hurry, and know that I must keep my curiosity in check for the time being, but be sure I shall insist upon satisfaction then, for I wish to be the first to wish you happy." Mrs. Banistre-Brewster fluttered her eyelashes at Jeremy, and he could almost feel the tap of a phantom fan on his arm. She was about to turn to go down the staircase when Jeremy heard the door behind him open.

"Jeremy," he heard a soft voice say.

He stood transfixed with horror as he watched Mrs. Banistre-Brewster's eyes open slowly with amazement and then fill with a gleam of maliciousness. He turned quickly to see Perdita with a stunned expression on her face, staring as though mesmerized at Mrs. Banistre-Brewster. For a moment the two ladies faced each other in silence, and then Jeremy said to Perdita, "It's all right, my dear, I will be with you in a moment. Pray return to your room."

Perdita bolted back into the bedroom like a rabbit down a hole, and closed the door quickly. The feelings that were going through her mind Jeremy could only guess, but he turned back to Mrs. Banistre-Brewster, trying with a supreme effort to collect his thoughts and to act with an ease he most certainly did not feel.

He smiled slowly and, matching Mrs. Banistre-Brewster's archness, said, "I fear you have caught me in a most monstrous lie. I must beg you to respect the secrecy with which Miss Chase and I married. She did not wish any news to be spread abroad until later, owing to the recent death of her uncle, but both Mrs. Chase and my mother were anxious that we did not have to wait too long to fulfil the dearest wish of the late Mr.

Chase. However, I know I can rely on you not to spread the news before the families see fit to make the announcement. You understand the displeasure that would cause to both families," he added with deliberateness.

"Oh no, of course not," Mrs. Banistre-Brewster said quickly, realizing the damage she would do to her social standing by antagonizing the two most prominent families in the neighborhood. "Why, Sir Jeremy, you know me to be the very soul of discretion. I will not say a word to anyone—but—Oh, I must wish you happy. Miss Chase, or I should say, Lady Dole, is such a charming young lady—so well liked in the neighborhood. She will make a charming mistress of Shotley Park. Perhaps you will permit me to tell the news to my sister, with whom I will be staying. She is so interested in all the news I bring of Byfold and Idingfold."

"No one, if you please Mrs. Banistre-Brewster," Jeremy said in a steely tone, and was delighted to see the consternation in Mrs. Banistre-Brewster's eyes. To forbid her to spread gossip under threat of social ostracism was to snatch the hope of Paradise from the damned. Before she could recover herself he bowed stiffly and said, "And now if you will excuse me, I really must find my man."

Jeremy turned and almost pushed Mrs. Banistre-Brewster aside as he started toward his own room.

Once there, he sat for some minutes on the end of his bed, frowning at the floor and wondering how the devil he had managed to get himself into such a coil. Finally he shrugged his shoulders and rang for Clamp.

The valet noticed that his master was upset, but put it down to the worry over Miss Chase. However, when Clamp was helping his master into the blue superfine coat, Sir Jeremy said, "I would be obliged, Clamp, if you would go downstairs and find out if Mrs. Banistre-Brewster has left the inn. If she has, then see that the horse is put to the dogcart and come back and tell me when that is done. We will leave for Hangarwood immediately. However, if Mrs. Banistre-Brewster is still here, wait until she leaves before carrying out my orders."

"Very good, Sir Jeremy," Clamp said, leaving the room quickly. He did not need to be told now what had caused his master's mood. Clamp knew, as well as anyone, the reputation of Mrs. Banistre-Brewster, and did not need to be warned of the damage she could do to Miss Chase's reputation if she found out that she was in the same inn as Sir Jeremy. However, Clamp might have felt a great deal more uneasy if he knew that the damage was already done.

— 5 —

Jeremy was reticent about his exchange with Mrs. Banistre-Brewster during the journey back to Hangarwood House. Perdita had finally plucked up the courage to ask the question that was uppermost in her mind, but even when she managed to ask him how he had dealt with Mrs. Banistre-Brewster, he would only say shortly, "It's all right. Don't worry," and the finality of his tone prevented her from asking for details.

In any case, Perdita's casting of Jeremy in the role of hero was by now so complete that she felt he was capable of solving any problem, and she was confident that he had managed to stifle even Mrs. Banistre-Brewster's wagging tongue, for no one would dare go against Jeremy's wishes. Besides, Perdita was content to leave that problem to him as she found that her recent ordeal had left more shadows behind than she had first thought that it would, and it was requiring a great deal of effort to keep her mind from dwelling on the more frightening episodes. She was therefore grateful that Jeremy refused to talk of serious matters and instead regaled her with amusing anecdotes of his experiences.

He was all too aware that the horrors of the past days could not be easily dismissed, and that it would take more than a good night's sleep to restore Perdita to her former self. He therefore wracked his brain for amusing stories to tell her and counted it a victory every time he made her smile.

He found that this attempt to keep her from fretting had the added advantage of keeping his own mind from the predicament that the encounter with Mrs. Banistre-Brewster had produced.

He simply wished now to get Perdita back to Hangarwood as quickly as possible, and apart from a brief stop at Sevenoaks to have some lunch and change horses, they did not pause in the journey.

The hired horse was a willing animal and the dogcart turned into the driveway of Hangarwood House just as the red ball of sun started to slide behind the black branches of the elms beside the house. Perdita drew in her breath sharply as the wheels crunched on the gravel of the drive. There had been many moments in the past days when she had thought that she might never see her home again.

However, she had little time to think sad thoughts, for as soon as the sound of the dogcart's wheel had been heard in the house, the front door was flung open and Aunt Charlotte, Jane, and all the servants came out onto the doorstep to greet her.

The wheels had barely stopped when the footman ran forward to hold the horse's head, and Bonder stepped up to offer Perdita a hand out of the vehicle, but she was not willing to give up her closeness with Jeremy so quickly, and she turned to him. He smiled and took her hand, and helped her gently to the ground. No sooner had her feet touched the gravel than she was engulfed in a crowd of arms and smiling faces.

"My darling child," her aunt said, hugging her close to her ample bosom, "what an awful ordeal you have been through, but you need fret no more. You are home where you belong, safe and sound, for which the Lord be thanked."

". . . and Jeremy," Perdita said with a shaky smile, looking at him over her aunt's shoulder with an expression of such gratitude and sweetness that Jeremy almost found that he had cause to be grateful to her captors.

"I don't know how you could be so brave, darling Perdita," Jane said, pressing forward into the group and clutching Perdita's hand. "I know that I would have died of fright long before I could have been rescued. Oh, let me look at you! I thought I might never see you again. Oh I can't believe you are home—and not harmed. Isn't Jeremy wonderful—and Clamp too—to have found you so quickly and saved you from those frightful men?"

Perdita nodded her head in agreement, but was unable to get a word in against Jane's torrent, and the press of servants who were moving her into the house.

As they entered the hall, Mrs. Chase started giving orders despite the fact that everything had been in readiness minutes after Sir Jeremy's groom had brought the news of Perdita's rescue. Betty was instructed yet again to be sure the Miss Perdita's bed was well aired and ready for her, and that it might be a good thing if the warming pan was put once more between the sheets to make sure that no damp had collected since the last time. Susan was told to see that Miss Perdita's nightgown was warming before the fire, and Mrs. Pargeter was reminded that the chicken broth which had been cooking for the last twelve hours would be needed at any minute. The reassuring answers did nothing to allay Mrs. Chase's fluster and she clucked around Perdita alternately hugging her and crying over her as they moved toward the staircase.

Jeremy stood thoughtfully on the outskirts of the melee and looked at Perdita as she was swept away to her bedroom. It was only when she had her foot on the lowest stair that Mrs. Chase remembered his presence. She allowed Betty and Jane to help Perdita up to her bedroom and turned to Jeremy with open arms.

"My dear Jeremy—don't think that I have forgotten you in the joy of the moment. Indeed, we owe the joy to you and to you alone. I dread to think what might have happened had you not acted so swiftly and so brilliantly. Oh, how can any of us ever thank you enough for what you have done! I am sure that we would never have seen Perdita again but for your efforts." Mrs. Chase reached once again for her handkerchief and dabbed her eyes, but before Jeremy could say anything she continued, "How you ever managed to discover where she was so quickly I will never understand, though I must hear all about it as soon as I have Perdita settled. Oh dear, I mustn't keep you standing here like this. I will tell them to take your horse to the stable and I insist that you stay to take dinner with us. Perdita of course will take dinner in her room, but Jane and I would be honored by your company.

"Oh, what would we have done without you? How can we ever sufficiently show you our gratitude? We will be forever in your debt."

Jeremy inclined his head slightly. "I need no thanks, Mrs. Chase. It would have grieved me as much as anyone had any harm come to Perdita. Do not thank me. My actions were purely self-interested. But I must decline your kind invitation to stay to dinner. I know that my mother is most anxious to hear that Perdita is safely home, and tonight I am sure that you would rather be with Perdita than entertaining a visitor.

However, I would be obliged if you would allow me to call tomorrow morning to see how Perdita goes on, and I would very much like to have a few minutes to talk with you privately. Would eleven o'clock be convenient?''

Mrs. Chase looked surprised, but said, ''Of course, my dear Jeremy, you are always welcome, at any time. I have always considered you and your brother, Christopher, as part of the family—and now more than ever. As for seeing me privately—why of course you may see me at any time that suits you. Oh, when I think of how we might all be feeling at this moment were it not for your actions!''

''Pray do not distress yourself at what might have been,'' Jeremy said quickly, seeing the tears start again in Mrs. Chase's eyes and watching her once more unfurl her lace handkerchief. ''Now it is important that we turn our attentions to getting Perdita's spirits back as soon as possible. I am sure that I will see much improvement when I come here at eleven tomorrow morning. Until then.'' He bowed over Mrs. Chase's hand and then turned quickly to go out of the door. Before Mrs. Chase had reached the top of the stairs she heard his dogcart going down the drive. She paused for a moment at the top of the stair, wondering what it could be that prompted him to ask for a private meeting with her, but then, realizing she had more important matters to attend to immediately, she went on to Perdita's room.

The surfeit of cosseting from which Perdita suffered that evening helped her to overcome the occasional fits of terror which welled up from within her and seemed to freeze her body in the warmth of the bed. Jane was the one most able to relieve these waking nightmares, but she had been told that Perdita must rest and that she was not to disturb her stepsister with her constant chatter. Nevertheless, the irrepressible Jane was unable to obey the command to the letter and when she had put her head around the bedroom door for the fourth time and said, ''I am not disturbing you, am I? I only want to tell you about the perfectly ridiculous man I sat next to at Mrs. James's tea in Russell Square,'' Perdita was forced to smile.

Mrs. Chase tried to chivvy Jane from the room, but Perdita stopped her. ''Oh let her stay. I am not ill, and it helps me to hear of ordinary things. I shall be right as a trivet by the morning in any case, but I do wish that I could have something more substantial to eat than Mrs. Pargeter's admirable soup.''

"I do not wish to run the risk of a fever setting in," Mrs. Chase said with a worried look, but was forced to give in to the combined pleas of both Jane and Perdita and had Betty go downstairs to see if there were any more of the lobster patties that they had had at luncheon.

A few minutes later Betty returned carrying a heavy tray reassuringly covered with plates under silver covers.

"I am not sure this is wise, my darling girl," Mrs. Chase said with a worried shake of her head as Perdita attacked the lobster patties as though she had never eaten before. "I am sure that Dr. Milton would advise a bland diet for a couple of days, but then I suppose you are not really ill. However, you have had a severe shock to your system and I do not want you succumbing to some fever.''

"Oh Mama," Jane said, "I daresay that Perdita was not fed at all by those awful men and it would be far more dangerous if she were to remain weak from lack of good food. I am sure that she was close to starvation when Jeremy found her. Is that not so, Perdita?"

Perdita nodded her head, glad to be able to get on with her meal and let Jane fight her battles for her.

Mrs. Chase made a few noises of dissent, but Jane realized that the day was carried and pressed home her advantage by saying, "We had an excellent apple pie last night, but as we were not very hungry—owing to our excitement at hearing of your release—I am sure that there is a good deal left. Do you think, Perdita, that you could manage some of that?"

"Yes please," Perdita said smiling, and then added more soberly, "I really don't think I shall ever look at food in the same way again. I shall never take it for granted, that is sure. It was so cold in the hut where the men kept me, and they only gave me one hot drink and some dry crusts of bread and a little water.''

"It is too terrible to dwell upon," Mrs. Chase said, sitting down heavily in a chair and clasping her hands at her bosom. "I live in hope that we shall soon hear that those villains have all been hung as they deserve.''

Perdita looked up quickly and her gray eyes were wide with horror. "Oh no, I hope they may be restrained and prevented from doing anything wicked again, but there was one in particular, called Henry, who saw that the others did nothing awful to me. It would be terrible if he were to suffer such a dreadful punishment. Indeed, I could not wish that upon any of them.''

"To be sure," Mrs. Chase said quickly, seeing, though not understanding, Perdita's distress. "They will probably be merely transported to the colonies, and once there may make a good new life for themselves having seen the error of their ways."

Perdita put down her spoon and pushed the food away. Though the men had frightened her and ill-treated her, she felt quite sick at the thought of them hanging by their necks from some roadside gibbet. The mere fact of having shared the same roof with them for a few days had served to make them human beings and not just objects to her, and the realization that they had feelings, however base they might be most of the time, made it impossible for her to regard them with complete animosity. The thought of the three bodies swinging slowly in the wind suspended by their necks made her shiver as though the same fate awaited her.

Mrs. Chase was bewildered at the effect her well-meant words had had on Perdita and quickly asked Jane to tell her step-sister about some of the new fashions they had seen in London during their short stay.

It was a subject close to Jane's heart and she had restrained herself for a long time. Now given the office, the words bubbled forth like water when a lock gate is opened. She launched into a graphic description of some of the new bonnets she had seen with high crowns and smaller brims than those seen in Byfold. "We must take note of these things," Jane said seriously, "for it would never do to be classed as country cousins when we make our come-outs this summer. Mama, you must promise that you will let us have fashionable clothes and not just things that Mrs. Oates makes up from her out-of-date copies of *La Belle Assemblée*. I was grateful that there was no occasion to wear my apricot silk, for I saw that I should have been laughed out of countenance had I worn it in fashionable company.''

"There is time to see to all that later," Mrs. Chase said with a slightly astringent tone. She had listened to Jane's grumbling about Mrs. Oates for several years, and was not prepared to insult the good lady no matter what Jane felt.

"You may be assured you will be well-dressed when you make your come-outs, but I will not have poor Mrs. Oates put to shame by denying her the pleasure of making at least some of your frocks."

Jane had to be satisfied with that for the time being, though she was determined to bring up the subject again when her mother was less preoccupied. However, she felt that having seen something of London now she would be in a better position to argue with her mother's adamantine insistence that, as Mrs. Oates had made clothes for her and Perdita since they were small children, she should not be denied the pleasure in seeing her work clothe them for the important event of their launch into society.

Jane realized that this was not the time to do battle and was quite content to turn again to the on-dits which had so delighted her in the few times she had dined out in London. She was an excellent mimic and Perdita was able almost to see with her own eyes the fat gentleman with the drip on the end of his nose who ogled all the pretty ladies without being the least aware of his own repulsive appearance. She was thrilled to hear that Jane had actually met someone who had been at a rout attended by Lord Byron, and though Jane could not give any details of his behavior or looks upon that occasion, Perdita felt that she was one step nearer to the object of her admiration.

By the time Jane had described the gowns of some of the more fashionable ladies she had seen, Perdita found herself quite relaxed, and Mrs. Chase, pressing upon her the sleeping draught that had been sent over by Dr. Milton and a glass of hot milk sweetened with honey, saw Perdita drift off into a quiet sleep soon after the clocks had struck nine. Mrs. Chase kissed the sleeping girl fondly on the forehead and she and Jane crept out of the room, leaving Perdita to her deep and dreamless sleep.

The sleeping draught coupled with exhaustion of mind and body kept Perdita asleep long after the rest of the household was awake the next morning. There was no question of her being awakened, and it was after ten o'clock before she rang the bell for Betty to bring her her chocolate and bread and butter. She found that the sleep had done much to restore her and she was in a much better frame of mind than she had been the night before. The visions of Crib, George, and Henry were beginning to fade into something between dream and reality, and Perdita was determined that she would, as far as possible, ignore the whole unhappy episode.

She had decided that a short walk in the garden with Jane and Frolic would do her a lot of good, and Betty was helping her into her russet merino dress when Jane burst into the room.

"Mama says that she wants you to come down to the drawing room as soon as you are dressed. She has been with Jeremy in there for at least half an hour. I wonder what they have been talking about? I was firmly told to go up to the schoolroom as Mama wished to speak to Jeremy privately. What can be going on? I should have thought that I might have been allowed to hear all the details of your rescue, but you are to go at once. Perhaps Mama feels you should make your thanks to Jeremy for rescuing you."

Perdita had an uncomfortable feeling that Mrs. Banistre-Brewster might have something to do with the summons. She had had time to wonder how Jeremy had managed to stop that wagging tongue so easily and was anxious to find out more of that situation. Besides, she had become increasingly aware that, no matter what the circumstances, it had been quite shocking to have allowed Jeremy to spend the night in her room, and this realization made her unnaturally reluctant to face him, even in the presence of her aunt.

However, to her dismay, when she opened the door she saw no sign of Aunt Charlotte and only Jeremy, dressed impeccably in a brown coat, buff riding breeches, and boots. He made an overwhelmingly handsome figure as he stood in front of the window and Perdita's heart seemed to leap like a fish within her.

As he heard the door open he turned and walked toward her saying, "I see you are much restored. It is good to see you looking so much better."

"It is you I have to thank for that, Jeremy," Perdita said, lowering her eyes and withdrawing her hand from his. She felt such an overwhelming rush of love for him that she was afraid that if he saw her eyes he might guess what she was feeling and the fear of making a complete peagoose of herself in front of him made her self-conscious and awkward.

She walked over to the piano and started to rearrange some dried beech leaves which stood in a vase on it.

"Perdita," Jeremy said in a voice which seemed to echo her awkwardness, "I have something important I wish to ask you."

Perdita turned toward him holding a spray of beech leaves. A thin ray of pale winter sun caught the silver-blond curls and gave them a radiance which made them seem to have a light of their own. The large gray eyes set in the pale face, and the russet of the dress, made up a picture which made Jeremy stare in silence at her. It was as though he were seeing her for the first time and some thought, some half-acknowledged reality stirred at the back of his mind, but he had business with her, one that he was finding difficult to embark upon. He took a deep breath and dismissed the ghosts of thoughts from his mind.

The silence had lasted only a fraction of a second, but there was something in Jeremy's expression, a wariness, a seeming reluctance to put forward the question he wished to ask her, which clutched at Perdita's heart with something like fear.

Jeremy saw the flicker of apprehension in her eyes and his mouth hardened with determination. "Perdita, I have come today to ask you to do me the honor of becoming my wife."

The words hung like Damocles' sword over Perdita. Her mouth opened in a gasp and her mind flew to the sight of Mrs. Banistre-Brewster's malicious gaze fixed on her over Jeremy's shoulder, and she realized at once why he had proposed.

"Oh no," Perdita said in horror. "No, Jeremy, please not." Then recollecting herself she said in a low voice which Jeremy could barely hear, "I am sorry. You do me a very great honor, and I thank you, but really I cannot—I do not think—" But no more words would come and Perdita ran from the room to the haven of her bedroom.

Once there, she allowed herself to examine the full disaster of his proposal. To have Jeremy ask her to marry him merely to still Mrs. Banistre-Brewster's malicious tongue was an irony she could barely comprehend. Since she had been a child, Jeremy had been her ideal man, and as she grew so had her love for him. For almost all of her life the words he had just uttered were the ones she had longed more than anything to hear, but to have them spoken by him from a feeling of duty and not from one of love, was an agony she had never dreamed of. In all the situations she had invented, he had come to realize slowly—or with a blinding flash—that she was·the one and only love of his life. How could she now marry him knowing that he had offered for her solely because he felt he had to? Besides, there had been talk last summer of a certain lady in London. Perdita had heard her aunt and Lady Dole whispering that an engagement might be imminent. It was bad enough that Jeremy felt he had to marry her, but to have him give up the lady he loved was something which wrung Perdita's heart. She could envisage *herself* being the one he loved and had, for honor's sake, to give up, but never had she thought of being the one he would be forced to marry.

Her dismal thoughts were interrupted by the door opening and her aunt saying, "My darling girl!" Perdita turned quickly and hoped that her face did not show the distress she was suffering.

Her aunt came over to the bed and drew Perdita to her. "Oh my darling child, I had no idea that you held him in such aversion. I had always thought that you liked him, and after his actions of the last few days I thought it more than possible that your liking might have turned to something deeper. But we all know that you have nothing to be ashamed about. No matter what people may say, your family will know that you could never do anything wrong and will love you. There must be some other way in which we can silence Mrs. Banistre-Brewster."

The expression of doubt on her aunt's face put the lie to her last sentence. Even as she spoke, Perdita knew that the only way she could save her reputation was to marry Jeremy, and if she did not, the slur would reflect on the whole family. She would have to marry him, and as quickly as possible.

"I do not hate Jeremy," she said in a low voice. "I—it is just . . ." But she found that she was unable to give the real reason for her reluctance to her aunt. Aunt Charlotte would have been practical and told her that many marriages were successful with far less affection on either side in the beginning. She could never have understood Perdita's pain in seeing Jeremy willing to sacrifice his future happiness for her.

"My dear, I know," Mrs. Chase said, "it is all too soon after your horrible adventure, and you have my assurance I would not have let him speak to you so soon were time not of the essence. If we are to prevent that dreadful woman's gossiping about you in the neighborhood, you must be married before she returns to Idingfold. There is nothing else to be done. She saw Jeremy coming out of your bedroom in his dressing gown, and knowing how people love to think the worst, I am afraid that even a full explanation would not stop her tongue. Jeremy is agreed that a wedding must take place within the next ten days, and it must be as quiet as possible. I daresay that when Mrs. Banistre-Brewster returns, most people will have forgotten the exact date of the wedding. We have good reasons for keeping it quiet: the recent death of your uncle, and the fact that we are still in Lent. You and Jeremy can go far away for your honeymoon and by the time you get back, no one will be bothered by what Mrs. Banistre-Brewster has to say. Everyone knows that she is a very malicious person and if you are married, no one will give her story much credence. Besides, you will be Lady Dole and people will not point the finger at you then.

"Now compose yourself and put your hair in order. I am sure that Jeremy will want to hear that you have come to see the necessity for the marriage. He is waiting downstairs for you." She patted Perdita's hand and smiled at her. "I told him that I thought that you were in a fragile state of nerves and did not quite comprehend what he offered. I daresay it will put his mind to rest to hear that you have decided to accept him. After all, it would not be very pleasant for him to have his name linked in such an unsavory way with yours. Dear child, I am sure that he will make you an excellent husband. He is a gentleman and will treat you well. Perhaps his manner is a little stiff, but he is kind and considerate, and kindness and consideration are so important in a marriage. I know that you think that love is more important, but believe me, an amiable husband is preferable to one who feels too much passion. Anyway, I am sure that by the time the year is out you will quite think yourself a ninnyhammer for having had any misgivings."

In the drawing room Jeremy had been having thoughts as troubled as Perdita's. He saw the imperative need for silencing the scandal which Mrs. Banistre-Brewster would start, but he was deeply distressed at the thought of having to force Perdita into a marriage she did not like. Although he had always regarded Perdita as his charge, he had long ago realized that she was in love with his brother, Christopher, and had become used to the idea that they would one day marry. He had, it is true, described what he believed to be their feelings as calf-love, and he ascribed to this his vague misgivings over the whole matter. Sometimes when he had watched Perdita and Christopher together, laughing and chattering as though there were no one else in the world, he felt strangely lonely to be locked out of their closeness and had dismissed them as a pair of children playing games of love.

He had seen the affectionate kiss which Perdita had given Christopher when he went off to Cambridge and heard the warm promises of undying friendship they had exchanged. He had surprised himself by feeling annoyed that she had not shown the same warmth of feeling when she had seen him off to the war.

But even though he knew that she felt close to Christopher, he had always supposed that she did not hold himself in aversion. Her letters sent to him in the Peninsula had been sweet and friendly, conveying so much warmth and youth that he had been reluctant to throw them away, and in fact still had them.

He knew he cared deeply about Perdita and had been glad to think that when she married Christopher he would still be able to keep an eye on her, but now the situation had changed radically and he had tried for the past twenty-four hours to convince himself that he could eventually make her find that he was not such a bad bargain. However, the look of horror on her face when she heard his proposal had appalled him. He felt as though a friend had driven a knife into his heart and the pain was one which he felt hardly able to bear. He had hoped that she would find his proposal bearable, but her look and her words had put paid to that hope.

He walked toward the window and looked out over the frost-gray world and wondered how he had ever allowed himself to get into such a tangle. He had spent a sleepless night trying to find some alternative, but his rash words to Mrs. Banistre-Brewster had made any other solution impossible. He had cursed himself for not having found a better answer, but there again he had realized that even though his words had been formed on the spur of the moment, he could not have thought of another way in which to explain his presence in Perdita's bedroom in his night clothes. Even if he had told Mrs. Banistre-Brewster the unvarnished truth, she would still have made capital of it.

Of all the women in the world he did not wish to see tied in a marriage she hated, it was Perdita, and he did not even have the comfort of thinking that he had much chance of making her happy. With the constant reminder of Christopher in the same house, he would be responsible for the misery of two of the people he cared most for in the world.

With a muttered "damn" he turned from the window in time to see the door open and a very subdued Perdita enter the room. Her eyes were downcast and there was a hesitation in her step which told Jeremy that she had not come to see the matter in a much happier light. He longed to be able to comfort her, but what use was his comfort when he was the source of her pain. He stood looking at her as she crossed the floor to him.

Her eyes glittered with unshed tears as she looked up at him, and her voice trembled slightly as she said, "I am sorry, Jeremy, but your proposal took me by surprise." She paused for a moment and then, taking a deep breath, continued, lowering her eyes, "But I think that I must be still suffering from the shocks of the past days and I did not answer you as I should. I am most honored by your offer of marriage and am pleased to accept you."

The last words were spoken in so low a tone and her eyes were so firmly fixed on the floor that Jeremy could barely hear her, but he took her hands and, matching her serious tone, said, "Believe me, I too am sorry that the proposal was necessary, but I intend to do everything in my power to make you happy, and I am sure that, if we try, we will deal very well together."

Jeremy's words did nothing to convince Perdita that his motives were anything other than she had surmised, but if he could try to make the best of the situation then she would too, and perhaps in time she might be able to make him feel less regret for his sacrifice.

She raised her eyes to his face and said, "Yes, I am sure that we will deal famously. I shall do everything I can to make you a comfortable wife."

Longing, with a feeling that was pure pain, to take her into his arms and kiss her, yet knowing how much worse the pain would be to feel her resistance or resignation, Jeremy simply raised her hands to his lips and kissed them gently.

"You have made me very happy," he said, and before the lie could become too much for either of them, he pulled away and said in a lighter tone, "I think perhaps it would be kind if we were to inform your aunt of our news. We will need to make plans rapidly, as I think it best if we marry as soon as possible."

"Yes, I understand," Perdita said, reminded once again that his sole reason for offering for her was to protect her name.

But Aunt Charlotte, when they went to her a few moments later, had been able to convince herself that this was a love match. In the optimism of her nature she had been able to believe that whatever it was that had put Perdita into such a fit of the dismals would sort itself out as soon as the two of them were married and the stresses of the past days were far behind them. She had no doubt that Jeremy would be an excellent husband, and Perdita's gentle nature would give him a wife to be envied.

She hugged them both, and kissed their cheeks and told them that she could not have wished for happier news, in between dabbing at her joyful tears with her handkerchief. Jane was then summoned and the whole scene repeated, though in this case, Jane, knowing the full extent of Perdita's feelings for Jeremy, was genuinely delighted that her step-sister should have achieved her heart's desire. The shadow of tears she saw in Perdita's eyes she attributed to those brought about by an excess of happy emotion, and did not question the muted replies that Perdita gave to her. It was clear that the dramas of the last few days had taken their toll on Perdita's nerves, and it was not surprising if, after they had all toasted the future happiness of the couple in a glass of Madeira, Perdita should complain of a headache and return to her bedroom.

It was not until some hours after Jeremy had left that Perdita reappeared and was then swamped by her aunt's discussing the wedding plans with her. It seemed that Jeremy had already made arrangements for procuring a special license and the wedding could take place at the end of the following week. Perdita looked up with a pale face at that news and said, "So soon?"

"Why, my dearest, you know that we cannot waste time, otherwise all of Jeremy's consideration will be put to naught. Mrs. Banistre-Brewster will be returning in a fortnight, and it is essential that you two shall be off on your wedding trip before she returns."

Jane's questioning look brought forth from her mother the full story of the necessity for the rushed wedding. Her eyes opened in understanding as she looked over at the white-faced Perdita. Unwilling to discuss Perdita's deeper feelings in front of her mother, it wasn't until well after they had all gone to bed that night that Jane, carrying a candle, made her way from her bedroom to her step-sister's room.

"Are you asleep?" she whispered as she quietly opened the door.

"No," Perdita answered from the shadows of the canopied bed.

"Perdita," Jane said, shutting the door behind her and coming over to sink down on the feather bed beside her step-sister, "please don't be so upset. I am sure that Jeremy is very fond of you and would not have offered just from a sense of duty. Perhaps he has been waiting for an opportunity to propose for years, and this seemed an excellent chance to follow up his heart's wishes. I am sure that he would not have asked simply to protect you from possible scandal if he did not feel warmly toward you. Why, if he did not care for you, he would not worry about your good name at all."

"Dearest Jane," Perdita said, reaching out a hand to clasp that of her step-sister, "I know that you are trying to comfort me, but real life is not like that in novels. I suppose happy endings are just figments of people's imaginations. I am determined to accept things as they are and make the best of the matter. Perhaps in time Jeremy may learn to love me a little. They say that proximity often inspires love, and I can only hope that it will be true in this case. But as for now, he has made it only too plain that he is marrying me out of a sense of duty."

"Oh how can you say that! I am sure it is not so."

Perdita looked down at the embroidered sheet and twisted it in her free hand. "He said so. He said to me that he was sorry that the proposal was necessary. Oh Jane, there is nothing that you can say that will make me think that he does not regret that necessity. And I—oh of all things, I would not have had him sacrifice himself for me.''

Perdita paused, shook her head, and took a deep breath. ''Well, I have made up my mind I shall not repine, and shall try to be as good and complacent a wife to him as he could want, and perhaps—one day . . .''

Her voice trailed off and she looked down at the sheet with such an expression of misery that Jane flung her arms around her. For a moment she could think of nothing to say that would be of any comfort. Jane sighed. ''Well,'' she said in a firm voice, ''you must take comfort in the fact that he does not hold you in aversion. He has always liked you. At least you are not in the unfortunate position of Belinda Laurimer, whose parents forced her to marry Lord Laurimer whom she detested openly. I hear too that now they are married he has been heard to say that he only married her for her fortune. Jeremy will never be unkind, and even if he does wish to have a *chère amie*, then you must just pretend not to notice and be grateful that he is civil to you.''

Perdita's gray eyes widened with horror at the thought of *chères amies*, and Jane realized that her last piece of comfort had done nothing to cheer her step-sister. ''Oh well,'' she said quickly, ''I daresay Jeremy will not want a *chère amie*. He is probably too old for that sort of thing anyway.''

That comfort was exceedingly cold as far as Perdita was concerned. She forebore to say so, as she realized that Jane was trying her best to make her feel better, but Perdita did not feel that she could manage much more of Jane's comfort, and pleading exhaustion, she urged Jane to go back to her own bed, with the assurance that she was sure that she would see things in a more cheerful light in the morning.

— 6 —

Though Perdita's feelings were unchanged the next day, she was soon able to bury them under the flurry of activity which preceeded the wedding. Although it was to be a quiet affair with no one but members of the immediate families present, the short time before the ceremony meant that many things had to be accomplished in a hurry.

Robert Chase was summoned home from Eton, much to his delight, to assume his role as head of the family and give the bride away. He paid his dues by submitting to the local tailor's fitting him with a new black coat and pantaloons, but having done that he absented himself from the talk of trousseaux, speculations on how Perdita would manage her new establishment, and all the other trivia which the ladies spent so much time discussing. He developed a method of disappearing like the morning mist soon after breakfast, and spent the days outdoors with his dog and his gun, only returning in time to eat an enormous dinner.

Perdita found that most of her days were taken up with fittings for her clothes, and some days she felt that she had spent all her waking hours standing in the schoolroom while Mrs. Oates danced around her like a demented hedgehog, her wrists encircled with little pincushions and her lips full of more pins.

Mrs. Oates was so busy with all the work she was doing for Perdita that Jane decided that it might be a good moment to bring up the subject of the dresses for her own come-out, and she made the rash suggestion that her mother might leave Perdita to the care of Mrs. Oates for a few days and come up to London so that they might engage the services of a London modiste for the clothes that Jane would need.

"For," as Jane said artlessly, "poor Mrs. Oates will be

quite worn out by the time she has finished Perdita's dresses and she will not want to make mine so soon after.''

Her mother's answer to this was to tell her shortly that she was a ridiculous chit of a girl and that if she had nothing better to do than to make such remarks, she had better take Susan and go through Perdita's underclothing to make sure that they now had enough nightgowns, petticoats, and knickers in the oak chest in Perdita's room.

Realizing that she had overstepped the mark, Jane left on the errand, knowing full well that her mother had checked and rechecked the clothes only the day before.

Perdita was meanwhile enduring the fittings as best she might. The discomfort of standing for hours with one arm raised, or being inadvertently stuck with pins, was nothing to the agony of hearing Mrs. Oates, dangerously simpering through her mouthful of pins, extolling the romance of the union of her dear Miss Perdita and Sir Jeremy. ''Who would have thought,'' she said, ''that when Miss Perdita came to me to have her first ballgown made I would be so soon making the gowns she would wear as Lady Dole.''

This theme was reiterated through the meticulous choosing of merinos, lutestrings, muslins, sarcenets, and jacconets; through the pinning and unpinning of countless necklines and hemlines, sleeves, gathers, and overskirts.

Despite Jane's protests that the gowns were old-fashioned, Mrs. Oates and Mrs. Chase were adamant in their opinion that the simple draped clothes were more suited to Perdita's tall figure than the elaborately decorated dresses with their padded hemlines which Jane insisted were all the rage at the moment. Jane risked another dismissal by muttering that she found the clothes very dismal. Perdita hoped that the clothes that Mrs. Oates was making for her with such care would not produce the same thoughts in Jeremy. She tried to remonstrate once or twice with Mrs. Oates about the paucity of trimming, but Perdita's kind heart got the better of her when tears sparkled in Mrs. Oates's eyes.

She was even overruled on the choice of colors, and the stronger tones which Perdita had felt might give her more maturity were overruled in favor of pale blues, greens, and pinks that her aunt told her were more suitable for a bride of her years. Perdita had particularly hoped that she might be allowed a silk in deep emerald green for the ballgown, but here too it was decided by the two older ladies that a pale green muslin with a draped fall and trimmed in Egyptian braid would be more suitable.

Perdita had to admit that the finished dress was pretty, but as her desire was to make Jeremy see her as a woman and not just a young girl, she felt that the dress might not be as successful as it could have been. It did, however, have a daringly low neckline, by Mrs. Oates's standards, and Perdita had to content herself with the hope that this would produce the desired effect on Jeremy.

Her aunt's avowal that it was the prettiest dress she had ever seen and her remark, "Mrs. Oates, you have excelled yourself. Why, I never saw anything in London to hold a candle to it! My dear Perdita, Jeremy will be so proud of you when he sees you in it" gave Perdita hope that Jeremy would at least notice her when she wore it, but she said nothing.

The issue of the wedding dress had been decided upon early in the week. Mrs. Oates would be so busy making the dresses for the trousseau that she would not have enough time to make a wedding dress for Perdita. It was therefore decided that she would wear her aunt's, simply having it taken in to fit her slender body and having an extra flounce of Brussels lace added to the bottom to make it long enough for her.

When the dress had been altered the effect was dramatic. The cream-colored satin underslip with its overskirt of lace made Perdita look like some gracious lily with her creamy white shoulders and long white neck rising from the froth of lace around the neckline. The cream satin bonnet with its lace veil and garland of white silk roses added to the ethereal effect, and even Jane was moved to silence for a moment.

Seeing herself in the cheval glass in the wedding dress for the first time, was, for Perdita one of the moments that became like punctuation marks in the hectic days of the week. Another was the moment when Jeremy arrived at Hangarwood House and, alone with her in the drawing room, produced a half hoop of diamonds for her betrothal ring. Though Perdita's hand had trembled slightly as he placed it on her finger, she was able to manage a creditable smile and to hold her feelings in check sufficiently so that she did not return his light kiss with too much fervor. However, the rest of the day she would secretly move her right hand over to feel the ring on her left, hardly daring to believe that it was there, and even at one moment allowing herself to daydream that it had been put there by a man who loved her deeply.

But she had little time for private thoughts, and the activities of the days sent Perdita to bed so tired that she fell asleep almost as soon as her head touched the pillow.

In just over a week since she had been returned to Hangarwood House she left it again, but this time not in a farm cart, but in the Chase carriage and seated beside her aunt, Jane, and Robert, dressed in the cream satin and lace and heading in the direction of the Shotley Park chapel.

Though she had not been successful in persuading herself that this was the happiest day of her life, Perdita was determined that no one else would know with what reluctance she set off to her wedding. If it was the travesty of all her dreams, no one else would be party to her innermost thoughts. If reality was unhappy, then she would pretend that the whole thing was a play. She would be some princess used as a political pawn in the game of destiny, setting out to marry a man she had never met.

Her resolution to lose herself in play-acting nearly left her as she started the walk down the aisle of the chapel on Robert's arm. The glimpse of Jeremy at the altar rail waiting for her to join him almost made her turn and run out of the chapel. She had envisioned this scene a thousand times in her daydreams, but then he had looked at her with joy, with love, or with an expression of conspiritorial happiness. Now his look was sober and enigmatic and it was impossible to guess his thoughts.

Within minutes, she found herself beside Jeremy at the altar rail. She had made the short journey without being aware of how many of the pews stood empty, nor was she conscious of the gaze of her Aunt Charlotte, Jane, and Lady Dole, nor of Christopher standing beside Jeremy. She was like a compass needle pulled inexorably toward its true north, and no one but Jeremy existed for her.

On the fringes of her mind she was conscious of the vicar addressing them and then she seemed to feel as well as hear Jeremy's deep baritone repeating vows which were poignantly bitter under the circumstances. She heard her own voice, clearer and steadier than she had believed possible, reiterating the vows, and then Jeremy slipped the gold ring on her finger and led her back down the aisle.

Through the rest of the celebrations, Perdita knew herself to be her father's daughter, as she acted the part of the happy bride to her family and the Doles. Once or twice she saw Jane give her a questioning glance, but her smile was so serene that Jane seemed to be satisfied. Only at the back of her mind did Perdita allow the thought of the coming moment when she must be alone with Jeremy without the unwitting support of the two families.

All too soon Aunt Charlotte was signaling to Perdita that it was time to change into her traveling costume and she was taken from Jeremy's side to the bedroom allotted to her at Shotley Park for her changing. She was helped out of the cream satin and into the dark blue lutestring with its high waist and its confining neckline topped with a neat white frill. The long tight sleeves ended just short of Perdita's fingers, and when she looked down they seemed to draw mocking attention to the two rings which shone on her left hand.

Luckily, Aunt Charlotte's damp-eyed torrents of advice and Jane's incessant chatter left Perdita with little time to say anything. Eventually the dressing was completed, the fur-trimmed pelisse buttoned down the front, and the bonnet with its matching trimming tied with a big bow under her chin. She went out of the bedroom with Mrs. Chase and Jane and started down the wide sweep of stairs to the hall where all the servants of Shotley Park and Hangarwood House were waiting to see her off.

Jeremy, looking tall and reserved, watched her silently as she came down the stairs. He held his curly-brimmed beaver in one hand, and was wearing a long greatcoat with a fur collar. There were last-minute hurried kisses, cries of good wishes, and a shower of rice, and Jeremy took her hand and was hurrying her down the steps and into the carriage.

The coachman cracked his whip, Clamp jumped up onto the groom's seat, and they were off down the driveway. Perdita craned her neck to catch a last glimpse of the waving family, her last link with safety, before a bend in the drive cut off the sight of them completely. Only then did she turn back to look at the man who was now her husband.

She had been afraid of this moment, when they were alone together for the first time, but Jeremy smiled at her and said in a matter-of-fact voice, "I hope that you like the way I have had the traveling carriage redone. It had not been used for some time and was in a shocking state. I think that Hobson has done an excellent job in the short time I gave him. Of course, if you do not like the color of the upholstery we can have it changed as soon as we get home."

Perdita, taking her cue from him, gratefully replied that she found the pale fawn broadcloth which covered the seats and cushions and lined the interior entirely to her taste and very handsome. She added that the springing of the carriage was the most comfortable she had ever experienced.

"You will find that necessary," Jeremy said. "The roads in France are very inferior to those in this country. Even the main roads to Paris are still unpaved and can be deuced uncomfortable if one does not have a well-sprung carriage."

"Are we going to Paris?" Perdita asked, all thought of awkwardness dissolving in the excitement of the prospect of a trip to a foreign country. Until recently the Continent had been closed to the English because of the war, and the thought of actually going to France made Perdita clap her hands with excitement.

Jeremy smiled at her childish enthusiasm and was delighted to see the apprehension leave her face. "Yes, I thought perhaps you might enjoy a visit to that city, and I shall enjoy hearing your views upon it. However," he said, the smile leaving his face, "if you would rather not go abroad, we can always spend our wedding trip in Brighton."

"Oh no!" Perdita said before she realized that he was teasing her. "Oh, you are funning. You know how much I have always wanted to go to the Continent, and especially to Paris. You will be the most wonderful guide, for I daresay you got to know it extremely well when you were there two years ago. Do you think that my French will be adequate? Mademoiselle used to say that my accent was very good, but that I confused the tenses of my verbs quite terribly. Oh, you must help me, and we will use the time on the journey to practice. The moment we leave England we will talk in nothing but French."

Jeremy smiled. She was after all just the adorable child he had always known, despite the lace and satin she had been wearing earlier. Without thinking, he reached out to put his hand on hers, but her quick intake of breath brought him back to reality with a jolt and he removed his hand quickly and thrust it firmly into the pocket of his coat.

Perdita did not fail to notice the aborted gesture and was again aware that their relationship was no longer one of simple friendship, and she fell silent. It was not until Jeremy, trying to rectify his blunder, returned the conversation to safe ground that she was able to relax again.

"We will be taking the carriage with us," he said, "but I have arranged to hire horses in France. Hughes and Clamp will be coming with us, but I am afraid that I did not have time to hire a maid for you before we left. I hope that you will be able to manage with maids at the inns we stay at until we get to Paris. I have a friend there who will help us find someone suitable. However, if this does not suit you, we can try to find someone in Brighton before we cross the Channel."

"Oh, I am sure that I shall do very well with the help of the maids at the inns," Perdita said. "I am surprisingly able to do up buttons, and even arrange my hair when in desperate straits."

She smiled up at Jeremy as she spoke, and he suddenly had such a ridiculous and overwhelming desire to take her in his arms and kiss her that he could only mutter a short, "Good, that's settled then," and turn quickly to look out of the window of the carriage.

Perdita felt as though she had been summarily dismissed, and the ease she had momentarily felt left her. She too turned to look at the passing countryside on her side of the carriage and no more was said by either of them until the carriage drew up at The King's Head in Pyecombe where they were to stop for refreshment while the horses were changed.

Seated before the fire in the private parlors of the inn, Perdita was able for a minute to forget the difficulties of her situation. The warm fire and the mulled ale lulled her and began to make the whole day seem more dream than reality. That, plus the stresses and exhaustions of the past days, caused her to doze off with her head against the squab cushions in the carriage when they resumed their journey, and she slept quietly as the horses trotted down the final stretch of road to Brighton.

Jeremy, watching her in the fading light, thought how adorable she looked with her head tilted against the cushions. He had been surprised by a glimpse of beauty when she had stood by the piano the day he had proposed to her, but now looking at her unobserved, he saw that she was really lovely. Of course, she was still only a girl, but the fine features and the pale sunlight hair gave promise of real beauty to come.

He sighed and leaned back against the cushions on his side of the carriage. It was not going to be easy to be married to someone as enchanting as Perdita and remember all the time that it was his brother that she loved. But here he was in this ridiculous situation setting off on a honeymoon with this girl knowing that she must be wishing it were Christopher with whom she was going to France. To look too far into the future was something Jeremy did not want to do, but he knew that Perdita meant too much to him to be treated as merely his partner in a marriage of convenience. In the long run, she would be his wife in every sense of the word, but that time was far off, and though her constant proximity might make it hard, he must remember what she thought she felt for Christopher and make no demands upon her. Only in this way was there a chance that one day she might see that what she felt for Christopher was only calf-love. He looked at her and smiled. She was, it was true, still more child than woman, but she was growing as a bud unfolds into a flower and he must give her time to abandon her childish dreams for reality.

Perdita did not wake until the carriage drew up beside the Steyne Hotel in Brighton, by which time Jeremy had been able to convince himself that he would have no trouble in remembering to simply treat Perdita with a restrained affection. However, he was nearly jolted from this belief by the sight of her face as she woke, enchantingly pink-cheeked from sleep, her bonnet slightly askew on her blond curls. A sudden feeling that he had been hit very hard in the solar plexus forced Jeremy to remind himself sternly that this was Perdita and not some light o' love. He handed her out of the carriage and led her into the hotel with a hard-won air of casual good manners.

Perdita, unaware of the battle he was waging, sensed a return of his reserve, which for a moment she had felt was beginning to melt. However, she had little time to think about this as the entrance hall of the Steyne Hotel was teeming with people, who, like the Doles, were waiting to sail to France on the *Princess Amelia* in the morning.

Not all of the company had had the foresight to bespeak

rooms, and the host was being accosted on one side by a fat woman with two small children clinging to her hands, and a red-faced man with a huge pile of luggage on the other. Both parties were insisting upon their prior right to the one remaining bedroom. Their voices were raised and the pandemonium was added to by a parrot who sat in its cage on the top of a mountain of luggage and screamed words in a foreign language.

Without any sign of haste or force, Jeremy made his way to the side of the landlord and said something to him in a low voice. The man immediately broke away from the arguing man and woman and came over to where Perdita was standing. Within minutes, porters had materialized to help Clamp upstairs with the luggage and had escorted Perdita to a pretty bedroom at the back of the hotel. There was a fire burning cheerfully in the fireplace and, relieved to be out of the rocking carriage, Perdita sank down on a chair and removed her bonnet.

Barely had she done so when there was a knock on the door and a maid came in, bobbed a curtsy, and asked if her ladyship wanted anything unpacked.

Perdita hesitated for a moment, savoring the strangeness of being addressed by her new title, and then directed the maid to unpack only the clothes that she would need for the night and the ones in which she would travel the next day. Having carried out these orders the maid left the room only to appear a few minutes later with a large can of steaming water. She placed this beside the washbasin on its stand and, unfolding the towels and laying them on the fender before the fire to get warm, she left the room again.

Perdita was glad to be able to wash off the grime and dust of the journey and luxuriated in the warm thick bathtowels, but the clock on the mantelshelf was ticking onward and when Perdita rang for the maid to help her into her blue velvet dress, the latter informed her that Sir Jeremy was expecting her in the private dining room at the back of the hotel and that he had bespoken dinner for six o'clock. Perdita hurried into her dress and quickly instructed the maid in how to arrange her hair. This done, she picked up her shawl just as there was a knock at the door.

Perdita opened it to find Clamp standing in the passage outside.

"Sir Jeremy's compliments, my lady, and Sir Jeremy wondered if you were ready to join him for supper, or whether you were tired and would prefer something sent up?"

"I am quite ready, Clamp," Perdita said, and pulling the shawl around her shoulders followed Clamp down the long passage to the staircase. At the bottom of the stair, Clamp turned away from the entrance of the hotel, which was still teeming with people, and walking down a narrow corridor opened a door at the end and showed Perdita into a low-beamed parlor whose far wall was almost entirely taken up by a large fireplace. The room was sparsely lit by candles and the nooks and crannies in the beams and the paneling seemed to soak up what little light there was, but a table was set before the fire and Jeremy was standing leaning against the mantelshelf. He came over to Perdita as soon as Clamp had ushered her through the door and, raising her hand to his lips, said, "I hope that you found everything satisfactory?"

His formal manner prompted Perdita to answer in kind and she replied that the maid had looked after her excellently and that her room was comfortable. There was a tense formality in their behavior, as though they were strangers meeting for the first time, and Perdita was grateful for the interruption of a waiter bringing their dinner. Some moments were passed as he served them the collops of lamb and the sauteed turnips, but after he had left, Perdita once again felt like a child at a grown-ups' party. Jeremy however began to tell her some of the plans he had made for their intended journey and Perdita picked up her end of the conversation as though she were joining him in some complicated and formal dance in which one misstep might trip the other.

As the evening wore on, Perdita felt herself grow more and more tense. In the few days preceeding the wedding, Aunt Charlotte had dropped some veiled hints about the wedding night. These had been confined to admonitions that Perdita was to remember that in all things her duty to her husband was paramount, and though this might require her to do some things which she might find a trifle strange, she should remember that men were different from women. Aunt Charlotte had muttered something about what St. Paul had said, but seemed a little unclear herself about his precise meaning. In any case, the whole discourse had been hardly enlightening.

However, Perdita and Jane had often speculated on what it

was exactly that married couples did with each other once they were on their honeymoon, and as young girls this curiosity had led them to examine the Bible with unusual thoroughness and they had looked up several words in the big dictionary in Mr. Chase's study. Neither tome had proved very fruitful and it was not until Robert had come home from his first half at Eton that the girls had found out anything very definite about the roles of men and women in marriage. Though Perdita and Jane had dismissed most of Robert's information as outrageous and ridiculous showing off, they had been given plenty of food for thought.

Despite Aunt Charlotte's rather dampening remarks, Perdita had felt that she might not find doing some of these things with Jeremy as unpleasant as her aunt had hinted. His touch on her hand caused strange, pleasant tremors in her body, and anything that involved being very close to him, Perdita felt could be nothing but pleasant. There was therefore a mixture of anticipation and shyness in her feelings that seemed to increase rapidly as they finished their dinner.

Jeremy, seeing her increased nervousness, knew at once what was troubling her. He had nothing but sympathy with her shyness, but was quite unable to tell her that she need not worry and that he had no intention of coming to her bed.

It was with some relief to both of them that Jeremy found an excuse to cut the evening short. At a little past seven o'clock, he rose from the table and said, "I think it as well that we have an early night. You must be very fatigued after your long day and the tiring journey. As we have to make an early start tomorrow so that the *Princess Amelia* can catch the morning tide, I suggest that we go to our beds now."

A blush crept up Perdita's cheeks, but Jeremy continued, "We will breakfast at seven so that we can be at the shore by eight. Clamp and Hughes will see to the luggage and the carriage, but we will be more comfortable if we can get one of the earlier boats so that we can get settled before the ship sails."

As he said this, he ushered Perdita through the door of the private parlor and led her upstairs. She was barely attending to his words, so full was her mind with anticipation of the time when they would be alone in the bedroom together. She strove to appear calm and was congratulating herself on her air of sophistication when her composure was rudely shattered when they reached her room by Jeremy's raising her hands to his lips and saying, "Good night, my dear. I hope that you will sleep well and be ready for our adventure in the morning." With that, he turned and walked down the corridor.

Perdita stood transfixed beside her bedroom door watching his retreating figure disappearing into the darkness of the passage. Her mind was a spinning top of different emotions. She had been so sure that he would accompany her to her room or at least give some sign that he would return later, but the finality of his words had given her no leeway for any expectation that he would come to her that night.

Worst of all, she was suddenly struck with horror that he might have guessed what she had assumed, and with a fiery blush flooding her cheeks she darted into the safety of her bedroom.

The conflicting thoughts and feelings kept her from sleeping much that night. Through the dark hours she realized that she had once again allowed herself to believe the fairy tale that everything would be resolved on their wedding night, and the marriage of convenience would prove to be one of passionate love after all. She had lived through many imaginary scenes in the past few days in which Jeremy would finally blurt out the truth that he loved her, and she would be free to run into his arms and tell him how much she loved him in return.

She now realized that her avowals to Jane, that she had expected nothing from the marriage except kindness, had not been true, and now admitted to herself that she had secretly hoped that once the ceremony was over she would find all the happiness she had ever dreamed of. Jeremy's brief, cool good night showed her that once again she had only indulged in idle daydreams and that the truth was that Jeremy had only married her out of a sense of honor.

Perdita lay in the deep feather bed, staring at the ceiling and wondering if she would ever be able to gain enough control of her emotions to be satisfied with the facts of her situation. It was becoming increasingly obvious that to wish for anything more than Jeremy offered was to wish for misery, and to display any sign of the love she felt for him would certainly merely embarrass him. It must be that he still yearned for the lady he had had to renounce and therefore to offer him affection was to court a rebuff. Perdita vowed to keep her feelings severely in check, so that at least she would not drive him further away. But it was not until she heard the church clock strike three that she was able to get her mind into sufficient order to get to sleep. She turned over to the cool, empty side of the bed, and with a determination to face the truth in the future she finally fell asleep.

The circles under her eyes the next morning told Jeremy only that Perdita was tired from the activities of the day before. His inquiries into how she had slept had only illicited the response that she had been very comfortable. She did not ask if he had slept well, but had she done so he would not have confessed to having spent a restless night himself. He had found that the vision of her asleep in the corner of the carriage had come between him and his own rest. At one point he had been about to leave his bed and go back down the corridor and assert his rights as her husband, but the thought of her horror, or worse still unhappy compliance, kept him to his own room.

Breakfast was an even more silent meal than supper had been, and it was not until they were walking down the street toward the shore that Perdita remembered her resolve to accept reality and make the best of it. It would never do for her to be a complete bore to Jeremy and she looked around for something on which she could comment.

Across from the Steyne Hotel the Brighton Pavilion's domes and minarets gleamed in the morning sun. This folly built for the Prince Regent, who had made the small seaside village of Brighton fashionable, was the source of much controversy. It seemed a harmless topic and Perdita turned to Jeremy and asked for his opinion of the building.

His remarks were enough to keep the conversation going until they reached the sea. At the shore the shingle was dotted with fishing boats which had already brought back some of the day's catch. Their nets were spread out to dry in the early sun, and there were buxom fishwives, their bare arms mottled red in the cold March air, gutting the fish and tossing them into large wicker baskets which other women would pick up and carry toward the market in town.

Everyone on the pebbly shore seemed to be in a hurry: the fishwives, the men in the boats, the merchants who came hoping to select the best fish, and even the waves, which as they hissed through the shingle seemed to have no time to waste.

Jeremy took Perdita's arm and, guiding her through the Medusan coils of ropes and nets, led her down toward the shoreline. She was glad of his assistance as the wet shingle was slippery and the pebbles rolled treacherously underfoot. They finally got through the line of boats and people and reached the edge of the waves. A small rowing boat was waiting a short distance offshore, bobbing like a toy in the lapping waves. Perdita hesitated a moment wondering how she was to reach the boat without ruining her clothes, when a large sailor, his trousers rolled above his knees, stepped forward and touched his forelock to them.

"The *Princess Amelia,* sir?" he asked Jeremy.

At Jeremy's nod he came forward, touched his forelock again to Perdita, and before she knew what he was doing had swept her into his huge arms and was carrying her through the waves and depositing her in the rocking boat. She was barely settled on the plank seat before she saw, to her amusement, the same procedure carried out on Jeremy, the sailor seeming to note no difference in their weights and managing Jeremy as easily as he had Perdita.

She was suddenly filled with the excitement of the adventure on which they had embarked. Even the boat was a new experience. She had been to the seaside with Aunt Charlotte and Uncle Matthew in the past, but she had never before been allowed in a boat. Aunt Charlotte had been much too frightened to allow the girls to take one of the excursions which plied up and down the shores. Now, sitting in the boat, Perdita's vivid imagination was fed by the new experience. She saw herself as a princess leaving her homeland forever as an exile. She tilted her chin up and turned to look at the ship which lay at anchor some way out to sea, and then turned as though to look at her beloved homeland for the last time.

Jeremy, catching her look, wondered if she were already regretting leaving home for such a long journey, but when she turned back to the ship her expression changed to one of fascination as she saw their carriage being swung up on the deck by a heavy sling, and she saw Clamp gesticulating at one of the sailors he obviously thought was not being careful enough.

"Oh, Jeremy, that's our carriage," Perdita said, excitedly

clutching his arm. "Oh, how fortunate that you decided not to take the horses with us, for how would they have got aboard?"

"In much the same way as the carriage," Jeremy answered. "They would have had slings of canvas passed under them and been pulled up by ropes attached to the slings."

Perdita looked at him wide-eyed. "I would think that they would hate that very much indeed. It must be very dangerous if they struggle."

"Indeed, they do not care for the experience much," Jeremy agreed. "Loading horses in the ships was not a job any man relished much when we went to the Peninsula. But of course the animals suffered more on that long journey than they would on this one across the Channel. My poor Fuego was a sorry sight indeed when I got him back to England. I thought for a while that he would never get over the experience of having been battered about through the Bay of Biscay, but I am glad now that I did not leave him behind in the Peninsula, where he would have had a very much worse fate than being uncomfortable at sea for a few days."

His mention of the Peninsula reminded Perdita that she knew very little of Jeremy's experiences in the war, and she decided that here at least was a safe topic of conversation in which to engage him during the journey. It would be one way of keeping her from thinking of more personal matters. However, there was no need for devising topics of conversation at the moment; the hull of the *Princess Amelia* was towering over them and the sailors were holding out hands to assist Perdita to climb the extremely flimsy-looking steps to the deck.

With encouragement from Jeremy, who followed close behind her, she managed to gain the deck without too much trouble and could then look around her. She was fascinated by the frenzied activity on board. Sailors ran hither and thither with ropes of all description, others stowed baggage and helped the passengers to board, and officers shouted orders at men scrambling up the rigging and on the lighters which swarmed around the ship like chicks around a hen, unloading the baggage and merchandise to be taken to France. However, despite the varied activity, every man knew his job so well that the whole thing was conducted with the precision of a dance, and apart from an occasional near miss, the men seemed to avoid each other with the grace of practiced athletes.

But all was not perfection. A splash and shout from behind her made Perdita turn from her position by the rail in time to see a quantity of luggage slip from its net and fall into the sea. Sailors grabbed for boat hooks and tried to rescue the fast-sinking trunks and valises. Perdita craned her neck, trying to see if any of the pieces of luggage were hers, but she was glad to see that she recognized none of them. Just then a cry of horror from behind her identified the pieces as belonging to the fat lady who had been trying to bespeak a bedroom for herself and her children the night before. The lady had started to scream abuse at the sailor who was trying to haul one of her sopping trunks aboard, and Perdita lost all sympathy for the woman when she started to set about the sailor with her umbrella when he was doing his best to aid the woman.

"It seems our friend is out of luck these days," Jeremy said at Perdita's side. "I trust she will not prove to be a Jonah and bring us a rough crossing. But I think we shall be given a smooth passage. There are no white caps and the sky looks clear."

"Indeed, it seems calm enough to me," Perdita said, having gratefully noted how still the ship was in the water. "I had imagined that the boat would be pitching and tossing and that I would have a hard time keeping my feet."

Jeremy smiled. "You will find things a bit different when we get further out to sea. The water close to shore is usually calm compared to the open sea."

Jeremy proved right, for once they had passed outside the wide circle of cliffs, the *Princess Amelia* started to lurch and wallow in a remarkably uncomfortable way. At first Perdita was unsure whether she was going to be able to stand the motion without succumbing to sea sickness, but Jeremy persuaded her to stay on deck for a while, advising her that she would find the confines of the cabin much more uncomfortable until she had become used to the movement of the ship. From somewhere he found a chair for her and a warm rug, and then he sent the hovering Clamp to find her a small glass of brandy.

She swallowed the amber liquid when Clamp returned and was surprised at the fierceness of its heat as it ran down her throat, but within a few minutes she felt a warm glow inside her and shortly after that began to think that the rocking motion of the ship was really quite pleasant. She said to

Jeremy that she had no idea that a glass of brandy could produce such a pleasant sensation. He laughed, and told her that she should remember that it should be taken by ladies only for purely medicinal reasons, and that he would be extremely put out if he were to find her drinking such strong stuff on any and every occasion.

Having seen her comfortably and drowsily ensconced in her chair on the deck, Jeremy went off to see if he could find out when they were likely to arrive in Dieppe. The weather could make a difference of several hours and he wished to see if he could find out whether there was any indication of bad weather brewing.

Perdita watched the horizon rise and dip above and below the ship's railing, heard the gulls screeching as they wheeled around the masts seeming to direct the sailors who were setting the sails. The rippling water scattered the light from the sun like sequins, and the monotonous creak and groan of the timber of the masts seemed to make a soothing lullaby. In a little while the motion of the ship and the warming influence of the brandy made Perdita doze off into a calm sleep.

When she awoke the sun was overhead and Jeremy was seated at her side. When he saw her eyes open he smiled and asked if she now felt like taking some luncheon. She found that the sea air had made her ravenous and she was pleased to accompany him down to a small dining room where they were served an excellent meal.

The *Princess Amelia* wallowed on through the Channel waters throughout that afternoon. Having taken a few turns around the deck with Jeremy and passed several hours reading her book, Perdita was quite pleased when suppertime came around. She found that the monotony of the sea on all sides of her and the confines of the ship were not to her taste and she had begun to wonder how people endured the months of sailing to India or other distant places.

She and Jeremy played a few hands of piquet after supper, but Perdita found that the sea air made her extremely sleepy, and well before eight o'clock she retired to her cabin. This time she did not even speculate as to whether or not Jeremy would join her. It was obvious that the cabin was for her alone. The worries of the night before, the wine at dinner, and the rocking of the ship prevented her lying awake, and almost before her head touched the pillow she was sound asleep.

She slept untroubled by dreams until a ray of sunlight beamed into the cabin and shone into her eyes. She woke to noise and commotion on the deck above her and, raising herself on one elbow, she looked out of the porthole and caught her first sight of France.

— 7 —

Her first impressions of France were ones which Perdita would never forget. Just sixty miles separated Dieppe from the coast of England, but those sixty miles might have been a thousand, so different were the sights which met Perdita's eyes from those that she had seen in Brighton.

Instead of the neat, understated rows of narrow houses, the delicately formed crescents and streets of Brighton, the houses in Dieppe stood tall and imposing in immaculate ranks facing the wide strip of greensward which edged the beach from the entrance to the harbor on the left, to the cliff and the ancient castle on the right. Everything seemed orderly and formal and, at first sight, too grand for the usual relaxed atmosphere of the seaside.

Perdita could not bear to be in her cabin when there was so much to be seen and, dressing as quickly as she could and giving her hair the minimum of attention, she pulled on her cloak, tied her bonnet ribbons beneath her chin, and made her way up to the deck.

Leaning on the rail she gazed with excitement at all the new things before her. As the ship made its way through the narrow entrance to the harbor, she could see more clearly the quays and the people on them. Dominating the entire harbor was a large crucifix erected above the pier, and even her delight in the newness and strangeness could not make Perdita think it other than a monstrosity. This ugly sign of the Roman Catholic persuasion of the country was mitigated by the magnificent towers of the Eglise St. Jacques which rose behind the houses that crowded the quay.

The somber gray and white of the buildings was enlivened by the brilliant red and blue costumes of the women working around the fishing boats. Perdita noticed that there were very

99

few men in evidence, and those that she saw seemed to be very old or very young. It seemed that women constituted most of the work force, but their enormous white headdresses which towered at least two feet above their faces made them seem in danger of toppling over as they went about their duties. The extravagance of their head gear seemed in no way to impede their work, nor make the women any less strong at accomplishing their tasks. As she watched, Perdita saw four of the women, barelegged to the knee, pull a large boat up onto the shore, while others hefted huge baskets of fish which were being landed from other boats. The whole picture was accompanied by the sound of wooden clogs clacking on the cobblestones and the voices of the women raised in an incessant and strident hum, like the noise of a disturbed wasps' nest.

"Well, what do you think of it?" said a voice at Perdita's side, and she turned to see Jeremy leaning on the rail beside her.

He was immaculate in a blue coat, beige pantaloons, and boots whose shine was like a deep still pool. He looked as though he had just stepped out of his dressing room at Shotley Park and not out of a cramped cabin. Perdita was conscious of her very hasty toilette and the fact that her hair was escaping from the confines of her bonnet in the sharp breeze. She raised her hand to her curls and quickly thrust them back under the brim of her bonnet before replying.

"It's so different from what I had expected. I had thought that the houses would look exactly like those we left in England— or if not exactly like, at least not as grand as these are. They seem to be like palaces instead of seaside houses."

"Wait until you see Paris. These will seem very simple by comparison. The French prefer formality to our way of doing things. They think that the English are just country bumpkins and have no polish, but then their aristocracy has always flocked to the court while the English aristocracy has preferred the privacy of their country estates.

"I had come, though, to tell you that we will be disembarking in a half hour. I found your cabin empty, and surmised that you might be on deck. If your bags are packed, I will send Clamp to get them so that we may be one of the first ashore."

Perdita had thrown her few night things into her valise as

soon as she had dressed and told Jeremy that everything was ready to be taken from her cabin. He went off in search of Clamp, leaving Perdita by the ship's rail to watch fascinated as the quayside approached and the details of the picture became clearer.

As the *Princess Amelia* had slipped through the narrow opening of the harbor of Dieppe, the activity on the ship had become more and more frantic, so that now, with the beach and quay only a few hundred yards away, the sailors were running back and forth manhandling ropes to be thrown to the waiting workers on the quay, and preparing the baggage and goods to be offloaded as soon as the ship was safely tied up.

When the ship had been finally made fast and Jeremy had returned, Perdita was thankful to find that she did not have to repeat the process of going down the narrow ladder into a bobbing rowboat. Here the depth of water at the quayside meant that she could disembark straight onto dry land, and within minutes she and Jeremy were safely ashore.

Jeremy then escorted her from the quayside to the Hotel de Londres where, he told her, he had arranged for rooms for the night. He explained that it might be some time before the carriage was unloaded and finding suitable horses for the journey was not something he wished to have hurried, therefore he had thought it best if they did not set off for Paris before the following morning.

Perdita was pleased to find that he was quite prepared to spend the day sightseeing, and, excited by her first time on foreign soil, she was delighted to have time to examine the ancient castle and to practice her French in the small shops in the market square. She could not resist buying a few souvenirs for Jane and her aunt, even though Jeremy assured her that she would find much more elegant things in Paris. In the end, though, it was he who insisted that she should have a small bottle of perfume which Perdita said smelled exactly like the roses at Hangarwood.

Early the next day they started on the road to Paris, and soon Perdita realized how uncomfortable she would have been in a carriage less well-sprung than their own. The roads were atrocious, with deep ruts and rocks and stones in abundance. Jeremy's horses, which had been left in England, would have had a hard time pulling the carriage over the rough ground, but the heavier horses which had been hired in Dieppe made light work of it, though their lumbering gaits made the carriage roll like a ship in a heavy sea.

Perdita was pleased that Jeremy seemed to show as much interest in the castles and ruins they passed as she did. It was pleasant to be able to get out of the carriage frequently and to explore all the places of interest. Her romantic mind peopled even the most uninspiring lumps of fallen masonry with knights and ladies in wimples with languishing airs.

On one of these early spring days, when the birds were singing especially loudly, and the world seemed imminently green and growing, Perdita's delight in a particular ruined tower prompted her to forget for a moment with whom she was, and she started to tell Jeremy the stories that were bubbling up in her imagination. Suddenly she realized that she was not talking to Jane or Christopher, and she stopped quickly, blushing.

But Jeremy smiled and said, "Go on. What did the princess do then? Surely she did not fling herself from the tower. There must be some way to find a happy ending for her."

Perdita looked at him and realized that he was not teasing her, and continued with her story, bringing it to a triumphant and happy conclusion.

Jeremy congratulated her warmly on the intricacies of the plot and from that day he encouraged her to tell him stories about the places they visited. Soon it became a game to see who could invent the most outrageous twist to the plot, turning then to the other to extricate the characters from their peril.

Jeremy found her happiness balm to his soul, though sometimes when she turned to him with a bright-eyed excitement he felt that playing the role of elder brother was not entirely to his taste. At those moment he had a wild urge to take her in his arms, to swing her in the air and kiss her until they were both completely out of breath, but he would quickly regain control of himself and Perdita would notice how his laughter would suddenly stop and how he would direct her notice to some feature of the landscape, or explain some custom of the country, bringing her firmly back to the real world.

At those moments she saw that she was boring him with her childishness and would become subdued and shy once again.

Jeremy, seeing the change in her, would feel an anger which he irrationally directed at her as much as himself, and their conversation would become stilted and formal.

Their progress, despite the roads and the sightseeing, was steady, and in the late afternoon of the seventh day since they had left Dieppe, Perdita caught her first glimpse of the city on the Seine. Soon the countryside gave way to the cobbled streets of St. Denis on the edge of Paris. But St. Denis was soon left behind and the narrow streets with their streaming gutters and overhanging houses showed that they were at last entering the city of Paris. Once they had negotiated these cramped streets, Perdita was awed by the way Paris opened out into wide avenues whose large houses with their steeply pitched roofs were set in formal gardens which hardly boasted one flower. The whole gave a feeling of organized grandeur, unlike the higgledy-piggledy arrangement of the London streets. She was reminded of Jeremy's telling her how the French aristocracy enjoyed the formality of the court, preferring it to the disorganization of the countryside. Thinking of those aristocrats brought another thought in its wake, and Perdita realized how recently these streets had heard the sound of the tumbrels taking those unfortunate people to the guillotine. It seemed impossible to imagine that these elegant streets had so recently played host to blood-thirsty hordes intent upon destroying all trace of their despotic rulers.

However, as the carriage turned a corner, Perdita's gloomy remembrances were dismissed by the sight of a flash of silver and she saw the twin towers of Notre Dame rising above the Seine.

She turned to Jeremy with excitement and said, "Oh, now I know we are really here! Really in Paris! When can we visit the cathedral? Can we go tomorrow? Oh, there is so much that I want you to show me here."

He smiled at her enthusiasm, but his answer brought her down to earth with a jolt. "I thought that after all these days of nothing but my company, you would enjoy having some female conversation. I wrote ahead to an old friend of mine, Natalie de Chervinges, and asked if she would perhaps be kind enough to show you around Paris. She will be much better informed than I about the modistes and milliners that you should partronize, and I have instructed her that you are to have whatever you wish. I am sure that you will want to return to England with all the latest gewgaws and fripperies."

Perdita found it hard to keep a smile on her face. She had been able to forget, over the past few days, that Jeremy had had no wish for this marriage. For the most part, until her chatter tired him, he had been attentive and charming, and even though he had not given the least hint that he wished to share her bedroom, she had allowed herself to fall into the trap of thinking that perhaps he was finding her congenial company at least. Now she saw that he had just been ruled by good manners and not by inclination. He had shown her the attentions of a kindly older brother who, now seeing a polite escape, could turn her over to someone else to be looked after, and could leave with a clear conscience.

Lost in her own thoughts, Perdita did not speak again as they crossed the Seine and she saw the whole of Notre Dame, like a ship sailing down the river on its island. On the other side of the river the carriage turned finally down the rue de Lille, and entered a cobblestoned courtyard. They drew up in front of a large house with an imposing front door, which was flung open before the carriage had stopped.

"Whose house is this?" Perdita asked, turning to Jeremy.

"Ours," he answered, smiling at the surprise in her face. "For the time being anyway. It belongs to my friends the Vicomte and Vicomtesse de Tournée. I met them when I was here in 1814 and again in 1816, and they very kindly wrote when they heard I was getting married, and offered us the use of their town house for our honeymoon. They are away for a couple of months, and I thought that you would prefer to stay here rather than in some hotel. There are so many people I would like you to meet and it will be easier to give parties here. However, if you would rather stay at an hotel I can always make other arrangements."

Perdita looked at the huge front door, which had now been opened, and the great chandelier lit hall inside, and felt overwhelmed by the prospect of living here, but obviously Jeremy was delighted to have the use of the house and it would be churlish to refuse the kindness of the de Tournées. "I am sure that this will be perfect," she said. "It is certainly very grand, and I am sure that I will find it very comfortable. How kind of your friends to lend it to us."

As they had been speaking Jeremy had led her up the front

steps to where two footmen in scarlet coats and powdered wigs were holding the doors open. Perdita felt that she was walking back into another century, and her first glance of the interior of the house did nothing to lessen her feeling of unreality.

The hall was decorated with elaborately inlaid and ornate pieces of furniture which were set in alcoves. The interiors of the alcoves were lined with mirror, which reflected and re-reflected the gilt sconces set against the mirror. Scagliola pillars edged the alcoves, and the walls between them were painted with classical scenes, as was the high ceiling.

To her right and left Perdita saw that the heavy mahogany doors with their elaborate gilt handles opened onto a succession of rooms which seemed to recede into infinity. Each room was as splendid as the hall, with walls hung with tapestries or brocade, or painted with more scenes of gods and goddesses disporting themselves on sugar pink clouds. Everything was a far cry from the comfortable and informal interior of Hangarwood House, and Perdita felt that she had walked into a museum. It seemed that the house on the rue de Lille was designed for nothing but immense parties, and Perdita began to wonder if she would find anyplace in which she could simply sit down and read a book.

She had not long to study the wealth of detail before one of the footmen came forward to help her off with her pelisse. Having done this he gestured another liveried footman (obviously of a slightly lesser rank, having a fraction less gold braid on his uniform) to come forward to show Perdita to her room. Neither man said a word, merely bowing and gesturing for Perdita to follow. Feeling that the whole staff might be composed of deaf mutes, Perdita turned to Jeremy with a questioning look.

"It's all right, my dear. The footman will see you to your room where you will find the maid that Natalie de Chervinges found for you. I believe that the maid speaks perfect English, so you will have no trouble in communicating with her. However, if you do not take to her, we will get rid of her tomorrow. When you have rested and changed, I will meet you in the yellow salon. One of the footmen will direct you to it."

In a daze, Perdita turned and followed the silent footman up the long curving flight of stairs. After walking down what

seemed interminable corridors, he opened the door to a bedroom which seemed almost as vast as the hall. The room was
paneled and painted with medallions of nymphs and shep-
herds in wreathes of roses. Great curtains of rose-colored
silk, swagged and tied with gold cords, hung from windows
which reached from the high ceiling to the floor. The bed was
tented with the same rose-colored silk, but instead of gold
cord the bed curtains were held back with ropes of silk roses.
Here, as downstairs, the furniture was elaborate with curved
lines and inlaid with a multitude of different woods to form
intricate patterns, the whole outlined and finished with delicately wrought ormolu.

Perdita was so overawed by the room that for a moment
she did not see the little maid standing on the far side of the
bed, but when the footman closed the door, the maid stepped
forward and curtsied to Perdita.

"Milady, I am Jeannette. Madame la Comtesse de Chervinges has arranged that I should be of help to you. Please
may I take your bonnet, and then perhaps I might help milady
into her sacque, so that you may rest before I help you prepare yourself for the dinner."

Perdita untied her bonnet and held it out to Jeannette.
"Thank you. Yes, I would like to rest for a short while. I
find that I am tired from my journey. I do not know where
my boxes and valises are, but perhaps you would see that
they are sent up and then you can unpack them while I am
resting."

"All is arranged; milady. The luggage will be in your
dressing room next door, and I will see to it and be so quiet
that you will not know I am there."

Having been helped out of her traveling clothes and dressed
in a wrapper by Jeannette, Perdita lay down to rest on the
vast bed and gave herself over to assimilating the surprises of
the last hour. She had not envisaged herself as the mistress of
a grand house in Paris, and she felt nervous at the thought of
having to rely on her schoolroom French to converse with
Jeremy's friends. So far the only ones he had mentioned
seemed to have titles, and the tales she had heard of society
in France made her wonder if she would be acceptable to
them.

These thoughts led her mind down its familiar paths of
fantasy and she saw herself as the tattered, beggarmaid bride

of a prince whose court snubbed and rejected her, while he failed to notice how badly she was being treated. So absorbed was she in her story that she was only aware that she had tears in her eyes, when she heard a knock at the door. Pulling herself quickly back to reality, she called for the person to enter and Jeannette walked in ready to help her into her evening dress.

However, Jeannette's next words made Perdita think that she was still in her fantasy world. "I have taken the liberty of putting out milady's green gown. It is the most suitable one, I think, for tonight's dinner party." The last words were uttered with some doubt as she held out the apple green muslin which Aunt Charlotte had thought so elegant.

Still not quite clear what Jeannette meant by a dinner party, Perdita said, "Oh no, not that one. I will need something less formal for tonight, perhaps the pink muslin would be better."

"*Mais non*, milady," Jeannette said firmly. "Tonight Monsieur le Duc and Madame la Duchesse de St. Prés will be dining. It would not be suitable to wear the pink dress. But this, when milady has put on her jewels, will be quite *comme il faut*."

Perdita looked horrified. Jeremy had said nothing about a dinner party. "I did not know that we were having people to dinner tonight."

"Why yes, milady, Auguste was told to prepare dinner for twenty."

Perdita had a moment of horror as she realized that this mode of living was probably the one that Jeremy expected to pursue, and the cozy *tête-à-têtes* that they had enjoyed on the journey to Paris would now become a thing of the past. Perhaps he would expect her to go to parties and routs every night and to entertain every manner of person from the *haut ton*. She found the thought considerably daunting, and sat in a daze while Jeannette performed miracles with curling tongs and comb.

When the maid had finished arranging Perdita's hair in a tumble of curls entwined with green ribbons, she fastened on it the large brooch from the emerald parure that had been her wedding present from Jeremy. When the rest of the jewels were in place, Perdita had to admit that she looked quite sophisticated and felt that perhaps she might manage to be the sort of hostess Jeremy wanted.

However, she still felt resentful that he had not given her any warning of the impending dinner party, and followed the footman who came to fetch her to the yellow salon with a look of prim displeasure on her face.

Jeremy was waiting for her, dressed in his evening clothes and looking altogether too relaxed to be anything but an irritant to Perdita, but his first word disarmed her.

"I apologize, my dear, it seems that Natalie thought that you would be bored if you did not immediately meet some of my friends. I do hope that you do not feel too tired tonight to entertain, and I hope that you will forgive me for not having been able to warn you sooner, but I am sure that you will be amused by the people who are coming, and they will be enchanted by you." He led her over to a sofa at one end of the room. "You will see a fine selection of Paris society tonight, and I shall be amused to hear your impressions of them later. I hope that you are going to find some pleasant companions among them."

He then proceeded to run down the list of guests and to give her brief accounts of each one, but the time was so short that the sound of the guests arriving interrupted the recital and Perdita was left to pray that she did not confuse Madame la Duchesse with Madame la Vicomtesse de Beaulieu, who was of very inferior breeding to la duchesse, the latter being able to trace her ancestry to Charles VI.

However, she found that remembering the ancestry and precedence of the guests was no worse than the feeling of inferiority that she felt at the sight of the toilettes displayed by the ladies. Mrs. Oates's dresses had done excellently for Idingfold, and might just have passed muster in some of the lesser haunts of society in London, but among the nobility of France, Perdita knew that she looked every inch the unfashionable country bumpkin. Only the emeralds, which were as fine as any of the jewels the other ladies were wearing, made her feel that she could hold her head up.

Her self-consciousness was in no way mitigated by the very open scrutiny that was delivered by some of the guests. One in particular, Madame de Frontenac, gave her a cool smile and a slow inspection when they were introduced. Perdita was further mortified to hear her say to Jeremy in French, "What a charming little girl you have married, Jeremy. Who would have thought that you would have fallen for such rustic charms. But I congratulate you, it must be so refreshing to be in the company of such innocence and artlessness.''

Perdita waited for Jeremy to give Madame de Frontenac a thorough set-down, but he merely replied in French, ''Indeed, Perdita is very refreshing company. She has kept me amused for the entire length of the journey from Dieppe. There are few other women, I believe, who could do that.''

Madame de Frontenac gave him a look from the corner of her eye and tapped him on the arm with her fan. ''Well, let us hope that after she has absorbed the polish of Paris you will find her no less enchanting.''

Perdita felt the blood rising in her face in impotent fury at this cool assumption that she would be improved by a closer knowledge of the French fashions and was about to say something she hoped would be cool and cutting, when a voice at her elbow said, ''Do not pay any attention to Elizabeth, she is merely jealous of you, and not having ever had any innocence herself, tries to pretend that there is no virtue in it. However, you have nothing to fear from her. She set her cap for Jeremy when he was here before, but he did no more than flirt with her—which did nothing to soften her sharp tongue.

''Now, I am sure that you must have already forgotten who half these people are. I am Natalie de Chervinges and I am sure that we are going to be the best of friends. My husband worked very closely with yours during the Occupation, so we got to know Jeremy very well, and I am looking forward to getting to know you as well. I would like you to feel that you can call upon me for help in anything at any time. I know how uncomfortable one can be in a strange city—I spent several years in London, you know, and I was badly in need of good friends.''

Glad for the offer of help, Perdita smiled at Natalie. ''Thank you, I know that I shall have many things to ask you. I am feeling very bewildered tonight. This is the first time I have been out of England and I am sure that I shall do something wrong and make Jeremy ashamed of me. I would be most grateful for your help. Could I ask you now to tell me who should take whom in to dinner? Jeremy started to tell me, but there was so much to take in that I have forgotten most of it. I know that Jeremy must lead in Madame la Duchesse, but after that I am afraid that I can't remember the order of precedence."

Natalie smiled. "You are quite right to be a little nervous about that. You would not believe how much importance some of these people place in such things. For myself, I prefer the more relaxed way of the English. However, if you are to survive in Paris society it is as well to get it right the first time. Few people do, and you will be considered brilliant if you manage to. Now here's the order in which they must go into the dining room—you need not worry about the table. Your butler has a list of the guests and will already have arranged matters." Natalie then proceeded to tell Perdita the order in which the guests should go in to dinner, and made it easier by following each name by a quick identification and some way in which the person could be remembered.

"It is much easier to remember a person when you know a little gossip about them," Natalie said easily. "I will, if you permit, call upon you tomorrow morning and then we can really have a good conversation about the people you are likely to meet. But for tonight—do you see Monsieur de Frontenac over there? The man with the large stomach and the very high points to his collars. Otalie de Beaulieu has been his mistress for almost thirty years." Perdita looked over at the vicomtesse, whose rosy cheeks were obviously due to art rather than nature, and regarded with amazement her heavily corsetted figure. She did not seem the sort of person to indulge in any fleshly passions other than eating, and Monsieur de Frontenac was balding and pasty-faced— hardly the image of Don Juan.

Natalie laughed softly at the amazement on Perdita's face. "Oh, it is true that they have long since given up any interest in giving free rein to their passion, but they keep up the flirtation lest anyone think that they are too old to relish the delights of the flesh. Monsieur de Frontenac makes a habit of confessing to his priest, but everyone knows that it is just a question of politesse to Otalie now."

"But doesn't Madame de Frontenac mind?" Perdita asked.

Natalie shrugged her shoulders. "Mind? *Mon Dieu*, why should she? Theirs was a *marriage de convenance* in any case, and his little affair keeps him away from her so that she can get on with her own life. Why would she want to have him around the whole time? And besides, it would be most embarrassing if it were thought that she were in love with her own husband.''

Perdita realized that there was some justification in Elizabeth de Frontenac's appraisal of her as an innocent. She realized that she had very different ideas about marriage from those held by Jeremy's French friends and she supposed that he had adopted their views and probably felt that he was not committing himself to more than a surface respectability when he married her.

Perdita was silent for a moment and her gray eyes had a speculative look as they followed Jeremy bending over the exquisite Elizabeth and seeming to hang on her every word.

Natalie, seeing the direction of her gaze and her expression, said, "Oh don't worry, *ma petite*. I am sure that your Jeremy loves you very much and that you will lead a very different sort of life from the one we do here.''

"Why do you say that you are sure that Jeremy loves me very much?'' Perdita asked, clutching at this straw.

Natalie looked at her and raised her eyebrows a fraction. "Because if he did not, he would not have married you. Why he could have had any woman he wanted—he merely had to lift a finger and she would have come running—but he chose you. So, *enfin*, you see it must have been you that he wanted— and indeed, why not, you are certainly the most beautiful woman in this room, and I am sure that your nature is equally beautiful.''

Natalie's compliments were very flattering, but Perdita reminded herself that Natalie did not know the reason for their marriage, and looking once again at Elizabeth de Frontenac, Perdita wished that, as well as looks and a sweet nature, she might have some of the poise and sophistication which Jeremy was obviously finding so fascinating.

At that moment the big double doors to the dining room were thrown open by two footmen and Perdita had to abandon her thoughts for the more pressing problem of trying to remember the rules of precedence which Natalie had just taught her. Natalie's thumbnail sketches proved of great help and Perdita was able to manage the whole thing with only one quick prompt from Natalie at her side. Within a few moments they were all seated at the long dining table, which was lit by a row of silver candelabra and covered with exquisite Sèvres plates and gold-rimmed wine glasses.

Even though she had managed the first hurdle well enough,
the meal proved uncomfortable for Perdita. The Duc de St.
Prés, on her right, had no conversation except for family
relationships and when he had closely questioned Perdita on
her ancestry and found that the Chases came from no more
than good yeoman stock, he lost interest and simply stared at
his plate with a disdainful expression. No matter what subject
Perdita brought up, she could illicit no more than a curt
"oui" or *"non."* She turned gratefully to the Vicomte de
Beaulieu when the second remove was brought in, but he
proved no better at light conversation than the duc, the vicomte's only subject being the tragic losses of houses and
possessions the émigrés had suffered during the years when
they had been forced to abandon their country. By the time
the footmen had removed the second course, Perdita felt that
she knew in detail the possessions of every member of the
French aristocracy.

With an almost audible sigh she turned back to the duc, but
the prospect of more boredom was too much and she determined to beat him at his own game.

"You were asking about my family," she began, and he
raised his bulbous eyes from his plate heaped with small birds
whose origins Perdita was trying to ignore. "Of course, my
father's family is quite well connected," she lied. "You
understand that I was adopted by the Chase family after my
parents died. My mother, of course, was a Chase, but my
father was the illegitimate son of the Tsar of Russia. His
mother was descended from Mary Queen of Scots, and his
cousin is the Duchess of Marlborough."

The duc's eyes lit up and for the first time there was a
glimmer of life in his expression. *"Tiens!"* he said, "that is
interesting. Now tell me how your father's mother happened to
bear a child to the Tsar?"

Perdita felt herself to be on safe ground now. Her ability to
invent stories had never failed her, and now the desperation
of boredom gave wings to her imagination. She set off, an
accomplished skater on thin ice, avoiding the mention of
actual dates but succeeded in bringing in a relationship with
Frederick of Prussia, Clovis of France, and Charlemagne.
Then, made daring by her own success, she even dropped a
hint about a remote but well documented connection with the
Emperor of China. The duc nodded and smiled, completely

enthralled with his dinner partner and never attempting to question even Perdita's most unlikely and blatant lies.

She was somewhat reluctant to have to turn again to the vicomte, but decided to try the same tactic on him, though this time her story was connected with great jewels lost by her family in the Middle Ages and huge properties destroyed by Cromwell in the Civil War. The vicomte, too, suddenly found that the new Lady Dole was a witty, attractive, and brilliant woman. He made a mental note to except her from his overall opinion that English women were built like horses and had no refinements. Perdita, playing her fish on her newly discovered lure, also found that the evening had become very much less tedious, but she was quite glad when the meal ended and she could lead the ladies from the table to the great salon upstairs.

Fortunately she was escorted up the stairs by two more footmen, as, never having been to the great salon before, she realized she would never have found it herself. The wine at dinner and her success with her ludicrous tales had banished her shyness and she almost laughed out loud at the thought of her leading the train of ladies on a hunt through the house as she opened one wrong door after another in the hopes of finding the grand salon.

The room was well named, as she found out when the footmen swung open the doors a few minutes later. Perdita could hardly suppress a gasp when she saw the sheer ostentation of it. Even so, she had to admit that it was beautiful. Mirrors panneled the entire wall opposite the long windows with their brocade curtains, a matching brocade covered the walls between the mirrors, and at each end of the room. Crystal chandeliers almost obscured the ceiling painted with the meeting of Mars and Venus, and an Aubusson carpet covered the floor which was the resting place for gilded and brocade-covered furniture.

Before Perdita could quite regain her senses, footmen had come forward to arrange the chairs in groups according to the wishes of the ladies, and soon they were seated and sipping dark chocolate from the small cups which were handed to them.

Elizabeth de Frontenac settled herself in a chair beside Perdita, saying, "I am so glad that we are to be informal and not ceremonious this evening. You English are so relaxed in your entertaining."

Perdita did not know what ceremony she was expected to carry out, but she was certainly not going to acknowledge this to Elizabeth de Frontenac, and so she said coolly, "Oh yes, I felt it would be more interesting for everyone if I were to show you the customs of my country. Jeremy so much prefers informality than too much boring ceremony."

Elizabeth cast her a speculative glance, and Perdita caught Natalie's eye and saw her smile and nod her head. Emboldened by this, Perdita continued, "My husband says that you were very kind to him when he was here before."

"He has spoken of me then?" Elizabeth said, her eyes glittering.

"Oh most certainly he has," Perdita answered. "He has often said how much you did for him. He confessed to having been almost embarrassed by your attentions—but you know we English are often mistaken into thinking that people who are less reserved than we are, mean more by their attentions than is intended."

Elizabeth looked a little disconcerted, and Perdita was hard-put not to smile at her discomposure. There was a moment's silence while Elizabeth tried to decide whether she had misjudged this young country girl. Perhaps she was not as innocent as she had first thought, but deciding that this was not the moment to join battle, she murmured, "I hope that *you* will not misjudge my friendship with your husband," as she rose.

"I am quite sure that you will not give me any reason to do that," Perdita assured Elizabeth in a voice that dripped sweetness.

With this parting shot lodged firmly between her shoulder blades, Elizabeth, more disconcerted than she had been for some time, made her way over to the duchesse and arranged herself on the sofa beside her.

The rest of the evening passed without any need for Perdita to unsheath her claws. She found most of the ladies agreeable and friendly, and Natalie in particular she grew to like more with every word they exchanged.

As the guests were leaving Natalie whispered to Perdita, "I know that we are going to be great friends. If I may, I will call upon you tomorrow and we will arrange what you would like to do. I believe that my modiste has several new fashions to show me. Perhaps you would like to come and see if there is something you would like."

Knowing that Mrs. Oates's efforts were not going to serve in Paris, Perdita agreed readily to the scheme and the two ladies set an appointment for eleven o'clock the following day.

When everyone had finally departed, Jeremy walked upstairs with Perdita. "You managed the whole evening admirably. I congratulate you. I have never seen the duc so fascinated by anyone before. What were you telling him?"

"Oh, I only told him about my family connections," Perdita said airily.

Jeremy raised one eyebrow and waited with a slight smile for further elucidation. Perdita, seeing the look, confessed to her flights of fancy, and was rewarded by the smile broadening into a grin, and at her confession of having admitted to a connection to the Emperor of China, the grin disappeared in a shout of laughter.

Delighted to have amused him, Perdita was about to indulge in some of the gossip she had heard that night when he stopped her short by saying, "You are the most surprising and inventive child. No doubt you will be the rage of Paris. But now you must be tired." They had reached her bedroom door and he raised her hand to his lips and abruptly left her.

Perdita was silent as Jeannette undressed her, and barely remembered to wish the maid a good night as she slid between the covers of the great bed. Her thoughts were at full gallop. It seemed that to Jeremy she would always be six years old, even though she was now his bride, and that if he was to see her in a different light, it would be up to her to make it impossible for him to think of her as a child. She had realized that night that she was very lacking in the sophistication and polish of the French ladies that Jeremy knew. She was reluctant to admit it, but perhaps Elizabeth de Frontenac had been right when she had talked about her acquiring more polish. Well, Natalie would help her with that, and she would most certainly be able to tell her how to choose her clothes, and how to shine in fashionable company.

Jeremy had called her a surprising and inventive child, but she would show him that she could be a surprising and inventive woman. There would be no more childish fantasy, no more play-acting. She would show him that she could be everything that a man could want in a woman.

Tomorrow she would start her reformation. Jeremy would no longer be allowed to dismiss her and go off in corners with Elizabeth de Frontenac.

There was a steely glint in Perdita's gray eyes and she failed to notice that she had stopped thinking of the course she had originally decided upon, that of being a complacent wife. She was now prepared to do battle to gain and hold Jeremy's affection.

— 8 —

Though Perdita saw little of Jeremy through the next few weeks, she was too busy with her own pursuits to worry about the fact that they were not having a very conventional honeymoon. Once she had put herself in Natalie's hands, there was little time to notice how seldom Jeremy was at her side. Perdita, having made up her mind that she would absorb as much polish as possible from Natalie, was too taken up with learning how to choose her clothes, what events she must be seen attending, and whom she should cultivate as friends. Natalie also saw to it that Perdita should understand what was, and what was not, permitted in a flirtation and how to deal graciously with any young man who became too ardent.

Behind Natalie's teaching lay her determination on two points: one, that Perdita should get to know and love Paris, and two, that she should return to England dressed in all the best and latest fashions that Paris could provide.

Therefore, the exploration of Paris, drives in the Bois de Boulogne, walks beside the Seine, and visits to the churches and cathedrals, the great houses with their collections of paintings, furniture, and other works of art, became as much a part of Perdita's life as the constant stream of parties and the consequent visits to Natalie's modiste—for it would never do, Natalie assured her, to be seen wearing the same evening dress twice. It had long since been evident to Perdita that Mrs. Oates's fashions were at least ten years out of date, and that the apple green muslin was enough to raise eyebrows even in the Assembly Rooms in Bath, let alone the opera in Paris. Mrs. Oates's old tattered and well-used copies of *La Belle Assemblée* had shown ladies in clinging draped muslins and silks, their only decoration classic embroidery *à la Greque* or *à la Egyptienne*. Perdita now realized that the skirts of her English dresses were much too long and that they hung straight instead of being padded at the hem to make them stand away from the ankles and give the wearer the look of some graceful chess piece. The gowns made for her by Natalie's modiste were given a great deal of trimming, and the necks and hems seemed to be embellished with whatever man or woman could devise.

Natalie was also strict with Perdita about choosing what suited her, instead of merely selecting a dress that she thought looked pretty. With her blond hair and her tall willowy figure, there was very little that did not suit Perdita, but Natalie was insistent that she should make for herself a very noticeable style, selecting from one, or at the most two, sections of the spectrum. They decided that she looked her best in all shades of blue, particularly those with tones of gray in them, but Perdita had more than a few moments of doubt when the modiste showed her one evening dress of a silvery blue velvet whose hem and neckline were decorated with a twist of gray-blue satin and gray squirrel fur. It was ruinously expensive, but Natalie assured her that Jeremy would think it money well spent when he saw her in the dress, and it was duly sent around to the house in the rue de Lille with the bill directed to Jeremy.

Perdita felt that the extragavance had been worth while when, the first time that she wore the dress, he looked at her intently and said, "That is a deuced pretty dress you are wearing. You should always wear that color. It suits you."

Pleased that he had noticed how she looked, Perdita answered, "I hope that you will still like it when you hear how much it cost. I am afraid that it was most terribly expensive."

"I shall consider any price reasonable to see you the most stared-at lady in the room tonight," he answered gallantly, but privately wondered if the dress was not a bit too sophisticated for Perdita, though he had reluctantly to admit that she carried it off with great style.

If Jeremy's reaction had been more gallant than ardent, at least he had noticed her, Perdita thought. In any case, Natalie had been so enthusiastic about the dress that Perdita felt more at ease at the dinner they went to that night than she had since they had arrived in Paris. Although Jeremy spent no more time than usual at her side, there were several young men who were eager to see that she was entertained.

Increasingly annoyed that he had not reacted more dramatically to her appearance, Perdita glanced over at him from time to time throughout the evening only to see him totally absorbed in whomever he was speaking to. Even more irritating was the fact that, all too often, his dark head was bending toward that of Elizabeth de Frontenac. Perdita heard him laugh in a way that he never did with her and she had an almost irrepressible urge to go over and slap that silly Elizabeth on the face, but instead Perdita decided to fight fire with fire and flirted outrageously with the young men who were beginning to seek her out at these parties. She was determined that Jeremy would notice how she could attract other men, but she never saw him look at her when she turned to see whether he had noticed her successes. Soon she began to see that she must take her enjoyment for its own sake and not because it might make Jeremy jealous.

Had she but known, Jeremy was all too aware of the stir she was causing, and the changes which had come over her since she had been under Natalie's guidance, and he was not at all sure that it had been one of his best ideas to have suggested that Natalie take Perdita in hand. It was as much as he could do to sit beside Elizabeth de Frontenac and listen to her silly chatter, knowing that Perdita was attracting the attention of every red-blooded man in the room, and he had more than once privately wished them all to the devil. Perdita's new elegance made her seem too much a woman sometimes instead of the young girl she was, and it had often been on the tip of his tongue to send her back to Jeannette to change out of the more revealing of her new gowns. However, he firmly reminded himself that she had been forced to sacrifice a great deal to accept his proposal of marriage, and if she wished to play at being grown up he would not spoil her fun. Besides, he knew that Natalie would not allow Perdita to make a fool of herself.

He therefore paid all her bills without a murmur and escorted her to balls, theaters, dinners, and the opera. He found the visits to the theater and opera less trying than the other parties as at least there it was only in the intervals that Perdita was surrounded by her ridiculous admirers. Increasingly, Jeremy found that he did not know the men and women who came to pay their respects to his wife, and to see Perdita becoming more and more at ease in fashionable Paris society made him feel as though he were merely becoming an unwanted appendage, or some boring old relative to be placated but not enjoyed.

Despite this, he could not, in honesty, fault Perdita's behavior to him. She always had a ready smile when they met during the day, and though she did not question him on how he passed his time, she never accepted an invitation without first making sure that he wished to attend the party. She was the picture of sweet civility, but he found her gentleness more irritant than balm, and ocasionally found himself answering her abruptly only to have to apologize a moment later. Part of his annoyance was that he had never before thought of himself as a short-tempered man, but he found himself less patient and tractable than he had believed himself to be.

Even though he knew Elizabeth de Frontenac to be shallow and vain, he found that one of the few ways he could control his restlessness and irritation was to flirt with her. At times he found her artfulness almost more than he could bear, and her sharp tongue made him wish she would not always be so critical of every other woman, but she served to draw some of his fire and it pleased him to give her some dagger-sharp set-downs.

He was so much in Elizabeth's company that Perdita began to believe that no matter what Natalie might say, Jeremy's relationship with Elizabeth had reached beyond that of an idle flirtation. Nevertheless, it was Jeremy whose emotions got the better of him first.

When April was just one week short of turning into May, Jeremy found that their stay in Paris had gone on too long.

Since the first day of their marriage Perdita had breakfasted alone in her room and had taken to coming downstairs just in time to go out with Natalie at eleven in the morning. The morning when he found that he no longer enjoyed staying in Paris, Perdita had not yet come downstairs when a letter for her from England was delivered to Jeremy in the yellow salon where he was taking breakfast. He looked at the address and was about to recall the footman and point out that the letter was not for him but for his wife, when he changed his mind and decided that he would take it upstairs himself. He climbed the first flight of stairs and made his way down the long corridor to Perdita's bedroom and boudoir.

He had reached the latter and had his hand raised to knock when he heard a gurgle of laughter and then a man's voice say something which set the laughter off again. Dispensing with the knock, Jeremy opened the door to find Perdita in a loose wrapper having her hair done by Jeannette, while two young men and Natalie sat in various places around the room. As the door opened, Perdita turned toward it and the wrapper slipped from one shoulder exposing a considerable amount of its creamy curve and the soft swell of the bosom below. She quickly pulled the robe over her shoulder, but not before Jeremy saw one of the young men look at her with unmistakable desire.

Jeremy found his fists clenching involuntarily and he started to step toward the young man. What might have then occurred no one could know, for Perdita said artlessly, "Oh Jeremy, I am so glad that you have come to join us. Louis de Salle was telling us such an amusing story. Louis, please tell my husband about the Comte de Lamoule."

"Not now," Jeremy said shortly. "I would be grateful if you would all allow me to see my wife alone for a moment."

The young men rose to their feet quickly and, kissing Perdita's hand, left at once. Natalie, sensing the atmosphere in the room, cocked a quizzical eyebrow at Perdita but got up and, muttering a brief "à bientôt," left the room while Jeannette, picking up some clothes lying scattered across the sofa, went quietly into the bedroom.

"What is it?" Perdita asked, thinking, from the expression on Jeremy's face, that he must have had some dreadful news.

Jeremy hesitated for a moment, and then held out the letter. "I thought perhaps you might want this," he said.

Perdita looked frightened and opened the letter quickly. "What has happened? Is it Aunt Charlotte or Jane?"

"I have no reason to think that there is any bad news," Jeremy said quickly. "Nevertheless, I think that it is time we started for home. I would like to be settled in the London house before the season gets started, and I am sure that you are anxious to see your family."

Perdita's eyebrows rose a fraction. "Why yes, I will be happy to see them. Have you decided upon a day for our departure?"

"If it is convenient for you, I would like to leave by the end of this week," Jeremy said, his tight lips the only sign of the anger he was feeling.

"Of course. I will tell Jeannette to start packing immediately. But Jeremy, is something upsetting you?"

"No, there is nothing," he said shortly, turning toward the door, and then as he opened it, he turned back to her. "Yes, there is!" His voice was sharp and angry and Perdita looked at him in astonishment as he continued. "I will not have my wife displaying her charms to every young man who wishes to ogle her. I had expected more breeding from you, and more delicacy of manner, but I come to your room to find you in a state of semi-undress, entertaining God-knows-what young men, and for what purpose, I shudder to think. You may be young and you may be all innocence, but I would have thought you to have had more sense and discretion than to behave in this way. Do I have to remind you that you are my wife and that I will not be made the laughingstock of all France by your silly, childish naivety? In future, you will not entertain men in your bedroom, nor indulge in these ridiculous flirtations which have made you the talk of Paris. Do you understand?" He glared at Perdita, but before she could answer he turned on his heel and slammed the door behind him.

Perdita sat with her mouth open staring at the mahogany door and wondering whether Jeremy had suddenly lost his senses.

Natalie noted Perdita's abstracted air when they met later that morning, and found herself having to repeat her questions a couple of times, but Perdita did not offer any explanation for her mood, and Natalie did not press for information. She had long since realized that there was something amiss in the marriage and had puzzled over what it could be. She knew that Perdita was very much in love with Jeremy, no matter how reserved she was with him in public, and having seen Jeremy in Paris before his marriage, she knew that for all his coolness, he was entranced by Perdita. Natalie had caught some of the looks he had directed at his wife when he thought that he was not being observed, and they were certainly not those of a man who was not in love.

Most telling of all to Natalie had been the look of blazing anger on his face when he had walked into the boudoir that morning and seen the way Louis de Salle looked at Perdita. Natalie had seen jealousy before and was well aware that a man indifferent to his wife did not nearly make a fool of himself over her. However, as she could not work out what was wrong and as she was aware that Perdita would not tell her, she shrugged her shoulders and set herself to seeing that Perdita was as amused as possible.

The news that the Doles were to return so suddenly to London surprised Natalie, but she covered her shock by merely saying, "I shall miss you very much, *ma chère* Perdita, but perhaps you will return soon. Now that all those dreadful years of war are over we are all able to cross the Channel easily."

"I shall miss you too, Natalie. I can't thank you enough for what you have done for me. You have been so kind, and you have turned me from a frumpish school girl into something resembling a lady of quality."

"To give you the direction of Madame Labouillière and Madame Fourment was not very difficult. Besides, I was doing them a favor to allow their clothes to be seen to such good advantage."

Perdita embraced her friend. She knew that she would miss the help and company of Natalie more than she could say, but at the same time she was looking forward to seeing Jane and describing to her all the sights and fashions of Paris. It would be pleasant also to have her own establishment. The London house could hardly be as large as the one on the rue de Lille, and she was sure that she would find it more to her taste.

The Doles' return to England was uneventful, though this time Jeremy seemed anxious not to waste any time on the journey and they covered the distance from Paris to Dieppe in five days rather than the seven they had taken on the way out.

Since his outburst in her boudoir, Perdita had noticed that Jeremy's behavior to her had changed. He was polite enough, but there was an abruptness to his manner that had not been there before. For his part, Jeremy had passed from surprise at his own vehemence in his reaction to the young men in Perdita's boudoir, to a gradual realization that his feelings for Perdita had suffered a distinct change. The protectiveness he had always felt for her had become laced with something that had nothing to do with simple brotherly friendship. The new, elegant Perdita could no longer be regarded as a child and the woman she had become was someone who was playing havoc with all his resolves and self-control.

Clamp was certainly not unaware of the change. In all the years he had been with Sir Jeremy, he had never seen his master so short-tempered. Usually the major was considerate of his servants, but now Clamp would find himself curtly told that the shaving water was not hot enough, the linen neck-cloths too starched or not starched enough, the Hessians and shoes not attended to with the usual care. At one of the hotels Sir Jeremy had turned to him and said, "Damme Clamp, I don't know what has come over you. You never used to give me all this trouble. I don't understand why a man who could get a good polish on my boots in a camp miles from any supplies, can fail to get a decent shine on them now."

Clamp's round face remained impassive, but as he closed the door behind him to go back to repolish the boots, he muttered to himself, "It isn't I what is giving the trouble. Gawd knows what's come over the major, but it's certain that marriage isn't suiting 'im."

Clamp had known for a long time that his master had felt more than a usual affection for Miss Chase—as she then was—and had always felt that something might come of it. But this marriage was a rum one if ever he saw one. Her ladyship obviously worshipped the major, and the major adored her, so why did they never share a bedroom? A day or two, perhaps, for a young girl of sensibility, but over a month! It was carrying sensibilities to extremes, Clamp thought, and no wonder the major was on edge.

However, it was not his place to notice, let alone speak, and Clamp went downstairs to the boot room of the hotel and attacked the offending boots with his mixture of champagne and blacking and his well-used deer's leg bone, until a new mirror could not have held more reflection than the Hessians.

Perdita found herself more pleased than she had thought she would be to be home in England. Although her French had improved dramatically from daily use, she still found it easier to converse in her native tongue, and the sense of familiarity made her feel less tense and watchful of her behavior once she was on her home ground. She hoped, too, that whatever was bothering Jeremy would dissipate now that he was back in familiar surroundings.

The house in Upper Grosvenor Street was a much less oppressive ambience than the house in the rue de Lille. Perdita found that the smaller scale and less imposing interiors enabled her to feel that she really was in a home instead of some vast palace. Jeremy had given her complete freedom to redecorate the house to her own taste, but the pale yellows of the drawing room with its finely proportioned windows she found pleasant and cheerful. Her own bedroom with its Chinese painted wallpaper and soft blue curtains and bedhangings she could not have improved upon, and her delight and liking for the new decorations that Jeremy had ordered to be carried out while they were on their honeymoon were so obviously genuine that Jeremy heaved a sigh of relief. He would not have begrudged Perdita anything, and most certainly did not want her to have to live in a house she disliked, but the modiste's and milliner's bills had been rather more than he expected and he was glad to be spared the expense of redoing the house at the moment.

For the first few days in London, Perdita missed the company of Natalie. The season was not yet in full swing and London was comparatively empty. In a couple of weeks the parties and balls would begin, but for the time being she was hard pressed to find someone with whom she could spend her days. Jeremy always seemed to be occupied. Almost every morning he would go to Gentleman Jackson's rooms at 13 Bond Street for a round or two with the master, or to the Fives Courts in St. Martin's Street to watch a bout. Even when he was not engaged in watching or taking part in boxing, he seemed to always be busy, and apart from taking dinner with Perdita most evenings, he was seldom at home.

Even when they were both in for dinner, Jeremy would go off
to his club directly afterward and Perdita would be left to
amuse herself as best she might. She knew that if she had
asked he would have stayed with her, but their conversation
had become stilted when they were alone together now and
awkwardness had become the keynote of their relationship.
She had not dared ask him if he were still angry at with her
about the incident in her boudoir as she did not want to raise
those demons, and instead she decided upon the safer course
of looking elsewhere for companionship.

As soon as it was known that they were in town, callers
began to arrive in the mornings, and a few tea parties and
afternoon visits were arranged. However, there were still
large parts of the day when she was left to her own devices
and Perdita fell back on her love of reading. The poetry
writing which had so absorbed her time before she was
married, was no longer a pastime to which she could turn
with pleasure. Since most of her poems had been of love
hoped for, she found it hard to turn to the subject of love
denied, and the epic poem she had been contemplating before
the kidnapping, she had given up as childish nonsense.

Some mornings, when the weather was fine, she would
walk out with Jeannette in attendance and Frolic, who had
been sent up from Hangarwood to greet her arrival in London. But the few paths in the Park soon became too familiar
to be interesting, and she did not know enough people to
make the walks more entertaining by stopping to gossip with
acquaintances.

She tried to fill the time with shopping expeditions in the
fashionable streets, but even these seemed flat without the
companionship of someone like Natalie with whom to discuss
the merits of a bonnet à la Hussar as opposed to a high
crowned one trimmed with swansdown. She walked the length
of Bond Street but saw nothing that she really wanted. She
wiled away a few hours with buying some gloves and a shawl
which had caught her fancy, but her wardrobes were so filled
with the things that she had brought from France that even
buying clothes did not hold any charms. Also it seemed that
after the admiration he had expressed over the blue velvet
dress, Jeremy would have hardly noticed if she had got
herself up as a Red Indian and worn nothing but feathers and
a leather skirt.

Her main pleasure became her visits to Hatchard's bookshop in Piccadilly and Hookham's Lending Library in Bond Street. After a short time these two places became the object of almost all her outings, and it was on the way to Hatchard's one day, with the faithful Jeannette and Frolic in attendance, that her eye was caught by a playbill affixed to a wall. Perdita had passed a hundred such bills on her walks in London, but this one stopped her. The notice was concerning a performance at the Sans Pareil Theater in the Strand, but the words which caused Perdita to stop were those of the name of the actor/manager of the company now at the Sans Pareil—the name, printed in inch-high letters was, Edmund Wycoller.

It had been many years since Perdita had heard anything of her father, and in fact she had almost begun to believe the story that he had been a soldier who had died in some remote country. To see his name blazoned in black and white brought her up short, and the years seemed to draw together until it seemed that she was again four years old and a laughing man with a voice that vibrated through the room was throwing her in the air and catching her in strong arms.

Perdita stared at the notice for some minutes, and then with a more determined step set off again with Jeannette almost running beside her. Perdita was brought back to the present and hesitated for an instant. She most certainly did not want the news to get back to the servants that she was visiting a theater in the middle of the day, and no matter how loyal Jeannette was she would be almost sure to say something to one of them, and then the news would spread until it would eventually reach Jeremy's ears.

Perdita thought quickly and then said, "Jeannette, would you be so kind as to take Frolic home. I should have remembered that the bookshop will be crowded at this hour and he does so hate a press of people. I shall never be able to give my mind over to selecting a book when I am worrying about his poor toes getting stepped on." She handed the lead over to the maid, who, with some surprise, took the dog.

"But milady, will you be all right by yourself?" she asked nervously.

"Of course. Don't worry, I will take a hackney carriage home."

The maid turned back with Frolic and Perdita waited until they were out of sight among the crowds sauntering along

Piccadilly, before turning and making her way, at a fast walk, toward the Strand.

She remembered enough about theater life to know that the front of the house would be closed at this hour, and once she had reached the Sans Pareil she turned into the alley beside it to find the stage door. A lugubrious man with a large nose on which trembled a monstrous wart, and eyes red-rimmed as a bloodhound's, sat on a rickety wooden chair just inside the stage door. He looked up as Perdita stepped confidently through it. Once again she was five years old and the man at the door was her friend Charlie, who had been nursemaid and companion to her when her parents had been busy. She was, in fact, about to call him by this name, when the man stopped her with, "Oi, where d'ya fink yer goin'?"

She turned to the doorman and realized that this was no longer the Charlie of her childhood. Her instinct was to reply simply, "To see my father," but again she realized that she was living in the past. Drawing herself up slightly she said, "Would you kindly tell Mr. Wycoller that a lady wishes to see him urgently."

Tom Hawkins had seen many ladies who wished to see Mr. Wycoller urgently, but this one did not seem cut from the same cloth as the others. He eyed Perdita's fine velvet pelisse with its edging of sable. He was not such a flat that he did not recognize a real lady when he saw one, so instead of his usual quick dismissal he said politely, " 'Oo shall I say wished to see 'im?"

"His—you may tell him Lady Dole would be glad to speak with him."

Eyeing her once again to make sure that he had not mistaken the situation, Tom sidled out through a dingy door which led to an even darker corridor, and Perdita was left wondering if she were not making a complete goose of herself. Perhaps it would be best to leave these bones of the past buried where they had been for the past thirteen years, yet on the other hand she knew that she would not rest in London until she had seen her father again.

It seemed like hours before she heard the sounds of a firm stride returning down the corridor. The begrimed door swung open and a man stood in the doorway. He was six feet tall with a heavy mane of graying hair crowning a broad brow.

He had thick eyebrows shading piercing gray eyes, which Perdita recognized as the source of her own. Although his figure was impressive and his features strong and beautifully shaped, it was the vitality he exuded that seemed to electrify the air around him, which was his most obvious quality. He stood in the doorway holding the door open with his right hand outstretched, and with his other hand he clasped a long cloak across his body.

Perdita looked into the gray eyes and the years and time dissolved as she said, "Father!"

Edmund Wycoller dropped his hand from his chest and held it forward in a sweeping gesture. He leaned forward from the waist and looked intently at Perdita, and the knuckles holding the door whitened. The pause went on vibrating in the silence, and then he said unbelievingly, "Perdita?" He let go of the door as she moved toward him, and swept the cloak behind him with a magnificent gesture, then held out his arms as she ran to him. For a moment they stood, too moved for words, holding each other silently, then Edmund Wycoller drew back a fraction, and in the voice that had filled auditoriums across the country he said, " 'O, she is warm! If this be magic, let it be an art lawful as eating.' "

Perdita's eyes were full of tears. "Oh, Father, I never thought that I would see you again. Oh, I have missed you so much!"

"Ah child—if you could but know how every waking hour of mine has been yours. I cannot believe it. I had entertained a hope that one day you might want to find me, that you might come to London and see the playbills—but then I feared that you might not even remember your old father's name."

"Father, how could I forget?"

"It was a long time ago, my darling; a long, long time ago, and you were such a babe. I knew that it would be best for you to forget me, but I entertained hopes that you would not. But why are we standing here in this drafty place? Come, you must meet the company; there must be a celebration. My daughter which was lost, is now found. Tom, go forth and find us the best claret—nay champagne—that this city can provide. Here, take my purse . . ." Edmund Wycoller pulled his purse from a pocket underneath the cloak and held it out to Tom, but before the latter could take it Edmund

Wycoller muted his extravagant gesture and taking a guinea from the purse held that out to Tom. "This should be enough. Two bottles, no less, but be quick about it."

Edmund Wycoller swung back toward the door, enveloping Perdita in the great cloak, and with his arm about her shoulder led her down the long corridor to the stage at the end.

The smell of old dust, of large enclosed spaces, the all-pervading, if faint, smell of grease paint and candlegrease made a part of Perdita which had long lain dormant return to life. She looked around smiling, and felt once more that she was that carefree child whose parents indulged her; whose life was a hubbub of noisy, laughing people who greeted everyone with effusive gestures and made minor tiffs, blood feuds, and any fondness, passionate love.

Edmund Wycoller led her out onto the stage which was lit by a few candles placed strategically around on rickety tables. In their flickering light, Perdita could see a company of people, some in theatrical dress, some in their street clothes, but all with scripts in their hands. She realized that she had interrupted a rehearsal, and had an impulse to turn and melt back into the wings as she would have as a child had she come upon this sacrosanct occasion, but then realizing that this time she would not be scolded for breaking up the rehearsal, she walked forward with her father.

He waited to speak until he had reached center stage, and Perdita noted with some amusement that he chose to approach his company from upstage so that they were forced to turn their backs on the auditorium. Though he had not said a word the entire company had turned as he came out of the wings leading Perdita, and they waited with an expectant hush until Edmund Wycoller had flung wide his arms, the cloak swinging in a dramatic arc revealing Perdita, and after a pregnant pause, declared, "My long lost daughter, Perdita."

For a moment there was utter silence. They all remained like a *tableau vivant* until a large lady sitting on a dilapidated chaise longue rose to her feet and swept toward Perdita.

"Oh my child," she said, enveloping Perdita in her vast bosom. "Your father has spoken so much, so much, of you that I feel you are my child too. Oh never was wanderer more welcome."

With a slightly impatient twitch of his cloak Edmund Wycoller drew the attention away from the lady. "My dear," he said turning to Perdita, "let me introduce you to the leading lady of my company, Mrs. Sarah Eddy." Before Mrs. Eddy could interrupt again, he swung his free arm in an arc to include the rest of the people on the stage. "By the footlights, my good right arm, Mr. John McEvoy . . . The lady in pink, our delicious rosebud, Miss Rosalind Delornay . . . Our stalwart and reliable Mrs. Sylvia Warburgh . . . The magnificent Mrs. Camilla Bass . . . The handsome Mr. George Branch (never was seen such a leg in a silk stocking) . . . Another fine actor Mr. Lawrence Pare . . . and ditto Mr. Theobald Duke . . . The two lovely ladies to our left—in blue, Miss Pamela Forrest, and in the cloak, Miss Emmaline Atwater. Ladies and gentlemen, may I once again present you my daughter, Perdita, Lady Dole."

There was only one response possible to this speech and Edmund duly got his round of applause before the entire company came forward to greet Perdita. It was obvious that her father had mentioned her often and there was no one in the company who was not familiar with her early years.

"Do you still remember how you hid in the wardrobe trunk when you were three?" Mrs. Eddy asked.

"Indeed I do," Perdita said smiling. "It seemed a good idea at first and then when I couldn't open the lid I was very frightened that no one would find me."

"Ah, but you had a wonderfully carrying voice, even for a three-year-old," her father said. "Why had I been in the middle of the storm scene in *Lear* I doubt not that I should have heard you above any wailing of wind or thunder."

"Your father has shown me the miniature of you that was done when you were four. You were such a pretty little thing then, but even prettier now," said Emmaline.

"Hear, hear," Mr. Pare and Mr. Duke said in unison.

Perdita felt a blush creep up her cheeks. It was a long time since she had been the recipient of such warm admiration.

"Ah, how the pretty thing blushes. 'Tis a long time since I managed a blush like that," Mrs. Warburgh said, cocking her round face to one side and looking at Perdita with a friendly smile.

"Perhaps no one ever gave you cause," Lawrence Pare said cheekily, but with a smile which absolved the remark from all malice.

"You young devil," Mrs. Warburgh replied. "Another remark like that and I will see that your tights are made so that you will be singing falsetto."

"Mrs. Warburgh is in charge of our wardrobe," Edmund Wycoller said hastily, perceiving the surprise in Perdita's face at Mrs. Warburgh's remark. "She can make a dish clout do for a king's robe, and were my sword as fast as her needle I should be the greatest fencer in the world."

At that moment Tom came in bearing two bottles of champagne, his red-rimmed eyes sparkling at the thought of being asked to share in the celebration and having leave to quit his post.

"Ah Tom, bring the bottles here, and go get glasses, my man. Would you have us drink from your boot? Or perhaps you intend that we sup straight from the bottle. I assure you my daughter is used to much better treatment. I'll not have her think that we are savages in the theater."

Tom put the bottles down on the stage and shambled off to get the glasses.

"Now, my dear, I want to hear so much, so much . . . all your life since you left my care," her father said as he led Perdita downstage to the sagging chaise longue. "Every thought, every feeling, I wish to share—spare me nothing. I must relive your life with you and make you my daughter again."

He sat down beside her on the chaise longue and, clasping both her hands in his, looked intently at her. "As beautiful as your mother, but who could be that—who indeed," he murmured and there was a sparkle of tears in his eyes. He was silent for a moment and Perdita did not dare interrupt the thoughts which were so obviously absorbing his mind. "Ah, but she is gone. Gone as the lilies and roses go." He raised his head. "But left me a daughter as fair as she, my blessed child. But no more of sad thoughts. My Perdita is found, and I will hear everything that has occurred since her grieving father let her go to lead a life he could not afford to give her."

"I have been happy," Perdita said, leaning forward to kiss her father's cheek. "But, oh how I missed you—and Mama. My aunt and uncle were all that was kind, and my aunt's daughter, Jane, as good a friend as it is possible to find. There was never a quarrel between us, and if I missed you and all of this—" she found herself imitating her father's expansive movement with her left arm, "I had much to keep me happy."

"And your marriage, when did that take place?"

"I was married only little over a month ago."

"And to a man you love? They did not marry you off for convenience sake, my sweeting, tell me?"

Perdita paused for a second. "I love my husband. He was my childhood hero. He and his brother lived in the village next to ours and were our constant companions. Jeremy is somewhat older than I—"

"No fault there," her father interrupted.

"—but he is considerate and kind and—and everything that one could wish," she ended lamely.

"You must bring him to see me so that I can ensure that he is a fit man to care for my precious daughter," Edmund Wycoller said sternly.

"Oh no," Perdita said quickly before she realized what she was saying.

"And why not?" her father asked drawing himself up.

"I—that is—he doesn't know who my real father is. You see, my uncle and aunt thought it would be better for me if it were not known that my father was an actor. We live in a small village and sometimes the villagers have strange notions about people with whom they are not familiar. It was assumed that my father had been a soldier killed fighting for his country, and that my aunt and uncle had adopted me upon my mother's death."

The circle of faces around Perdita took on a variety of expressions: the older members of the company looked sympathetic, while the younger ones glared in indignation.

"No, no," Edmund Wycoller said, "fret not. I understand. There are those that consider actors nothing but rogues and vagabonds, and your uncle was wise to protect you thus from any slur that might attach to you. But would your husband not understand—our profession is not entirely unacceptable in the best circles. One must remember the beautiful Dorothea Jordan; loved by a king's son, no less."

"But, my dear, she was not his wife," Sarah Eddy interrupted.

"No, no, not his wife," Edmund Wycoller agreed sadly, "but better to the Duke of Clarence than any wife he might have had, and more enchanting than his German princess."

"I am sorry, Father. If you think I should, of course I shall tell Jeremy about you, and will bring him to see you, but . . ." Perdita did not dare tell her father that she had good reason for not wanting to tell Jeremy anything which might give him cause to dislike her. He was no snob, but at the present she had no wish to do or say anything which might prompt an outburst of temper.

"No, child. You will know if and when your husband should be told. I am content to have found you, to know that you are well and happy, but you will be able to get away to come to see me from time to time, will you not?"

Perdita put her arms around her father's neck. "Now that I have found you again, no one will ever be able to prevent me from seeing you. Even if it must be in secret, I shall come as often as you will have me. Oh, it is so wonderful to be back in the theater with you, with all these kind people. I had forgotten how much I missed all this."

"Ah, my blood runs in your veins," Edmund Wycoller said. "To have once experienced the essence of the theater, its own rare air, is never to be complete again without it. Why, were things but different in your life, I would have you treading the boards with me in no time at all. You have your mother's grace and it would not take long to turn you into the perfect Cordelia—or perhaps Miranda?" He cocked his head on one side and looked at her speculatively.

"Come, let the poor child be herself for the time being," Sarah Eddy said. "Besides, the champagne waits and we are all developing a monstrous thirst for the stuff."

The words were like scraps thrown to starving dogs. Within seconds, John McEvoy and Theobald Duke had the bottles open and with giggles from the Misses Forrest and Atwater and gallant remarks from the gentlemen of the company, the glasses were filled and toasts drunk to the return of Perdita to the bosom of her theatrical family.

"For you are to regard us all as that," Mrs. Eddy said. "I should consider it the greatest honor were you to think of me as even a pale substitute for that wonderful mother that you lost." Her eyes swam with tears at the thought of the poor motherless child.

"Ah, come now, Sarah, Perdita has not been motherless. You heard her say how excellent a mother her aunt has been to her. Welcome her to your bosom, by all means, but do not treat her as a starving orphan of the storm," Edmund Wycoller said testily.

"Edmund, I am merely assuring the poor child that she has a true friend in me, and should she wish for an older woman to love and guide her, I should be honored if she would turn to me."

Perdita could see how magnificent Sarah Eddy would be as Lady Macbeth, as the actress turned a look of monumental disdain upon Edmund Wycoller. "I should be glad of your advice and affection," Perdita assured her hurriedly, before the brewing squabble could cloud the reunion.

Mrs. Eddy turned to her. "My dear, I am so glad that you so perfectly understand me. I had no intention of usurping your dear aunt's place. I was merely offering the open hand of friendship to you. *You* were aware of that even if your father mistook me." She could not resist a toss of her head in Edmund Wycoller's direction, but he chose to ignore it and contented himself with refilling the glasses.

Two hours had passed before Perdita remembered that she was supposed to have been merely collecting a book, and, worrying that her absence might be giving cause for alarm at Upper Grosvenor Street, she hastily made her adieux, but not before her father had drawn a promise from her that she would return to the theater tomorrow morning.

She bade the company goodbye, and they watched her leave the stage and make her way toward the stage door.

Unable to let the moment go without some gesture, Edmund Wycoller pointed toward the corner from which Perdita had left and said, "That child needs a father."

There was a suitably reverent silence from the company, then he turned back to them. "Very well, ladies and gentlemen, Act three Scene two—'My lord, my lord . . .,' Mr. McEvoy. . . ."

— 9 —

For the next few days, Perdita found her mind so caught up in the excitement of finding her father, and the renewed acquaintance with the life of an acting company, that for the first time in years she found herself thinking of things other than Jeremy when she was alone. It seemed that her father's world called to something which had lain dormant or barely recognized in her, and now the theater was making all the things which had set her apart from the life at Hangarwood and which had prompted her to write poems and heroic verse, seem to fit into place in her nature.

The vitality that she found within the confines of the Sans Pareil Theater, the voices declaiming Shakespeare as though the worlds were luscious ripe fruit, the passions (real and feigned), the laughter, the teasing, the bawdy jokes, the brilliant imitations of people in public life or met in the street, all seemed to give excitement and purpose to Perdita's life.

She took to leaving the house in the mornings as soon as she could without causing too much speculation as to her change of habit, and would make her way toward the Strand. Somewhere on the way she would find an excuse to send Jeannette home, but after the third day she could see that Jeannette was puzzled by, if not suspicious of, her actions. Perdita knew that she would have to devise some way to get to the theater without leaving the house with Jeannette.

She mentioned her difficulty to her father and the assembled company when she met them, hoping that their fertile minds would devise a plan for her.

It was the pretty little Pamela Forrest who came up with an answer. "You could always use Madame desVignes' shop," she said.

Edmund Wycoller turned a look of grave displeasure on the

giggling girl. It was well known that Miss Forrest, for all her tender years, was not as pure as her innocent blue eyes and pretty pink cheeks would make her seem. "I will not have my daughter using such a place," he said severely. "Madame desVignes may make some very pretty bonnets, but everyone knows that her real business is running a house of assignation."

"I wasn't suggesting that your daughter use it as such," Pamela said, pouting prettily. "Perdita would merely tell her coachman to leave her there and call for her later. She could easily slip out of the shop once he had gone and run through Lumley Court and be around at the stage door in a trice."

"What if the coachman should know about the place and gossip about his mistress below stairs. No, it will not do. Another way must be found. I will not have my daughter's good name compromised in any way. We must think of an alternative."

But Edmund Wycoller's urging produced no results and after ten minutes when furrowed brows and heads in hands produced nothing more than a few sighs, he was forced to say, "Well I don't like it above half, but I suppose it is the only way. Would you very much mind the arrangement, my darling? Can you trust your coachman?"

"I do not believe that Hughes will know of Madame desVignes' reputation. He has never been to London before this year. He is unlikely to think more than that I am visiting a new milliner's. Besides, I can sometimes take a hackney carriage and not have Hughes drive me all the time, so he will not know how many times I go to Madame desVignes'. But I do not know how to become acquainted with Madame desVignes. Will she not need some sort of payment for using her shop? She would think it strange if I arrive day after day and then rush out again a few minutes later."

"Oh, I can arrange all that," Pamela said helpfully. "I am an old friend of Madame desVignes and she will be happy to oblige. As you will not actually be using one of her rooms, I am sure that she will not want any payment, and if you were to buy a bonnet or two—which would be as well if your coachman is to be convinced that your visits are genuine—I daresay Madame desVignes will be quite happy to provide any story necessary, should the occasion arise. Leave it all to me. I will see Madame desVignes today and you may direct your coachman there tomorrow morning. Her shop is at Number Eleven Maiden Lane, just behind the theater. All you have to do is wait until the coachman has gone, and then slip out of the side door and down the alley at the side, then cut across the next opening on your right and you will find yourself opposite the stage door.''

"I shall wait outside the stage door for you," Edmund Wycoller said firmly. "Should you not appear by half past eleven, I shall come to Madame desVignes' and make inquiries for you. Perhaps it would be best if I were to await you there.''

"Oh no, Papa, I think that might cause too many questions. Besides, I shall manage very well, I assure you, and it would be foolish for you to wait there when you have so much to do in the theater. If I am not at the theater by half-past the hour, you may assume that I was unable to get away.''

Edmund Wycoller had to be satisfied with this, for no amount of persuasion would move Perdita from her firm opinion that he should not waste his time waiting for her at Madame desVignes' when he still had many things to do with the casting, lighting, and staging of *Richard III*, which was in the course of production. Mrs. Eddy added her plea for good sense to overrule his natural feeling for the safety of his daughter, and in the end he gave in with a good grace, saying only that he would be constantly going to the stage door to watch for Perdita.

The following day when Jeannette brought Perdita her morning chocolate and hot roll, Perdita said airily, "I will not need you this morning. I have heard of a wonderful milliner, but as the shop is some way off I shall take the barouche. Please inform Hughes that I shall need him at a quarter to eleven.''

Hughes was therefore the only member of the household who saw Perdita go into the shop of Madame desVignes in Maiden Lane. With his instructions to come back in an hour to fetch her, he drove off down the narrow cobbled road, turned his horses down Southampton Street, and made his way homeward by the Strand. As he passed the Sans Pareil Theater, Perdita was already walking into Lumley Court on her way to the theater.

However the journey did not take her the couple of minutes

she had expected. She had just turned into the narrow gap between two houses which stood opposite the theater stage door, when she noticed a pile of garbage, standing in one of the deep doorways, give a heave. Thinking some rat or mangey dog was about to run across her path, Perdita stopped quickly, but a half-stifled sob made her look more curiously at the pile of refuse. She walked forward a step and as she did so she could hear the sound of someone breathing. She was leaning down to see who it was that was hidden when her father stepped out of of the stage door of the theater.

"Perdita, what can you find so intriguing about that pile of refuse?" he asked, and then as she did not move, continued impatiently, "Come, I have been waiting for you."

Perdita looked up. "There is someone here," she said.

Her father walked forward and with the toe of his boot pushed aside some of the clutter of bones, rags, paper, and bottles. A pair of bright brown eyes, in an exceptionally dirty face, peered out of the darkness of the shadow.

"Come out, sirrah," Edmund Wycoller called in his most strident voice. "What do you think you are doing lurking in doorways and frightening innocent young ladies. Come out, I say, and at once."

"Come on," Perdita said in a gentle voice, "no one is going to hurt you."

There was a short pause and then the rest of the refuse fell over with a clanking of bottles and bones and a small boy rose out of the heap and took a tentative step forward.

Perdita crouched down so that she was level with the boy's face and said, "What are you doing here? Are you lost?"

The child looked at her with terrified eyes, but he did not say anything.

"Dumb," Edmund Wycoller said, "probably deaf *and* dumb—ah, what tragedies we see all around us!"

Perdita was not so inclined to jump to conclusions. "No," she said, "not dumb, just terrified. What has frightened you so, sweetheart?"

The boy looked at her as though she had taken leave of her senses. In his seven years he had never been addressed by any endearment, and this elegant lady in her fine fur-trimmed pelisse who was kneeling in the filth of the alley had just called him her sweetheart. The child took a tentative step toward Perdita and she held out her arms.

The gesture was unfamiliar to the boy, but the meaning was plain, and he walked forward to Perdita and into her arms. Without a thought that the child smelt quite terrible, and was undoubtedly verminous, she clasped him in a warm hug. "Come now," she said gently, "what is your name?"

"Freddy," the child said, his mouth against Perdita's fur collar.

"And Freddy, do your parents live near here?"

"Ain't got no parents," Freddy answered.

"No parents? You poor child—well then, where are your guardians?"

The child pulled back from Perdita's arms and started as though to run off, but Edmund Wycoller's hand descended firmly on Freddy's shoulder and spun him around to face Perdita again. "Answer the lady, boy," he said sternly.

The child gave a frightened glance at the big man towering over him and decided that compliance was his best defense. "I come from Mr. Brownlow's. 'E 'ad me from the orphanage almost a year ago, but 'e was bad, so I runs away and 'id from 'im. 'E's been looking for me. I 'eard 'im walking about and calling an cursin' and sayin' 'e'd kill me when 'e found me—so I stayed 'idden."

"It's all right," Perdita said soothingly, "no one is going to hurt you."

"Mr. Brownlow killed Tommy. 'E beat 'im to deaf, 'cause 'e wouldn't go up the chimbley. I don't want to be beat to deaf, and I don't want to go up no more chimbleys—I don't—I don't." With the last words Freddy's mouth drooped at the corners and the tears started to run down his filthy cheeks.

"I won't let anyone beat you to death," Perdita said firmly, the tears starting in her own eyes. "You don't have to worry any more, Freddy, I won't let you go back to that monster, Mr. Brownlow. Come, my darling, I'm going to take you into this nice place here and we will see that you get some new clothes." She looked at the thin rags which barely covered Freddy's boney little frame. "I think you'd like something to eat, too." She stood up and took Freddy by the hand as she turned to her father. "We'll have to take him to the theater until we can contact the authorities and work out what is to become of him, father."

"I'm not sure . . ." Edmund Wycoller began. He was

beginning to think that he might be called upon to play a greater part in Freddy's life than he might wish.

However, Perdita said firmly, "We can't leave him here. He must have something to eat and somewhere to go where the dreadful Mr. Brownlow can't find him. He is freezing and very hungry. We must find you something to eat at once, Freddy."

Freddy's eyes grew large and a glimmer of excitement sprang into their brown depths. "I ain't 'ad noffink to eat for two days," he said meltingly, and then to test this new-found fairy godmother, "Could I 'ave some bread and drippin'?"

"I'm sure you can," Perdita said cheerfully, leading him by the hand toward the stage door, while a dubious Edmund Wycoller followed at their heels.

As they went through the stage door Perdita turned to Tom and said, "Could you perhaps spare a moment, Tom, to be so kind as to fetch two large pieces of bread and dripping and some milk? Here is a shilling. That should be enough, but please hurry. Poor little Freddy has not had anything to eat for two days. Oh, and if you can find some good hot soup, I am sure that he would like that too."

Freddy, who felt as though he must be dreaming, was too amazed to speak and he let Perdita lead him down the corridor toward the stage. When they arrived there it was to find the permanent company gathered, some of them in their costumes for *Richard III*. Mrs. Warburgh had been going through the wardrobe trunks, trying to suit costumes to parts and fitting them on the people who would be playing the characters. The tunics and cloaks, the long kirtles and elaborate headdresses made Freddy think that he had been brought into some exotic kingdom. The glow of the candles lighting the stage did nothing to lessen the feeling of unreality and he stood still, clinging to Perdita's hand and staring at the strange creatures before him.

There was a dying murmur as one by one the company became aware of the ragged urchin clutching Perdita's hand, but she stepped forward, dragging Freddy with her, and said, "This is Freddy. My father and I found him in the alley by the stage door. He has been very badly treated by a horrible man, and as he has no family, he was forced to run away. I thought perhaps he could stay here until we can think of what to do with him."

The word *we* rang like a death knell in Edmund Wycoller's ears. Ever since he had seen Perdita hold out her arms to the bedraggled Freddy, he had been very much afraid that his daughter's return might prove to be not an entirely unmixed blessing.

He was about to remonstrate with her and remind her that only seconds before she had been talking of contacting the authorities, but Mrs. Eddy stepped forward in her full dress of Richard III's wife, Anne. "Why the poor, poor child. Of course we will look after him. He must be fed and washed, and no doubt when some of the grime is removed he will prove to be quite a taking little thing. Just look at those beautiful eyes."

Freddy looked up at the imposing lady in the vast scarlet cloak edged with ermine and the great golden crown on her head, and was sure that here was the Queen of England.

Perdita tugged at his hand. "This is Mrs. Eddy. Say how do you do, Freddy."

Freddy was a little taken aback by the fact that the Queen of England had a name much like the rest of her subjects and was struck dumb for a moment, but another tug at his hand galvanized him into action. The other boys in Mr. Brownlow's chimney-sweeping establishment had once speculated on what it was like to be the King or Queen of England, and one boy had informed the others that he knew for a fact that everyone meeting the royal couple were required to bow until their heads touched the ground. Freddy therefore bent double, and trying also to comply with Perdita's request, said to his knees, "How d'ye do, Queen Mrs. Eddy."

The assembled company laughed, but Mrs. Eddy was entranced. "Ah, what a sweetly pretty greeting," she said, bending to give Freddy a kiss, thinking better of it at the last moment, and instead giving him a friendly pat on the head. "I know what you would like. Come here, my dear boy, I just happened to put a sweetmeat in my reticule this morning. Something told me that it might come in handy today."

She led Freddy off to the back of the stage and soon Freddy's chatter could be heard from the dark corner. Once the floodgates had been opened it seemed that he would never stop talking, but the arrival of Tom with two enormous pieces of fresh bread lavishly slathered with beef dripping gave Freddy such a good alternative use for his mouth that he was silent until the last crumb had been swallowed and washed down with the flask of milk and the soup.

Mrs. Eddy and Perdita watched the child eat with a look of complacent pleasure on their faces, and when he had finished Mrs. Eddy said, "Now you will go off with Mrs. Warburgh, Freddy, and she will wash you and find you some lovely clothes to wear. Then when you are washed and have been made tidy, you may come back here and Lady Dole and I will decide what we are going to do with you."

Freddy knew better than to argue with the Queen of England, and though the idea of being washed held no great joy for him, he submitted to the ministrations of Mrs. Warburgh with good enough temper, only letting fly with one of his more unusual words when she insisted on digging firmly into the tender recesses of his ears with a soapy cloth. However, when he was presented to the company an hour later, it was hardly possible to recognize him as being the same child as the filthy urchin that Perdita had brought in.

Mrs. Warburgh had been unable to find any modern children's clothes to fit Freddy, but had finally pulled out a satin suit which had been used for one of the Babes in the Wood, which was just Freddy's size. When he was presented to the company in a lawn shirt with his satin waistcoat, coat, and breeches, it was obvious to all that Mrs. Eddy had been right when she said he had the makings of a very taking child. The bright eyes in the thin face and the thick mop of dark curly hair were quite arresting, but beyond that it seemed his miserable past had not broken his spirit and now cleaned and fed he carried himself with an air which would have done credit to a young prince.

Something of his past life had been told to the company while he had been off being washed and clothed. He had confided in Mrs. Eddy that he remembered nothing except the orphanage from whose dismal and unfriendly walls he had been taken by Mr. Brownlow with two other boys. The boys were technically apprenticed to Mr. Brownlow, Mrs. Eddy had gathered, and he was supposed to see that they were reasonably looked after and taught a trade. However, the laws, as everyone listening knew, were so lax that in fact Mr. Brownlow could treat the boys as though they were his possessions, without any fear that he might be prosecuted. No one ever came to see that he was feeding and clothing them, and even the death of Tommy had been passed over by the magistrates, when Mr. Brownlow had persuaded the constable sent to look into the matter that it had merely been a tragic climbing accident. The mortality among climbing boys was high, and the explanation had caused no ripple of doubt.

Freddy's description of how the children had been forced to climb the chimneys, the slower and more frightened ones being hurried in their jobs by lighting the fire underneath them, brought exclamations of horror from several of the company. Freddy's vivid description of his terror at having to climb up the pitch-dark chimneys by himself, choking on the soot which he dislodged and often meeting rats on the narrow ledges which were his only foothold, had brought tears to Mrs. Eddy's eyes.

Perdita particularly felt a fierce sympathy with the child. She knew from experience the overwhelming hold that fear could get on one, and the despair of being in a situation from which one could see no escape. The emotions which she had tried so hard to bury, engendered by her kidnapping, rose up in the form of anger at the evil Mr. Brownlow.

"We must do something to see that Mr. Brownlow is brought to justice. He must not be allowed to have any more small boys in his charge. He must be punished, transported, put in jail! Oh, I shall go straight to Bow Street and see that he is arrested this very day."

"Indeed, it shall be done," Mrs. Eddy said, worried by the near hysteria in Perdita's voice. "We will all make sure that Mr. Brownlow is severely punished and that Freddy is kept safely. But we must first of all make arrangements for Freddy. Unfortunately, I know that the law is very lax when it comes to punishing the masters of apprentices, and at all costs Freddy's name must not be mentioned, as then there might be a chance that the authorities would make us give him back to Mr. Brownlow."

"Freddy must be kept safe at all costs," Perdita said with anguish. "Mr. Brownlow must never be allowed to have him back."

"Do not fret, my love," Mrs. Eddy said. "We will keep Freddy with us and just inform the justices that they should investigate Mr. Brownlow thoroughly. I am sure that your father will be able to hide the source of his knowledge yet convince them that they should take swift action. There is no one in whom I would have greater trust for such a task. Who else can wring tears from an audience as he can?''

She turned and smiled at Edmund Wycoller, who realized that his fears had become reality and that he was about to become the champion of climbing boys. He shrugged his shoulders, acknowledging to himself the futility of argument, and merely said, "As you say, my dear, as you say."

However, he was not so complacent when Mrs. Eddy added to Perdita, "Your father and I will make ourselves responsible for Freddy's upbringing. Why, Freddy may show some talent for the theater. It is obvious that he has that vital quality, presence, and he may prove to be an asset to the company in time. Perhaps he might even start his career in the production of Richard III. He would make an excellent little Duke of York. You have not yet cast the part of the young Richard, have you Edmund? It is an easy enough part and I shall take it upon myself to coach young Freddy so that you may rest easy knowing that you will not have that to add to your burdens."

Edmund Wycoller felt that this morning's events had somehow cast him in the part of audience rather than his usual starring role. He did not altogether like the feeling of being out of control of the situation, but was not sure how he was to manage to wrest the reins back from Perdita and Mrs. Eddy.

His relationship with Mrs. Eddy had been a long one, and indeed it was well known that she was his wife in all but name. Her care for him and her knowledge of his likes and ways made him a great deal more comfortable than he would have been without her, but Sarah had never before asserted herself so positively. Edmund Wycoller had always known that she was a woman of strong will, and he had found it restful to let her manage the everyday trivia of their lives, but she had always taken great care that her iron fist was enclosed in the most comforting velvet glove, and had always subtly implied that *her* wishes were *his*. However, this time he had a feeling that he would be brazenly overruled should he not agree to her plans. On top of this, he knew that if he were to refuse to house and feed the young Freddy, he would most certainly be cast as the villain in his daughter's eyes. He had no wish to fall so swiftly from her grace and he therefore eyed the little boy and muttered that perhaps there was a chance that he might do for the small part in *Richard III*.

"Ah Edmund," Mrs. Eddy said, smiling at him and binding him more firmly to his unwanted commitment, "I knew that your heart was too great to allow this poor, poor child to suffer further injustice. Perdita, how proud you must be to have such a compassionate father."

"Indeed I am," Perdita answered, throwing her arms around her father's neck and kissing him warmly.

Feeling the kiss to have something of a Judas touch, Edmund Wycoller flinched slightly, but Perdita was unaware of her father's reluctance. Since the meeting in the alley, she had been wondering how she would explain the presence of Freddy to the Upper Grosvenor Street servants, and in any case had felt that Jeannette might not be too pleased to have the care of a rather outspoken street urchin. The solution put forward by Mrs. Eddy and ratified by her father was therefore one which she felt had a great deal of merit. Also, the thought that Freddy might, if he proved to have the ability, find a way of making a living for himself seemed to add even more virtue to the plan.

"Freddy," she said, turning to the little boy who stood silently as the Queen of England had decided his future, "did you hear that? You are to stay with Mrs. Eddy and Mr. Wycoller, and perhaps if you are very good and do just as you are told, you may be allowed to take part in one of their plays and to become a great actor."

"Ah, take part perhaps," Perdita's father said quickly, "but it will be a long time before it can be said that he is a great actor, if ever." Things seemed to be getting too much out-of-hand, and seeing visions of Master Freddy's name appearing above his own on the playbills, he realized the time had come to put a stop to such an excess of hopes.

"Well no, of course, not quite a great actor yet," Perdita said quickly, seeing the steely glint in her father's eyes, "but perhaps one day, Freddy, if you work very hard, you may become famous, and earn a lot of money. You would like that, would you not?"

Freddy nodded, as it seemed to be expected of him. He still had very little idea of what went on in this vast room with all the seats facing the platform on which they stood. But the pretty lady had promised him that he would never have to go up a chimney again, she had produced bread and dripping as if by magic, and if she said that he would like something, she must surely be right.

Perdita had been so taken up with her plans for Freddy's future that she had quite lost track of time, and it was not until Pamela Forrest reminded her that she had been away from Madame desVignes' millinery shop for nearly an hour that Perdita realized that she would have to hurry if she were not to be seen getting back into the shop. She kissed Freddy fondly and promised to come the next day and bring him a surprise. Mrs. Eddy and her father were warmly thanked for their kind and generous hearts, and Edmund Wycoller thought for the first time that there might be something to be said for the plan, but after she had run down the corridor and out of the theater he realized that his newly restored daughter had managed to turn his life totally upside down in under an hour.

Perdita's thoughts were much taken with the events of the morning for the rest of the day, and when she and Jeremy set out later that evening to dine with Lord and Lady Martineau, he noticed that she was even quieter than usual. Perdita was seeing for the first time the sharp contrast between her life and that of so many of the people who inhabited London. It seemed to her wicked that she should have been so ignorant of the suffering and poverty, or to have regarded it as only part of a drama, when it made up the life of the majority of the people. She determined never again to lose sight of the fact that, no matter whether or not she had her heart's desire, she was a very fortunate person.

However, these thoughts were almost totally eclipsed later that evening. The party was a crush. Although the season was not yet in full swing, the drawing rooms and ballrooms were beginning to get more crowded and supper and dancing for fifty was becoming a more common way of entertaining than the small dinners for sixteen or twenty people which had marked the days of late April and early May.

The company at Lord and Lady Martineau's that evening was of such size that supper had been served at a number of small tables set in the grand salon. Perdita was enjoying the conversation at her table when a Miss Ponsonby, whom she had met on a previous occasion, leaned toward her and whispered, ''I see Sir Jeremy is seated next to Miss Smith-Fenton. I daresay she is quite out of countenance with you.''

Perdita, not knowing what Miss Ponsonby was talking

about, answered, "I am sure that Miss Smith-Fenton has nothing to dislike me for. Why we have barely spoken two words."

"Ah, Lady Dole, what a diplomat you are," Miss Ponsonby said. "I am referring, of course, to the on-dit of last season that your husband was about to offer for Miss Smith-Fenton. I had heard that she had even started to collect her trousseau, but of course that was just gossip. Nevertheless, everyone noticed how attentive Sir Jeremy was to her, and they must have driven in the Park together at least a dozen times. However, you have certainly put paid to her hopes. I heard that her mama was quite put out at having the expense of paying for another season in London for her daughter."

Perdita hardly knew how to answer this conversation, but she made some noncommittal answer and turned as quickly as she could to the gentleman on the other side of her and tried to engage him in some quite unexceptional conversation. Miss Ponsonby, however, had sown a more devastating seed than even she had intended, and Perdita found that the rest of the evening her eyes were constantly drawn to Jeremy and Miss Smith-Fenton.

Here, at last, was the actuality of the vague specter which had haunted Perdita—the lady whom Jeremy had loved and whom he had been forced to relinquish to save Perdita's name. She could not help studying Sylvia Smith-Fenton's dark good looks and wondering whether Jeremy really preferred brunettes to blonds.

Her mind kept hearing Miss Ponsonby's words and her eyes kept trying to find any look of regret or sorrow in Jeremy's face. By the time they were riding home in the carriage she could not resist saying to him, "You were sitting next to an extremely striking lady at supper. Was that not Miss Smith-Fenton, about whom I have heard so much?"

Jeremy glanced at Perdita, paused for a moment, and then said, "I have known Miss Smith-Fenton for a long time. Her brother and I were at Eton together and then we served together in the Peninsula. He was killed there soon after I was wounded. He was a fine man and a sore loss to the regiment."

He seemed reluctant to say more about Miss Smith-Fenton and Perdita was left none the wiser about his feelings for the lady, but she felt the gulf between them widen.

From time to time as the carraige rattled through the dark

streets, Perdita glanced over at Jeremy, his dark head tilted against the squab cushions, seemingly unaware of her presence and off in some dream which Perdita was sure included Sylvia Smith-Fenton. A leaden ache seemed to pervade her body as she wondered whether he would ever cease to regret the necessity for marrying her, and whether *she* would ever be able to sit next to him in a carriage, put her hand in his on a dance floor, or endure his presence in a room without longing and longing to run into his arms.

She had hoped that by the time they returned from France, her proximity and their shared experiences would have begun to break through the barrier he had put up between them, had thought that he might, just once, have kissed her on the lips and found that it was more enjoyable than he had imagined. But once or twice she had reached out her hand to touch his only to see him pull away quickly as though he was repelled by her. Only on one occasion had he shown any sign that he thought of her as his wife, and that was when he had found her in the boudoir with Natalie, Louis, and Antoine, and though briefly she had hoped that this meant that he was jealous, she had all too soon realized that it was only that he did not approve of his wife's behaving in the French manner.

Tonight, as with so many other nights, as soon as the carriage arrived at Upper Grosvenor Street, Jeremy handed her out of the carriage, walked with her up the steps to the door, and, having seen her inside, turned again to go out to his club. However, this time before he left he caught her by surprise by saying, "Perhaps you would care to drive in the Park with me tomorrow afternoon if you have nothing better to do? It has been some time since we drove together."

The invitation caught Perdita off guard. "Oh, I cannot— that is, I was invited to go to take tea with Mrs. Prendal. She is an old friend of my mother's, but I could have one of the footmen take a note to her. I am sure that I will be able to see her at some other time."

"No, don't put yourself to the trouble," Jeremy said slowly. He seemed about to say something else, but shook his head, briefly wished her good night, and was out of the door before Perdita had a chance to insist that she would far rather drive with him than take tea with Mrs. Prendal.

Although she was at a loss to know what had prompted the unusual invitation, Perdita was annoyed with herself for having missed an opportunity to be with him. If she were to take his affection from Miss Smith-Fenton, Perdita knew that she must use every occasion she could to make Jeremy notice her, for despite the fact that there were a number of young men in London, as there had been in Paris, willing to flirt with the lovely Lady Dole, men who obviously found her an attractive woman, neither these nor the new clothes and the polished manner she had learned from Natalie, seemed to be able to find a chink in Jeremy's armor of polite indifference.

If only she had that attribute that Mrs. Eddy had, that her father had to a high degree, and that the rest of the theatrical company talked about, that elusive quality they referred to as "presence," perhaps, Perdita felt, she could force Jeremy to fix his eyes on her the way he had on Sylvia Smith-Fenton.

Perdita lay in bed thinking that if "presence" were a thing that could be learned, then the one person who could teach it would be her father.

Perdita sat up in bed, her eyes glowing. When she saw her father the next day she would ask his opinion, and enlist his aid. She would not let that dismal little Miss Smith-Fenton get the better of her.

Perdita did not have a chance to ask her father for his help when she first saw him the next day. When she arrived at the theater he was not waiting for her at the stage door, and as she walked through into the little hall where Tom sat picking his teeth with the end of an old goose feather, she heard voices raised in one of the dressing rooms. The tone of them did not sound as though someone were reading from Shakespeare, nor that a normal conversation were taking place, and she turned to Tom with a question in her eyes.

He sucked the end of the quill, took it from his mouth, and said, "You brought us a pretty kettle of fish, m'lady. Your father ain't 'alf up in the boughs about young Freddy. Seems a good meal and a comfortable night's sleep brought out the devil in 'im."

"Oh dear," Perdita said, walking quickly in the direction of the dressing rooms which lay to the right of the entrance. She walked down the row until she came to the open door of the one from which the noise was coming. As she went through the door the sight which met her eyes gave her an almost uncontrolable urge to turn tail and run. Her father was holding a squirming Freddy by the ear, while Mrs. Warburgh, in floods of tears, was being comforted by Mrs. Eddy. As Perdita approached she saw the cloak that Mrs. Eddy had been wearing the day before clutched in Mrs. Warburgh's arms as though it were a dying child.

At the sound of Perdita's steps her father turned and with a voice that would have reached Whitehall, roared, "Well, miss, and look what you have foisted upon your loving father. Here's an ungrateful wretch who no sooner has been cossetted, fed, and clothed to the top of his bent, turns upon his benefactors and brings them to the brink of ruin." As he ended this speech, he gave a tweak to Freddy's ear and the boy let out a howl.

"Aye, howl, howl," Edmund Wycoller said, turning to Freddy. "You'll howl louder when I turn you back to your rightful owner, Mr. Brownlow."

The howls rose to screams and Edmund Wycoller let go of the child's ear and said, "Quiet! This caterwauling would raise the dead and most certainly alert the watch to your whereabouts. If you want to remain safe, you'd better keep your mouth shut."

Perdita had by that time reached Freddy's side. She knelt down beside him but turned a furious look upon her father. "Father, how could you threaten poor Freddy with sending him back to Mr. Brownlow? You should be quite ashamed of your lack of heart. There, there," she said, turning to Freddy, whose screams had now turned to snuffling sobs, "My father did not mean his threat. No one is going to send you back to Mr. Brownlow, no matter what you have done, but what is it that you have been doing, Freddy, to put everyone in this taking?"

"I only tried to make meself a cloak like Mrs. Eddy was wearing'," Freddy said, wiping his nose on his sleeve before Perdita could pull a handkerchief from her reticule. "They said I was to be a prince and a prince needs a red cloak."

Perdita looked at the piece of red velvet which Mrs. Warburgh was clutching to her bosom and light dawned on her. "Oh Freddy, you didn't try to make yourself a cloak out of Mrs. Eddy's, did you?"

"I fought vere was enough for ve two of us. 'Er's was very big," Freddy said sulkily. "But vey all took on so, you'd 'ave thought I'd murdered 'em."

"You might as well have, you wretched child," Edmund Wycoller thundered. "Do you have the slightest idea how much that cloak cost us? Red velvet at a guinea a yard is not something that I can afford to have cut up for a child's plaything. That cloak has been treasured and cherished for years, and now, you young jackanapes, you have ruined it."

Mrs. Warburgh, to add drama to the statement, held out the cloak, and Perdita saw that her father had some justification in his claim that it was ruined. A large square had been hacked out of the middle of it and it was now little more than a very expensive rag.

"Oh Freddy," she said, "that was very naughty of you," but seeing his lower lip tremble, hastily continued, "however, I am sure that you did not mean to do anything bad. In future, you must not take anything that does not belong to you, and most certainly must not cut things up without pemission. Now go to Mrs. Eddy and Mrs. Warburgh and say that you are very sorry and will not do anything bad again."

She led the subdued Freddy across to the two ladies, who were eyeing the scene which had been taking place, and Freddy mumbled, "I am very sorry, Mrs. Eddy, Mrs. Warburgh. I won't do it again."

It was impossible to resist his obvious penitence and Perdita having shown the reason behind his naughtiness, Mrs. Warburgh could not hold on to her anger any longer. She and Mrs. Eddy accepted Freddy's apologies, though they could not help adding that it had been an exceptionally naughty thing to do.

Perdita was meanwhile searching in her reticule. She pulled out three gold coins which she held out to Mrs. Warburgh. "Here, I know that it is not enough for a new cloak, but perhaps you will be able to find a second-hand one for this."

"No, no, child," her father said, stepping forward and closing her hand over the money, "I shall take no penny from you. Mrs. Warburgh will contrive, I am sure of it, and we may find something that will do as a substitute. Besides, I have every intention of docking Master Freddy's salary when it comes due." He glared at Freddy, but there was no fire in his glance, and apart from lowering his eyes Freddy seemed unmoved by the threat.

But Perdita continued, "Please, Papa, I would very much like to make what amends I can now. After all, if it were not for me, you would not have Freddy here at all, and you are looking after him. At least let me do this."

Common sense overcame Edmund Wycoller's higher feelings, and seeing the justice in Perdita's assertions he accepted the money with a fine pretense of someone only doing it to satisfy her conscience. The money was handed over to a placated Mrs. Warburgh who, secretly knowing that she could get velvet just as good as that in the cloak for half a crown a yard, excused herself quickly lest her restored good humor should make Freddy think that his crime had not been a heinous one after all. The kernel of the drama having been well-digested, Mrs. Eddy took Freddy in hand with a "If I keep you occupied, perhaps you will not have so much time for devilment," and led him off to start teaching him his lines, and to begin to try to eradicate the fine thick Cockney accent which embellished his speech.

As the door closed behind Freddy and Sarah Eddy, Perdita found herself alone with her father for the first time that week. The activity of the theater had made it impossible for them to find time to be alone together in the all too short moments that she could get away from home.

"Well my dear," Edmund Wycoller said, sinking down before one of the mirrors into a dusty and rickety chair, "it seems that we have very few moments in which to talk together, and there is so much to talk about." He paused for a second, but before Perdita could say anything he continued, "Oh, when I look at you I see the most beautiful legacy your mother could leave me. You are so much like her. That same hair, like sunlight sifting through the leaves of a beech wood, that smile—sometimes, my darling child, when you smile I feel myself a young man again, and see my beloved Lavinia as she was when I first met her.

"Did I ever tell you how we met?" Perdita shook her head and waited for him to go on.

"She was a year younger than you are now." Edmund Wycoller's voice grew soft and his sight seemed to retreat behind his eyes. "I can see her still as she came down that road in Suffolk. She had been visiting a friend in the neighborhood of Hadleigh and I was there with a group of strolling players with whom I was then associated. I had never seen a girl so lovely. There are no words to tell. She 'bereft me of all words, only my blood spoke in my veins,' to paraphrase the Bard. But it seems that she saw in me too something she recognized as being of meaning in her life. On what pretext I forget, but we stopped and spoke to each other, to ask the time of day, to inquire directions, to admire the countryside?

Those facts have gone now, but I remember how her voice thrilled through my veins and set the seal to all I had believed was in her of my happiness.

"We met often, daily during the time I was at Hadleigh. Luckily, her friend was a romantic young soul and was happy to assist us in our meetings. Love grew, and when it was time for me to continue on my journeying, she agreed to come with me. Of course she was not of age, but she declared that she would not be parted from me, and to force your grandfather's hand to permit our marriage—she was under age of course—she came with the troupe as we wended our way up through Norfolk. There was nothing improper in our relationship. I took care that she was chaperoned by an older member of the troupe, with whom she stayed—a Mrs. Morgan, I recollect. But after a month of that it became clear to your grandfather that his daughter was adamant and that no matter how unsullied her name was in fact, it would be hard for him to persuade society that a young girl who had spent a month with strolling players was a suitable match for any member of the quality.

"We were married, and a year later you were born. I cannot believe that there was a happier little family the length and breadth of the British Isles. Of course, we were not rich. We lived for the main part in down-at-heel lodgings, but with my scant wages and the small allowance your grandfather made us, we managed, and in any case we lacked for nothing, for love was a god we worshiped and who blessed us with an open hand. What days, those were, what days! I think back and cannot remember any days then that were not filled with sunshine and laughter. And then, when you had just turned five and your little brother was born, she was taken from me with the babe. The light went out. My life was a dark and empty cavern. Those times were as much of hell as I ever wish to know. I could not think clearly, I could not eat, nor drink, nor work, nor see any hope for the future, and when your uncle offered to take you and bring you up as his own child with his wife and stepdaughter, I could not think that it would not be for the best for you. It could not break my heart more to lose you, I thought then; it was already in such small fragments. But oh, and oh, I came to know that it was not so, and when time had healed me enough to allow me to start to live again, I came to regret my decision. Many was the time that I thought of going to your uncle and asking, nay demanding, that he give you back to me, but then I would think how you would be settled in your new home, how he would be able to give you all the things that I could not, and I turned back to my life and threw my energies into my work. But always there is, and always there will be, that corner of my heart, which I hardly dare contemplate, where you and I and my beloved Lavinia live in the happiness we once knew.''

Edmund Wycoller looked down at his hands clasped in his lap and then raised one hand slowly to wipe away the tears which were rolling slowly down his cheeks. Perdita got up from the couch and went over to him to put her arms around his shoulders.

''Oh father,'' she said pressing her face against his with the tears running from her own eyes. The tears were for her father, and for her dead mother, but they were also joined by tears of regret for the happiness that her parents had known and which she would never have. She could imagine the total unity of love and thought which had warmed and lightened her parents' lives, and knew that it was denied her. She sank into her father's lap and sobbed against his shoulder like a child.

''My darling girl, don't cry so. Do you cry for me? Nay, nay, my little one. I have long since lived without tears, and grown to cherish the knowledge that the love that your mother and I had for each other was a rare treasure, and like most things rare cannot be measured by amounts. What we had was more than most people ever dream of having. We were lucky and I thank God now for the days he gave, and no longer curse Him for the days that were taken. But do you cry for me? Tell me, my angel child, what is hurting you so? Tell your old father, that he may put it right.''

He rocked her in his arms and she felt that here at last was someone she could talk to, who might understand how she felt, and with whom it would not be disloyal to discuss her problems with Jeremy. ''Oh Papa, I—to hear you talk of such happiness—I should like so much to know it in my own life.''

''What is this? What are you telling me? Is your husband not kind to you? Does he mistreat you, betray you?''

Perdita pulled back a little and said in a low voice, "No, not that. It is just that I don't think he loves me—and—and oh Papa, I do love him so much."

It was if the long pent-up flood of her feelings for Jeremy, the restraints of the past weeks which had become unendurable, had been unlocked by the loving concern of her father and his warm memories of his own happy marriage. Perdita told him of the reason why she had married Jeremy, of how he had merely offered for her out of a sense of honor to protect her name when, having saved her from the kidnappers, he had been found coming from her room by Mrs. Banistre-Brewster. She told her father how he had been kind but distant to her, how he barely seemed to notice her, and finally confessed that he had never come to her bed.

The tale of her kidnapping caused her father to pull her to him in an agony of dismay at the thought of her danger, but it was her final confession which made him draw back with an expression of incredulity.

"My darling girl, surely, you are not telling me that your aunt would permit you to marry a man who prefers those of his own sex?"

"Oh no," Perdita said quickly, "at least I am sure that is not the reason for his behavior. I think that he still loves a lady that he was courting last year and whom he had to give up for my sake. I have been told that he was on the point of offering for her, and no doubt would have done but for the coil that he found himself in when he had saved me from those awful men."

"My child, no man, however much in love with another lady in the past, could fail to succumb to your charms once he was married to you. The whole idea is preposterous. The man must literally adore hair shirts and self-flagellation to behave in such a manner. You are ravishingly beautiful, you have a nature both gentle and sweet, you have grace and intelligence—all the attributes a man could want. The man must be made of stone who would not desire you."

Perdita had to smile at her father's strong defense of her, but she said, "The trouble is that he does not really notice me, or rather that he still thinks that I am the little girl he knew years ago. He is kind to me, and indulges me in every way, but it seems that he barely sees me, at least not as a woman. I have tried hard to make him see that I am quite grown up now. When I was in Paris I bought many clothes that were certainly not designed for children, and I thought that perhaps once he really noticed that I had grown up he would begin to love me a little, or at least to find that he had not made such a bad bargain after all.''

''Bad bargain! Pshaw! No man could possibly think of you as a bad bargain. The fellow's a scoundrel. I have a good mind to horsewhip him. He'd take notice then. But, my pretty dove, if you love this man, we must do something. He shall be forced to notice you. Now what is needed?''

Edmund Wycoller held Perdita by the hands and, getting up, stood looking at her for a minute. ''Beautiful,'' he murmured, ''certainly beautiful. Graceful, yes, but we need more. We need perhaps a touch of theater, a hint of drama.'' He cocked his head on one side and then said, ''Now child, leave the room and show me how you would come in were you entering a ballroom, or the salon at some party, with Jeremy by your side.''

Perdita, with a question in her eyes, said nothing but did as she was told, going out of the door and entering again in her normal fashion.

''Ah, now there at least we can make an improvement,'' Edmund Wycoller said. ''Go out again and when you come back, pause for a moment in the doorway. At a ball you will not have to consider the door itself, so I will not bother you with ways to open doors, but stand for a second in the doorway and survey the room, then, and only when you have made a sufficiently long pause, enter the room. Don't be in a hurry. Come in slowly, and walk without looking to right or left toward your destination. For our purposes now the chest in the corner will suffice. Tell yourself that it is the one person in the world that you wish to see. Now begin.''

Perdita duly went out of the room again and reentered trying to remember her father's instructions, but she found that it was not as easy to acquire the perfection of timing that he demanded. ''No, no, child, pause in the doorway, and look slowly, slowly around, not like an owl on a post. Take your time. You are seeing, but the purpose is to be seen.

Know that all the eyes in the room are on you. Know it, know it, but do not care. Give them time to be aware of you, time to wonder why you are standing there. Curiosity focuses all eyes. Now again. Out of the door and reenter."

As Perdita walked out of the door this time she ran into Mrs. Eddy, who had deposited Freddy with Pamela and had come to see why Edmund and Perdita had not come to see the rehearsal. Her look of surprise as she saw Perdita turn and walk back into the room changed to a smile as she heard Edmund say from within, "That's better, but look for someone. No, no, you have not found him yet. Even if you know where he is, look in the other direction first. You must build up the suspense until everyone wants to know what you are looking for, then you will have their attention, and then you may move. Out, out. Try it again."

"Learning to make an entrance, my dear?" Mrs. Eddy said, as Perdita came out of the dressing room again. "Well, you have the greatest teacher in the world, you will soon master it." She went into the dressing room with Edmund and stood with him as he watched Perdita come back.

This time she concentrated on her father's advice to remember that all eyes in the room were on her. Her imagination took charge and she saw herself as some great lady whose admirers were legion, who was so used to flattery and adulation wherever she went that the whole thing was a bore to her. She paused in the doorway, looked slowly into the left-hand corner of the room, letting her eyes form a smooth arc as they swung from that corner over to the right, moving her head with a graceful flow of action. Then she allowed herself to see the chest in the corner—a beloved friend, long lost; her one and only love taken from her by cruel fate and now restored. She smiled, the smile coming slowly from her lips to her eyes, she clasped her hands in surprise and delight in front of her, and then opened her arms a little way and walked toward the chest as though to the welcoming arms of her lover.

"Bravo," Mrs. Eddy said. "Edmund, she is your daughter indeed. I have never seen anyone grasp the idea so quickly."

Perdita smiled and turned to her father for his approval.

"Yes, my dear, I think you understand now. Timing—it is all in the timing, and that one great art of knowing that you are the center of attention. Once you *know* that, you will be, and I defy Sir Jeremy to be unaware of you."

Mrs. Eddy cast him a questioning glance and he said, "It is Perdita's story, but perhaps she will not mind your knowing about it." He looked over at Perdita, who nodded. "It seems that this foolish husband of hers—for reasons I will not go in to at the moment—appears not to notice her. We have decided that he will be forced to see that she is the most beautiful woman in any gathering they choose to grace. I doubt that there are many who can equal my Perdita for beauty, but beauty, like a flower, can go unnoticed unless it announces itself in some way, and I am teaching my daughter to know that she will be the center of attention wherever she goes."

"Oh indeed, my dear, you will be. Your father will give you just that polish, you may be sure. I always think of myself as an ancient king's favorite. I find it helps to imagine myself a totally different person, don't you know?"

"Oh yes, I do that too. I always used to imagine myself as different people when I was a child: Queen Elizabeth, Mary Queen of Scots going bravely to her beheading, a poor ragged orphan, when I was afflicted with a fit of the dismals, or—oh, any number of people. I am afraid that I still make up stories to myself when I am alone, or do not have much to do."

"Ah, perhaps if we do not make an actress of you we will turn you into a playwright," Edmund Wycoller said. "The theater is sadly lacking in new plays, and perhaps you will be the one to remedy that."

"Why, that would be a perfect idea!" Mrs. Eddy said, turning to him eagerly. "Perhaps Perdita could write the curtain-raiser for our *Richard III*. There is little time, of course, but if we helped her, perhaps it could be done. Just think, Edmund, how delightful it would be for you to act in a play written by your own daughter!"

"But my dear, Perdita is not a writer. How can she suddenly produce a play from nothing but the wandering thoughts of a young girl?"

"Well she can try. There will be nothing lost in that. You said yourself, not two days ago, that you were having trouble finding something suitable. Something that would not involve a troupe of singers or a performing dog or horse, something which could be acted before one backcloth and would require but the minimum of props and elaborate clothes. Let Perdita try. You may still look elsewhere, but it will do no harm to let her try her hand at such a thing, and you and I may advise her on the techniques. Why, she might write whole plays for you if she can succeed in this."

While Mrs. Eddy had been speaking, Perdita had been turning the suggestion over in her mind and finding that the more she thought of it, the more the idea appealed to her. She had plenty of time on her hands during the day and although she had not returned to the epic poem she had been on the point of starting before her kidnapping, she missed the occupation of writing. By having a purpose for it, she felt it would be more easily resumed.

"Oh Papa, do let me try. I have been writing poetry since I could hold a pen and have written several small plays for Jane and our friends to act in. I would love to try my skill at devising a one act play for you. As Mrs. Eddy says, you could still look for other alternatives, so that if mine is not suitable you would not have wasted any time. Oh, please let me try."

"Poetry, plays? Bring me some of your work when you come to see me tomorrow and have some ideas for a plot in your mind. Perhaps you might try a short piece in verse. Not too many characters, mind you. Perhaps five or six, and short, three scenes, or at the most four, but short. We do not want the audience tired out before they see the main play."

Perdita ran forward and put her arms around her father's neck. "Oh I would so like to be part of your company, Papa, and in this way I can be. It is so wonderful to have so much to think about. I have been at a loss for things to do, but now I shall have my entrances to practice and shall have the play to think about. Oh, I shall not sleep tonight so that I may think of a million ideas to propose to you tomorrow."

The idea of writing a play for her father was so entrancing

to her, and she was so deep in thought when she left by Madame de Vignes' front door an hour later, that Perdita did not notice a woman staring at her from the other side of the street. Even if she had, she would not have recognized the lank hair and snaggle-toothed face of Peg Diver, with whom, but for Jeremy's timely rescue, she might have had an all too intimate acquaintance.

Perdita's present problems with her marriage had managed to make her almost forget her kidnapping, and apart from the moments when something reminded her of her terror at the hands of George, Henry, and Crib, most of those events had been erased from her mind. But Peg had cause to remember the incident with more fidelity.

When her Henry had not returned to London for some days, after she had seen Clamp, Peg had occasionally felt uneasy, but Henry was often absent from London and she had told herself that she was getting silly in the head. However, when a filthy street urchin had brought her a crumpled note some two months back, she had gone quickly to Newgate. A small bribe to the guards, and she had been allowed to speak to Henry for almost ten minutes before she was hustled out of the prison. When she went back the next day it was to be told that he had been tried and sent out to the ship that was to transport him to Australia. But Henry had told her enough in the ten minutes for her to realize that she had been the unwitting cause of his deportation. Henry's description of the small cove with the round face and the cauliflower ear was brief, but enough for Peg to know that the man who had visited her asking for information as to Henry's whereabouts was the man who had been instrumental in seeing him sent to jail. Henry had also given a graphic description of the tall gentleman with the deceptively languid air and the pale blonde girl who had been kidnapped and taken to Otley Green.

After Henry had left the country the knowledge of what she had done had rankled in Peg's heart like a thorn, and she became obsessed with taking some sort of revenge. She had dismissed the idea of murder, for although she felt quite capable of carrying it out, she was too much the realist to think that she might not be discovered and made to swing for it, and even for Henry she was not prepared to go that far.

Henry had told her that it was the tall, dark-haired man who had given the orders, and that the round-faced man, Clamp, was only his servant. It was therefore Jeremy who became the object for Peg's revenge. From Henry's description he had obviously been a man of quality, and Peg surmised that he was almost certain to be in London for the season. She had taken to neglecting her calling in favor of hanging about the streets of fashionable London in the hours when the *haut ton* were going to their evening's entertainment. Peg soon developed a sixth sense about where the fashionable parties were to be held, and long before the first carriages arrived she would be in some shadowy doorway where she had a good view of the guests arriving.

She had waited in wet and fair weather for more than three weeks before her patience was rewarded. One evening outside the house of Lord and Lady Donahue she saw a tall, dark gentleman hand a slender blonde lady from a carriage. Peg looked intently at the couple, and heard the gentleman say to the coachman, "You may return for us at midnight, Hughes. Oh, and I would be grateful if you would send word to Clamp not to wait up for me. I will be going straight to my club."

The way the man moved, as though time would wait for him, and the name, Clamp, were all that Peg needed to be sure that she had at last found her victim. It was not difficult for her to follow the carriage back to the mews and to seek out one of the young stableboys.

Peg had no clear idea how she would pursue her quarry, nor how long it would take her to find out something that would give her some hold over the Doles. She was no stranger to drawing out people's confidences and soon, in the privacy of the hayloft, she had got the young stableboy to discuss everything he knew about his master and mistress. There had been some talk about the hurried wedding, but that had proved only to have been impatience on the part of the bridegroom, though the funny part was that Sir Jeremy and Lady Dole never seemed to share a bedroom. He mentioned the kidnapping and the drama that had caused, but Peg hurried him through that recital, knowing more about it than she could be told by any stableboy. The boy talked on, trying to impress Peg with the knowledge that drifted down the

backstairs and unaware that Peg was barely listening to him.
There seemed to be nothing that Peg could use, but she had
time, lots of time, and sooner or later Sir Jeremy or Lady
Dole would do something that they did not want talked about.
Peg was beginning to think about making her way home when
the boy said, ''I'm glad I'm not married to her ladyship. Sir
Jeremy must be deep in the pocket to keep her in bonnets.
Hughes, the coachman, has to drive her to the milliner's,
Madame Devines or somefink, every day. Who could need a
new bonnet every day?''

Peg's heart skipped a beat. So Lady Dole was already
playing Sir Jeremy false, was she? Madame desVignes was
well known to Peg, and she was well aware that the shop was
only a front for her real business of arranging discreet assignations and hiring out private rooms for a few hours. Hugging herself with delight, Peg only stayed with the boy long
enough to find out exactly when Lady Dole went to Madame
desVignes', and having acquired that information, she returned to The Wattles with a light heart.

She took the precaution of watching Madame desVignes'
for the next few mornings before she did anything further,
and was happy to see that Lady Dole did indeed arrive
punctually at eleven every morning and seemed to be in the
shop for over an hour every day.

The third afternoon, she called on Annie Milligan in The
Wattles. Annie was the only person in the street who could
read and write, and Peg carefully dictated a letter to her.
After that was done, she folded the piece of paper carefully
and then found among the flotsam of humanity who fre-
quented the area, one who seemed reliable enough to deliver
the letter to Sir Jeremy Dole. Having set her plan in motion,
Peg returned to her trade with a feeling that at least, in part,
she was making amends to her Henry.

The note was delivered to Jeremy as he was dressing to go
out to dinner with Perdita. Clamp had just helped him into a
black coat and was fastening the straps of his tight black
pantaloons under the soles of his evening slippers. Jeremy
held out his hand idly for the letter as it was presented to him
and, looking with an expression of disgust and puzzlement at
the extremely grubby piece of paper, unfolded it delicately
with the tips of his fingers. As he started to read, the look of
disgust turned to one of anger. Clamp glanced up at his

master's face and did not like the look he saw there. Sir Jeremy seldom lost his temper, but when he did the whole world seemed to shake.

"Who delivered this?" Jeremy asked, turning to the footman who still hovered at the doorway.

"I've never seen the man before, Sir Jeremy. Not the sort one would expect to see in these parts, sir, but he was very insistent that you would be interested in the note."

Jeremy's frown deepened and he dismissed the footman with a wave of his hand. He looked at the note again. The writing was the work of someone not at home with quill and paper, but despite the splattering of ink and the occasional misspelling, the message was plain. The note said: "Do you ever wonder who it is that your wife meets at Madame desVignes' at eleven o'clock every morning?"

Jeremy was well aware of Madame desVignes' true business, and was in no doubt of the message's intent. However, his first instinct was to crumple the note and wish the writer to the devil. He was quite sure that Perdita had never even heard of Madame desVignes, and he found it impossible to think that she would ever have any interest in meeting a lover. The whole idea was ridiculous and unthinkable. She was an innocent. She was certainly without guile and the ability to scheme. Nevertheless, he could not quite understand why this letter, this revolting parcel of lying insinuation, should disturb him so much. But it had been written by someone who had a grudge against him; someone who would try any trick to disquiet him and plant discord in his marriage. Jeremy clenched his teeth, as though there were not enough problems he had to face in this marriage, without someone's trying to make more trouble.

Over the past month the realization that he was deeply in love with his wife had been something which had tormented him. He knew that she loved Christopher, that she had only married him because of the threat of scandal, and those thoughts had made Jeremy impose upon himself an iron discipline which every day he found harder to maintain. He had found that the only way he could keep his feelings in check was to spend as little time as possible with Perdita and to treat her with a cool formality which prevented her showing any signs of sisterly affection to him.

More than once, though, he had in desperation decided

that the time had come to end the charade one way or another; to get out of her life completely and let her find what happiness she could on her own, or alternatively to tell her of his feelings and hope that she could return them to a slight degree. However, the latter course had always been aborted by the thought that if he failed he might lose what little affection she had for him, and he had instead worked off his passions by long sessions in Jackson's Boxing Saloon and nights gambling at his club.

Now, unwilling to think about the note and its implications, he stuffed it into the pocket of his coat and went downstairs to meet Perdita.

— II —

Despite his assurance to himself that the note was purely a fabric of vicious lies, Jeremy found that it was like a thorn in his mind, and that the longer it lodged the more it absorbed his thoughts. He knew that by spending so much time away from Perdita he was forcing her to find her own amusement, but he had always felt that her love of Christopher was so paramount that it had not crossed his mind that she might look for love elsewhere. However, he dismissed this thought quickly. The note was just lies—all lies. But even so, he found he could not entirely dismiss the suspicions that had been aroused.

As he sat in the carriage with Perdita, he found himself constantly glancing over at her as she sat looking out of the window on the far side of the carriage. She was unaware that she was being watched, and Jeremy was able to drink in the calm profile, her long neck rising in a graceful curve from the silk shawl thrown around her shoulders, the fragile angle of jawbone, and the lips that had always enchanted him with the way they closed together with the subtle simplicity of flower petals. Surely something so perfect, so tranquil could not be deceiving him. As he looked he had an almost overwhelming desire to pull her to him and tell her in no uncertain terms that she was his and his only, and that he would share her with no one. But knowing that such a sudden declaration was out of the question, he could only sit and look at her.

Her silence and composure did nothing to dampen his inner turmoil, and he wished that she would speak so that he might bring up the subject of the note, or of Madame desVignes. Even as he thought this, he realized that this desire too was totally impractical. She would look at him as though he were mad, which he was beginning to feel he was, and the chasm between them would widen again.

He had to admit that nothing in her bearing could possibly be interpreted as being out of the ordinary, and his reason told him that she could not so suddenly change from the innocent young girl whom he had married into the sort of practiced, scheming woman who could meet a lover by day and sit beside her husband with such composure the same night.

As they jolted over the cobblestones and the lights from the street and the passing carriages illuminated Perdita's face, he found himself time and again on the point of opening some leading conversation with her which might at least tell him whether she knew of the existence of Madame desVignes. Once he even steeled himself to show her the note and ask her outright whether there was any truth in it, and his hand was halfway to his pocket before he could stop himself and tell himself that he would not be helping his cause by doing such a thing. If it were not true, she would hate him for even suspecting her, and if she should acknowledge it to be the truth, he would find it even more painful than not knowing. He cursed himself for a gullible fool and tried, once again, to forget that he had ever received the letter.

However, he could not keep himself from noticing Perdita's every action that evening. It was as though his nerves had been grafted onto her and every flicker or movement on her part, every nuance of expression, was immediately noted and stored in his brain.

Had he not been in such a state of heightened awareness, he might have missed the way in which she entered the grand salon where their host and hostess were waiting to greet them. He watched Perdita make her salutations and then saw her stand for a minute looking about the room. The minute seemed to draw out to eternity as she turned her head slowly from left to right and allowed her eyes to make a circle of the room as though there were one particular face that she was looking for. There was an inner stillness in her which nevertheless carried the tension and fascination of a cat poised to spring. Several quizzing glasses were raised and directed at her, and a silence spread around her as groups nearby turned to look. Jeremy found his possessiveness aggravated by these attentions, and he reached out his hand to touch her arm and lead her further into the room, but before his hand could touch her a smile of delight came to her face and she walked away from him toward the far corner of the room.

Jeremy's eyes followed her and he saw her approach a young man who stood just out of reach of the candlelight. With a feeling of intense anger which made him feel as though a fist had landed hard in his stomach, he saw Perdita lean forward and kiss the man on the cheek. Jeremy saw the man take both her hands in a familiar manner and hold her at arm's length while his eyes took in her whole person. It was not until Jeremy had thrust his way through the crowd of people and almost reached Perdita's side that he recognized the man as his brother, Christopher.

The flame of anger in him turned to icy cold. The truth that he had been living with for the past months was made visible and tangible. Jeremy knew a jealousy of which he had not known he was capable. He had been able to convince himself over the past month that he could bear to live with the fact that Perdita would never love him as she loved Christopher, but the sight of the two of them together made him realize that he had not begun to come to terms with his feelings.

Summoning all the self-control of which he was capable, he reached out his hand to his brother and said in as normal a voice as he could manage, "My dear Christopher, I had not thought to see you in London so soon. I trust it is not because you have been rusticated."

Christopher laughed and clasped his brother's outstretched hand. "Jeremy, it's good to see you. No, even the tutors at Cambridge are human enough to allow a man some time off every now and then. I am here to greet Jane and Mrs. Chase when they arrive tomorrow, and to pay my respects to my brother and sister-in-law. I may say that I have never seen Perdita look more fetching. I always had a suspicion that she might become quite personable if she could come out of her dream world and pay more attention to her attire, but who would have believed that the grubby child who hid in the barn with me to escape her French governess would turn into a beauty of the first water? Why Perdita, 'pon my oath I don't believe that there is a woman in this room to touch you. Paris most certainly suited you."

Perdita smiled. "What a gull-catcher you are, dear Christopher, but it is no good trying your arts on me. You are not the only one with a long memory, and I remember too many set-downs to swallow your compliments now. However, out of friendship I am content to let you practice your arts on me so that you may have enough address to set your cap for one of the ladies you will meet this season.''

Christopher looked somewhat sheepish at this last remark and Perdita cocked a quizzical eyebrow at him. ''Ah, do I detect that I have hit the mark? Who is she, Christopher? Do I know her?''

Christopher grinned and said with mock formality, ''I am not at liberty to divulge her name, but, yes, you do know her. However, I am not practicing my arts on you, my delicious Perdita. I had hoped that you would think that I had perfected them, for what should your perfection deserve but perfect compliments?''

''Bravo! That was beautifully spoken. What can I do but blush and accept such a ravishing compliment, no matter how much my delightful modesty must make me deny its truth. But come, tell me how you fare at Cambridge, and why you did not let me and Jeremy know that you were coming to London? Where are you staying? You must, of course, come to Upper Grosvenor Street. It is your home, you know.''

''I would not for the life of me disturb the newlyweds in their bliss. I should feel myself quite unwelcome in a matter of minutes and no doubt be quickly sickened by the billing and cooing that would pass for conversation. Please spare me that. Besides, I am lodging with a friend from Cambridge, George Wilkins, and however much I might enjoy your company, my dearest sister and brother, I am afraid that you would not make such good cronies for the activities I have in mind. Also, there is a strong possibility that Jeremy might decide to come it strong when he realizes that I intend to run through my patrimony in the shortest possible time, and that I have no concern for the future at all.''

''You may be sure that if you do any such thing you will be the recipient of my heaviest brotherly advice, no matter where you are lodging,'' Jeremy said, trying to match the bantering tone of the conversation. ''Don't forget that I am your trustee until you come of age, and shall have no compunction in cutting you off without a farthing if I feel that you are playing fast and loose with your inheritance.''

''You don't frighten me in the least, brother. When have

you ever failed to sport the blunt and to get me out of any scrape? I cannot be convinced that marriage has turned you into a clutch-fist. Why Perdita's dress alone must have cost a small fortune. Not that it is not extremely handsome and worth every penny of its cost. The wreaths of silk cornflowers are an exceptionally pretty touch.'' Christopher raised his quizzing glass and examined the gray silk gown with its padded hem and wreaths of bright blue flowers which had been one of Perdita's more outrageous extravagances in Paris. He lowered the glass and continued ''Besides, I am sure that my adored Perdita will plead for my cause, and even the hardest heart could not refuse her anything. Why one tear from those incredible eyes would melt the stoniest heart. No, dear brother, I advise you to pay up, and gratefully, for I would not wish your withers to be wrung by seeing Perdita in tears on my behalf.''

Christopher's words were more potent than he had intended. Jeremy had visions of how agonizing it would be to have Perdita taking up Christopher's cause, and he said abruptly, ''I think it is time that Perdita and I spoke to some of the other company. No doubt we will be seeing you again before you go back to Cambridge?''

''Why indeed,'' Christopher said, somewhat surprised at his brother's quick change of mood. ''I had hoped to call upon you tomorrow afternoon if that is convenient?''

''Of course,'' Perdita said warmly. ''You may find Jane and Aunt Charlotte there too, for they expect to be in London before noon and I am sure that they will waste no time in coming to see us.''

''Until tomorrow then,'' Christopher said as Jeremy took Perdita's arm and led her away.

The combination of seeing Christopher and at once being at home with his ridiculous chatter, and the feeling that she was in command of herself and her surroundings, thanks to her father's coaching, helped Perdita enjoy the evening more than any since she had arrived in London. The two young men who flanked her at dinner were both captivated by the light-hearted and beautiful Lady Dole, and both felt that the season might have much to recommend it. They both resolved to see that they were invited to as many balls as possible where she was to be a guest, and they made up their minds to pay court to her. Both had heard rumors that her marriage to Sir Jeremy had been one of convenience and that he spent more of his time at his club than he did with his wife. They both felt that a neglected wife of Perdita's charms was exactly what was needed to add a touch of excitement to what might otherwise be a round of tedious parties.

Jeremy, unaware of the rumors circulating about his marriage, was feeling anything but the complacent husband that evening. From time to time, when he glanced down the table at Perdita, he saw her laugh and talk with an animation he had not seen since they had been married. By the time that the third remove had been put on the table, he had convinced himself that Perdita had known that Christopher was to be there this evening and that that fact accounted for her unusual liveliness, and for the way she had obviously been searching for him when she entered the drawing room. As the evening wore on, he found it increasingly hard to convince himself that he enjoyed seeing her so happy, and encouraged her to leave the party as soon as it was politely possible to do so. By the time they were on their way home, he was almost wishing her a fit of the dismals and only replied in monosyllables to her enthusiasm over the arrival of Christopher. This of all things he could not endorse, as he could find no comfort in the fact that it was his own brother who had produced this change in her usual demeanor, and when he handed her down from the carriage it was with an abruptness that she had never seen before in his manner to her. His good night was equally short, and she wondered if possible his old wounds were paining him. However, before she could inquire he had turned on his heel and left the house.

Her concern for his well-being was allayed the next morning when he seemed to be more in spirits, but she did not spend long in his company as she was anxious to get to the theater to see her father and know whether Freddy had committed any further outrages.

The Sans Pareil was in an unusual state of calm and buoyant feeling when she arrived there an hour later. Freddy had behaved impeccably for the last twenty-four hours, and was improving so fast with his mastery of polite English that her father was forced to admit that he might make quite a good Richard of York. Edmund Wycoller had also had some success in finding suitable actors to round out the cast at a hearing at the O.P. and P.S. Tavern in Russell Square the night before. To add to his good humor, he had been approached by two members of the ton who had offered him handsome sums for the privilege of being allowed to play two of the minor parts in *Richard III*. Even the fact that Perdita could not give him good news of ideas for the curtain-raiser did nothing to dim his spirits.

"Do not fret," he said, "the muse will seek you out when you least expect it. Do not strive to make it dance to your tune, but let your mind be receptive to the ideas that will fall like starlight upon you." His elegant speech, Perdita recognized as another sign of his high spirits. His absorption in other matters was also apparent, as he turned back to the task of rehearsals, turning his energies and talents toward blending the cast into a harmonious whole. Perdita stayed for a few minutes to watch the proceedings, but she realized that she was only in the way, and after a shorter time than usual she left the theater and went back to Madame des Vignes' to await her carriage. She wiled away the next half hour in selecting the bonnets which she had promised to buy from Madame des Vignes.

However, her heart was not in the selection of the silk bonnet with the straw-colored feathers decorating the brim, nor in the emerald green one made *à la Hussar* which had a very dashing air to it. Perdita was longing for the hour when Jane and Aunt Charlotte would arrive to visit her in Upper Grosvenor Street.

By the time she finally reached home and found a newly delivered note from them saying that they would call at four o'clock that afternoon, Perdita was in such a state of excitement that she could not settle to any task. It seemed to have been years since she had seen Jane, and there were all the sights she had seen and all the fashions she had discovered with which she wished to regale her step-sister. The clock hands seemed to crawl around the face of the long case clock in the drawing room and she felt she had sat for years waiting before she heard a knock at the door and heard Jane's and Mrs. Chase's voices in the hall.

They had barely handed over their pelisses to the butler before Perdita had swept down the stairs and enfolded them both in warm hugs. It was not until the first ecstatic greeting had been exchanged that she saw that Christopher had followed them into the hall. She greeted him in the same informal manner and started to lead them all upstairs to the drawing room.

Christopher, however, shook his head at her invitation to take a glass of Madeira with them and said, "I have no doubt that you ladies will have all sorts of interesting things to say about the latest fashions in Paris, exclamations to be made about the hang of Perdita's new curtains and the elegance of the coverings for the chairs, but I must beg you to excuse me the delight of hearing about such things and to take the liberty of leaving you to talk to my brother on some important matters."

So saying, he turned to go toward the library which led off the hall, but not before Perdita had intercepted a glance charged with meaning which passed between him and Jane.

Had her aunt not been present she would have immediately demanded to be party to the secret, but in case it should be something that Jane did not want to discuss in front of her mother, Perdita tactfully kept silent. But as soon as the door of the drawing room had closed behind the three ladies, Jane blurted out, "Perdita, you must wish me happy!"

Mrs. Chase's fond smile echoed her pleasure in her daughter's words and she added, "Indeed, is it not wonderful news? Nothing could give me greater happiness than to have both my daughters marry into a family as delightful as the Doles, nor could I wish for two more charming and kind men than Jeremy and Christopher to look after my darling girls. It was your good example, my dearest Perdita, which put the idea into the children's heads. Of course, I told them that they were much too young to think of marrying yet, and that Jane must have her come-out and Christopher get his degree from Cambridge before any proper announcement can be made in the *Gazette*, but as family we had to share the news with you and Jeremy."

Perdita could only reply to this news with a frenzy of good wishes, hugs, a few tears, and many smiles. To see the two people she loved best, next to Jeremy, united in marriage was the most wonderful things that she could imagine.

"Christopher has gone to break the news to Jeremy," Jane said when at last she could break free of Perdita's joyous embraces. "I expect that Jeremy will say that he is too young to contemplate marriage, but we are willing to wait until he has finished at Cambridge, though I do not know how I will be able to bear to wait that long. I declare that I shall in all probability elope with Christopher to Gretna Green before the two years are up.''

''You'll do no such thing,'' Mrs. Chase said severely. ''I shall keep you under lock and key if you mention such a dreadful thing again. You will find that two years passes very quickly, and then you will have the rest of your lives to spend with each other. Gretna Green indeed! Such childish nonsense! I declare that I think that you are too young to even think of betrothal when you can talk in such a fashion.''

Mrs. Chase folded her hands in her ample lap, straightened her back, and tried to look severe, but Jane knew all too well that her mother would forgive her anything and had in any case not taken seriously the talk of Gretna Green. However, she could not resist continuing to tease her mother and said, ''Darling Mama, I know it is not the impropriety of eloping that upsets you, but the thought that you would be deprived of wearing yourself to a raveling in the course of arranging a large wedding party. I fully intend to make up for the way you were forestalled from ruining your health over Perdita's wedding. With me you may find a thousand delightful worries to deprive yourself of sleep: you must consider for many hours whether I would look more fetching in satin or silk and whether the lace should be Brussels or Honiton. You may toss and turn over the vexed question of how many new gowns I shall need for my trousseau and whether the bonnets should be trimmed with ribbons or swansdown. After that, you may ponder the difficulties of choosing between six or eight bridesmaids, and who they should be and who will be offended by not being asked. Then you have the question as to whether young Tommy Lovejoy would be an asset as a page, or set the church in an uproar by loosening his pet mouse in the congregation as he did two Sundays ago. You will have to debate the knotty problem of the bride cake and whether it should be decorated with bells or bows. That will occupy you for the first year, and then the following year you may keep your mind busy in deciding upon the number of lobster patties the guests will consume and how much claret and champagne should be allowed to keep the party merry and yet not inebriated. Just in case you should find time hanging on your hands, I will suggest names for the guests which you will know to be quite unsuitable and you will have to persuade me at length that Mr. X. will be insulted if he is not asked and that he will be in a fury if he is not put in a more important pew than Mr. Y. Oh darling Mama, nothing on earth will prevent me from allowing you to work yourself into a decline on my behalf.''

By the end of this speech Mrs. Chase and Perdita were laughing at Jane's suggestions and Mrs. Chase's half-hearted remonstrances to try to stop Jane's torrent of ridiculous chatter only produced more outlandish ideas. It was this merry group which Jeremy and Christopher interrupted when they entered the drawing room a few moments later.

"It seems that the news Jane has brought you has produced an unseemly mirth," Christopher said, turning to Perdita. "I do trust that you do not find the whole idea as ludicrous as it would seem from your expression."

"Oh no, I cannot think of anything that could make me happier than to see you and Jane married and to know that we will be brother and sister twice over. Darling Christopher, I must congratulate you, not only on having won the dearest person on earth, but having been inspired to ask her to marry you.'' Perdita took Christopher's hands in hers and then embraced him warmly. She was so overcome by the delight she felt in the news of the engagement that she did not note Jeremy's puzzled look, but she became conscious that throughout the rest of the visit he said little, and sat watching the animated group with a speculative expression.

It was not until the three guests had left some hour later that she was able to speak to him of his reserve.

"Have you some misgivings about this betrothal?" she asked him after the front door had closed behind their visitors and they were in the drawing room again.

"I? No, for my part I am delighted that Christopher has chosen someone as good-natured and loving as Jane. Besides, on the practical side, she has a good portion, while he, as a younger son, would not otherwise have found it easy to keep up the sort of establishment that he has been used to. No, for my part it would seem an excellent arrangement."

"But you seem to feel some reserve about the matter," Perdita persisted.

Jeremy looked at her thoughtfully for a moment and then said slowly, "It was on your behalf that I felt some reservation. Are you not at all upset by this news? I have long been aware that your feelings for Christopher were above the ordinary. You can tell me. Will you find it difficult to see him married to your step-sister?''

''I—feelings above the ordinary for Christopher?'' Perdita said, amazed. ''Jeremy, you of all people must know that he and I have been as brother and sister since I came to Hangarwood House as a child. He was a wonderful companion when Jane and I were young, and our friendship has only grown through the years, but do you imply that I felt some romantic attachment toward him? I assure you that this was never the case. Oh, how could you have thought that?'' Perdita smiled, but Jeremy's face remained grave.

''I must beg your pardon then,'' he said. ''It had always seemed to me that you had taken a particular delight in Christopher's company, and perhaps I have misread into this more than was actually there.''

''Indeed, you misread the situation. I can only repeat that I have felt no more for Christopher than a sister might feel for a brother. Why he is so little older than I that I could hardly think of him in terms of a romantic attachment. To have known someone as a ridiculous young hobbledehoy schoolchild, would not induce the sort of love and admiration I hold for—''

She stopped, realizing that she had nearly said too much, and turned away before he could see the color rise in her cheeks.

Jeremy was so stunned by her total denial of any romantic attachment to Christopher that he did not know how to reply. Perdita, taking his silence to mean that her near avowal of love for him had produced the reaction she most feared—embarrassed dismay—felt a matching embarrassment. It was the closest that she had come to a declaration, and having met with so little response she felt that the only thing to do was to make as hasty a retreat as possible, and excusing herself on some pretext she left the room.

Jeremy was left feeling that someone had taken a spoon of his brains and given them a rapid stirring. He had been so convinced that Perdita was in love with Christopher that he had at first almost refused to grant his blessing on Christopher's betrothal, when the latter had found him in the library some hours back. However, he had realized that he would not be able to prevent Christopher's marrying some day, and to deny him his choice of an eminently suitable bride would call forth some awkward questions. He had therefore given his blessing with as good a grace as he could muster, but had been tormented by the effect that the news might have on Perdita.

Her initial delight had somewhat surprised him, but thinking that perhaps she was merely putting a good face on the situation and hiding her true feelings, Jeremy had waited until the guests had left before offering her a shoulder to weep on. When she had refused to react to his offer and had instead declared, with obvious honesty, that she had never entertained any romantic feelings for Christopher, Jeremy was left to wonder what sort of fool he had been making of himself over the past month. If her affection was not taken by Christopher then surely she was heartfree, and in such a case perhaps there was a chance for him. But then he remembered her last words. She had said that her feelings for Christopher was hardly the basis for the sort of love and admiration she felt for— and then she had abruptly stopped, realizing that she was speaking to her husband.

If, when he had married her, she had not been in love with Christopher, it was obvious that in her eyes he, Jeremy, had behaved in a most unfeeling manner. His careful formality with her, his rigid withholding of all gestures and words of affection could only have made her feel that he did not care for her. Even if then he had not understood the full extent of his love for her, had he known she was heartfree he might have allowed himself to realize sooner just how much he depended upon her for his happiness.

His lean face held an expression somewhere between remorse and self-loathing as he strode back and forth upon the hearth rug, his hands clasped behind his back while he wished with all his heart that he could have the last months to live over again. Had he been less blinded by his suppositions, his failure to see Perdita as a woman rather than a child, he might have persuaded her that her own husband might be a worthy recipient of her affections. But now—the words rang in his head, "the sort of love and admiration I hold for—"

It was obvious that through lack of attention he had thrown away that one thing which he now wished most of all to have.

Through the rest of the afternoon the agony of his own foolishness gnawed at him, and even a fast ride through the

Park later that evening did nothing to dispel the devils which tormented him. It was during the ride that the remembrance of the note he had received added its voice to those which were bothering him, and on returning to the stables with his horse he could not resist seeking out Hughes and asking him casually whether Lady Dole had ordered the carriage for the following morning.

"She did not tell me otherwise, Sir Jeremy. I am always at the house by half past ten o'clock," Hughes answered.

"Ah yes," Jeremy said casually, "Lady Dole was not sure whether you understood it to be a standing order."

"Why yes, Sir Jeremy. I always pick her up from the house at half past ten and drive her to Maiden Lane, to the milliner's. She did not tell me differently when I brought her back this morning, and I presumed that she would need the carriage as usual tomorrow."

"Quite so," Jeremy said, fighting to keep his voice normal, but his agony had multiplied a hundredfold as he turned to walk the short distance back to the house.

Knowing himself to be unfit company for anyone that evening, he cried off taking Perdita to the card party they were to attend, but knowing that Christopher as well as her aunt and step-sister were to be there, he had no compunction in letting her go on her own. He made his way instead to Watier's where he proceeded to drink a great deal of white brandy and to play several hands of whist for considerably higher stakes than was his usual practice.

It was not until the watch had called four in the morning that Jeremy found his way back to Upper Grosvenor Street and allowed a sleepy-eyed Clamp to get him to his bed.

— 12 —

Perdita had enjoyed the card party that night, especially as Jane and Christopher had been there and plans had been made to drive together the following day. However, at the back of her mind was the memory of the conversation she had had with Jeremy that afternoon. The more she thought of it, the more puzzled she became as to how Jeremy could have believed her to have been in love with Christopher. She had always felt that her feelings for Jeremy were too dangerously obvious and it had seemed clear that she regarded Christopher solely as a brother. Never in her wildest dreams had Christopher ousted Jeremy from the part of the romantic hero, and it amazed her that Jeremy should have put such a strange interpretation on the situation.

However, as she thought about it, she began to see how, with a wild stretch of the imagination, her easy manner with Christopher could be seen as something more than simple affection. It was true that Jeremy's reserved manner had produced a shyness in her that was in sharp contrast with the openness she felt with Christopher. The pains she had taken to hide her feelings from Jeremy had perhaps been extreme, but how could she show him how she felt when she knew she would be rebuffed? Even before she had known about Sylvia Smith-Fenton, he had seemed unwilling to let her touch him, and had never given the least sign that he wished for more show of affection. Now, since his recent meeting with Sylvia Smith-Fenton, he had been very much on edge, showing signs of shortness of temper which Perdita had never seen before, and which she took to mean that his feelings for Sylvia Smith-Fenton were still deep and he was hating the fact that he had been forced into marriage with a woman not of his choosing.

It was strange, Perdita thought, how she had always cast Jeremy as her hero, but her heroes never behaved as he was doing now. They took poison, died in battle against insuperable odds, or exiled themselves to foreign lands when they were crossed in love. They did not just get short-tempered and remote. She began to wonder what she would have felt like if Jeremy had gone into exile or killed himself, and found to her surprise that she would have thought him more of a fool than a hero. All in all, she much preferred the more human reaction he was adopting, which at least gave room for hope of improvement.

She was thoughtful and silent later while Jeannette prepared her for bed, her mind revolving on the contrary attributes of heroes and humans.

Though in the end she knew that she preferred to live with a human, the old habits of dramatization would not die easily and soon she found that Jeremy's misapprehension had become the grit that was turning to pearl in her mind.

She lay in bed staring at the bed curtains, but seeing on them a dramatic scenario based on love mistaken and unspoken. The play took shape before her eyes to become the idea for the curtain-raiser she was to write for her father. It would be one such as Mr. Congreve might have written, with many closely timed entrances and exits, and a denouement involving overheard conversation and screens or masked balls, and mistresses dressed as maids.

However, as she continued to elaborate on this idea, she realized its impracticability. The staging would be too complicated and the action would have to run too long for a one act play. Better to devise a tragedy in which the misunderstanding leads to disaster. An ancient Greek, or perhaps Roman setting. A Roman consul who marries a young woman for political advantage but thinking that she loves a younger man, remains remote, not realizing how much his young wife loves him. She takes poison, thinking that there is no hope for her love, and only on her death does the consul realize that he loves her.

Perdita became so involved with her story that the light of the single candle burning by her bedside began to flicker as it burned to its socket. Perdita blew it out and lay staring into the dark, too concerned with the plot to worry about sleep.

After a while she became disenchanted with the idea of a

sunlit Rome. It would be too cheerful a light for the drama she envisaged. Better the bleak northern winter of a Hebredian Island where the sea, pounding on ragged rocks, would be heard in the background. Also the formality of the classical manner would be less easy to manipulate to her ends than the raw boldness of a medieval kingdom. Perhaps to add even more romance it could be set in the time of King Arthur. A king of some far island must send for a young bride to consolidate a treaty. His younger brother is sent to escort the princess (a touch of Tristram and Isolde, but with a different ending). The bride arrives and is shy and in awe of her splendid bridegroom, and since she is more at ease with his brother, the King presumes them to be in love. He is cold and seemingly indifferent. Here an evil and plotting chamberlain could try to poison the king's mind against his queen, accusing her of infidelities. The queen is so distraught at her husband's indifference and increasing coldness that she takes poison, or stabs herself with a dagger, whichever should prove the most practical and dramatic. Only when he finds her dying does the king reveal his love for her, and he too takes poison, or plunges the same dagger into himself.

Perdita's eyelids began to close, and she wisely decided to leave the more trying decisions between poison or daggers until the morning. She pulled up the bedcovers and slept.

The reawakened delight in writing and allowing her imagination freedom to devise the play, flesh out the skeletons of characters, and hear in her mind their words, so absorbed Perdita the next morning that she did not notice that Jeremy was not in the library as usual when she came downstairs to go out. During the drive to Madame desVignes', she was busy going over her dialogue, and before she knew it she had arrived at the milliner's.

She was so eager to discuss her ideas with her father that she could hardly contain herself for the necessary minute which it took for Hughes and the carriage to leave the street outside the shop before she could run out of the side door and down the alley to the theater.

As she turned the corner of the alley toward the stage door, she saw her father waiting impatiently for her outside. At the sight of him, she ran forward and flung herself into his arms. She kissed him warmly in her excitement and he returned her embrace with equal enthusiasm, but before he could even utter a word in greeting she said, "Oh Papa, I think that I have the most magnificent idea for your curtain-raiser. Don't you think that a melodrama of seemingly unrequited love would be an excellent subject?"

Her father cocked a quizzical eyebrow at her, but before he could say anything she went on, "I feel it would be best as a tragedy, as it would hold more excitement than treating the subject from the comic point of view, but you must tell me if you think that a melodrama set in the time of King Arthur might be too much in the same vein as *Richard III*. Oh, not that I am comparing my skill to that of the Bard, but perhaps the audience would not consider it a pleasant evening to have to listen to too much sorrow and despair. I suppose it could be a comedy, but I thought that it would be too difficult to contrive it all in one act—that is, the sort of plot which I had in mind."

Her father had been holding her in his arms and looking at her with love and amusement as she babbled out the words in her excitement. Finally he laughed and bent to kiss her forehead. Then, putting his arm firmly around her shoulders, he said, "Come, I think that all these ideas are quite wonderful, but let us discuss them in the comfort of the theater and not out here in the alleyway. I feel that we might have a more profitable discussion inside where we can consult with the scene designer, Mrs. Warburgh, and such people as will be concerned with the staging. Besides all is a-bustle inside and I am needed. Come, a pen and paper will not come amiss so that you can capture every fugitive idea."

Perdita smiled happily at him, leaned her head on his shoulder, and allowed herself to be led into the theater.

By now the full cast for *Richard III* had been assembled and the activity of a theater in the throes of producing a major play were well underway. Islands of actors gossiped in corners, or mouthed lines as they stood at the back of the stage or in the wings. Property men ran back and forth with bits of furniture or objects, scene painters put finishing touches to backdrops or wings, the stage manager called instructions to men hidden high up in the flys, and Mrs. Warburgh and her minions ran hither and thither putting a tuck in here or cutting a seam there. The whole scene reminded Perdita of the deck of the ship just before she and Jeremy had sailed from Brighton.

The noise inside the theater had increased tenfold since Perdita had been there the day before. The usual sounds of voices reciting was augmented by the sound of hammering and sawing. The smell of grease paint and the musty smell of disuse were now blended with that of oil paint and sawdust and the faint sickly odor of coal gas as the new lamps were fitted in the footlights and in the brackets around the proscenium arch.

Everywhere she looked there was activity, and as soon as Edmund Wycoller appeared on the stage he was surrounded by a horde of people asking questions. One wanted his opinion on whether the backdrop for the first act should show the same street as the one in act three or whether by dint of manipulating one of the wings the character of the street could be changed enough to make the backdrop serve for all the street scenes in the play.

"I do not wish to skimp on this production," Edmund Wycoller said boldly. "We must have a second backdrop. See that it is done."

The designer was immediately replaced by Mrs. Warburgh, holding out a pair of crimson hose. "Would you consider these suitable for your appearance in act four when you are seen as the king for the first time? I had thought that they would be a striking contrast to the purple velvet doublet and cloak, and as the other men in the scene will all be wearing shades of browns and grays, yours would be the only colored hose. I thought that this way you would be instantly recognizable as different from the rest. But perhaps you feel them to be too gaudy?"

"No, no, I like your idea. It will pull the king from the common horde and underline the fact that he has been translated to a higher level. But be sure that I have the brown hose for the earlier acts. It will make a pleasing touch."

"Yes, exactly," Mrs. Warburgh said, going off happily with the red hose streaming like a banner from her arm.

It was then the turn of two of the carpenters having trouble with the wings for act two, which would not fit comfortably at the side of the stage when they needed to be moved out of the way. It seemed that the two men needed each other to have enough courage to question the great Edmund Wycoller, and the smaller of the two repeated every word the other said, so that it seemed that the theater had suddenly developed an echo. When they had eventually finished their lengthy explanation and it had been deemed perfectly feasible to reduce the size of the wing by one foot, they went off muttering to each other with pleasure.

Next there was the property master with a question about the throne for the king, and after him one of the amateur actors who came to inquire whether he should speak his lines in a bold proclaiming tone or whether his character called for a less forceful rendition of the words.

"What part do you play, sir?"

"Why that of Lord Grey, in act one, scene—"

"Yes, I am aware of when you make your entrance. Lord Grey is a courtier. Speak your lines in a courtly tone and that will suffice." Edmund Wycoller dismissed the man with a wave of his hand.

"Yes, yes, with a courtly tone. Of course, that is the perfect way. I see that now. It will read well that way. I have already committed to memory my first speech and shall be ready to rehearse it whenever you see fit." It seemed that the amateur would never be shaken from his position at Edmund Wycoller's side, but the old actor was used to dealing with such limpets and turned quickly away from the man, taking Perdita's arm with a gesture which bespoke a certain urgency and left the amateur with only the sight of Wycoller's fast disappearing back.

Her father led Perdita over to the scene designer, made a few suggestions for the street change, and then said, "John, talk to my daughter for a moment while I discuss McEvoy's makeup with him. My daughter is going to write our curtain-raiser and I would like you to see if you can devise something suitable for the backdrop. Help her all you can, for this is an early attempt of hers and she may not have yet considered all the technicalities of her entrances and exits and what is possible in the small space allowed for the action. It would be as well if she fully understands the limitations which will be imposed upon her before she gets too deeply into the writing."

Perdita turned to ask her father whether this meant that he had definitely decided to allow her to write the playlet, but Edmund was already walking off and was surrounded by a new circle of questioners buzzing about him like flies around a horse on a hot day.

Perdita turned back to John Cassell, who was ready to

listen to her ideas. By the end of the next hour she found that the limitations imposed by the strip of stage, which was all she would have to work with, had helped her rather than hindered her. The boundaries that Mr. Cassell had drawn to the action helped her more closely define the thread of the plot and this was making her see her characters more clearly.

All the action could take place in one room in the castle. The king could be found here talking to his evil chamberlain and discussing his new queen. The chamberlain could be laying the ground for his evil machinations whereby he hoped to discredit the queen and the prince and leave the road to power open to himself. The queen and the prince could be found here by the king, and the latter could observe the ease with which she treated his brother compared with the formality with which she treated him. The room would be where finally the queen, distraught at her husband's obvious lack of love for her, would confess her love of him to her lady-in-waiting, and proclaim her determination to set him free of her by her death. The king would find his queen dying in the same room and would hear her confess her love with her dying breath.

As Perdita and John Cassell talked, she became more and more eager to get home to start working on the dialogue for the play. She thanked Mr. Cassell and excused herself, and only taking time to seek out Freddy and make sure that all was serene around him, she broke through the hordes around her father and, having told him how helpful she had found John Cassell, bade him goodbye and made her way out of the theater.

Once home she could hardly wait to seek the seclusion of her bedroom and its little writing table, so that she could sit down with her ample supply of paper and newly sharpened quills and begin her drama.

She was so engrossed by the lives and complex romance of her King Andrew and Princess Moyra, and had just decided to change the ending so that it was the king who took poison, that three hours had passed before she was drawn back to the present by Jeannette's coming to tell her that her step-sister and Mr. Dole were waiting for her in the drawing room.

Perdita put her quill to one side and ran downstairs to greet Jane and Christopher, but when she entered the drawing room Jane looked at her in surprise.

"Are you not coming after all?"

"To what am I supposed to be coming?" Perdita asked.

"Why you promised that you would ask Jeremy to drive you in the Park this afternoon so that you could see the perch phaeton and the new bays Christopher has hired. He is to take me up with him, but as you know there will only be room for the two of us. Oh Perdita, don't tell me that you had forgotten? And where is Jeremy?"

Perdita had to confess that all memory of last night's arrangement had slipped her mind, and that she had no idea where Jeremy was at the moment. Jane's obvious impatience and annoyance was as much engendered by the thought of insufficient people seeing her fetching new outfit and her very pretty bonnet as it was with the fact that she might have to forego her friend's company. It was obvious to Perdita that the new clothes must be seen and admired at the fashionable hour in the Park, and she sent at once to find out whether Sir Jeremy was in the house.

The servant left on his errand and a minute later Jeremy entered the drawing room.

"I understand that you wanted to see me urgently," he said to Perdita after he had greeted Jane and his brother. "Is there anything that I can do for you?"

His distant, almost unfriendly tone, Perdita was forced to ignore in the prior claim of Jane to her concern. "Yes, Jeremy," she said, "I am afraid that I have been very stupid and quite forgot that I had arranged to ask you to take me driving in the Park this afternoon. Christopher and Jane are eager to go and thought that it would be amusing if we all went together. Unfortunately, there is not enough room in Christopher's phaeton to take us all up, so I must ask you if you would be good enough to take me in your curricle."

"I would be honored to escort you," Jeremy said icily and without the flicker of a smile. "I will send at once for the curricle and will be ready within the half hour." He paused, then gave her a penetrating look and added, "I daresay you have had so many things to think about that something so trivial as a drive in the Park with your husband might well slip your mind."

He turned to leave the room, but not before he had seen a blush rise to Perdita's face. As he closed the door behind him a frown settled on his forehead, and he anticipated the drive with an annoyance that he might not have felt had he not spent some of the morning hours in Maiden Lane.

Peg's letter, Hughes's confirmation that Perdita had visited Madame desVignes' several times, and the new-found knowledge that she had never entertained any romantic feelings for his brother, had so worked upon Jeremy's mind that he could not prevent himself from finding out whether Perdita was indeed meeting some man at Madame desVignes'.

He therefore had left the house some time before Perdita had come downstairs that morning, and had made his way to Maiden Lane. Once there he had established himself in a coffee shop opposite the milliner's whose windows gave him an uninterrupted view of the shop across the street. A little after eleven he saw Hughes and the carriage drive up to the door of the milliner's and he saw Perdita go into the shop. Jeremy waited to see if any man that he recognized would follow her, but much to his surprise he saw Perdita come out of the side door a few minutes later and set off down Lumley Court. Without thinking of what he could say, should he confront her, Jeremy left the coffee house, crossed the street, and followed Perdita down the alley.

He saw her turn to the right into a narrow way between two houses. As he got to this point he stopped and looked to see where she had gone. He was just in time to see her run toward a tall distinguished man that he had never seen before, who held out his arms to Perdita and embraced her with obvious affection and familiarity.

Jeremy watched while the two of them talked. He saw the man's smile and his look of possessive love as he gazed down at Perdita. He saw Perdita's smile and the animation of someone in the presence of a lover. He saw the kisses and the way the man put his arm protectively around her shoulder and led her into a door opposite the alley in which Jeremy was standing.

A feeling of such intense rage filled Jeremy that he was unable to move for a minute. He had heard of people being so angry that they did not know what they were doing, but until this moment he had never believed that such a strong emotion could be true. Now he knew that it was not only true but perfectly possible for even the most self-controlled person to commit murder. If the man who had led Perdita away had been in front of him at that moment, Jeremy knew that he would have tried to strangle him with his bare hands. His first thought was to follow Perdita and the man and demand satisfaction, but the door had shut firmly behind the two of them and Jeremy had enough sense to realize that to go beating on a locked door demanding to be let in so that he might murder someone would not be a feasible or practical course of action.

The red rage which suffused his brain started to die down slowly, and he realized that standing impotently in the alley was unlikely to improve matters. There was nothing for it but to return home and try to clear his confused thoughts and calm his seething anger.

As he walked home he found that his main preoccupation and anger centered on the realization that another man had touched *his* Perdita. When, in the past, he had thought her to be in love with Christopher, he had made up his mind to stand out of the way of their love, but it had been *his* choice to do so. He had considered the matter to be dependent on his permission. Never before had he stopped to think that she might not realize that he was there to order her life and control her destiny, and that she might think that she had a perfect right to decide the direction of her own feelings and choose the man that she would love.

Now seeing her walk into the arms of a stranger, seeing her look on him with affection, and finding that he, Jeremy, was apparently irrelevant to her happiness, he began to see in a miasma of fury that he had blithely assumed something that was totally unsubstantiated.

Perdita, it seemed, could choose whom to love without his help. The fact that she was his wife did not, at the moment, add any fuel to the feeling that she had betrayed him. Whether or not they had been married, Jeremy knew that he would have felt just as angry, just as rejected, and that it was his own possessiveness, and no legal or spiritual bond, which caused this feeling. He had never realized before how he had taken it for granted, despite their problems, that Perdita was his, and the thought, striking him now, was dismissed hurriedly as he was in no mood to see himself as having overstepped the mark, let alone been downright absurd in his assumptions. All he would entertain was the knowledge that she had no business falling in love with any man without his express agreement, and the fact that she had found someone whom he did not even know, and had managed to have a number of assignations with him, was made even more intolerable by the fact that she had never even bothered to tell him.

Had he not been so angry, so upset by the scene he had just witnessed, Jeremy might have laughed at his own arrogance. But no pinprick of humor was to be allowed to explode the balloon of his *amour propre*, and he clung to his fury as a child to a favorite toy.

He regained the house without being conscious of the streets he had crossed nor the time it had taken him, and went straight to the library without bothering to acknowledge the greeting of the footman who stood ready to take his hat and cane.

He spent an hour in which his fury threatened to choke him before he heard Perdita come into the house and he rose from his chair with the express purpose of confronting her with what he had witnessed that morning. But with his hand on the doorknob a vestige of sense assailed him and he realized that he was not prepared to demean himself in her eyes by acknowledging his jealousy, or worse still, the fact that he had spied upon her. He sank back into his chair, stared at the fireless grate, and stayed there, fluctuating between sorrow and rage and devising every sort of action from suicide to murder until the footman came in to tell him that her ladyship wished to see him in the drawing room.

He was both pleased and annoyed at seeing Jane and Christopher with his wife. He realized that their presence prevented him from allowing himself to vent his wrath on Perdita, but it also prevented him from having the whole matter out in the open with her—a situation he was beginning to feel might be a lot better than having to spend any more hours in his terrible state of unknowing.

With a supreme effort he managed to control his voice and ask her pleasantly what it was that she wanted, and to acquiese graciously to her request to be taken driving in the Park. However, he could not resist throwing out a seemingly trivial remark which he felt might mean more to her than to the others in the room. His feelings suffered a new jolt when he saw the blush rise in her face just before he left her.

Her appearance a quarter of an hour later in a vastly becoming outfit consisting of a gray silk, high crowned bonnet decorated with pink egret feathers and a gray silk dress trimmed with pink ribbons, did little to soothe him. Had she been quite out of looks, sallow skinned and lack-luster of eye he would have been better pleased, but the brightness in her gray eyes and the pink flush to her cheeks showed that she, at least, was finding life agreeable. Jeremy found that he was clenching his jaw so hard that it hurt as he helped her up into the curricle.

If Perdita noticed his taciturnity she did not comment on it, and in any case, no sooner had they entered the Park than they were greeted by one friend after another. Many of them were old acquaintances of Jeremy's but a few were Perdita's new-found friends. In all cases the compliments paid to Perdita did nothing to quell the anger seething in Jeremy.

The two couples drove side by side down the wide carriage road for some way while Jane and Perdita exchanged comments on the turnouts to be seen, and chatted amiably of the more outlandish members of the dandy set who used the fashionable hour in the Park to show off their latest extravagances in dress and behavior. Christopher seemed pleased to join in the light banter and to encourage Jane's comments on some of the people that they saw. Jeremy was further infuriated that his three companions did not seem to notice his silence, nor inquire what had put him out of sorts. He sat staring straight ahead with a look of stony disapproval on his face.

It was not until they were nearly at the end of the carriage way and about to turn back that Christopher finally said, "You are unnaturally silent, brother. I believe that you have not said ten words since we met. Has some disaster overtaken the family, or are you merely brooding on the follies of fashion and the vanity of mankind in general?"

Jeremy looked over at Christopher as though he wished him to the devil, and said in an icy voice, "No, I am only silent because it seems to me that you, Perdita, and Jane are saying all that is necessary. I do not feel my wit or wisdom can compete with Jane's and I know that Perdita is a far better judge of fashion than I am. Besides, the grays are fresh this afternoon and I would not like to endanger life, limb, and my good name as a whip, by having the curricle run off and my fair bride and myself thrown into some ditch."

"Very well," Christopher answered, "I will let you off

with that excuse for now, but I cannot think how Perdita can put up with you if you are such a dull fellow at home. Tell me, Perdita, is he always as silent as this? For if he is, then marriage must have a seriously dampening effect on a fellow's nature, and perhaps I should think again before I commit myself to such an action. I have no wish to spend my life in a situation where my spirits are permanently lowered.''

Perdita smiled. She too had been wondering why Jeremy was so silent, but she only said, ''No, I cannot complain of his silence usually. He is more often only too ready to point out things of interest to me. However, I am sure that you will never find your spirits lowered when you are married to Jane. Indeed, I am quite sure that you will find her a companion who makes even the trivia of life a great deal more interesting than it is normally.''

At that moment Mr. Wentworth, one of the young men who had found Perdita so enchanting at the party two nights ago, rode up and sweeping off his hat paid his respects to the company before saying directly to Perdita, ''Lady Dole, I have not seen you driving in the Park these last weeks. I hope that we may expect to see the Park decorated with the rarest flower in London more often now that the season is in full swing. Sir Jeremy, I must complain. It should be made a punishable offense to deprive the rest of society from a daily glimpse of your lovely wife. I must cry shame, sir, on your selfishness, but will be content to forgive you if you will grant me the privilege of inviting your wife up beside me in my curricle when you are too busy to drive her out yourself.''

Jeremy favored the young man with a scowl and said coldly, ''I am afraid, sir, that my wife does not drive with anyone but me.'' With that, he flicked the whip at the grays, pulling away from Jane and Christopher and leaving a very perplexed young man staring after the curricle as it disappeared into the crowds. Mr. Wentworth began to wonder if perhaps the rumors that Sir Jeremy neglected his wife were grossly exaggerated and, crushed, he turned his bay horse and cantered off in search of less dangerous flirtations.

Perdita, surprised at Jeremy's rudeness, looked over at his angry face. Some months back she would have quailed before his expression, but her time in France and the discovery of her father had given her a new self-assurance and she said,

"My dear Jeremy, why are you in such a taking? I am sure that Mr. Wentworth meant no disrespect in his remark."

Jeremy stared straight ahead at the grays' ears as though he was about to bite them and said, "I do not wish you to endanger your reputation by being taken up in a carriage by any Tom, Dick, or Harry who wishes to add to his consequence by being seen with you. I do not wish to have to constantly remind you that you are my wife and that any unseemly behavior on your part directly reflects upon me. You might perhaps allow yourself a little regard for my feelings and not persist in allowing your friends to feel that I am some doddering old fool who can be cuckolded with impunity."

Perdita was so taken aback by this outrageous remark that she could only stare at Jeremy to see if this were some awful idea of a joke. Apart from the one time when he had found her in her boudoir in France with her friends, she had never seen him so angry, and there was certainly nothing in her past knowledge of him that had prepared her for this curt overbearing stranger who sat beside her now.

He stared straight ahead at his horses and seemed not to notice that he had struck Perdita dumb. She was finding that the outrageousness of his remarks, having obviously not been intended as a joke, were causing her amazement to turn into anger. How dare he put poor Mr. Wentworth to shame, and to shame her, too, by his behavior. Besides, his insinuation that she might be capable of playing him false was insulting in the extreme. He had been strange before they came driving and his curt remark to her in front of Jane and Christopher had put her to the blush then, but no he was acting in a most outrageous manner.

To imply that being driven by a friend in the Park at the fashionable hour would be used as evidence of infidelity was beyond enough. Even the most recently married women could be seen out driving with friends without tarnishing their reputations in the slightest. Why she could have named several ladies of impeccable virtue who were driving in the Park at this very moment with men who were not their husbands.

Her own mounting indignation eventually overcame her reluctance to join battle with him and, matching his controlled iciness of tone, she said, "I do not believe that I would be endangering either of our reputations were I to accept Mr. Wentworth's offer. You know yourself that it is perfectly unexceptional for a lady to be driven in the Park by the merest acquaintance. I am sorry that you should have found it necessary to give such a display of bad manners to a young man who meant nothing but the courtesy by his invitation. Your insinuations to me I will ignore, but I am astounded that you should speak to me in that way."

Jeremy turned to her with a look of thunder. "I believe, madam, that being several years your senior, I may be permitted to know more about the on-dits of this town than you do. I assure you nothing casts more of a slur on a husband than to have his wife making sheep's eyes at a lot of wet-behind-the-ears calflings. I must insist that you adhere to the code of behavior which I lay down for you."

The anger which Perdita had felt at Jeremy's actions now turned to a roaring blaze, and in a voice trembling with indignation she said, "I shall find it very hard to adhere to your principles if they are to be as harsh as those you outline now. Besides, to treat me in this manner implies a lack of respect for my feelings and trust in my good judgment. I must tell you, Jeremy, that I do not intend to be the sort of wife who allows herself to be brow-beaten and bullied by her husband. I wish to live with you in harmony, but not at the expense of letting myself be subjected to these outrageous insults. You should be well aware that I am not the sort of woman to cast her husband in a poor light."

He gave her a look which might have intimidated the most courageous, but the glower in his dark eyes and the way his eyebrows drew together under the brim of his hat only made Perdita straighten her back and prepare herself to do battle. She had known him too long to think that he was a cruel man, and whatever was prompting him to be so short with her must obviously have root in some pain, his wounds, or some sickness in its early stages. She was about to inquire whether he was ill when he said, "I wish that I could have such confidence in you, but I know I cannot."

Perdita stared at him in disbelief. "Jeremy, what possesses you? There is nothing that I have done which you could find in any way humiliating to you, and if there is, why then tell me, for I assure you I have done nothing intentional to harm you. There was that incident in France, but you know that was an unwitting mistake. Natalie told me that it was quite acceptable in France, but I understand your feelings on the matter and have never repeated the offense.''

"I am not speaking of your time in France," Jeremy said shortly, not looking at her. "I realize that you made an innocent mistake that day, and perhaps I was too harsh with you, but I do not wish to pursue the subject. In any event, it is time that we returned home."

The drive back to the house was conducted in stony silence. Perdita wracked her brains to think what it was that she had done that could have been misinterpreted. The only secret she had from Jeremy was that of the identity of her father, but if he had found out that she was meeting him, then surely he would simply have confronted her with it, and not merely insinuated terrible things about her. Just to be the daughter of an actor did not make her a whore, as Jeremy had implied. Even the fact that she had been less than open with him about her parentage would not have produced this icy anger in the Jeremy she had always known.

As their silent drive continued, Perdita began to feel more and more angry that he should accuse her of things she had not done, and never would do. She began to wonder how she would manage to get through an evening in his company, but as soon as they entered the hall of Upper Grosvenor Street, he said, "I shall not be dining at home tonight, and may not return until late. You will have to go to Lady Dowson's with your step-sister and aunt."

With that, he turned on his heel and went into the library, shutting the door firmly behind him. Tempted for a minute to run after him and force him to give her an explanation for his behavior, Perdita stared at the door, then thinking better of it, she turned and went quickly to her room to calm her seething mind and to try to lose herself in the more understandable characters in her play.

— 13 —

Perdita's mood did not lighten as the hours progressed and she was in no humor to attend Lady Dowson's rout that evening. She sent a footman with a note of apology to Lady Dowson and another note to her aunt to say that she had the megrim. She then tried to put the incident with Jeremy out of her mind and to concentrate on her play.

The actions of her King Andrew and Queen Moyra were certainly less perplexing than Jeremy's, and indeed if they did not dance to her tune she could always close the desk on them until they did behave.

She was sorely tempted to reverse her recent opinion that real life had more merit than imagination, but she was not yet prepared to feel that her real Jeremy had gone forever. Whatever was upsetting him would no doubt be resolved one way or another in the course of time, and better by far that she should use her energies to write her play than to brood uselessly over Jeremy.

She pulled her chair up to the writing desk and, clearing her mind of everything but her characters, got to work. She managed a very acceptable first scene where King Andrew was seen speaking with his chamberlain, Douglas MacPhearson; the speeches flowed easily and seemed almost to write themselves, and she found that her king was beginning to develop a character which was not only appealing as a hero, but would explain his inordinate reticence with his bride.

After a while the play became so absorbing that Perdita became quite unconscious of the passage of time until the candle on her writing table guttered out. Impatiently, she got up and lit the ones in the sconces on the wall, then removed one to put in the candlestick on the desk, but by the time she was ready to put pen to paper again, she found that the first easy flow of words had completely dried up.

She got up again, walked around the room, noticed that it was getting chilly, and went to the chest in the next room and pulled one of her shawls from it. Wrapped in that she sat down at the writing table again and determined that she would bend her characters to her will and make them speak the lines she wished them to say. This second scene dealt with the relationship between Prince James and the queen. In Perdita's mind's eye, she could see the dark-haired Lawrence Pare as the prince, and the fair Pamela Forrest as the queen, but she knew that they would not thank her for introducing them to the stage and leaving them there without any lines to say.

She struggled with the dialogue while the floor around her became covered with crumpled pieces of paper. The real problem was the queen. Prince James had become articulate at last, but the queen refused to do anything but stand around with downcast eyes.

Perdita crumpled another piece of paper which joined its fellows on the floor, and with a sigh turned again to the battle.

Jeremy meanwhile had spent most of the evening in Brooks's Club in St. James's playing a few desultory games of whist. When that had become tiresome he moved on to the higher stakes at the faro table at Watier's. There he met several old friends and the glasses of claret that he took with them seemed to revive his spirits. However, when one of them innocently started to tease him about his married state, his bad humor returned. The cheerful claret struck him as being a very insipid drink and he called for a waiter to bring him a glass of white brandy.

He had consumed a number of these glasses when a friend that he had not seen since his days in the Peninsula, Major John Jenks, came into the club. Jeremy and John had seen a lot of each other during the campaign and had even managed a few excellent runs with the foxhounds in Portugal and Spain when the rigors of war allowed it. Normally Jeremy would have found John's company much to be desired, but Major Jenks's first words dispelled any joy that Jeremy felt in seeing him.

"Jeremy! I had heard you were in town and had hoped to run into you at Lady Dowson's this evening. I was looking forward to meeting your bride. The on-dit is that you have captured the most beautiful woman in London. Trust you to have no feelings for your brother officers and to marry her before any of us had a chance to try to cut you out. But I understand that she is not well. I hope nothing serious? Lady Dowson could not tell me more than that she had received a note from Lady Dole excusing herself on the grounds of ill-health."

It was the first that Jeremy had heard of Perdita's refusal to go to the party, but he was unwilling to explain to his friend that he and Perdita had barely been on speaking terms when he had last seen her. Instead he answered, "No, nothing serious. She was just fagged out. Too many parties. You know how it is once the season starts, and she is not used to so much gaiety. I thought it best if she stayed home tonight."

"And you so ungallant as to leave her on her own? Fie upon you, Jeremy, a newly married man! You will have to attend to your wife better than that or you may find yourself losing her to others more attentive," John said, laughing. But he was not prepared for the angry glower his speech produced in Jeremy. John raised his eyebrows a fraction, but quickly turned the conversation to reminiscences of the campaign in the Peninsula.

He found, however, that Jeremy's attention was not on the activities of Wellington's army. He suddenly rose to his feet, cutting John Jenks off in mid-sentence, and with barely a word of apology called for his hat and cane and left the club.

Jeremy had hardly been listening to his friend after he had mentioned the absence of Perdita from Lady Dowson's party. The mention of her name had pierced through the comforting layers of brandy and had reawakened the jealousy which had plagued him for the past few days. John Jenks's remark on the lack of attention he paid to his wife, and how someone else might prove more attentive, rubbed salt into the wound. He began to imagine all sorts of assignations that she might be having, as the canker of suspicion swallowed up the last vestiges of rationality. He had visions of her running upstairs as soon as he was out of the house, and going off to meet her lover, safe in the knowledge that her husband would not be home for hours. The picture in his mind turned to one of her inviting the lover to the house and of the two of them locked in a passionate embrace in her bedroom, while the rest of the house slept.

He did not wait for a hackney carriage to be called, but strode off in the direction of Upper Grosvenor Street. He covered the distance almost at a run and, reaching the front door, rapped imperiously to be let in. He almost flung his hat and cane at the footman who opened the door to him, and without a word started up the stairs two steps at a time.

His drink-befuddled mind had not allowed him to think what he would say should he find his wife in the embrace of her lover, but so convinced was he by this time that he would discover her with someone, that he flung open her bedroom door without knocking. As he stepped inside he turned toward the bed but was brought up short by the fact that it was empty and un-slept-in. He was about to go downstairs and demand of the footman where his wife had gone, when he suddenly became conscious of Perdita sitting at her writing table at the far end of the room in a circle of candlelight.

Perdita had turned in surprise when she heard the door thrust open, and she was even more surprised when she saw that it was Jeremy. He was swaying slightly on his feet, and she had never before seen him in such a state. At first she thought that he was ill or injured, but his first words made her realize that he was only the worse for drink.

"Where is he?" Jeremy demanded.

"Where is who?" she asked in surprise.

Jeremy looked around the room. He was finding it a trifle hard to focus properly, but even in his fogged state he could find no sign of the presence of any other person. His searching eyes settled on the crumpled pieces of paper on the floor and he began to realize that Perdita had been writing, not engaged in some illicit dalliance. However, the evidence of his own eyes that very morning pointed to the fact that she had a lover, and if she had not invited him to her house this evening, at least it was obvious that she was pouring out her heart to him on paper.

Jeremy closed the door firmly behind him and walked over to the writing table with his hand outstretched. "Let me see what you are writing," he demanded.

Perdita instinctively made as if to hide the piece of paper which lay before her, but Jeremy snatched it quickly from beneath her protecting elbow. He looked intently at the page. The words swam a bit under his eyes, and it took him a little while to see that the suspect letter was written in the form of verse speeches. He saw the names of Prince James and Queen Moyra beside the speeches and it slowly dawned on him that he was not looking at a love letter but at part of a play. Sheepishly, he handed the paper back to Perdita.

She stared at him, waiting for him to make the next move, but when he said nothing she broke the silence. "I am trying to write a play, Jeremy, but I would rather that no one saw it until I have finished it. What did you think I was writing?"

Jeremy was not prepared to answer this question with the truth. In the pause, he had become aware of her bare arm lying creamy and smooth in the circle of candlelight, and as the seconds drew out his mind became more and more fixed upon it. Without conscious thought he reached out his hand to touch it. The silkiness of her cool flesh under his hand seemed to act like a lighted tinder to the explosive feelings that he had kept in check for so long. All the passion and the desire which had built up in him since their marriage seemed suddenly to become a tidal wave washing away all sane thought and any restraints.

Never, with any of the other women that he had known, had he been so completely the slave to his feelings. Always he had retained a thread of coolness, a rationality which had kept control even at the height of passion, but now he was no longer in control and desire seemed to swallow him up and use his mind and body as though he had no part in the proceedings.

His hand closed hard over Perdita's arm and with one quick movement he pulled her from her chair and into his arms. Before she was fully aware of what he was doing, his other hand came up under his chin to force her face up toward his, and his mouth came down on hers with a bruising fierceness.

Perdita had a sudden sickening memory of another angry grasp, of an evil face distorted with lust close to hers. Jeremy's hold on her was so like that of the revolting Crib that she could not help pulling back frantically and striking at Jeremy. Her resistance seemed to make Jeremy even more violent and she struggled to break free of his vicelike grasp. The similarity to Crib, in his completely alien behavior, made her feel terrified of Jeremy. It was as though some pet cat had suddenly turned into a tiger which was intent upon devouring her. Jeremy's face came toward hers and his mouth came down onto hers hard and brutal. Perdita tried to move her face away, but as she moved, his hand under her chin closed to hold her head firmly and he continued to kiss her with a cruelty which made her cry out.

The sound of her protest only seemed to make Jeremy more callous and inflexible. One hand slid from her waist down her body and with a fluid movement he picked her up and carried her over to the bed.

The last time Perdita had been picked up in his arms she had longed for the moment to continue forever; now she felt terrified by this stranger who seemed almost unaware of his own actions. She had longed, in the months since they had been married, for Jeremy to come to her and to make love to her, but now there was so little of love in his touch that she felt revulsion instead of desire.

Was it possible that this was the way it was between all men and women? But even as he pushed her roughly onto the bed she knew that what he was showing her was a travesty of love. This was not the way it was supposed to be between them. This was not the Jeremy who had cared for her and protected her. It must not be like this between them. She struggled against his arms and tried to push him away from her, but her "No, Jeremy, no," was met with only more unyielding strength.

He seemed to have lost all sense of hearing, and Perdita felt that she had ceased to exist as a person to him. She felt real terror as he pulled away the fine lawn of her nightgown and his mouth began to explore her body with a hungry intensity. The tears were running down her cheeks as he continued to touch every inch of her. But slowly, despite the roughness of his caresses, his practiced hands drew a response as he awakened her body to sensations she had never felt before. Mesmerized by the feelings he was inducing in her, she reached up her hands to touch the silky smoothness of the skin on his back and then ran her fingers down the hard muscles on either side of his backbone. He drew in his breath sharply and seemed to pause for a moment, as though he had just awakened from a dream. His kisses lost their fierceness and his touch became more tender. His mouth came back to her with a softness she thought she would never feel. More sure and less frightened, she began to return his kisses, and found his hands touching her as though she were the most precious thing in the world. He murmured words of endearment in a voice she had never heard him use before, and which made her whole body vibrate as though he were a violinist turning her into the instrument of his music.

The fire that had burned in him lost its anger and at the same time its warmth became transmitted to her, so that her passion began to match his, and with more delight than she had ever imagined possible she felt him enter her and their two bodies moved into a unity that was unquestionably the most beautiful thing that had ever happened to her.

Nothing in Perdita's imagination had prepared her for the joy she felt as she gave herself to the moment and to Jeremy, and in the end she had no will but his, and no being save that which he touched and possessed.

Later she turned into his arms, and the last thing she felt before she slept was his lips on her hair and the strength of his arms around her.

She slept deeply as though bedded in a warm cloud of comfort, and dreamed of worlds filled with glowing sunshine and bird song. She woke the next morning, reluctant to leave the bliss in which she lay cocooned, but when she reached out her hand to touch Jeremy and to make sure that it was all true, her hand found nothing but space, and her eyes opened quickly to look over at the other side of the bed. There was no sign of Jeremy, and she thought with panic that she must have dreamed the whole thing, but her body told her that their lovemaking had been real. She sat up in the bed and saw that the daylight was streaming through the curtains and flickering over the rumpled bed, the crumpled sheets of paper on the floor, her discarded nightgown, and the stub of candle which had burned itself out in the candlestick on her writing table.

She got out of bed and found herself a new nightgown, and after having bundled the other at the back of the cupboard, she got back into bed and rang the bell for Jeannette. When the maid arrived with her tray of hot chocolate and thin slices of bread and butter, Perdita asked casually whether Sir Jeremy was up and whether he had taken his breakfast yet.

"*Oui*, milady, Sir Jeremy left more than two hours ago. He told Clamp to pack his bag as he was needed down in the country. He said that you were not to be awakened, but he left this for you.''

Perdita reached out her hand for the folded piece of paper which Jeannette handed her. She could hardly believe that after last night, Jeremy could have left her without a word, but perhaps there had been some bad news from Shotley Park.

She did not want to be seen reading the note, as she felt that it would contain some very personal message, and she wanted to be alone to savor it in peace. She therefore waited with impatience while Jeannette drew back the curtains and tidied the room, but when the door had finally closed behind the maid, Perdita opened the piece of paper and read:

My dear Perdita,

I know that no amount of apologies will be sufficient to redress the wrongs of last night, and to save you the embarrassment of having to see me, I have returned to Shotley.

After last night's miserable episode there can be no mending matters between us, and I have therefore decided that it is best if I do not share the same roof with you.

You are, of course, free to use the London house as your own, and I will inform my bankers to pay any bills you submit to them.

I hope that some time in the future we may be able to meet without distress, but for now I think it best if I remain in the country.

I have the honor, Madam,
to be your humble and obedient
servant,
Jeremy

Perdita read the letter through three times, but much as she tried she could find no hope or comfort in any line. She lay on her bed feeling as though her veins had suddenly been filled with ice water.

It was obvious that her resistance to him last night had finally set the seal of Jeremy's dislike of the marriage. He had married her to save her honor, he had treated her well, apart for a couple of outbursts of temper, and then for her to have met his advances with resistance and protest when he finally asserted his rights as a husband must naturally have filled him with disgust for her.

Perdita stared sightlessly at the bright day outside the windows of her bedroom and felt the whole world slip away from her as she was swallowed up in her misery.

How could she have been so idiotic to have tried to deny herself to Jeremy. Certainly he had caught her by surprise and had been rough and strange with her, but her aunt had told her to expect some things that she might find unpleasant. What a fool she had been. If only she had not always felt that life could be manipulated like the characters in her poems and stories. Reality was seldom perfect, but last night—last night had ended perfectly for her, and if she had had the restraint and sense to be patient, she would not have lost that bliss that could have become part of her life. Now, through her own stupidity, all hope of having Jeremy as her real husband was gone forever.

It was well over an hour before Perdita could regain enough control over herself to ring for Jeannette and tell her that she was suffering from a headache and that she did not wish to be disturbed. Jeannette went off knowing that it was not a headache that was bothering her ladyship, but something that had been in Sir Jeremy's letter.

"For," as she said to the cook, "milady was looking all sunshine when I took her breakfast tray to her, and when I came to remove it she looked as though she had lost her last friend. It must have been something in Sir Jeremy's note. Franks said that Sir Jeremy was more than a little foxed when he came home last night. I hope that they have not quarreled. *Le bon dieu* protect me from ever falling in love. It brings more trouble than anything."

The cook, a spinster of ripe years, agreed heartily and having clucked over her poor young lady, decided that nothing would be more cheering for her than a couple of nice mutton chops for her luncheon. Having devised the correct remedy for all troubles of the heart and mind, she turned with a satisfied air to her stove to make sure that the heat was correct for her culinary panacea.

Upstairs Perdita had no such easy remedy. Several times she had crumpled Jeremy's letter and thrown it into her wastepaper basket, only to retrieve it a minute later and lovingly smooth out its creases. It was an agonizing letter to read, and yet his hand on the paper was the closest thing that she had of him at this moment. His words brought pain, but the memory of his presence that the handwriting evoked was something that she needed intensely.

It was almost eleven o'clock before Jeannette knocked tentatively at the bedroom door and, upon being told to come in, said, "Milady, Hughes is waiting with the carriage. He would like to know whether he will be wanted this morning?"

"Oh no," Perdita said in a distraught voice. "No, tell Hughes that I will not be needing the carriage today." Then recollecting that her father might be waiting for her at the theater, she added, "Wait. I would like him to deliver a note to the Sans Pareil Theater in the Strand."

Perdita got up and went over to her writing table and wrote a note to her father explaining that she had a headache and would not be able to come to him at the theater that day. She added that she hoped to be able to see him the following day, and then, sanding and folding the paper, she wrote her father's direction on it and handed it to Jeannette.

Once the maid had left, Perdita stared thoughtfully at the desk. It was probable that the word would quickly spread among the servants that she had sent a letter to an actor. But now it seemed pointless to hide the fact that her father was Edmund Wycoller. If Jeremy no longer cared about her, why should she continue to deny her father. Anyway, he was now the only man alive who cared for her. This lowering thought brought tears to her eyes, but she told herself firmly that there was no help in crying, and that if she were not to weep herself into a decline she must take herself in hand and try to occupy herself with things which would not remind her of Jeremy.

With this new resolve in mind, she decided to get dressed and see if a walk in the Park with Frolic would not put her mind in better order and help her decide what her next step should be. The fresh air might at least lift some of the misery which sat on her like a leaden devil. She turned toward her dressing room, but as she walked past her writing table she saw the page of the play she had been working on when Jeremy had walked in the night before. She looked down at the last words she had written.

It was Queen Moyra speaking to Prince James:

"No more, nor less than brother, always
You will be a cherished guest within my heart."

Almost without thinking, Perdita's hand reached for a quill and, dipping it into the ink, she crossed out the lines and quickly started to write others. Without knowing she did so, she sat down on the chair beside the desk and started to write in earnest. This time the floor did not become littered with crumpled paper. The words seemed to flow from the misery of her heart, and the lines the queen spoke to her lady-in-waiting were those that Perdita herself might have said to a close friend when speaking of her love for Jeremy. The despair and unhappiness of the past few hours were miraculously condensed into the ink which flowed across the pages.

Before Jeannette came up to the bedroom to tell Perdita that luncheon was served, the second scene was complete and the third and final scene, well underway.

Jeannette was pleased to see her ladyship occupied, and noted that the pink was back in her cheeks. Whatever had been in the letter had obviously not been that tragic after all, and the report she later took to the cook was satisfactory to both ladies.

Perdita, having barely finished her luncheon, was in the drawing room and was just preparing to go upstairs again to continue with her play when she heard the butler open the front door. A second later Jane burst into the room.

She hardly waited to embrace Perdita before saying, "You must come to Vauxhall tonight. Christopher is getting up a party of his friends who are here from Cambridge, and we need you and Jeremy to be our chaperones, otherwise we shall be obliged to take some terrible old quiz. Oh, of course, I don't mean Mama, but she is already engaged to play cards with some of her cronies, and the other mamas are all engaged in something or another. The problem is that Christopher's friend George Wilkins is very much taken with Lucinda Pierce. Her mother is the most terrible dragon, and will only agree to Lucinda's being one of the party if it is suitably chaperoned. I said that you and Jeremy would lend the whole thing respectability. Mrs. Pierce is the most terrible snob and the minute I mentioned Sir Jeremy and Lady Dole, she quite melted and said that she was sure that you would see that Lucinda was not compromised in any way. I promise you, Perdita, those were her very words. As though George would seduce her the minute she set foot inside the Gardens. Now, don't make any excuses. You see that you have to come or you will be in all our bad graces. Oh I do hope that Jeremy will be reasonable, but I am sure that you have learned to wind him around your little finger by now and will be able to persuade him to see that to refuse would be the most disagreeable thing that he could do, for if Lucinda does not come, George will cry off, and if George fails us, Christopher will take it into his head that Vauxhall is poor stuff, and I do so want to see the cascade and the fireworks. So you must tell Jeremy that he is bound to like it.''

Perdita allowed the torrent of words to come to a stop before saying, "I will come, if you wish, but I am afraid that Jeremy has had to go down to Shotley for a few days.''

"To Shotley!" Jane said, as though it were the most thoughtless thing that Jeremy could have done. "Why did he go to the country at this time of year? There is nothing to do down there now. What possessed him to leave London at the height of the season?''

Perdita was in no mood for a full confession and instead said simply, "He merely said that he had some urgent business to attend to.''

"But when will he be back? Perhaps we could put off the party for a day or two, but it is most provoking of him to have run off just when we need him the most.''

Perdita was forced to smile wryly. To label Jeremy's behavior as provoking when to her it was as though he had signed her death warrant seemed so ironic that it was hard to reconcile the two viewpoints. She had to admit to Jane though that she had no idea when Jeremy would be returning, but assumed that he might be away for some time.

"Oh how disobliging he is,'' Jane said. "Now what are we to do? I am not sure that Mrs. Pierce will consider you sufficient for all your title, and it would be the most terrible thing if she were to decide to join the party. She is terribly disapproving of everything and liable to put a damper on the whole proceedings. There is no room for gaiety when Mrs. Pierce is around. I have only met her once, but I must confess that if I were George I would think twice about marrying anyone with a mother like that. After all, one is bound to meet one's mother-in-law from time to time, no matter how far away one sets up one's establishment. Lucinda is extremely pretty and very sweet, but I am not sure that I would consider her prettiness and sweetness ample compensation for her mother.''

Jane's chatter was lifting some of Perdita's gloom, and she apologized for Jeremy's lapse and regretted that she had insufficient stature to be a responsible chaperone on her own. She was regretful that she would not be needed in the party, as she had come to think that an evening spent at Vauxhall with Jane and her friends would be infinitely preferable to one spent at home with only her own thoughts for company.

''Is there not some other mother who would be less dreadful than Mrs. Pierce who might be persuaded to come with you?'' she asked.

''No, of the other three, one has said the Vauxhall always brings on her rheumatics, another has a husband in bed with a quinsy sore throat and cannot leave him, and the other is already engaged to have dinner with some friends. Well, I suppose I must beard Mrs. Pierce in her den and try to persuade her that you are such a model of respectability that even the Archbishop of Canterbury could not exceed you in propriety and morals. I shall have to use all my powers of persuasion.''

''Perhaps it would help if I came with you?'' Perdita said.

''Oh no, indeed, I am afraid that I had to tell a tiny fib and assured Mrs. Pierce that you were thirty-five, very proper, and knew absolutely everything about the evil ways of young men and how to foil them. I am afraid that if she saw you she would believe none of it, especially when she sees that you are nothing like as old or ugly as you appeared from my description.''

''You are a monstrous child! Really, Jane, you might spare my reputation a trifle when you start spreading these stories about me. Much as I would like to help you, I do not wish it to be thought that I am a dreary old antidote.''

''Well no one who sees you will think that, but you must agree that for this matter it was more expedient that I told a few little untruths. There will be no harm come to Lucinda in any case. George is so enamoured of her that he treats her as though she were made of porcelain. There is no doubt that her reputation is safer when she is with him than at any other time in her life. Oh, but now I have thought, even if Mrs.

Pierce agrees to your being responsible for us on your own, that still leaves a problem of an escort for you. Is there anyone that you know who you could ask to come with us? Perhaps some elderly gentleman so that you would not be thought to be forming an unsuitable liaison while Jeremy is out of town?''

Perdita was almost tempted to say that there was little danger of Jeremy's being annoyed by any liaison she formed now, but instead thought for a moment and then said, "I think that there might be someone I could ask. He is,'' she said truthfully, "old enough to be my father, but if he is not busy, he would come, I am sure. I will send a note at once to ask him to accompany us, and if you wait, we may get his reply within the hour.''

Perdita went over the the writing table between the windows of the drawing room and quickly wrote a note to her father. She was sure that his expansive nature would add to the enjoyment of the evening, and for her part she could think of no one else whose company would be tolerable to her at this moment.

Perdita's despair had produced a recklessness in her. With her life and happiness in wreckage around her, she no longer felt it necessary to take care that the truth about her parentage was not discovered. What did it matter what people would think of her or how she might be shunned. Everything paled into insignificance beside the fact that Jeremy had left her. Better now to turn to the world of the theater, where at least she would know warmth and humor and an interest to fill part of her empty life.

She sent the note with a footman and settled down to await the answer with Jane. Jane, as usual, was vibrant with gossip about the people she had met and Perdita found herself drawn into the animated discussion. Jane's comments were shrewd and perspicacious though often a bit harsh, and several times Perdita felt she must defend someone whose character was being mercilessly caricatured. At one point Jane was moved to say, "I don't believe that there is anyone in the world that you dislike, Perdita. I cannot for the life of me imagine how you can avoid being insipid, but somehow you do. I confess that I would very much like to have your sweetness of nature. Jeremy is a very lucky man indeed. I must try to copy you, otherwise I shall have Christopher constantly comparing me unfavorably to you.''

The return of the footman with a note from her father provided Perdita with an excuse for not replying. It was obvious that in a day or two Jane would have to know the real reason for Jeremy's absence, but the longer she could put off telling Jane, the more time she could give herself to gain some sort of equilibrium.

The note from Edmund Wycoller said that he found the honor of the invitation to join the party for Vauxhall too much to decline and that he would therefore trust this evening's rehearsal to his understudy. Perdita, omitting the opening and closing salutations, read the letter aloud to Jane, but when she mentioned the rehearsal being trusted to the understudy Jane said, "You are not speaking of Edmund Wycoller, the actor?"

"The very same," Perdita said, smiling at Jane's open mouth.

Jane flushed with excitement. "How do you know him? It seems that you must know him quite well. Do you think that he will enjoy our party, or will he find us very boring?"

"I am quite sure he will enjoy it immensely. As for knowing him, I knew him before I came to Hangarwood, he was a—a friend of my mother's. You will find him amusing company, and I assure you that he will be very pleased to get to know you. I have spoken of you often to him. However, perhaps it would be as well to tell Mrs. Pierce that he is an old friend of the family and try to imply that he is someone other than an actor—if she should ask. I do not feel, from what you tell me of her, that she would find it acceptable to have her daughter chaperoned by an actor!"

Jane laughed. "No, I daresay that piece of information would send her up in the boughs. I shall say that he is a gentleman that has been known to our family for many years and simply leave it at that. However, remind me to inform Lucinda that she is not to tell her mother his true calling, for Lucinda is sure to recognize him when they meet. Oh, I am so delighted that he will come. I have never met an actor before and am sure that they are the most amusing company. I am almost glad that Jeremy could not be here.''

Perdita could not quite agree with the last sentiment, but ignoring it she said, "I am sure that you will be enchanted by

Mr. Wycoller, and I look forward to seeing both of you fall head over heels in love with each other.''

''Oh Perdita, don't tease, you know that there is no one that I could possibly love but Christopher. Nevertheless, perhaps it might be fun to see if I can make Christopher a little jealous.'' At that she picked up her shawl and, kissing Perdita goodbye, left to go to Mrs. Pierce's and persuade the lady that the evening's entertainment would be conducted in a most respectable manner.

— 14 —

It had been a long time since Perdita had seen her father away from the theater, and then, with her child's eyes, she had not recognized the effect that he had on other people. When she was tiny he had seemed godlike to her anyway and it had not struck her as unusual that he should produce the same sort of awe in others. But now, in the paths of Vauxhall, where the little lights that hung from the trees and edged the paths gave the whole setting an unreal quality, and where the artificial cascade, the theaters and the pavilions on the grounds gave Edmund Wycoller as good a setting as his own theater, he shone and sparkled.

The admiring eyes of the young girls in the party, the cockalorum pride of the young men at being able to say that they had actually conversed with the great Edmund Wycoller, was fuel to his fire. The desire to show off his power to his own daughter added yet another degree of valor to his performance, and performance it was.

They had barely arrived at the Gardens before it became quite clear that Edmund Wycoller was the star of the evening. He was too consummate an actor to strut and declaim and call attention to himself, but Perdita saw the art of underplaying and timing brought to perfection. If attention should wander from him for a second he would go silent, but with a silence that resounded like gongs, and within seconds all the eyes would be focused on him again. But the occasions for this device were rare and for the most part the young men and women hung around him like children around Santa Claus.

George Wilkins, who had had the privilege of seeing Mr. Wycoller play Shylock, had blushed crimson when first introduced to him. He bowed as deeply as if he had just been introduced to royalty and said, "I never thought, sir, that I would live to have the great honor, the privilege, of actually touching the hand of the great Edmund Wycoller himself. This is a moment I shall treasure all my life, you may be sure of that, sir."

Edmund Wycoller dismissed George's effusive compliments with just the right amount of gratitude mixed with humility and proceeded to win all hearts by turning the subject to stories of the disasters that had overcome him during his career on the stage. He told of adamant magistrates who had to be wooed to grant permission for the strolling players to perform in a drafty barn. He told of incidents where the company had put on their plays despite permission's being refused and of the consequences when the constabulary, aided by dogs, had put the company to rout. Everything was acted out with such vigor and realism that the events seemed to be repeated before the party's eyes.

"You can imagine," Edmund Wycoller said, "the lack of authenticity when the all-powerful Prospero is chased down the village street by a pack of curs, a large tear out of the seat of his trousers and a village urchin shouting, 'Show us yer magic then.' I neatly crowned the child with my staff *en passant*, and the stars he saw were all the magic he got that night."

He then proceeded to act out the moment when, in his first attempt at Hamlet on the London stage, he had tripped on his sword as he prepared to unsheath it for the fight with Laertes, fallen against the curtain, pulled it down over himself, and promptly fallen into the orchestra pit. The description was so vivid that the party was crying with laughter by the time Edmund Wycoller had finished, and even Perdita found that she could not remain down in the mouth when her father was telling his tales.

As the party moved through the walks toward one of the clearings where a juggler was performing, Jane managed to detach Perdita from the group around the actor.

"You are right, Perdita, he is the most charming man in the world. What does Jeremy think of him? And why, oh why have you never told me before that you knew him?"

Perdita was tempted to make up some story, but the time for stories seemed to be past, and all deceptions seemed pointless and useless. She sighed, looked for a second at

Jane, and then said, "I suppose it doesn't matter your knowing now, but he is my father."

Jane stopped dead in her tracks, her mouth opening. "But I
thought—you always said that your father was a soldier."

"Yes, Uncle Matthew advised me to put that about so that
I would not suffer the social ostracism which would accompany the knowledge that my father was an actor. I was told,
when I first came to Hangarwood, that I must tell no one the
true profession of my father, but I do not see why you should
not know."

"Ostracism! To be the daughter of the great Edmund
Wycoller! Why he is received everywhere. He has even given
command performances at Windsor Castle, so Christopher
tells me. I have never heard anything so pudding-brained. Far
from being ostracized, you would be immensely sought after
if it were generally known!"

"I suppose it does seem a little ludicrous, but you see he
was not always as famous as he is now. When my mother
was alive, he was a struggling actor in the provinces and
would scarcely have been acceptable then. Besides, we are in
a more sophisticated society in London than we were in
Byfold. You can imagine how Mrs. Banistre-Brewster would
have delighted in the information that my father was a strolling player," Perdita said sourly. "But Jane, I would be
grateful if you would not tell anyone what I have just told
you. I do not think that Aunt Charlotte would be pleased to
know that the news is common knowledge, and I and—I
would rather that Jeremy did not find out either."

"You mean that you have not told Jeremy? He would be
delighted with your father. Besides, you know that Jeremy
does not give a feather or a farthing for that sort of village
snobbishness."

"Please, don't tell him. There are reasons I will tell you at
some other time why it is best that he does not know, so
please be careful what you say to Christopher, for he mustn't
tell Jeremy either. You must promise me that you will not let
Jeremy hear about this."

The intense look of anxiety on Perdita's face made Jane
stop in her attempt to encourage her step-sister to be open
with her secret, and instead she said, "Very well, if that is
what you wish, I shall be as silent as the grave, you can trust

me. But what are the reasons you have for not telling Jeremy yourself?''

Perdita looked down the path to where Christopher had detached himself from the group around Edmund Wycoller and was now coming back toward Jane and Perdita. "I can't tell you now. Come to see me at Upper Grosvenor Street tomorrow at eleven and I will tell you all then.''

Jane had barely time to agree before Christopher was at their side.

"What sisterly gossip are you two indulging in? Surely nothing that can be as amusing as the tales that Mr. Wycoller is telling us. Come, we are all making our way to the cascade so that we may have a good vantage point from which to watch the fireworks. If we don't hurry, we will never secure a good place.''

Christopher linked his arms through those of the two girls and hurried down the paths, which were becoming increasingly filled with people, all hurrying on the same mission.

The artificial cascade at the end of the path was even more spectacular in the gathering dark than it was in daylight. The hundreds of little lights which were arranged in the trees overhanging the water, and in the ferns and grasses which were planted among the rocks beside the pool, twinkled in the tumbling waterfall and seemed to dance and prance over the surface of the constantly moving water.

Christopher stopped and the three of them watched the scene in silence for a while, then Jane sighed and Christopher turned to her to watch her delight in the spectacle. At that moment the entire crowd of people let out a great "O-o-oh" as the blue, green, red, and brilliant white lights of the fireworks blossomed like giant dandelion clocks in the night sky. As the sparks began to fall to earth, another burst of color exploded against the blue-black darkness. Jane clutched Christopher's arm and he put his head close the hers, smiling at her enchantment with the glorious spectacle. Suddenly Perdita felt desperately alone and she longed and longed for Jeremy to be standing close to her, hugging her to him in the way Christopher was now hugging Jane. As though in answer to her wishes, she felt someone touch her arm and turned quickly, half expecting to see that her desperate longing had conjured up the one person she wanted to see, but as she turned her head she saw that it was only her father who had come to her.

Her eyes betrayed her disappointment and Edmund Wycoller said in a low voice, "What is wrong? What troubles you, my sweeting?"

Perdita turned away and shook her head. She could not trust her voice at the moment as her unhappiness reasserted itself with redoubled strength. Her father took a firm hold of her arm and silently led her away from the group and back down the now almost deserted paths where only a few latecomers were making their way toward the fireworks. Finding a seat in a quiet alley of pleached lime trees, he sat her down and seated himself beside her. He reached over and took her hands in his and looked at her silently for a moment.

"Now my dove, tell me what that husband has done now?"

Perdita looked up surprised and then a shadow of a smile crossed her face. "Is it so obvious?" she asked.

"Only to those that see with the eyes of love," her father answered. "But tell me. I had so hoped that things were better between you."

Perdita took a deep breath and tried to steady herself before answering. Finally she said, "He has left me—he wishes us to spend the rest of our lives apart."

"Apart! For what reason?"

It took Perdita a little while to steel herself to admit the truth to her father, but eventually she said in a soft voice, "I have not been a—a—dutiful wife."

He pulled her to him and patted her, but it was obvious that his last words had stunned him. "A dutiful wife? What do you mean? How could you not have been a dutiful wife? Ah, there is some other that you love, and that jackanapes of a husband has threatened to set you aside for that! I have never heard of such absurdity! Now, now you will be better off without him and then you may go to your lover. It will all be for the best that way, my dearest, you will see."

"I do not have a lover," Perdita said miserably. "I only love Jeremy."

"No lover? Then why does your husband accuse you of being an undutiful wife? The fellow must be queer in the attic. Fit for Bedlam, nothing less. Let him go, dear heart, he is not worth a mote of your affection. Let him go and good riddance to him.''

"I don't want to let him go, Father. I love him. I want to be his wife, but I have made such an awful mistake, and now there is no hope that he will ever love me.'' Tears welled in Perdita's eyes and her father absentmindedly reached for his handkerchief, frowning as he thought.

"Dry your eyes,'' he said firmly, "and blow your nose. There will be no remedying the matter until you can give me a clear idea of what it is all about. If you wish to cry, you may cry after you have fully apprised me of the situation. Now start at the beginning. Why do you believe yourself to be an undutiful wife?''

The commonsense tone that her father adopted helped Perdita to regain control of herself. Although she found it hard to put the case of her distress into words, she eventually said, in a barely audible voice, "We had a quarrel yesterday. I was angry with him. I know I should not have been, but I thought that he was being very unreasonable and I told him so.''

"My dear child, is that all?'' Edmund Wycoller said, smiling at her.

"No,'' Perdita said, unable to meet her father's eyes. "He—later—late last night he came to me in my room and I—I—refused him, or at least I tried to. Oh I know I did not behave as a wife should, but he surprised me. After our quarrel, I had not thought that he would come to my room for the first time since we were married. I know I should not have resisted him. He is my husband, and Aunt Charlotte told me that my duty was to submit, and if things had been different between us, I should have welcomed him, but he was so strange and he frightened me. Now I have lost him forever.''

Edmund Wycoller looked at her for a second with an uncomprehending expression on his face, then he said, "Yes, well, I always said that the fella sounded like a sapskull and a blackguard, now the proof is here. What man in his right senses would leave his wife because of an innocent reluctance, a modesty in carnal matters! Good God, half the men in England would be separated from their brides if that were cause enough! What does he suppose an innocent young girl would do when approached by some lunatic who leaves her alone for several months and then comes raving to her bedroom in the middle of the night? The man is mad—stark staring mad! He ignores you, he quarrels with you, and then comes and forces himself upon you. By heaven, no daughter of mine shall have to live her life with such a madman. The best thing for you, my dear, is to get a bill of divorcement. I am sure that you would have no trouble. You may think you love him, but let me assure you that it is just a passing fancy. You are too intelligent to love a man as queer in the attic as that one. Mind you, when society gets to hear of what he is about, he will be the joke of the century, for who would believe a man would set aside an angel like you for the sin of innocence? He will be the butt of jokes from Land's End to John'o Groats. Why he will probably be forced to end his life in far Australia to avoid the scorn, the ridicule, the rampant revenge that I and the rest of of society will pour upon him."

Perdita was unable to join with her father in his castigation of Jeremy, though she was warmed by the fierce defense offered to her, but more immediate problems had to be solved before Jeremy's exile to the Antipodes could be considered. There was no doubt that she could not pretend for long that Jeremy had left town for only a short time. Despite her father's conviction that she was to be the toast of London, she was not so sure that society would rally to her side and she dreaded the slights she would have to suffer once Jeremy's intentions were known, and even more the insincere condolences which would be offered by some of her new acquaintances. It became increasingly plain to Perdita that she did not wish to remain in Upper Grosvenor Street, and that she would prefer to hide in some remote corner of London or the country until the scandal should blow over.

Her mind followed this line of thought as her father continued to mutter over Jeremy's insanity, and finally she interrupted his tirade with, "Papa, I cannot stay at Upper Grosvenor Street, and no matter what you think, I do not want to drink scandal broth with anyone. Jeremy has made it clear that he will see that my financial needs are met, and although I would wish to be no burden upon him at all, I think that I must avail myself of his offer until I can see my way clear to making my own living. Perhaps I should look at once for a small house somewhere. I believe the village of Kensington is very pleasant, and far enough away from the center of Lon-

don so that I would be quite unnoticed, yet not so far that I
would be prevented from seeing you."

Her father's eyebrows crept up his forehead as she outlined
these plans, but when she had finished he said, "Kensington?
A small house? What rubbish is this? You will naturally make
your home with me, your father. Those of us in the theater
are more tolerant than the rest of society, and you need fear
no slurs cast upon you when you are in my protection. Why,
you may join the company itself and if you wish to earn your
living you will be able to in that way. Indeed, I foresee that
you will be the rage of London. The theatrical dynasty of
Wycoller will ring beside the name of Kemble down the
centuries. There is so much for you: Ophelia, Desdemona,
Miranda, Cordelia, your own namesake in *The Winter's Tale*.
The Bard might have written all these especially for you. I
shall play your Hamlet, your Othello, your Prospero and
Lear, and your alter-father, Leontes."

Edmund Wycoller's eyes sparkled at the thought of the
great father and daughter team they would make, and all
thoughts of Jeremy's misdoings were forgotten in the excitement of the future he saw spreading before him and his
daughter.

"Your life is about to begin," he said expansively, waving
his arms to the pleached limes around them. "Tonight you
will return home and pack your bags, and at first light you
will join Mrs. Eddy and myself at the house in Bull Inn
Court. There is still plenty of room even with the young
Frederick in residence." He glared briefly at Perdita, but
went on, "Speaking of which, *there* is one admirer you have
already, and I daresay with his attentions you will have little
enough time to be downhearted. Now, what do you say? Is it
not an excellent plan? A silver lining to your cloud, to be
with your father and those that adore you?"

"I only wish that it were so simple, Papa, but I cannot
simply disappear and reappear on the stage of the Sans Pareil."

"And why not, pray?"

"First, I must tell my Aunt Charlotte. She will have to
know what has happened, and I expect that she will want me
to return to her—though I cannot think that I would be
comfortable at Hangarwood House, with the Doles in the next
village. Also, I must at least tell Jeremy my direction. There

may be papers and things that he will have to send to me, so he must know where I can be found.''

"He does not deserve such consideration."

"I believe he does. Besides, I do not intend to make a greater drama than is necessary. The situation is hard enough as it is without going to lengths to exacerbate the matter. Besides . . ."

"Besides what?"

"I would like him to know where I am in case he should ever want to find me," Perdita said, lowering her voice almost to a whisper.

Her father looked at her for a moment and then reached out his hand to touch hers. "You really do love him, don't you?" he said gently.

Perdita nodded.

"Ah well, I will not chide you for that. If men were to merit the love of women, there would be few of us with the affection we need to make us happy. But try not to put too much hope into your love. Things may come about, but you must act as though they will not and make a new life for yourself."

"I will try, Papa," Perdita said, raising her eyes to him. "But you must not be cross with me if I fail sometimes."

"No, no, my dearest, never. I would never scold for a foolishness of the heart. Now, we must find the rest of the party before it is discovered that their chaperones have been derelict in their duty. Tomorrow, when you have had a chance to settle your plans, you can send a note to say when I may expect you, but come soon. Your old father needs you."

Perdita hugged her father and rose with him. Silently he put his arm around her and without a word they retraced their steps until they found the party about to seek the solace of shaved ham and the famous Vauxhall punch. The spirits of the company were such by that time that Perdita's quietness went unnoticed by all but her father. From time to time he glanced at her but was content to leave any further action on his part until she had joined him at his house in Bull Inn Court.

Perdita spent a troubled night after she returned from Vauxhall. Most of it was taken up with composing a letter to Jeremy. As she had said to her father, she did not want to leave him with no idea of how to find her, but at the same time she was still reluctant to tell him that she was going to stay with her father. The fact that she had kept that secret from him would be yet another reason for him to hold her in dislike. She therefore simply stated that she was going to live with an old friend of her mother's and that she could be contacted at 12 Bull Inn Court. Further elaboration seemed unnecessary and unwise, and she eventually sealed the letter ready for the post in the morning.

To her Aunt Charlotte she would need to be more direct and open, but the thought of how, firstly, to explain the situation between herself and Jeremy, and secondly, to tell her aunt of the fact that she had found her father and was now proposing to live with him, gave her another set of problems to worry about. She knew that once she had explained to Aunt Charlotte that the marriage had turned out to be a disaster and that Jeremy wanted nothing further to do with her, her aunt would realize the impracticality of Perdita's returning to Hangarwood House. However, she might not feel so sanguine, after having spent so many years protecting Perdita from the consequences of having a father who was an actor, to hear that Perdita was proposing to throw off all convention and take to a life on the stage. But the more she thought of it, the more Perdita realized that it was the best answer that she could devise for her future life. It would, at the very least, give her some occupation and a means of earning her own living, for she had no intention of being a burden to Jeremy any longer than she needed to be.

As the dawn seeped through the curtains, Perdita found that she was becoming more confident in her decision and less fearful of the disapproval of her aunt. At last she was about to undertake a life which was entirely her own, one for which she would be entirely responsible and which would be free of all deception. If it were not the one she wished for most, at least she would be able to live without lies and confine her fantasies to the stage of the theater.

By the time she had had breakfast and had dressed, she felt a great deal more composed than she had been the day before, and she went downstairs to await the arrival of her step-sister.

Jane was more than usually prompt in arriving. It had, in fact, taken a great deal of self-control on her part not to arrive at Upper Grosvenor Street an hour before she was expected. Although her night had not been sleepless, she had woken early consumed with the desire to find out how Perdita had found her father, how often she had seen him, and how she had managed to keep his presence and identity secret from Jeremy. But the overwhelming question was what had happened between Perdita and Jeremy to make the former so anxious that Jeremy hear nothing of the identity of her father.

Jane barely kissed her step-sister, and did not wait to be seated on the satin sofa in the drawing room before she demanded an explanation.

Perdita proceeded, for once uninterrupted, to give a full account of her early life and repeated the reasons she had been given for keeping silent about the true profession of her father. Although Jane kept quiet, her face registered such expressions of outrage, dismay, or sorrow that Perdita was sometimes hard put to continue. Nevertheless, Jane remained silent until Perdita had finished her story, but then said, "But now you may make a clean breast of it. There is no one who would not think all the more of you for having such a notable father."

"I cannot do that," Perdita said slowly. "Oh Jane, there is so much more that I must tell you."

The tone of her voice stopped Jane's exuberant defense of Edmund Wycoller. "What else is there? Why can you not tell Jeremy?"

Perdita paused, took a deep breath, and said slowly, "Jeremy wishes us to live separately."

Jane's mouth fell open, but for once there was no following torrent of words.

"Oh Jane, my marriage has not been what I had hoped. In fact, it has been the disaster I feared it might be. It was obvious from the first day after our wedding that Jeremy had married me merely to save my reputation. Oh, he was all that he should have been in kindness and attention to my wishes, but he—that is, he made it plain that he had no interest in me as a woman. He treated me as though he were my kind older brother."

"You mean the marriage was never consummated?" Jane asked wide-eyed.

Perdita looked a little surprised at the blunt statement, but smiled as she realized how typical it was of Jane to come right to the point.

"No—that is, not until quite recently. I had given up all hope that he would come to me as a husband, but the other night, after we had quarreled and he had left the house in a rage, he returned and came to my bedroom very late. I do not know how to explain to you, but I was surprised and he seemed so different, not his usual kind and gentle self. It was as though a stranger were forcing himself upon me. I—I resisted him, and though he—well—although things happened, I know that he was angry that I should have tried to resist him. After all, he was only asserting his rights, and Aunt Charlotte had warned me that I might not like it, though— well that is not important now. Anyway the next morning he had left and Jeannette brought me a letter he had written before leaving for the country. In it he told me that he felt it best if we never lived under the same roof again. Oh Jane, what am I to do? How could I have been so foolish as to deny him when he is the only man I have ever wanted?"

Jane got up and walked over to her step-sister, seated herself beside her, and put her arms around her.

"I cannot believe that all this has happened. I did not really believe you when you told me, before your marriage, that Jeremy was only marrying you out of a sense of duty. I was sure that he had felt more than the ordinary affection for you. I have seen him look at you several times when you did not notice, and I could have sworn that he was more than taken with you. I mentioned it to Christopher later and he said that Jeremy has always loved you—since you were a child! He could tell by the way he always brought your name up whenever he was home from the war, or when he wrote asking for news of the goings-on at Shotley or Hangarwood. Christopher said that Jeremy would never ask directly about you, but more by way of an afterthought, which is a sure sign of more than common interest in a person. Also, Christopher said that he once found a whole bundle of the letters you had written to Jeremy when he was in the Peninsula, all neatly tied up with tape and obviously much read, and when he teased Jeremy about them, Jeremy flew into a rage such as Christopher had never seen before, so I cannot see why he behaved so strangely once he had made you his wife. The whole thing is very perplexing. But what are you going to do now?"

Perdita, whose head was spinning with the revelations Jane had imparted, took a few minutes before she could bring herself back to the present.

"I did not know. Well, it can mean nothing now. It is clear that Jeremy's feelings for me have changed. It is best that I do not think about what you have just told me, for indeed it can only make me more unhappy to think that but for a series of unfortunate incidents, things might have worked out differently. I must not allow myself to refine upon it too much. I have decided to live with my father, and perhaps join him on the stage. I must set my mind to the future and not allow myself to wonder what might have been. I have spent too much of my life in a dream world, or hidden away from the truth in fantasy. Now I shall keep my fantasies and imagination to the inside of the theater. In any case, the truth is that I shall be with people who love me and will have much to absorb my mind. I shall most certainly stand in need of both of these things."

"What are you going to tell Jeremy?"

"I still do not wish to tell him that my father is an actor. It could make no difference to him now, but I would rather he did not have anything further to hold against me. I have written to tell him simply that I am going to make my home with a friend of my mother's. I did not specify the name of the person, but it is the truth in its way. Papa was a good friend to my mother as well as being her husband. Then I shall have the companionship of Mrs. Eddy, my father's leading lady, and young Freddy, a climbing boy that she and my father have taken into their care—I will tell you that tale at another time—so he will keep me company too."

"You have not mentioned Mrs. Eddy before," Jane said.

"Oh, have I not? Well, Mrs. Eddy shares a home with my father. I hope you are not too shocked, but, well, things like that are more usual in the theatrical world, for none of the company treats their relationship as anything strange."

"I can understand completely," Jane said, nodding wisely. "No doubt after the love your father bore your mother he would not wish to give his name to another. I think that it is very romantic, and if my mother should kick up a dust about your living with your father and a woman who is not precisely his wife, I shall tell her so."

"I pray you will do no such thing. I feel that Aunt

Charlotte would be better served if she were not made aware
of Mrs. Eddy's existence in the house. If necessary, I shall
say that my father employs a housekeeper—which is very
nearly the truth. Oh, Jane, it does seem that no matter how
hard I try I must always remain silent about something, or tell
a different story to everyone, and I do not like it above half.
One of my worst tests will be to tell your mother about what
has happened. If she is to be at home this afternoon, would
you tell her that I would like to see her privately for a half
hour or so?"

"I will tell her that she must cancel all other engagements
as you have something very important to say to her," Jane
replied.

She left a few minutes later, replete with as much information as she could digest in one sitting, and Perdita, for her
part, found that her confessions to Jane had left her feeling
that she might be able to deal with her life after all. With her
new confidence she was able to direct Jeannette to pack
almost all of her clothes with the excuse that she would be
visiting friends for several weeks while Sir Jeremy was away.
She surprised herself by being able to be quite composed
when she gave the butler the address where she might be
reached, and left instructions that the house was to be kept in
readiness for Sir Jeremy as he had not yet made firm plans
and might return unexpectedly.

However, her confidence nearly deserted her when she
went to see Aunt Charlotte that afternoon. Jane had tactfully
arranged to go out driving with Christopher, so Perdita and
her aunt were undisturbed. Even so, it took Perdita some time
to get to the point of her visit and, having stumbled around
the subject of Jeremy's quittal of Upper Grosvenor Street, she
had to repeat the explanation twice before her aunt had been
able to grasp the full extent of the disaster.

Mrs. Chase had immediately insisted that Perdita pack her
bags and return to the bosom of her family, and had then to
be persuaded that for Perdita to join her father at the theater
was a more reasonable alternative. Mrs. Chase had to send
for her sal volatile at that point, but had rallied and finally
conceded that it was perhaps the best solution. She saw the
difficulties inherent in Perdita's return to Hangarwood House
with the Doles so nearby, besides Mrs. Chase, having performed the mental discipline of releasing Perdita from her

charge at her marriage to Jeremy, was finding it difficult to imagine Perdita as her responsibility again. The subtleties of the situation Mrs. Chase realized would be difficult to assess, and as there was a reasonable alternative which seemed to be to Perdita's liking, she was soon able to wave the sal volatile bottle away and embrace Perdita with genuine affection untinged with any misgivings about the future.

Perdita was glad that the situation had now been resolved in a manner agreeable to all, and having promised her aunt that she would be a constant visitor in London and a faithful correspondent once Mrs. Chase had returned to Hangarwood, she made her way back to Upper Grosvenor Street and the final supervision of her packing.

At last it was finished and Perdita, dispensing with any grand farewells to the servants, entered the carriage that Hughes had brought around from the mews and instructed him to drive her to Bull Inn Court.

As the carriage rolled down the street and turned into Grosvenor Square, Perdita felt that one whole part of her life was being cut off from her forever. The Perdita who had grown up loving Jeremy was about to become some shadowy figure of fiction, and she would soon not even remember what it felt like to be his wife. But for the moment the ache in her chest and the tears which blurred her vision were a painful reminder that such a moment had not yet been reached.

— 15 —

Edmund Wycoller had spent almost as much time in thought after the evening at Vauxhall as Perdita had done. His opinion of Jeremy had not changed very much, but he had come to realize that Perdita was very much in love with him still. He had toyed with the idea of going down to Shotley and facing Jeremy and even calling him out. However, on more mature consideration he realized that neither move would be particularly helpful to Perdita at this moment. The best he could do was to put no obstacles in her path, so that if Jeremy decided that he had made a terrible mistake, it would be possible for him to come back to Perdita as easily as possible.

He realized that one thing that he could do would be to regularize his own situation, so when Perdita arrived at Bull Inn Court it was to be told that she was invited to her father's wedding, which would take place the next day.

Mrs. Eddy had been somewhat surprised. Not, she admitted to herself, by the suddenness of the proposal, but that he had decided to propose at all. Edmund however explained his motives, though couching them in sufficiently lover-like phrases to make the lady able to accept without loss of face. "You see, my dear," he ended, "I cannot pretend to you that my feelings for you are those of the raptures of young love, but I am comfortable with you, you understand me, and I know you to be a woman I can happily imagine sharing the rest of my life. You would therefore be doing me a great kindness by marrying me."

It was a proposal that Mrs. Eddy had no reservations about accepting, and having sent Mr. Wycoller off to get a special license, looked out a suitable bonnet for the occasion and having told Freddy he was to be best man, all that was left was for her to invite Perdita to be her matron-of-honor.

The morning after Perdita's arrival the party therefore set off to St. Martin's-in-the-Fields, where the vicar had promised to perform the ceremony. All was beautifully carried out, including a few tears from Perdita and a couple from the bride herself, and then the wedding party returned to the theater where once again Tom had been detailed to purchase several bottles of champagne.

The universal high spirits and good humor were only slightly ruffled at one point when Edmund Wycoller said with mock distress that now it would be necessary to reprint all the playbills with the name of Sarah Eddy changed to Sarah Wycoller.

The suggestion was not met with approval by the new Mrs. Wycoller and she drew herself up to her full height and turned an icy smile upon Edmund. "My dear," she said sweetly, "I think you may spare yourself that trouble. With my reputation, it would be hard for my public to recognize a new name. It would somehow make it seem that the name of Eddy, which carries so much weight on a playbill at present, were suddenly put to naught, and with it the actress herself."

"My dear," Edmund Wycoller said quickly, "I had only hoped that with Perdita joining the company you would think it impressive to have three Wycollers on the bill."

"I see your reasoning, my dearest," Sarah continued, with her smile now seemingly carved out of marble, "but I feel that you have overlooked the confusion to the public should one of their most respected actresses suddenly disappear and reappear as quite another person. It might take years for them to resolve the matter, and during that time, think how much money would be lost at the box office."

Edmund Wycoller would have been ready to take exception to this assertion at any other time, but he had no desire to argue with his new wife on their wedding day, and decided to give the matter more thought at another time. Today, celebration was in order and his gracious concession to his wife's wishes allowed the festivities to continue without any cloud hanging over them.

At one moment he had drawn Perdita aside and without divulging the real reason for the precipitous marriage had said earnestly, "I hope that you understand that my marriage to Mrs. Eddy means no disrespect to your mother's memory."

His face was so filled with anxiety that Perdita could

hardly repress a smile, but said, "No, dear Papa, it would be hard to accuse you of a rash and sudden second marriage since my mother has been dead these fourteen years. Besides, I am sure that she is looking down from heaven and wishing you all the joy that you and Mrs. Eddy, I mean Mrs. Wycoller, deserve."

"Thank you, my dearest," her father said, "but I think that we must have you call your step-mother by a less formal name. I am sure that she would be happy for you to call her Sarah, for you have had enough mamas."

In the following weeks, Perdita was swept up in so much activity that she had very little time to brood about her past mistakes and wonder whether Jeremy ever thought of her. Edmund Wycoller had made up his mind to keep her as busy as possible and he pressed her to finish her play and at the same time told her that he had decided that she should play the queen herself. He therefore embarked on an intensive course of instruction for Perdita, for he had no intention of letting his only child appear in public and make a fool of herself. When he was not able to instruct her himself he turned her over to the new Mrs. Wycoller.

Edmund Wycoller did not need to be told that the play Perdita had written was based largely on her own experience, and he felt that she would therefore be familiar enough with the emotions to act the part of the queen with a good deal of authenticity. Nevertheless she needed to know a lot about stagecraft and he began to give her a grounding in the basic rules of acting. She must never, he said, upstage another actor by making him turn his back to the audience to address his lines to her; she must never cut another actor's applause or laughter by following her cue too soon; she must appear natural in movement and yet always speak her lines to the auditorium; she must produce her voice from the back of her throat and not just from her lips, and must project and ennunciate so that the softest whisper could be heard by those patrons in the "gods" at the top of the house.

He taught her how to move gracefully in skirts with trains, skirts with panniers, in medieval dress, and even how to walk like a boy when she would be required to play parts in hose and doublet. He taught her how to play to another actor; to adapt her acting so that her part balanced with the overall scheme of the play. She learned how to stand and how to sit, and what to do with her hands and her feet and how stillness can be more effective than movement, but how movement, if subtly performed, can convey a whole character in one action. But above all she learned that the audience is paramount and that never, never should she forget them for one minute so that she could sense their mood and manipulate it to the order of the play. She also learned that although she should be conscious of the audience, she should never let them know it, so that they could be taken with her into the fantasy that was being woven for them in the flickering light of the gaslamps.

From Sarah she learned about stage make-up, how to use a fan and the old-fashioned language it conveyed. She learned the graces expected of an actress, and the nuances of voice that can be used in a love scene.

By the end of the second week, Perdita thought that her mind would explode with all the new knowledge, but she was an apt pupil and made few mistakes. However, beyond the fact that she was quick to learn the techniques, her father found that she had that extra, mystical quality which enables an actress to seem to put on the skin of her part, and to draw the audience with her into the fantasy.

Watching her rehearse one of the scenes of her play with Lawrence Pare as Prince James, Edmund Wycoller forgot at one moment that he was watching his daughter and waited tensely to see if the king's suspicions were right and if the girl on the stage was really in love with the younger man. Edmund watched the queen move over to the table, pick up a bowl of flowers, and bend her head to smell them, and from her relaxed, semi-abstracted air as she made the gesture, she told plainly that she had only half her mind on the conversation with the prince and that all she felt for him was an easy friendship.

Edmund Wycoller clasped his hands in his lap and his eyes shone at the grace of the performance. Then, brought back to reality, he felt a surge of immense pride when he realized that his daughter had the makings of a consummate actress.

When the scene was finished, he went over to her and took her in his arms. "I think that I will never have a prouder moment," he said, kissing her on the forehead. "I knew that you would be a credit to the name of Wycoller, but I never imagined that you would be its brightest star. You have much to learn, of course, but the essential flame, the spirit is there. Without it you might have become a good actress, but with it you can find greatness.''

Perdita hardly knew what to say. She knew that her father's praise was not given easily, even to her, but over the past two weeks she had found that when she was on the stage acting a part, she felt more sure of herself than when she was in her real life. In her childhood the stories that she had made up for herself and for Jane and Christopher had been her escape when things seemed too boring or too difficult. Now she could put on another person as easily as she might put on a new dress, and forget the misery of losing Jeremy.

They were in the final week of rehearsal when Jane came to see Perdita in the theater. It was the first time that Jane had seen the backstage of a theater and she was intrigued by the mundane, almost tawdry things, which in the light of the footlights took on a glamorous quality. She was amazed how the actors and actresses could become completely different people when they slipped out from the wings, how they could, in the blink of an eye, resume their everyday personas when they came off stage, as though stepping in and out of different pairs of shoes.

Jane was most impressed with Perdita's performance. As children they had often improvised plays, and although Perdita's fertile mind had invented most of the plays they acted, she had never shown herself to be the skilled actress that Jane saw on the stage now. As she watched the play in rehearsal, she felt that she was seeing a stranger instead of her step-sister.

However, as Perdita's play unfolded Jane found another interest in it. She remembered the conversation she had had with Perdita after her engagement had been announced, and how they had laughed at the fact that Jeremy had believed Perdita to have been in love with Christopher. Now Jane saw how that idea had been clothed out to become the play that was being enacted.

Jane watched as John McEvoy as King Andrew spoke to his chamberlain (played by Edmund Wycoller) about his fears that his young bride had fallen in love with his younger brother while traveling from her homeland. Jane watched the chamberlain, scheming for power, malign both the king's brother and his queen. She saw the queen's despair over the king's remoteness and saw the chamberlain foster her misery by telling her how the king was in love with another lady. Finally, Jane watched as the king was driven to take poison to free his wife so that she could go to the man she loved, and saw the deathbed reconciliation of the king and his bride.

There were obvious differences between the play and Jeremy and Perdita's real lives, but the misunderstandings were similar enough. Christopher had been adamant that Jeremy loved Perdita and Perdita most certainly had never wavered in her love for Jeremy. From what Perdita had told her, Jane believed that Perdita had never dared tell Jeremy she loved him, and she had hinted that there was a lady whom he had been forced to give up for her sake. Who had told Perdita that, Jane did not know, but nevertheless it would have been cause enough for Perdita to have kept her feelings to herself. The trouble was that both Perdita and Jeremy were too self-sacrificing, Jane decided, whereas a few minutes of openness might have saved them from the coil and misery that they were in now.

As though to underline her thoughts, Edmund Wycoller stopped the rehearsal at that point and said to John McEvoy, "You must make it clear to the audience that although the king is in love with his bride, he is reluctant to force his attentions upon her. He is a noble man, a good man, and the thought of forcing himself upon a lady who does not love him is anathema to him."

Jane watched in amazement to see that although Perdita had written the play, the idea her father had put forward had not really occurred to her. Seeing it so much from the queen's point of view, she had not realized how a man, married to a woman whom he thought did not love him, might feel.

Jane almost clapped her hands and whispered, "Oh yes." There was no one in the empty seats beside her or on the stage who could hear her words, but she suddenly began to have an idea of how she could get Perdita and Jeremy back together again.

She sat through the rest of the rehearsal, barely able to concentrate on anything the actors were saying or doing, though once or twice the lines were so apt, so valuable to her forming plan that she had to clasp her hands tightly to prevent herself clapping with excitement.

By the time the rehearsal was finished, Jane was in a fever of anxiety to be off. She needed to see Christopher and to confer with him. Perdita had told her not to let him tell Jeremy about her father, but Jane saw no reason why Christopher should not help her plan in another way.

She was distracted as she spent the time required by politeness with the cast after the rehearsal was over. The only thing which roused her from her thoughts was the firm pressure of John McEvoy's hand. She looked up into his dark blue eyes, and at his extremely handsome face, and had to remind herself quickly that Christopher was the handsomest man in the world. However, she did allow herself to feel that Perdita's life was not totally without reward.

She drew away from John McEvoy and walked over to Perdita. "You will most certainly take London by storm, my dearest sister. How stupid we have all been to have kept you hidden in the country, ignoring your talents. I shall bring a party to the opening night and shall tell everyone all the time, except when you are making your speeches, of course, that you are my sister. I shall bathe in your reflected glory. Oh, I can see that I shall be invited everywhere just on the possibility that I might introduce people to you. Which, of course, I shan't as I don't want to be completely overshadowed by you."

Perdita smiled and said, "You are, above all people, the most ridiculous and darling person I know. But you may stop your speeches now as I can see that you are all a-fidget to get back to Christopher. I do thank you for having been so polite as to have sat through the whole rehearsal. I know that it has taken all your willpower, but I do not wish to put too much strain upon you."

Absolved from further talk, Jane was indeed only too happy to be able to leave the theater and go in search of Christopher. She was barely through the front door of her mother's house and did not even stop to remove her bonnet before she wrote a note to be taken to Christopher at his lodgings at once.

The wording of the note was so imperative that Christopher did not stop even to get his hat before rushing around to Charles Street to answer the ambiguous but urgent summons. Once there, he brushed past the butler as soon as the door was opened and only asking the whereabouts of Miss de Marney, ran up the stairs two steps at a time to arrive breathless in the drawing room. He stopped surprised in the doorway to see a smiling and seemingly composed Jane sitting on the sofa doing some embroidery.

"What the deuce do you mean by sending me such a note?" he asked. "I thought that you were on your death bed at the very least. 'Come at once. Waste not a second. I must see you on a matter of life or death!' Really Jane, I must protest. I risked my reputation by coming out into the streets without my hat. What is so urgent that it couldn't have waited until I had had nuncheon?"

"I was afraid that you might have had plans to go to the fight this afternoon, and I wished to catch you before you left your lodgings. I knew that I would have to make my message seem very urgent to prevent you from seeing Tom Cribb fight. Besides, it *is* urgent," Jane added, seeing the cloud cross Christopher's face at the thought of the great mill that he was missing.

"Christopher, I have thought of a way of getting Perdita and Jeremy back together," Jane added quickly. "I know that she is as much in love with him as she ever was, and quite miserable without him. You told me that you thought Jeremy must have windmills in his head to have left Perdita, and you have agreed that we must find a way to make them see how foolish they are being, and I think I have found that way."

"Oh good," Christopher said, "but couldn't the idea wait until after the fight?"

"No," Jane said firmly, rising from the sofa and going over to him and putting her hand on his arm. "Come over here and sit down, and I will explain everything.

"I was at the theater this morning watching a rehearsal of the play Perdita wrote. I did not know before what it was about, but it appears it is all about love undiscovered, and I know that she was writing about herself and Jeremy. Of course, she does not clearly understand how much Jeremy loves her, but she was weaving a romance and it served her purpose to make King Andrew in love with his wife—"

"King Andrew?"

"Yes, the hero of the play, the one who is really Jeremy. You see, King Andrew thinks that his brother, Prince James, is in love with Queen Moyra and therefore he will not speak of his own love, and Moyra thinks that King Andrew is not in love with her and has been told that he is in love with someone else, so of course she is very shy with him. King Andrew is therefore even more convinced that Queen Moyra does not love him, and then when he sees how easy she is with Prince James his fears are increased, though of course Prince James and Queen Moyra merely feel friendship for each other, and—''

''Oh, for pity's sake, Jane, do slow down and tell me why the play should make you think that it in any way resembles the relationship between Perdita and Jeremy?''

''Why, but you must see. Jeremy told Perdita that he had always thought she was in love with you. He only discovered that she was not when she was so obviously happy for the two of us when we announced our engagement, and she told me on another occasion that someone had said to her that Jeremy was about to marry another lady at the end of last season. She was sure that he still loved that lady.''

''Well, that's ridiculous. I told you that Jeremy has always been in love with Perdita. As for thinking that she was in love with me, that's ridiculous too. He could not have thought anything so absurd. Well, I mean I am very fond of Perdita, and I hope that she is of me, but we have never been in love with each other. It would not have done. She is kind and sweet and pretty, but there is too much reserve in her manner for me. She's much more to Jeremy's style than mine.''

''Yes, I know, dearest, but that is not the point. The point is that Jeremy *thought* that she was in love with you, and I believe that is why he was so cool toward her. He never wooed her, and he made her feel that he was marrying her solely out of a sense of duty because he had compromised her in front of Mrs. Banistre-Brewster. So of course Perdita thought that he had only married her to be honorable, and *she* was too reserved to show that she adored him, and so the whole thing became a travesty, and then something happened, I am not quite sure what, and he became very peculiar—''

''I am not surprised,'' Christopher said grimly.

''What do you mean?'' Jane asked.

''Well it is deuced difficult for a man to live with a woman he loves and still feel constrained not to touch her, if you know what I mean? It would take someone with my brother's willpower to have spent so much time with Perdita without going mad.''

"Oh, yes, well, I think I understand what you mean," Jane said, blushing and looking at the toes of her shoes.

"I hope so," Christopher said gruffly, "for you may be sure that I shall not treat you with such restraint once we are married."

"No, indeed, I should certainly hope not, but then dearest Christopher, we know that we love each other, and Perdita and Jeremy do not. Oh, but do please stop getting me off the line of my thoughts and making me quite unable to think of anything except marrying you."

Jane was not however permitted to think of Perdita's problems for some while as Christopher remembered that he had not kissed his fiancée properly that day and remedied the oversight without delay.

When at last Jane was able to remember what it was that she had wished to speak to Christopher about, several minutes had passed, but then she pulled back from her comfortable place in his arms, smoothed her dress, and said, "We must stop thinking about ourselves for a minute and get to grips with the problem of getting Perdita and Jeremy back together. You see, I believe that if he could see Perdita acting out their own story, or at least a rough simile of it, he would understand that Perdita loves him and then all could be put to right, but you are the only person who can get him to the Sans Pareil Theater to see the play, and I cannot imagine how you will do that."

"I doubt that he will come if he knows that he will see Perdita," Christopher said with a frown.

"Oh, he need not know that," Jane said airily.

"What do you mean? You told me that Perdita had insisted that he be told where she was. He's not such a dunderhead not to be able to put two and two together and know that if he goes to the Sans Pareil, ten to one he'll run into Perdita."

"She didn't tell him that she was going to be at the theater. She told him she was living with an old friend of her mother's. She didn't even tell him that she was living with her father, because she didn't want Jeremy to know that her father was an actor, and if she had told him that she was staying with Edmund Wycoller, Jeremy might have taken exception. Not knowing that it was quite proper, you understand?"

"Stop, Jane. Are you telling me that Edmund Wycoller is Perdita's real father?"

"Oh yes, didn't I remember to tell you that? Actually, I don't think Perdita wanted me to tell you, because she was afraid you might tell Jeremy."

"It seems that you have forgotten many things to tell me. When did Perdita find out that Mr. Wycoller was her father?"

"Oh, she always knew that. After all, she was five when she left him to come live with us. It was just that her uncle, my step-father, told her not to tell anyone that her father was an actor. He did not want her ostracized by the narrow-minded society of Byfold. Perdita always knew who her father really was, but it wasn't until she saw his name on a playbill, here in London, that she was able to find him again. When Jeremy said he didn't want to live with her anymore, it seemed reasonable for her to go and live with her father and try to make her living by going on the stage. She is very much against taking any money from Jeremy, you know. I think it is quite foolish, but I suppose it is her pride again. Anyway, Mr. Wycoller thinks it is good for her to have something to do, and besides she has turned out to be a very good actress."

"Oh lord," Christopher said, clapping his hands to his head. "I really don't believe I am able to take in so much at one time. It is worse than my philosophy tutorials at Cambridge. But, Jane, now that Perdita has started on what may be a very successful career on the stage, are you sure she doesn't want to continue with it? I mean, I can't see old Jeremy allowing his wife to tread the boards. He wouldn't think it at all the thing. Though come to think of it, he is so besotted with Perdita he might allow it if she wanted it very much, but I don't think she should count on it."

"Christopher, you are very stupid sometimes. Of course, Perdita doesn't care a fig about the stage compared with Jeremy. She would much rather be with him, and would give everything up if she thought that there was a chance of really being his wife, and living with him again. No, what we must do is make Jeremy realize that she loves him."

"And you want me to go down to Shotley and tell him?"

"Oh no, that would do no good. He wouldn't believe either of us. He must hear it from Perdita herself, and she will never tell him directly. I believe the only hope is for us to get

Jeremy to see the play. When he sees Perdita saying the lines she wrote, I am sure that he will understand that she is drawing on her own feelings and experience. Your role is to persuade Jeremy to come to the first night with us, without telling him that Perdita is in the play, or even at the theater. I am afraid that if he knew that, he would not come. We must just get him there and let the play do the rest.''

Christopher looked thoughtful for a moment. ''Well it might work, but what if it doesn't?''

''Why then, we'll have to take them both by force, lock them in a room, and not let them out until they have confessed their feelings for each other.''

''Ha! Do you really think that anyone could force Jeremy to do anything he didn't want to?''

''That's neither here nor there at the moment, but don't be so poor-spirited. I for one shall not give up until those two are happily together again. But for the moment we must devise a way in which we can make certain that Jeremy comes to the play with us.''

Christopher's brow furrowed again. ''I don't know how that's to be done. Jeremy's settled down at Shotley and obviously has no intention of returning to London this season.''

''But the house is still open. The servants are still there. Couldn't you tell him that there is a frightful row going on and that he must come back and sort it out?''

''No, that won't do. He'd just send a note to the butler telling him to arrange matters.''

''Well perhaps you could write and tell him that there has been a dreadful fire, or could find someone who absolutely had to see him, his man of business perhaps, or an old army friend who had fallen upon hard times and needed his help.''

''Can't think of anyone who could persuade him to come to London if he don't want to. You know Jeremy, so damned practical. He'd send his man of business instructions to come to Shotley, and write directly to his army friend to ask what he needed. Anyway, there's no one in the army that he would come all this way to see—except . . .'' Christopher frowned and became silent for a moment while Jane looked at him expectantly.

''I don't know if I dare approach him, though,'' Christopher continued, ''but Jeremy would come running if he called. But I don't think he would agree to such a plan. After all, he's a very important man. Hardly likely to want to get involved in the love problems of one of his officers.''

"Christopher, for heaven's sake, who are you talking about? Who wouldn't want to get involved?''

"The Duke of Wellington, of course. He was as fond of Jeremy as he was of any of his officers. Thought very highly of him. Even sent a personal letter when Jeremy was wounded to say that the 15th Hussars would be only a shadow of a regiment without him. But I don't suppose he would want to get involved with Jeremy's private life.''

"Well, you can ask him and see. You must go to him and try to persuade him to get Jeremy to come to him in London on the twenty-fourth, then we can be sure Jeremy will be in London at least the day before the performance and we can take him to the theater the night before he sees the duke.''

"The duke'll never do it. Don't see how I can ask him to.''

"Well you must think of a way, for do it you must," Jane said firmly. "Besides, it is well known that the duke has a romantic heart. One hears that he had several *chères amies*, including that Harriet Wilson.''

"Jane!'' Christopher said aghast, "where do you hear such things? You really must not admit to knowing them.''

"Oh, I wouldn't mention it to anyone but you. I am not such a peagoose, but that does not signify at the moment. We must keep in mind the fact that you have to ask the duke to send for Jeremy. Now come, sit down here and write to ask him for an appointment. I am sure that when he knows that you are Jeremy's brother, he will see you.''

Jane firmly led Christopher over to the writing table and put a piece of hot-pressed paper in front of him. Christopher, looking as though he was signing his own death warrant, picked up the quill and began to write. "I might have imagined slaying dragons for you with a light heart, but I never imagined that you would put me to such a severe test as this,'' he muttered.

Jane smiled. "Oh dragons, there would be no point in slaying them. I shall think more highly of you for doing this than if you were to face ten dragons.'' She put her arms around Christopher's shoulders and hugged him, and the worry on his face cleared.

"There,'' he said finally, sanding the wet ink and then

folding the paper. He wrote the address on the outside and stood up with the paper in his hand. "I will see this is delivered at once, but I shall expect you to spend the rest of the day in prayer. If I am to face the duke, I shall need all the terrestrial and heavenly help I can get."

"Oh Christopher, I shall most certainly pray for your success, but the duke is sure to listen to you, and after all, he cannot eat you."

"I wouldn't be too sure of that," Christopher said with a wry grin as he opened the door and left the room to pursue his errand.

— 16 —

In all events, when Christopher returned to Charles Street late that afternoon, he had certainly not suffered any slights or set-downs from the great man. In fact, he was so elated by his meeting and the way the duke had greeted him that he bounded into the drawing room, where he found Jane cursing a tangled skein of silk and on edge with impatience to hear how things had gone.

"You know, I can't think how he has got such a terrible reputation," Christopher said as soon as he had kissed his bride-to-be. "He was all that is affable to me, and very easy to talk to. Seems he knew one of m' tutors at Eton. Funny chap we used to call Jellyhead behind his back (his real name was Jemmersted). The duke was very amused at the nickname. Seems they had been at school together and old Jellyhead had been a bit of a prig even then. Well, I confess I never thought the duke would be so human. He even offered me some of the port the Portugese government had given him. Dashed good stuff. Of course, it was a bit early in the day to be drinking it, but when you consider that it was sort of the spoils of war—"

"Oh Christopher, do stop. I don't want to hear about any wretched port or silly tutors. Tell me what the duke said about our scheme to get Jeremy to come to London?"

"Oh that," Christopher said idly, walking over to the mantelpiece and fiddling with the spills in a vase on it. "He thought it was a splendid idea. Seems Jeremy had spoken to him once or twice about Perdita when they were in Spain. When I told the duke that she and Jeremy had had some sort of misunderstanding and that their marriage seemed to be in danger, he said he would do what he could to help us set things right."

"Oh Christopher, that's wonderful," Jane said, jumping up from the sofa and running over to hang on his arm. "Did he write the letter, and has he sent it? You know that the twenty-third is only four days off."

"The duke did better than that. He offered to make up a party for the play himself. Said that he was supposed to go to some boring musical party that night, but that he would cry off. He said that he much preferred the theater to all those screeching ladies or violins. He wrote to Jeremy and invited him then and there. He read me the letter. It was masterful. I mean, it was all very polite and suchlike, but there was no doubt that it would take a brave man to refuse the invitation. Anyway I don't think for a moment that Jeremy will want to. Seems he and the duke haven't met since they were in Paris, so it stands to reason that Jeremy will not refuse."

"Oh, I do hope so," Jane said, frowning. "I have such hopes of this scheme putting to rights all Jeremy's and Perdita's misunderstandings. You may be sure that I shall be in a fever of anxiety until I hear that he is definitely coming. I shall be able to think of nothing else."

"Not even me?" Christopher quizzed, turning from the fireplace and taking her in his arms.

"Don't be silly," Jane said, allowing herself to be drawn against his new Stultz coat. "I shall never stop thinking of you for the rest of my life, you know that."

It seemed that Christopher needed more proof and the next hour was taken up with a conversation which both found so immensely interesting that all thought of Jeremy and Perdita quite left their heads.

But by the time a note arrived from the duke two days later, Jane was greatly relieved to hear that Jeremy had agreed to form part of the party to go to Apsley House for dinner and on to the theater later.

Jane's next anxiety was caused by the thought that if Jeremy saw the playbills before the time they reached the theater, he might cry off at the last minute. However, Christopher took her severely to task and said that she was getting herself up in the boughs about nothing if she thought that Jeremy would have time to study the playbills in the few hours he would be in London before the party. "Besides," he said, "there is no reason why Jeremy should connect his Perdita with the Miss Perdita Wycoller on the bills. Plenty of aspiring actresses have been calling themselves Perdita since Mary Robinson was known by that nickname.''

Jane's fears were somewhat allayed, but she was anything but composed for the two days that remained before the opening performance of Perdita's play. Even the pressing problem of what to wear to dinner at Apsley House was pushed to one side while she worried about whether or not her plan would succeed. She realized that she was going against Perdita's wishes by allowing Jeremy to find out that Edmund Wycoller was her father, but Jane excused the betrayal by telling herself that she was not exactly telling Jeremy who Perdita's father was, and that he might have discovered it by himself in any case.

Her other worry was that her mother might say something indiscreet when she saw that Jeremy was also at Apsley House. The duke had included Mrs. Chase in the party, and although Mrs. Chase had been surprised at the invitation, Jane had assured her that it was only given because Christopher had met the duke recently and in the course of conversation had told him that his sister-in-law was about to appear in her own play. Mrs. Chase seemed quite happy with this explanation, but Jane could not think how to explain why Jeremy was to be of the party, and decided to let matters rest until they actually met face to face. How then to prevent Mrs. Chase from saying to Jeremy that Perdita was in the play was a problem that Jane and Christopher decided to defer for the time being.

On the night, Christopher came to Charles Street to collect the ladies, both of whom were somewhat agitated at the thought of the evening ahead. Mrs. Chase's main concern was with meeting the duke himself. He had been the hero of the country for some time and to meet him face to face quite made her think that she would have her palpitations. Jane might have been just as disturbed at the thought of meeting the great man, but her awe and apprehension was overlaid by the more pressing problem of preventing her mother from giving the game away.

As they were settled in the carriage Jane decided that she could not leave things to chance, and turning to her mother blurted out, ''Mama, Jeremy is to be of the party tonight. It is all part of a plan that Christopher and I have to get Jeremy and Perdita back together again. The duke knows all about it, but no one is to tell Jeremy that Perdita is acting in the play we are to see tonight. Promise me that you won't tell him anything about Perdita when you see him.''

Mrs. Chase raised her gloved hands to her cheeks. "Jane, how wicked of you not to have told me this before. Why, I shall not know what to say to Jeremy. After the way he has treated Perdita, I declare I shall probably need my smelling salts. How could you put me in such an uncomfortable position, you naughty child?''

"There was no help for it, Mama, I am afraid. I thought that you might refuse the duke's invitation if you knew beforehand that Jeremy was to be at Apsley House, but you must see that this might be the way of getting Perdita and Jeremy back together, and I felt that you would not mind being sacrificed for such a good cause.''

"I am not sure that Jeremy deserves Perdita. He certainly has behaved in a very reprehensible fashion to her, if you will excuse me, Christopher. I know he is your brother, and I have always been very fond of him, but he most certainly put Perdita in a very difficult situation.''

"I quite understand, Mrs. Chase, but Jane and I believe that there was more to matters than met the eye.''

"I assure you, Perdita would never do anything wrong,'' Mrs. Chase said drawing herself up.

"Oh no, ma'am, I did not mean to imply that, but Jane and I are of the opinion that there has been a great deal of misunderstanding between them and we have hopes that the events of this evening may put them right. As you know, Mrs. Chase, Perdita is still in love with Jeremy, and I am quite sure that Jeremy is really deeply in love with her. If only we can get the two of them to realize that this is the case, I am sure that they can be happy together again.''

Mrs. Chase looked mollified, but shook her head as she answered, "I do hope you are right. I am quite sure that Perdita is still very fond of your brother, and of course I would do anything to see her happy, but I still do not know how I am to look Jeremy in the eye.''

"If it is any comfort to you, Mrs. Chase, I am sure that Jeremy will have just as much trouble in facing you. He has no idea that any of us are to be at the duke's tonight, and I have it in my heart to feel a bit sorry for the man.''

Mrs. Chase nodded. The thought of Jeremy's discomfort

helped her to see the problem from another angle and she determined to be as civil as possible to him. After all, if Jane and Christopher were right and this evening could bridge the chasm between Jeremy and Perdita, it would be more uncomfortable to have the remembrance of uncharitable things said once the couple were back together. She determined that she would do her very best to say nothing exceptional and to try to carry off the evening with the utmost sophistication.

Jeremy, it seemed, had much the same thoughts, for although his initial surprise at seeing Mrs. Chase, Jane, and Christopher, was apparent to them all, he quickly rallied from his expression of discomfort and was so polite and friendly that Mrs. Chase found herself warming to him despite herself.

Jane noticed a strained look in his face, but he seemed determined to make things as easy as possible, and as he bowed over her hand he said, "My dear Jane, it is a great pleasure to see you and your mother here this evening. May I congratulate you upon your looks. Obviously my brother is still on his best behavior and you have not yet realized the grave error you have made in becoming betrothed to such a scurrilous fellow."

"I have great hopes that this is just the beginning of your awareness that your brother is one of nature's true gentlemen," Jane answered smiling. "He is everything that I have ever dreamed a fiancé to be and I know that he will make me a wonderful husband."

There was something like pain in Jeremy's eyes when Jane made the last remark, and she quickly changed the subject and said, "But tell me, did you leave your mother in good health, and is all well at Shotley?"

"My mother is in fine health and spirits, thank you, and Shotley is still standing despite all the ravages that tenants, weather, and general decay can do to a place. I sometimes feel that with an estate, however hard one works, one is simply keeping pace with dilapidation and that to stand still and do nothing for even a day, is to invite utter desolation to descend upon the place. However, I have thrown caution to the winds to accept the duke's invitation. He seemed insistent that I attend the party this evening. It appears that the performance at the theater is something above the ordinary. Have you ever seen this fellow Wycoller act? I understand that he is the master of his craft and some say even better than Kemble or

Kean, but not having seen him myself, I can give no opinion on the matter.''

Jane was grateful that dinner was announced at that moment and that she did not have to answer Jeremy's question. She did not want to have to admit that she had attended a rehearsal of one of the plays that they were about to see, and furthermore had even made the acquaintance of Mr. Wycoller.

She was led into dinner by Lord Munsel, who was a member of the party with his wife, and was grateful to find that she was seated at dinner between Lord Munsel and the duke and that Jeremy was at the far end of the table.

Lord Munsel she found to be a not altogether agreeable dinner companion as he insisted upon talking to her as though she was only five years old, and asking her such inane questions about her come-out that she could barely resist giving him some pert answers, but she managed to hold her tongue and give his lordship only unexceptional answers. However, she was able at one point to give vent to her feelings by making a face at Christopher who sat across the table from her when his lordship turned to speak with Mrs. Adams who sat on the other side of him.

Lord Munsel added to his misdemeanors by saying to Mrs. Adams in a carrying voice, ''That Miss de Marney seems like a pretty little thing. It is refreshing to find a gal of her generation with such pretty manners.''

Jane turned to the duke to find him regarding her with a twinkle in his eye and was delighted when she could address remarks to him. He honored her by discussing his most memorable battle with her, and told her some amusing anecdotes which had occurred at Waterloo. Although his description of the battle was almost word for word that which she had heard from Jeremy in the past, it nevertheless pleased her to hear it from the hero himself.

At one point she glanced down the table to Jeremy and caught him with an off-guard expression on his face which thoroughly endorsed her feelings that, despite his apparent composure, he was far from happy. There was a strained, tired look to him which Jane felt was more indicative of his real feelings than the affable manner he had assumed before supper.

Catching her glance, the duke said, ''We must see that

your plan works, Miss de Marney. I can't have one of my officers in such a state. Bad for morale."

Jane was about to retort that as Jeremy was no longer in the army it was not morale which concerned her, but his happiness, but she caught the twinkle in the duke's eye and merely nodded and said, "I have every intention, duke, of seeing that my plan does not fail."

"That's the right idea," the duke answered. "Never go into battle with the thought of failure in your mind. Be prepared for retreat, but never for failure. I am quite sure that you will not give up until you win this battle, and with that determination I know that you will win."

His words gave Jane new courage and when the party set off for the theater she had a resolute line to her mouth and her eyes held a steely glint.

"I'm glad that I have not displeased you," Christopher said seating himself in the carriage beside her. "I would tremble for my life."

"Don't be absurd," Jane said laughing and holding out her hand to him. "I would never be angry with you."

Christopher was so much in love that he found no difficulty in believing her, and the ride to the theater was passed in comfortable conversation.

Jane had one moment of disquiet when the carriage arrived at the theater and she saw Jeremy walk over to one of the playbills affixed to the wall of the Sans Pareil and start to bend close to examine it. Jane ran over quickly and caught his arm and led him firmly inside before he could see too much.

The duke had hired the stage box and the adjacent open box beside it. The Sans Pareil, being a small theater, boasted only two enclosed boxes, one on either side of the stage, and the duke escorted Jeremy and Jane into the enclosed box and seated himself with Lady Munsel beside him. He insisted that the two ladies have the seats furthest from the stage so that they would get a better view of the proceedings, and having firmly told Jeremy that he and Jane were to sit in the front row, he settled his other guests in the other box and sat down behind Jeremy. Jeremy had picked up his playbill and was studying it closely. Jane looked across at the duke, and slowly, like a great eagle closing one eye, he gave her a long wink.

Jane could barely stop herself from staring at Jeremy's face to see if there was any reaction to the name Perdita on the playbill. She saw his lips tighten a fraction, but Jane could not decide whether the name itself had caused the reaction or whether he had deduced something.

In any case, she could not resist leaning toward him and saying, "They say that Miss Perdita Wycoller has a great deal of talent. Do you see that she not only acts, but has written the first piece to be performed tonight?" Despite Perdita's admonition, Jane could not refrain from adding, "I suppose that being the daughter of the great Edmund Wycoller, she might be expected to be unusually gifted."

The abstracted nod that Jeremy gave to this information gave no inkling as to whether or not he yet had any suspicions of who it was he was going to see on the stage that night.

Jeremy, however, was fighting to control many different feelings. The name on the playbill had opened a Pandora's box of memories which he had been trying to keep confined since that night several weeks before when he had stormed into Perdita's bedroom. Even though he had no suspicion that the Perdita on the playbill was anything to do with his wife, the events of that night were like a raw wound to him still. He had tried with all his might to put them out of his mind. His own behavior on that occasion filled him with the deepest revulsion. He had never before believed that he could have behaved in such a manner, and every avenue of excuse, his suspicions, his frustrations, his misapprehensions, seemed only to deepen his self-loathing. That Perdita was totally innocent of all that he had suspected her of was the one thing that stood out clearly. Even if he was still unable to explain her meeting with the stranger in the alley behind Madame desVignes', he knew now that she had never cuckolded him.

It had been an unusual feeling of total cowardice which, in the sobering light of day, had prompted him to depart for Shotley before Perdita was awake on the morning after that fateful night. He had hardly known what to say to her in his note, and to face her would have been far worse. In any case, her brief reply had told him plainly that she wanted nothing further to do with him.

At Shotley, Jeremy had tried to immerse himself in the problems of the estate and he had launched a couple of extremely radical projects, hoping that the risk involved would keep his mind from continually harking back to the disastrous mess he had made of his marriage to Perdita. However, it now seemed that even the most outrageously perilous of those schemes was about to yield enormous profits, and the thought that he would not have Perdita to share his triumphs with made him wish with all his heart that he could have drowned himself in failure rather than ride the lonely wave of success.

The invitation from the duke had come at a time when his restlessness had become acute, and the sound of the theater party and meeting with his old Commander in Chief seemed to offer a release from his miserable and solitary thoughts. However, when he found that Mrs. Chase, Jane, and Christopher were of the party he nearly turned tail and ran, and only the most rigorous self-discipline had enabled him to maintain a pose of being quite at his ease.

But now the name Perdita leaped at him from the playbill in his hand, and he wondered whether he would be able to endure an evening watching a lady who bore his Perdita's name but none of her attributes. He smiled wryly to himself; if fate were determined to punish him, it was certainly being effective.

At this point the gaslamps in the auditorium dimmed and the curtain rose to show a room in a castle. The setting was austere. Gray stone walls rose at the back of the stage, with only one narrow window to break their massive shape. A rough tapestry hung from the wall and the room was furnished sparsely with two chairs and a table. A man was standing gazing out of the window with his back to the audience, but as the curtain rose he turned slowly to address an older man standing at the table also with his back to the audience. The first man spoke and walked slowly to the front of the stage; as he did so the older one turned and there was a burst of applause as Edmund Wycoller faced his audience. Jeremy barely suppressed an exclamation. Before him was the man to whom Perdita had run so joyously that day he had followed her to Madame desVignes'.

Jeremy leaned forward tensely in his seat. He could not be mistaken. That leonine face, with the thick gray hair, the broad shoulders, it was indeed the man into whose arms Perdita had run. A feeling of anger and sickness swept over Jeremy so that for a moment he had to shut his eyes to blot out the sight of the man who had been responsible for his total lack of self-control and his subsequent misery.

Edmund Wycoller's voice spread across the auditorium like a thick coating of oil as he insinuated to King Andrew that it was Prince James, a man her own age, whom the queen loved. The words could almost be seen seeping like poison into King Andrew's veins.

The scene played on. There was a fanfare of trumpets from offstage and Queen Moyra, attended by her lady-in-waiting and Prince James, entered from stage right.

Jeremy half rose from his chair, but a firm hand from behind him pressed him back into his seat and he sat staring as his own Perdita, dressed magnificently in queen's robes, swept into the room and curtsied deeply to the king.

Jeremy's mind raced. Perdita, the adopted child who had spoken so little of her real father, whose name before she had been adopted by the Chases had never been mentioned. But somewhere in the dim recesses of his memory Jeremy could see himself about to enter the library at Shotley just after Perdita had arrived at Hangarwood, and could hear his father say to his mother, "She will have to forget the name Wycoller. It would never do for it to be known that her father is an actor. Matthew Chase is quite right. She must be taught never to mention it, and the quicker the better."

That little girl, bewildered and alone, having to deny the father that she had loved, taught to be ashamed of him. Jeremy's jaw tightened. How could they have done that to his Perdita. He had never realized what a burden she had carried throughout her life. No wonder she had felt that she must meet her father in secret, in out-of-the-way places where she felt safe from discovery, must keep the fact of her parentage even from her husband, who had never allowed her to come close enough to him for confidences. Jeremy's fists clenched so hard that his fingernails dug into the palms of his hands.

He was brought back to the action on the stage by words which were being spoken and which seemed to raise echoes in his mind. The king, convinced that his wife loved his younger brother, was seemingly cool to her. But she did not love Prince James, and confessed to the lady-in-waiting that the king's coldness to her was making her miserable, and that if only she had the courage she would declare her love for him. Each new revelation homed like a barbed arrow into Jeremy's heart.

Jane, watching him rather than the play, saw the tension in his back, saw the frown deepen between his eyebrows and the whitened knuckles of his hands, and she could barely refrain from clapping her hands as she saw the plan she had conceived begin to work.

The play swung to its climax. The king, persuaded by the reticence of his bride that she did not love him, became more and more reserved and finally, believing that the kindest thing that he could do for her would be to kill himself so that she could marry his brother, swallowed a vial of poison. Only as he lay dying did the queen find him and hear with his dying breath that he loved her. Striken that she must live without him, she drained the bottle of poison and died with him.

The curtain fell, but before Jeremy could come out of his trance he felt Jane's hand on his arm and heard her say, "Come, I think that we should go down and congratulate Perdita."

Jeremy hesitated, unsure of what he could say and feeling that he would be the last person in the world Perdita would want to see, but a stern voice from behind him said, "Go on, Major."

Jeremy rose and Jane led him with a firm grasp down the staircase and through the door which opened onto the back of the stage. She began to lead him down the passage toward the dressing rooms, but Jeremy stopped.

"No, Jane, I can't see Perdita. You see we had—well, really a quarrel. I behaved very badly toward her, and she will not wish to see me."

Jane turned and gave him a very prim look. "Oh, I know all about that, but if you don't know by now that Perdita feels about you exactly the way Queen Moyra felt about King Andrew, well—well, I shall wash my hands of the pair of you and let you spend the rest of your lives in utter misery. Now come on. Just say—oh, for heaven's sake, you know what to say to the woman you love."

She turned and pulled a bewildered Jeremy after her to a half-open door at the end of the corridor. She poked her head around the door and as she did so said, "Darling Perdita, you were marvelous, but I have someone who has much more important things to say to you."

She pushed Jeremy into the room and firmly closed the door behind him. Perdita, turning from her mirror where she was taking off her makeup, sat as though turned to stone with a cloth halfway to her face. For a moment she and Jeremy stared at each other in silence.

He found that he could hardly get his breath, but he finally managed to say in a husky voice, "Perdita, how do I make amends? There are no excuses, but I misunderstood so much, and have been so foolish—no, worse than foolish. You see, I did not know about your father, and then when I saw you with him outside the theater, saw you run into his arms, I thought—but that is no excuse for the way I behaved."

"You saw me?"

"Yes, in the alley, behind Madame desVignes'. I was sent a letter and—Oh Perdita, I am so ashamed, but I got suspicious and followed you."

"A letter? From whom?"

"I don't know, some lying troublemaker, and it doesn't matter now. All that matters is that I have been so totally miserable without you and that I really think that taking poison might be a good idea. Though if there is any chance—any chance in the world that you could—that your generous heart would let me try to make amends— Oh, Perdita, I would so much rather live with you and spend the rest of my life trying to show you how much I love you."

He stood with his back to the door, knowing that the next few seconds would change his life one way or another forever, and he felt as though he were suspended by a thin thread between heaven and hell.

Perdita's eyes opened wide and a smile began to touch her lips. She got up swiftly from her chair and ran across the floor to him. Flinging herself into his arms she pressed her face against his chest, neither of them knowing or caring that his exquisite coat was being ruined beyond redemption by the grease paint on her face. "Oh, please don't take poison. It would be such a terrible mistake, and it seems that we have made more than enough mistakes already. Jeremy, I have been so unhappy without you, and I love you quite terribly. I should have told you that long ago, but I thought that you only married me to save me from Mrs. Bannistre-Brewster's gossip, and then I was told you had given up your heart's love for me, and I was so sure you disliked our marriage very much, and wouldn't want to know how much I loved you."

"Not want to know that you loved me? My darling heart, it's the only thing in the world that I do want to know. As for there being anyone else—I think there was never anyone for me but you since the day I rescued you from the horrible little boy. Do you remember?"

"Of course I remember. You were my hero from that day on, but I was so much in awe of you that I couldn't believe that you could ever really love me. I dreamed about it, but didn't believe it could truly happen."

"And I was so sure that you loved Christopher that I did not dare say anything. I thought you hated the idea of having to marry me. Oh my love, what an absurd parcel of misunderstandings we have made for ourselves. Oh how I wish we could blot out the past and start again."

"All but the loving."

"Yes, but we will never keep silent on that again. You need never be afraid to show me your love, and I—Oh Perdita, where do I begin?"

She raised her face to his and his mouth came down onto hers with a kiss that she had dreamed about, gentle at first and then seeming to absorb her so that their selves became warm and whole, rounded and surrounded by love.

The door of the dressing room opened and Edmund Wycoller, dressed as Richard III, looked around the door. The couple lost in each other's arms was quite unaware of the intrusion, and after a second Edmund withdrew.

Closing the door behind him, he sighed. "She would have taken London by storm. She might have even outshone the great Siddons. What a loss, what a loss." He wandered off in the direction of the stage shaking his head sadly, but the smile on his face was beatific.

About the Author

Corinna Cunliffe was born in Surrey, England, and spent her early childhood on a farm in Hertfordshire. During World War II she was sent to the United States. After the war she returned to England and completed her education, but her American ties proved strong and she returned to the United States where she worked for *THE LADIES' HOME JOURNAL*. After her marriage and the birth of her son, Corinna Cunliffe went with her wine importer husband to live in the Burgundy region of France. Following her divorce, she returned to London, where she worked for *HOMES AND GARDENS* and *GOOD HOUSEKEEPING*.

Her hobbies are painting, reading, cooking, gardening, visiting old houses, interesting gossip, and voyages of discovery. She now makes her home in Vermont in a small house with large views.

SIGNET Regency Romances You'll Want to Read

(0451)

☐ THE REPENTANT REBEL by Jane Ashford. (131959—$2.50)

☐ FIRST SEASON by Jane Ashford. (126785—$2.25)

☐ A RADICAL ARRANGEMENT by Jane Ashford. (125150—$2.25)

☐ THE MARCHINGTON SCANDAL by Jane Ashford. (116232—$2.25)

☐ THE THREE GRACES by Jane Ashford. (114183—$2.25)

☐ A COMMERCIAL ENTERPRISE by Sandra Heath. (131614—$2.50)

☐ MY LADY DOMINO by Sandra Heath. (126149—$2.25)

☐ MALLY by Sandra Heath. (143469—$2.50)

☐ THE OPERA DANCER by Sandra Heath. (143531—$2.50)

☐ THE UNWILLING HEIRESS by Sandra Heath. (097718—$1.95)

☐ MANNERBY'S LADY by Sandra Heath. (097726—$1.95)

☐ THE SHERBORNE SAPPHIRES by Sandra Heath. (115139—$2.25)

☐ THE CHADWICK RING by Julia Jefferies. (113462—$2.25)

Prices slightly higher in Canada.

**Buy them at your local
bookstore or use coupon
on next page for ordering.**

Other Regency Romances You'll Enjoy